1

My Alien Contact

1

War & Pieces

by

Vernon Gillen

All of Vernon's novels and books are available at Amazon.com

ISBN - #

978-1792657030

To The Reader

Now I know that you men do not like "love novels" but, in this novel I had to show the love that grew between a human man and the alien hybrid that he met on an alien ship. This love grew and gave me the novel you are about to read. But this is not a love novel. It is a novel with the added romance needed to do what was needed in this novel. I still added plenty of action for you action readers.

Vernon Gillen

Dedication

I dedicate this novel to President Donald J. Trump. I finished writing this novel on Christmas morning of 2018 just before daylight. For the first time in many years I am happy this Christmas. For so many years we were shamed if we said Merry Christmas. Even when other Republicans were in _OUR_ White House they caved in to the Liberal Communist that hated God, Jesus, and Christmas. Now we finally have a president that is standing up to the Communist in the United States.

Thank you President Trump for speaking out for us Christians. Thank you for the hard work you do for our country and I pray for you daily. May God bless you and your family.

And for you Republicans in Congress and the Senate; you're about to be voted out of office for going against President Trump. He is the best thing that has happened to this country since President Washington. And one more thing Mister Trump.

Build That Wall

Contents

Chapter 1

First Sighting

Every once in a while two friends got together and went out at night to hunt wild hogs and sometimes wolves. They were a gutsy couple of men considering that the woods in central Texas also held large wild cats. This was why both men carried rifles with large capacity magazines.

A few years earlier Bubba had inherited fifty acres of land that banked on the local lake. The land had many dangerous animals but he considered the wild hog the most dangerous. He was sixty four years old now and carried a CAR-15 with a forty round magazine and holographic sight. Just in case he needed them he also carry two more thirty round magazines on these nightly hunting trips.

Rick was forty five years old. He carried a SKS rifle with a thirty round magazine. Like Bubba he also carried two extra loaded magazines. They were both true believers in the saying; "I would rather have it and not need it than to need it and not have it."

A storm had come through earlier that evening but the skies were clear with a full moon. It was a perfect night for hunting wild hogs. Wild hogs can ruin a rancher's fields making it almost impossible to drive a tractor over. After discovering a place where the wild hogs had rooted up a large area the night before Bubba called his friend Rick and they decided to go hunting. When it got dark the two men grabbed their rifles and headed out into the woods.

Just under an hour later Bubba and Rick came to the area where the hogs had rooted up the field the night before. Suddenly they heard one hog not far away. Where there is one hog there were usually more. Bubba and Rick spread out about ten feet apart and then started walking towards the sound of the hog. Before long they came to a small clearing where in the full moon they could see seven to ten hogs rooting around.

Bubba turned on his laser sight and put the green dot on the side of the head of one large hog. When he pulled the trigger on his CAR-15 the hog went down. Then both men fired at will at anything that moved. As the black hogs ran Bubba stood by a large oak tree for cover. Not knowing where the gunshots were coming from three hogs ran right by him. Hogs have large razor sharp tusks that can slice a man's leg open. As they ran by Bubba he opened fire again stopping one hog close to him and another one a few feet past him.

Rick had a close call of his own. When Bubba fired his first shot and the hogs started running two of them ran right at Rick not knowing that he was there. Not wanting to get his leg chewed up he quickly climbed a tree. From about four feet up the tree he fired killing one of the hogs. Then he dropped down to the ground and shot two more hogs.

Finally the shooting stopped leaving five of the wild hogs dead. The two men walked back to Bubba's home and got Bubba's truck. Then they drove down to where the dead hogs were and loaded them in the back of the truck.

"One of these things almost got me." Bubba told Rick as they loaded the hogs in the truck.

"Me too." Rick said. "But we have enough pork to make a lot of sausage now."

"Now we just need a couple of deer." Bubba added.

Suddenly the two men saw a light that seemed to hover through the trees a few hundred yards away. As they watched the light it vanished as quickly as it appeared.

The two men then got in the truck and took the hogs back to Bubba's house where they spent the next three hours buttering them. For a while neither of them talked about the light. With some luck they would shoot a couple of deer and make some really fine venison sausage. After a while they talked about the light that seemed to float through the trees but dismissed it as just something that they only thought they saw.

Bubba and Rick quartered the hog meat and placed it in a large refrigerator to chill overnight. It would be much easier to finish cleaning the meat the next day when it is cooled off. After a few cups of coffee Rick got most of the meat and went home. He had the industrial size meat grinder and could handle grinding the meat much quicker than Bubba.

Bubba went straight to bed. He was tired and it would be daylight soon. After just a few hours of sleep he got up and started working on finishing the meat. Rick had taken the bigger hogs with him leaving only two small hogs with his friend. Now it was a matter of removing all of the meat from the bones. As he did this he had to place the meat back in the refrigerator to keep it cooled off. Just before noon he had finished removing the meat from the bones and rested for a while.

Bubba got a cup of coffee and sat on his couch. After turning his TV to Fox News he set back to enjoy his coffee. As he sat there he thought about the light floating through the trees again. *What could it have been? Was there really something there or was it just their imagination as they thought?* The light was visible for only a few seconds so maybe it was just the moonlight reflecting off of some shinny leaves. As he continued to watch his TV he dismissed the light as a play of shadows and shinny leaves.

As couple of hours later Bubba was grinding the meat when there was a knock at the door. It was Rick. Bubba waved for Rick to come in and then continued grinding the meat.

"I could not sleep when I got home." Rick said. "All I could think of was that light we saw in the woods."

"It was probably just the moonlight reflecting off of some shinny leaves." Bubba dismissed it again.

"But at one time there was that red light that came on for just a second or two." Rick reminded his friend.

Bubba stopped the grinder. "You're right." he said remembering the red light. "I saw it too."

"Do you believe in UFO's?" Rick asked.

"Actually I do." Bubba agreed. "Look at the trillions of stars in the night sky. Those are just suns like our own with planets orbiting each one. That would be trillions on trillions of planets. I cannot believe that there is only life on Earth nor could we be the more advanced of all planets."

"What do you mean ... we are not the most advanced?"

"Believing that we are more advanced than any other people on another planet is just as arrogant as thinking that there is only life on Earth." Bubba commented.

Rick said nothing for a few seconds. Then he asked; "Do you think that it was or could have been a UFO?"

Bubba started the grinder again. Over the noise of the grinder he yelled; "Could have been."

Bubba was almost finished with grinding the meat so Rick went into the den and watched the TV until the meat was finished. When all of the hog meat was ground he put it in vacuum bags and then placed the bags in a small chest freezer in the den. When he got some deer meat he would grind it up, mix it with the ground pork and spices and mix it all into sausage.

Bubba saved the small intestines of the two small hogs to make link sausage. When he shot a deer he would use the small intestines from it as well. After cleaning the intestines from the hogs he coated them with salt and placed them in a zip lock bag. Then he placed the bag in the freezer with the ground meat.

Finally Bubba was finished. All he needed now was one large buck but deer season would not start for another few days. Now it was time to sit down with Rick and plan the opening day hunt.

As the two men talked they decided on who would hunt where. Both of them had their areas where they planted rye grass and filled feeders with corn. Game cameras had shown that they had done a great job of drawing in the big bucks. But everything would change when others across the fence started shooting that morning. As others started shooting the deer would get nervous and their habits would change.

It did not take long for the conversation to turn back to the light floating through the trees in the woods. Rick wanted to go out that night and try to find it but Bubba did not want to. He

11

did not know why but something about the light put fear in his heart. It was like remembering that he had a bad nightmare but he could not remember the nightmare itself.

Finally Bubba gave in to Rick's hounding him and agreed to go back out into the woods that night.

"I'll hunt hogs not a light." Bubba said.

"And if we see the light again?" Rick asked.

"Then we'll see what it is."

At that time the news reporter started showing a video taken from a cell phone. It showed a large light moving just above the water and across the lake. Then the man that shot the video was interviewed. He told how that he saw the light as it passed over him. He was night fishing and heard nothing. The light flew across the lake and disappeared in the distance.

Bubba and Rick were both quiet. They knew then that the light was not the moonlight reflecting off of shinny leaves. They also realized that they had come close to a real UFO.

That night Rick and Bubba went into the woods. Both carried their cell phones and rifles. They only wanted to take pictures of the UFO but that was not to happen. For just over five hours the two men slowly walked the roads through the woods on Bubba's property. Many times they stopped to listen but heard no hogs. One time they heard a cougar down by the lake but it was not there when they got there.

About two hours after midnight Bubba and Rick stopped and listened one more time before heading back to Bubba's home. After listening for a few seconds Rick broke the silence.

"See any lights?"

Bubba snickered. "No. Do you?"

"Not sure if I really wanted to."

Bubba lead the way back to his house as Rick fallowed. It was a bit on the cold side so the men quickly got into the home and took off their jackets. Bubba built a fire in the fireplace. They talked over the hunt but mostly talked about the light that they did not see that night. Again they wondered if they had not seen anything before but there was that report on the TV about a mysterious light floating over the lake. It had to be true but neither men believed that they would ever see it again. In fact they both found peace in not seeing the light again.

By time Rick left the temperature outside had dropped down to just above freezing. Bubba's older joints started reminding him of the arthritis he had in his shoulders. His ankles and hips did not feel much better. After adding wood to the fire in his fireplace he sat down with a cup of hot apple cider.

Fox News was telling stories about thousands of people marching north out of Central America. Then the news turned to the elections and other things. At five in the morning Bubba turned the TV to a local news channel out of Waco. He often watched this channel for the weather reports not the liberal biased; so called news. As he waited for the weather report to come on he fell asleep. Then he woke up minutes later to a reporter talking about the light floating over the lake.

At first Bubba thought that the reporter was talking about the light being seen over the lake a couple of nights earlier but then realized that this light was seen only hours earlier. He wondered how he and Rick had missed the light but, it could have been over the lake and they never would have known it. They could not see the lake for all of the trees. During the few minutes that they were at the lake they did not see any lights.

Bubba fell asleep again and woke up about five hours later. He had missed the weather report but learned that the UFO had returned the night before. *What was it looking for? Was it looking for anything? If not then what was it doing?* These questions ran over and over in his mind. Then suddenly the phone rang.

"Did you see the news?" Rick asked before Bubba could say hello.

"Looks like we missed it." Bubba said with a yawn.

"Want'a go out again tonight?"

"Not really." Bubba explained. "But you can if you want."

"You're right." Rick said after thinking about it. "We need to stop walking the woods so much just before deer season."

"I'll fill the deer feeders later on today so they will be ready on opening day."

"Great." Rick was thankful. "That will save me on some gas."

The two men talked for just a few more minutes finalizing their plans for opening day of deer season. When Bubba hung up his phone he got up and made coffee. The temperature outside had dropped down to just below freezing. After getting a cup of coffee he put on his heavy military coat and stepped outside.

The camouflaged coat was warm but the wind still cut through it. He felt for the wild animals that had to live in it but he would try his best to relieve one of the big bucks of their torment in a few days. After a few minutes of standing in the wind Bubba took his cup of cold coffee back into the warm home where he rebuilt a fire in the fireplace.

After refilling his mug of coffee he went to his computer and got onto his diary.

> "I must admit that looking for the light that Rick and I saw the other night scares me. I do not understand this fear. It did not look like any UFO like what was reported on the TV. Why does this scare me so much? Maybe I might go out a little from the house and look again for myself tonight. I will have my trusty AR-15 with me with the forty round magazine in it. What can stand up to that not to mention the two extra thirty round magazines I will have?

Bubba sat back in his high back chair and looked over his desk. It was a large oak desk that he inherited from his parents. After a few minutes he stood and went to lay down on his bed. When he woke up it was daylight.

The coffee pot was off having turned itself off after two hours of not being used. However the coffee was still warm so he turned the pot back on and refilled his mug. Then he went out on his front porch and sat in his chair.

Bubba's home was at the top of a hill overlooking a small part of the lake. He looked over the lake knowing that in the daylight he would not see any UFO's. The lake was beautiful from his porch and he enjoyed sitting there and watching the lake often. After finishing his coffee he got up and began moving firewood into his home.

Using a canvas fire log carrier he began to move firewood from an area on his porch that held one quarter of a cord of wood. He took the firewood into his home and stacked it beside his fireplace. When he had a stack about four feet long and three feet high he stopped. Then he spent the next hour moving firewood from the two cord stack in the front yard to the porch. By then he was tired and went back into his home to watch his TV.

Trying to catch up on the news he watch Fox News. The local stations never told the truth about anything concerning the Republican president or other national news. He only watched local news out of Waco for the weather reports. At least they did tell the truth about local things.

Four caravans of people; literally thousands of them were coming out of Central America and were moving through Mexico with many of the first caravan were already in Tijuana Mexico. Taunting the border patrol by climbing the fence was a constant thing. But the government deployed an Entry Denial System (EDS) which emitted a sound wave that made a person feel like their skin was burning. It did not hurt anyone but no one could stand against it. They quickly ran back to the Mexico side of the fence.

Bubba and Rick had talked many times about what they would do if these people came over to the United States side. It would overwhelm Welfare and other government programs that were set up for American citizens. But they agreed that as long as the EDS was working they would think more on deer season opening in a few days.

Bubba drove into town and got four, fifty pound bags of whole corn for his and Rick's feeders. Bubba proudly hung his

CAR-15 in a gun rack by the back window of the truck. His truck doors were locked so he did not worry to much when he came out of the feed store and saw two young men looking at the rifle.

"That's why I have the doors locked." he told the young men. He did not recognize the men as any of the locals.

"What could you do to stop us if we wanted it ... old man?"

"You see this bulge on my left side?" Bubba told the men. "It's not a BB pistol."

Bubba had his Concealed Handgun Licenses (CHL) and carried a Ruger P-95. The magazine held fifteen rounds of 9 millimeter. Another round chambered gave him sixteen shots if he needed them.

The two young city boys stopped smiling. They thought that this old man would be a pushover but they found out different. As he walked up to the driver's side of his truck the young men left. With a big smile on his face Bubba drove around to the back of the feed store to load the corn he had just bought.

When Bubba got to his property he drove straight out to his deer feeder. After dumping two of the bags of corn into it he drove to Rick's feeder and put the other two bags in his feeder. Looking around he looked up wondering if he would see the UFO. It was still daylight so he knew that he wouldn't. Then he drove back to his home and burned the four empty bags along with trash from his home.

It was not all that cool that night as Bubba sat on his porch looking over the lake. He hoped to see some hint of a UFO so that he would know that it did exist. He worried that either it did exist or he and Rick were going crazy. He sat there for many hours before going in to watch his TV.

The local news reporter talked about the UFO that had been seen a few nights earlier. Then suddenly the cameraman turned the camera to look over the lake. Far off in the distance was a light floating over the lake again. Bubba ran outside and looked at the lake. A few seconds later he saw the light. It was real. Using his binoculars he could see that it was not just a light but an aircraft not of this world. Then suddenly it took off; straight up

16

into the sky and was gone in a second. With nothing else to see outside he went back to watch the local news reporter to see what they were talking about.

The reporter was a young woman that was so excited that she could hardly talk. From time to time she had to stop and catch her breath. Finally the news station turned to other news.

Bubba made a mug of instant coffee and added some chocolate syrup to it. The chocolate cut the bitter taste of the instant coffee. Then he went back outside and sat down to watch the skies again. After a couple of hours he went back inside and went to bed.

It was a restless night for Bubba as he tossed and turned in his bed. Now he knew that the UFO was real. He saw it. The idea of seeing the UFO caused him to be more scared than he was before. *What was it about the UFO that scared him?* He wondered about this until he finally fell asleep around three in the morning.

The next morning Bubba woke up to someone knocking on his front door. He got up and threw on a pair of shorts. Then he went to the door and opened it. It was Rick.

"Did you see the news this morning?" an excited Rick asked. Now we know it was real."

"I saw it last night." Bubba explained as he made a pot of coffee. "Then I went out on the porch and saw it myself as it floated across the lake."

"All they showed was a light."

"I looked through my binoculars and saw it real good." Bubba said. "It was defiantly an aircraft but not from here."

"Was it a helicopter?"

"No. When I said that it was not from here I mean that it was not from Earth."

"Are you sure?"

"Well ..." Bubba said. "Unless our military has aircraft that fly that slow ..."

"A helicopter can fly slow."

"This thing was round and about five times bigger than a helicopter and the lights on it were brighter than anything I had ever seen before."

When the coffee was made the two men filled their mugs and went out on the porch. After sitting in their chairs the conversation went back to the UFO. Later it changed to the deer hunting which would start in two day.

"I'll be here around five in the morning." Rick told Bubba.

"You know me. I'll be up and already waiting on you." Bubba said with a smile. "By the way. I put two bags of corn in both feeders."

"Thanks." Rick said with a heavy sigh. "I'll pay you back later."

"Just buy four bags next month."

"Okay."

Rick told his friend good by and left. Bubba knew that he would be getting up in a few hours. But seeing the UFO haunted him and he began to shake from fear. This was turning out to be causing him problems but why. It bothered him so much that he stayed in the house all that day.

Chapter 2

The Chip

It was four in the morning of opening day for deer season. Bubba had already been up for two hours. He was watching a special on the Waco Massacre. He had always thought that the place burned down because of the government but two people that lived through the fire said different.

One man said that through the smoke filled hallways he saw someone pouring gasoline in the floor. Then the man lit a match and dropped it and the flames shot up. A woman said that David had said many times that if the government tried to force their way in he would burn the place down.

Suddenly a knock at the door shocked Bubba back into reality. "Come in Rick."

Rick opened the door and came in. When he looked at the TV he said; "Oh I saw that last week. Janet Reno should be executed for the murders that she committed there."

I don't know." Bubba disagreed. "Two of the people that came out while the place was burning down said different."

"What do you mean?" Rick asked.

"You said you saw the show." Bubba reminded Rick. "A man that came out said that he saw another men pouring gasoline on the floor and then set it on fire with a match. A woman said that David said a few times that if the government tried to come in he would burn the place down."

So what do you think happened?"

"A high ranking FBI agent said that they launched ninety-three smoke and teargas canisters in the building and those things get pretty hot." Bubba took a breath and added; "I think it was a combination of the government's teargas and smoke canisters and someone on the inside setting fir to the place."

"But I still think it all started with the government and Janet Reno." Rick said in anger.

"Oh I agree and the government had no business being there anyway."

"They said that David had four fully automatic rifles but those are protected by the second amendment." Rick replied.

"Not really." Bubba suggested. "All of our rights are governed by laws so that no one will take that right to the extreme."

"Watch it now." Rick quickly warned his friend. "That's how the Liberal Communist are trying to take your AR-15 and my SKS rifle. They say that we are going to the extreme by just owning them."

"Yeah well ... lets just see them come to get my guns and we will see how many of them die for their stepping on my second amendment right." Bubba warned. "Anyone that comes to get my guns is a Communist and I will fight them with all of the power I have. I have no problem shooting a Communist."

The two men allowed this conversation to help them forget the morning hunt. With about an hour before daylight they grabbed their hunting rifles and left the house. They wished each other good luck and went their own ways to their deer stands.

A few minutes later Bubba sat in the plastic seat that he had wired down to a milk crate. The eastern sky was already turning a very light blue. He took a drink from his canteen and sat it on the ground beside him. Now it was just a matter of waiting for that big buck to come along.

Suddenly a bright light flashed over Bubba as it flew just above the trees. Then it stopped and came back to hover above him. Afraid to move he just sat there knowing that the aircraft knew he was there. Then just as quickly as it came it also left.

For a long time Bubba did not move. He just sat there sometimes slowly looking around for any deer. But the UFO had scared any animals around him away. After about thirty minutes he knew that he would not see any deer and stood. Then he realized that the sun was up. When the UFO hovered over him it was still down. Some time had passed; maybe thirty minutes without his knowing what happened. He had heard of people that were abducted having missing time. Did the UFO take him for a few minutes? If so then why?

Bubba went back to his home and found Rick already there sitting on the porch.

"Did you see it?" Rick asked as he stood. "It flew over the trees just before daylight."

Yeah I saw it." Bubba admitted but was reluctant to say anything about the missing time. Then again was there any missing time. Could he have fallen asleep and that was all that happened? That had to have been what happened. "It flew right over me."

The two men went into the home and sat down with cups of coffee. All Rick wanted to talk about was the UFO. Bubba wanted to watch the local news to see if there was anything about the UFO. That fear of the UFO was churning in his stomach again but now worse than ever. Bubba loved Rick like a brother but this was one time that he just wanted to be alone. Finally Rich had, had enough of Bubba not wanting to talk and left.

As Rick shut the front door Bubba sat there watching the TV. There was nothing about the UFO so he turned the TV back to the Fox News channel. Over six thousand people in two different caravans from Central American had threatened to rush our southern border with Mexico. Because of this the President had just given permission for the troops on the border to use lethal force if they needed to.

"About time." Bubba said out loud. "We can't protect our borders without the use of rifles." Bubba felt for the people but he felt that they should obey our laws as well. "Let'em rush the border now."

Bubba's head was hurting. As he rubbed the right side of his neck he felt something hard just under the skin and close to the back of his skull. By putting a small mirror behind his head and looking into another mirror in front of him he could see that there was defiantly something there. Without wasting any time he

21

called Rick and asked him to come over. All he told Rick was that it was important. It seemed like hours but about thirty minutes later Rick drove up.

Bubba went outside and met Rick as he got out of his truck. "Look at this." he told Rick as he pointed at what was under his skin.

"I can't see it very good." Rick said." Let's get inside and use a bright light."

The two men went into Bubba's home and sat on the couch. Rick turned a bright light to show on Bubba's neck and looked at the spot where Bubba was pointing.

"It looks like a pimple with something black under it." Rick told Bubba. "There is something there that is surrounded in puss."

"Can you get it out?" Bubba asked.

"It's kind'a big but it should come right out."

Rick pulled his knife and used the point of it to cut the skin over the head of puss. A tiny black object slid right out. Scraping it with his knife he showed Bubba what it was.

Looking at the black thing on Rick's knife Bubba said; "It looks like a piece of burned wood."

"I think it is."

"What do you mean?" Bubba asked.

Remember last summer when we were working on our deer stands and we were burning some dead limbs?"

"Yeah!"

"Remember when I was using the shredder and got to close to the fire?"

"Yes … and?"

"The shredder picked up something and threw it." Rick advised. "It hit you in the neck but when it stopped bleeding you forgot about it."

"Oh yeah." Bubba remembered. "But this should have got infected long before now." Bubba said. "Why is it just now getting infected?"

"Don't know but it did." Rick said. "Is this why you asked

me to come over here?"

"I was wondering if maybe …" Bubba said before deciding to say nothing to Rick. He thought that during the missing time the UFO may have picked him up and placed a tracking device in his neck. But he had not even mentioned the missing time to Rick yet.

"You were wondering if maybe … what?"

"Oh nothing." Bubba said. "I guess I just got scared with something so big in my neck."

"It's not that big." Rick laughed at Bubba.

Rick said that he had a lot to do and left, still laughing. Bubba sat back down on the couch and looked at the piece of burned wood that Rick removed from his neck. The more he looked at it the more it began to look metallic.

Bubba got up and looked through the junk drawer. Finally he found a magnet that came from a tiny speaker. When he hovered the magnet above the black thing in his hand he got the surprise of his life. The black thing flew up to the magnet.

"It's metallic … made of some type of metal." Bubba said to himself.

An old question began to form in Bubba's head. *Did the shredder still throw it into his neck of did the UFO place it there?* It did not matter if it was a piece of burned wood or metal. It was still there. Those in the UFO would not have picked him up just to placed a piece of burned wood in his neck. But they might have picked him up and placed a tracking device in his neck. Therefore; could the black metal thing be a tracking device? He knew no one that could check it out to find out.

The next morning Rick came back to go hunting again. Bubba knew that Rick believer in the possibility of UFOs because he saw it. He decided to tell his friend about the missing time and the black metal chip.

"Do you think it is a tracking device?" Rick asked.

"I don't know."

"Take it to David." Rick suggested. "He has all kinds of electrical devices for testing things. He might be able to see if it is emitting a signal."

"Yeah … your right." Bubba said. He felt better. Now he would find out if it was a tracking device or just a chunk of black metal.

"You going hunting this morning?" Rick asked Bubba.

No." Bubba said just loud enough for Rick to hear him. "I'm going to see David."

Okay then." Rick said. "It's off to shooting a buck I go."

Rick left out the front door and went to his deer stand. Bubba got another mug of coffee and walked out on the porch. He sat in his chair and looked over the lake. He hoped to see the UFO again but, the early morning was quiet. As the sun came up he found himself sitting there holding an empty mug. He got up and went back in the house. After refilling his mug with coffee and sat on the couch.

After turning the TV to the local news channel Bubba looked at the black chip again. It was triangle shaped. Then he noticed that it was smooth as well. After a few more minutes he put the metal chip in his pocket so that he would not forget it when he left for David's house.

Around eight in the morning Bubba got up and went to his truck. After cranking the motor up he just sat there thinking about the chip. He wondered if David might laugh and make fun of him. Then he realized that he no longer cared. He had to find out if it was a tracking device or just a chunk of black metal. He put the truck into gear and then left for David's home.

A few minutes later Bubba drove up into David's driveway. David came out and met Bubba at his truck.

"Haven't seen you in a long time." David said.

The two men shook hands and then Bubba got to the point of his visit. He told David about the light that he and Rick had seen and then about the black piece of metal.

"I think that … maybe … that UFO put this in my neck." Bubba admitted. "I need you to tell me if it is emitting a frequency so they can track me."

David looked at Bubba like he was crazy and then asked;

24

"Rick saw this ... UFO too?"

"We both did ... a few times."

"Okay then." David said. "Let's get inside and see what this thing is."

Both men went into David's home and into a back room. The walls were covered with electrical devices and a large oak desk and folding table had HAM radios and other radio equipment on them. David pushed a few things on his desk aside and lay the black piece of metal on the desk. Then he got one of the electrical devices and plugged it in. Instantly the needle on the front of the device shot to the right.

"I haven't even set it yet." David said talking about the device. "This thing of yours is defiantly emitting a frequency of some type."

For the next thirty minutes David worked on learning all he could about the black metal. Then he said that he was sure that it was a tracking device emitting a frequency to be tracked. Bubba started shaking.

"You okay man?" David asked Bubba.

"Yeah ... I guess." Bubba replied as he sat in a chair. "That means that they have already taken me at least one time."

"If you never noticed this thing under your skin before then you might have only been taken one time ... the other day."

"Do you believe in UFOs?" Bubba asked David.

"Oh yes." David replied. "I've heard things over these radios that would curl your toes up."

"What kind of things?"

"Mostly just noises." David said. "Background static. Everything out there gives off frequencies ... noises heard over radios. I've discovered that some of those noises are communications and not from Earth. But ... for now ... I can't prove anything."

"You need to keep it to study it more?" Bubba asked.

"If you don't mind." David agreed.

"Go ahead. I don't need it."

A few minutes later Bubba left and went straight to Rick's

25

home. He told Rick what he had done and what David had said about the black piece of metal.

"David called it a chip and said that it emitted a frequency for tracking." Bubba told Rick.

"Well now they can't track you or find you if he has the chip."

"Yeah but they'll find him thinking that I am there."

"Better warn him." Rick advised.

Bubba got on his cell phone and called David but there was no answer. After hanging up Bubba's phone rang. It was David.

"Sorry man. I was sitting on my throne."

"On your ..." Bubba replied. Then he realized what David was talking about. "Oh!"

Bubba warned his friend about the chip and that the UFO might come there and grab him. David was actually hoping that they might. It was something that he had hoped for all of his life.

"Why do you think I wanted to keep it?" David asked.

"You're crazy." Bubba told David. "Why would you want them to take you?"

"I don't really know." David said. "It's something that I have kind of planned on ... all my life."

The two men talked for a few more minutes. Bubba put his phone back in it's case on his side and looked at Rick.

"He wants them to come get him." Bubba told Rick. "He said that it is something he has been planning on all of his life."

"He is a bit on the weird side you know." Rick advised.

After that Bubba went back to his home. All the way home he shook from fear. Knowing that the UFO had already got him once he was more scared than ever and yet there was suddenly a drive in him to go into the woods that night. He did not want to but he felt that he had to. It didn't make any since.

Once home Bubba made some coffee and sat on his porch with a mug of it. He looked over the lake half way hoping to see the UFO but knowing that it did not come out during the day. *Where did it stay during the day? What was it doing there?* He sat there wondering about these and other things. When his mug was

26

empty he went backing his home and watch the TV for a while. He could not explain it but he caught himself watching the clock on the wall waiting for it to get dark. The more he thought about it the more scared he got.

Was this drive to go into the woods that night something that the UFO was doing? He actually felt that if he did not do it then he might come to some harm. But if he did go into the woods that night and the UFO picked him up again he might still come to some harm. It was enough to drive a man mad.

Then suddenly Bubba realized that it was dark outside. For a while he could not move. Then he realized that he was no longer scared. After standing he went to his gun rack and got his CAR-15 rifle. After putting on a jacket he walked out onto his porch. As he stood there he noticed someone driving up his driveway. It was David.

David drove up to Bubba's home and quickly got out of his truck. "They were at my house." David yelled at Bubba.

"Who?"

"The Grays." David said. "They probably thought that you were there because the tracking device was."

"How did you get away?" Bubba asked.

"They just walked into my home and looked around." David was almost out of breath. "They looked around and then left. While they were there I could not move."

"They didn't take you with them?"

"Only one of them even looked at me." David replied. "It was like they paid me no mind. They didn't even care that I saw them."

"They probably knew that no one would believe your story anyway." Bubba said.

David sat down on the porch steps and tried to calm down. "Why didn't they take me?"

"That's right." Bubba said with a smile. "You want them to take you."

"Not now. Not now that I've seen them."

"You said that they were the Grays?"

"Yeah!" David said. "Gray skin ... big eyes ... the whole bit."

David finally noticed that Bubba was holding his CAR-15. He asked Bubba what he was doing and then asked if he could go as well. Bubba did not care.

"You don't look scared anymore." David said as he noticed that his friend was so calm.

"I don't understand it either." Bubba mentioned. "I was sitting on my couch scared to even move. Then I noticed that it was dark and I was no longer scared. It's like something is driving me out into the woods. It's just something that I have to do."

"They are controlling you somehow."

"But you have the chip so ... how?"

"I don't know man but it does seem that they are." David said.

"Go in my house and grab my Ruger 10/22 rifle." Bubba told David.

A few minutes later David came out of Bubba's home with the rifle and they were on their way into the woods. Neither man knew what to expect or what they would do if the UFO showed up. Bubba's fears returned and he was scared again. But he still had the drive to go into the woods. David on the other hand still looked forward to being picked up by the UFO. It was something that Bubba could not figure out.

Chapter 3

Abducted

Bubba and David were in the woods for about thirty minutes when they started hearing wild hogs rooting nearby.

"You got a bunch of them out here don't you?" David asked quietly.

"One is to many." Bubba added. "Just one can mess up a field so bad that you can't drive a tractor over it unless you do it slow. Even then the tractor wants to throw you off."

As the two men listened to the hogs they decided not to shoot any of them. David was not much of a hunter and the hogs scared him. They scared him but being abducted by a UFO did not.

Bubba lead the way around the hogs until they came to another clearing. Suddenly a bright light shined down from above them. It was the UFO and they did not even know that it was there. There was no sound at all as it hovered above the two men. The next thing Bubba knew was that he was laying on what looked like a stainless steal table. He could not move.

The entire room looked to be made of stainless steal. He lay on one of two tables and David was laying on the other one. Three small creatures stood around the table that David was on. They seemed to be doing something to him but David was out cold and feeling no pain.

The creatures were about four feet tall but they did not have the large heads that he had always heard about. They were wearing masks that looked to maybe be breathing systems. Maybe they could not breath Earth's air which filled the room for his and David's sake.

Bubba looked around. His head was the only part of his body that he could move. The table that he was on was warm; not cold like stainless steal usually was. Bubba's fears returned and he began to shake again. Then he heard a soothing voice behind him.

"It's okay." the female voice said. "We won't hurt either of you."

Not being able to see the one that was talking to him Bubba asked what they wanted. Then a figure stepped around to his right. She was almost six feet tall and looked to be part human.

"My name is Becka and yes ... I am half human."

"And half what else?" Bubba asked.

Becka smiled and said; "Half what you call ... the Grays."

"These are Grays?"

"Yes." Becka informed him.

"But they do not have the big eyes and large heads."

Becka thought for a moment. "Oh those are hoods to help them breath your air. That's why they wear those masks right now."

"You said that you are not going to hurt us." Bubba reminded her. "Then what are they doing to my friend?"

"They are placing a ... I think you call it a tracking device in his head. You two won't be taking it out like you did yours."

"So it was a tracking device." Bubba said.

"You carried one for many years but it stopped working. With our superior technology we still sometimes depend on batteries ... just like you. We just placed that one in your neck until we could get you back up here and replace the one in your head."

"I don't want one in my head." Bubba insisted. One of the Grays looked over because of his raised voice.

"I'm sorry Bubba but I have no control over that."

"You know my name?"

"Of course." Becka said. "Like I said ... you have been with us many times over the years."

"Why am I just now learning this?" Bubba asked. "Why have I not had any hints that you have even been around here before the other day?"

"That's the way they do it." Becka said. "They come get you

when you are asleep and you never know it."

"Why are you so interested in me?"

"Despite the rumors that you hear about the Grays they really are interested in your sperm." Becka informed him. "In the past you have told them stories and they all like hearing them.

"Why is my sperm so important?"

"I don't know for sure but you have fathered three hybrid males."

"Like you?"

"Yes but I am a female."

"I can tell that." Bubba admitted. "You have nice boobs."

Becka smiled. "Thank you."

"Where are ... my boys?"

"Not on this ship but that is all I know."

Bubba just lay there for a moment and then asked; "What will happen to me now?"

"They will put you to sleep and then replace the tracking device in your head."

Bubba tried to move some but couldn't. "My back is hurting. I am sixty four years old you know."

"If I could trust you not to get off of the table ... would you like to sit up?"

"Oh yes please. I'll sit right here." Bubba promised.

Becka helped Bubba to sit up. It was like the force that held him down was turned off. Once he sat of the side of the table he felt the force pulling down on him again.

"You couldn't run if you wanted to." Becka said with a smile.

"Yeah! I can feel it." Bubba replied. "Just how many times have you taken me?"

"Oh I don't know." Becka said. "Maybe twenty five times including this one." She looked into Bubba's eyes and saw fear again. "You're scared."

"Well wouldn't you be?"

"But they will put you to sleep before putting it in your head ... actually through your sinuses and behind your eyes." she tried to ease his mind. "The other ones don't care if you suffer."

"The other ones?" Bubba asked.

"There are those that come here and perform experiments on humans but they are not from our planet." Becka told Bubba. "They are the Zims."

"What do you call yourselves?"

"I am simply a hybrid but the Grays are from Stylus." Becka told Bubba. We are at war with the Zims."

The Stylus were finished with David who was still knocked out. They took their instruments to another table that extended from a wall and left them. Then they got new instruments and walked over to Bubba.

"You need to lay back now. They won't hurt you." Becka said. "They actually like you."

As Bubba laid back he asked; "They like me?"

"You have been very helpful in the past." Becka said. "I will talk to you later."

One of the Stylus laid something on Bubba's forehead and he passed out. When they finished the thing on his forehead was removed and he woke up. He had a slight headache but that was all.

"You will have a headache for a while." Becka said. "You feel like walking?"

"You'll let me walk around?"

"You and I walk around every time we come get you." Becka answered. "They just wipe your memory before taking you back so … you just don't remember."

"I wish you would let me remember this time." Bubba quietly mentioned.

"I can talk to them and ask for you if you want."

"Would you?"

"Sure." Becka said with a smile. "I like being around you."

"Now I'm to old for you." Bubba said as he joked about their age difference.

"How old do you think I am?" Becka asked.

"You look like your about twenty years old but, you're a hybrid so I don't know."

"Thank you but ... I'm ninety-six." she told Bubba. "We hybrids live to be about three hundred."

Bubba stood with Becka holding onto him. He felt hands on his other arm and looked over to see one of the Stylus also helping him. After a few seconds he stood on his own.

Bubba looked at the Stylus helping him and could see through the mask that covered his face. He could see that it showed no emotions on it's face.

"Do they ever smile?" Bubba asked Becka.

"They don't show any emotions." she said. "If you try to scare one of them they might jump a little but that is all. There are two things that they cannot understand about humans. Your emotions and large breast."

"Don't take this the wrong way but ... you have nice ... boobs."

"We female hybrids grow breast because of the human DNA in us but all Stylus are flat chested. The female's breast will go some with milk if they are pregnant but that is all."

As Bubba and Becka walked down a hall he looked at the other Stylus around him. "How can I walk around without a breathing mask and the Stylus out here don't wear them either? They had to back there."

The air on Stylus is almost the same as that on Earth." Becka advised. "Earth's air has more oxygen in it so you will get tired soon from a lack of enough of it. Don't worry. You just have to rest more than me but the rest of the ship must use the air of Stylus. That means that you have to breath it right now."

Every time Bubba and Becka started to walk by a Stylus they would get against the wall. "Why do they get against the wall when we pass them?" he asked.

"Humans are very violent but most of these Stylus know you."

"If they know me then why are they still scared of me?"

Becka let out a heavy sigh. "Ok! I'll tell you."

Becka lead Bubba into a lunch room where they sat at a table. Holding his hands she told him about the Stylus' fear of humans.

"When the Zims take a human they do not care how much pain they cause them. The Zims also place something in their heads that they can use to control that human. Then they send the human to us as a weapon."

"What kind of weapon?" Bubba asked.

"Sometimes they carry explosives and sometimes they are just send to sabotage something like this ship."

"I don't think I like the Zims."

Becka smiled and leaned in towards Bubba. "We don't either."

"Why are you at war with them?"

"They sometimes attack our ships but ... mostly because of how they treat humans."

"How can I keep from being taken by them?" Bubba asked.

"Your tracking device also lets us know if the Zims try to get you." "How long will it take you to come to my rescue?" Bubba asked.

"Less than a minute."

"How can you get here so quickly?"

"During the day we hide at the bottom of the lake."

"Where are we right now?

"On what you might call a mother ship." Becka told him. "Soon we will go to a small ship or ... aircraft as you might call it. Then we will use it to take you and David back."

"How do you keep our telescopes from seeing this ship?"

"Right now we are hiding on the back side of your moon. This ship stays here."

Becka and Bubba got up and walked around a little more Finally it was time to send him and David back. Becka warned Bubba not to tell anyone about the tracking device in David's head. She also asked one of the Stylus if Bubba could keep his memory of this visit. The Stylus agreed.

Becka turned into a room where David waited on a floating table. Becka gave Bubba a quick kiss on the cheek and then backed up. The next thing that Bubba knew was that he and

David lay on the ground with their rifles beside them. Seconds later David woke up.

"What happened?" David quickly asked Bubba.

"I don't know." Bubba said. "I just woke up myself."

Bubba and David stood and walked back to Bubba's home. All the way back David was asking Bubba questions but he could not answer them. He knew the answer to most of them but Becka told him not to talk about the; visit as she called it. Once in the safety of his home Bubba made a pot of coffee. Then he and David went out on the porch with full mugs of the liquid courage.

"I still … kind of wish we had been abducted." David said.

"I don't." Bubba admitted. "You can go if you want."

"But we could learn so much from them."

"I don't think so." Bubba said. "From what I've heard they just hurt you in all kinds of ways."

"But still …" David said as his mind went deep into thought.

After a while David went home leaving Bubba sitting there wondering if he should have told his friend that he got his wish. It would have meant so much to David to know that he had been abducted but Becka warned him to say nothing to anyone. At least they allowed him to remember what happened. If he broke his word to them they might go back to blanking his memory. He did not want that.

The next few days went by slow for Bubba. He could not get his abduction out of his mind. He also could not get Becka out of his mind. She was beautiful even though she was only half human. She looked to be about twenty years old if that old but she was thirty-two years older than him. She was a bit to thin for his taste but he did not really care. It was not like they were dating.

A week after he and David had been taken Bubba got another urge to go out into the woods at night. This time he did not do it. After a few hours of watching his TV he went to bed. Suddenly he began to rise off of his bed. He floated towards the wall of the bedroom and then right through it. He continued to float upward as he picked up speed. Then he passed out.

Bubba woke up a few seconds later laying on one of the tables. This time no force was holding him down. He sat up on the side of the table just as Becka walked in.

"Have a nice trip up here?" Becka asked Bubba with a big smile.

"Well ..." Bubba said. "Floating through my bedroom wall was a new experience for me. How do you do that?"

Actually you floated through it at light speed." Becka told him. "It just seems that you're traveling slow. You see ... at that speed you would pass through anything."

"So I floated here instantly?"

"Pretty much."

Bubba thought for a moment and then simply said; "Wow!"

"That's how we bring everyone here and send them back." Becka said. That's also how we travel from here to our planet and back. That way instead of hitting something in space which would destroy the ship we fly through it."

Bubba stood and walked out of the room with Becka. This time she took him to the control room and allowed him to watch as other Stylus flew the craft. Suddenly the craft flew into space and around the moon. On the back side of the moon it docked with the mother ship. Then Becka lead Bubba out of the control room and to a metal door. When the door opened they walked into the mother ship.

Bubba and Becka walked back to the lunchroom. There they sat down to talk. He looked around at the other Stylus and tried to figure out what they were eating.

"They're all eating the same thing." Bubba told Becka.

"It's called muka." Becka told him. Muka is made from a plant that grows on Stylus. It's highly nutritious and all they eat." After seeing his interest she asked; "You want to try some?"

Bubba thought about Becka's offer and then agreed to try some. She got up and walked over to the food dispenser. Then she came back with a small bowl of white paste. Then she lay the bowl and a spoon in front of Bubba. He looked at the white paste and then back up at her. He smiled and took the spoon in hand.

After dipping the spoon in the white past he tasted it.

Bubba looked back up at Becka and smiled. "It's sweet … almost to sweet."

"Go ahead and eat it." Becka advised him. "It's good for you too."

Before leaving Bubba had two more bowls of the muka. He could have eaten more but the other Stylus were already looking at him. They had never seen anyone eat so much.

Becka had only one bowl of the muka but she enjoyed watching Bubba eat his fill. As they walked down the hallway Bubba asked her why they came and got him this time.

"I just wanted to see you again."

"They came back to Earth just to do something you wanted." Bubba said with a frown.

Becka stopped walking and looked down at the deck. "There is another reason." she said barely loud enough for him to hear her.

Seeing that Becka was upset Bubba asked her what was wrong. She only turned and continued walking. Then she turned into another room that looked to be a storeroom for supplies. She turned to face Bubba and told him what was bothering her.

"They want us to mate." Becka said. "It's never been done before … a human with a hybrid."

"They want it but do you?"

Becka smiled and said; "Actually I would do it."

"But why?"

"Bubba … you have only known me for a few days but I have known you for many years." Becka said as she continued to smile. "The Stylus may not have many emotions but because of my human DNA I do."

"Exactly what emotion are you talking about?" Bubba asked.

Becka's face changed to a more serious look. "I like you very much."

"Why don't they just take sperm from me while I slept and impregnate you with it?"

"Because I asked them to do it this way." Becka finally

37

admitted. "They liked the idea."

"So you actually want to get pregnant with my child?" Bubba asked.

"I do not actually want to get pregnant but I do want to be with you." Becka held Bubba's hands and added. "I wouldn't mind having your child."

"And if I refuse to do this would they still take sperm from me anyway?"

"No." Becka replied. "The Stylus do not force things like this. The Zims do."

"Can I have time to think this over?" Bubba asked.

"I guess so." Becka said. "The Stylus were just thinking that it would be the first time this was done. It's just another experiment to them."

"And what is it to you?"

"I would like to be with you and if I get pregnant then so be it."

"Let me think this over a while."

"Do you want to be with me?" Becka asked.

"I like walking with you and I wouldn't mind being with you." Bubba admitted. "You're beautiful."

Becka smiled and said; "Then think it over. We will contact you again in a week."

Bubba was taken back to his home where he woke up laying in his bed. For a while he just laid there before getting up. By then the sun was up a little and it was time to make some coffee. However; he had been up all night with Becka so after the first mug of coffee he went back to bed and fell asleep again.

Chapter 4

Refuge

Bubba woke up again around noon. After making more coffee and filling a mug he went out on the porch and sat down. Not knowing what to do he prayed.

"Father; I don't call on you much but my life is really crazy right now. You know what the Stylus and Becka want me to do but … what do you want me to do?

Bubba sat there on his porch looking over the lake. His mom's voice started repeating the Ten Commandments in his head; especially the one that said; "Thou shalt not commit fornication." Was this God giving him an answer to his prayer? He did feel uneasy about it not so much for breaking one of the Ten Commandments but because Becka was not human. He also had a problem with getting a woman pregnant just because others wanted her to have a baby.

With his coffee mug empty Bubba went back in his home and refilled it. Then he sat on the couch to watch his local news. As soon as he turned the TV on he saw that the reporter was showing videos of a UFO that was seen flying close to the lake during the daylight hours that morning. The reporter said that the video was taken only two hour earlier. His got Bubba's attention.

Hunting always helped Bubba to think so he grabbed his CAR-15 and went into the woods. He still had over six hours of daylight left so he knew that the Stylus would not be coming for him. *Why were the Stylus flying during the daylight that morning?* It did not make since but he figured they had their reasons.

Suddenly Bubba woke up on one of the tables on the UFO.

Then he realized that he could not move. He wondered what they were doing. Someone on the other table screamed from pain. *Where was Becka*? When the man on the other table screamed again Bubba realized that he was not on Becka's ship. These had to be the Zims.

Pain was not something that Bubba looked forward to. What did these Zims want from him? He was able to roll his head and look around some. This was not the same examination room as the one on Becka's ship.

To his left was a bench that extended from the wall. Two men and an older woman sat on it. They just sat there staring straight ahead as if they were in a trance. Then Bubba noticed the Zims walking over to him.

"Oh shit." he said as fear filled his mind.

Then suddenly the room shook as if the UFO had hit something. The Stylus found Bubba and were attacking the Zims' ship. The Zims that were walking towards him had stopped and were looking around. The room shook again as the Zims' ship was hit again by the weapons of the Stylus' ship.

One of the Zims looked at Bubba and then pointed at him. The next thing he knew was that he was waking up on the ground. Then suddenly he woke up again but on the Stylus' ship. Becka stood beside him.

As Bubba sat up on the side of the table Becka walked over to the other table and tried to ease the mind of the man on it. He was the man that had been screaming on the Zims' ship. Bubba looked at the wall but only saw the old woman sitting on the bench. She was still in a trance and stared straight ahead.

Bubba stood and walked over to the other table. When the man saw a human there he finally stopped fighting the Stylus and calmed down. That was when Bubba realized that the man was his friend David.

"Bubba." David said. "What's going on?" He shook from fear.

"It's okay David." Bubba assured his friend. "These are the Stylus. They will not hurt you."

40

"How do you know?" David said as he shook uncontrollably. "They were cutting on me a few minutes ago."

"No David. Those were the Zims; a different race of beings. These are the Stylus."

"They need to knock him out so they can patch up what the Zims were doing." Becka told Bubba.

"They're going to knock you out and fix the cuts on you." Bubba told David. "You'll be okay."

One of the Stylus placed the small device on David's forehead and he passed out. Becka grabbed Bubba's hand and walked him out into the hallway. Then they went into a small room with tables and chairs. It was a smaller version of the lunchroom on the mother ship.

"What happened?" Bubba asked Becka. "I was hunting and then I was on a Zims ship. Then just as some Zims started to walk over to me the room shook. Seconds later I was back in the woods and then suddenly up here."

"The Zims are trying to grab all of the humans that we are watching for some reason." Becka warned. "When they grabbed you we were on the bottom of the lake. Your tracking device alerted us to the Zims grabbing you so we surfaced and attacked them in space. They tried to send you and the others back but we grabbed all of you when they did."

"Maybe that is why I am dizzy."

"Yes." Becka advised. "You went through to much at one time. Like I said ... the Zims do not care about humans or the damage they do to you."

"Well thanks and ... tell the Stylus I said thanks."

"They may not speak but most of them know your language." Becka said. "You can tell them yourself."

I never hear them talking." Bubba mentioned. "How do they communicate with each other?"

"They use telepathy but only a few humans can hear what they are saying."

"Evidentially I am not one of them."

Becka smiled. "No you're not."

Bubba looked up at the small food dispenser and asked; "Could I get some of that muka?"

"You hungry?"

"No not really." Bubba said with a smile. "I just like the stuff."

Becka started laughing. It was the first time Bubba ever heard her laugh. "Of course." she said. "Go get some."

Bubba stood and started to walk to the food dispenser when the ship shook valiantly. Suddenly water started coming into the ship. Becka grabbed Bubba who had fallen to the floor and took him to the room where he and David were sent back to Earth from. She called it the transport room. Instantly they were transported back to the earth's surface.

Bubba woke up before Becka. He shook her causing her to wake up. Then they stood. Bubba looked around and realized where they were.

"That's the lake so my home is up there a ways." he said as he pointed up the hill.

This time Bubba lead the way. As they worked their way up the hill Bubba saw his CAR-15 laying on the ground. Realizing that this was where he was when the Zims grabbed him he grabbed his rifle and continued to lead Becka to his home. Finally they reached his porch where Becka stopped. She had never seen his home before and looked it over.

"Will we be safe here? She asked.

"I have almost three thousand rounds for this rifle." he advised her. "We're safer here than on your ship right now."

Becka fallowed Bubba up the steps and into his home. Again she looked around. All of her life she had been on Stylus ships where almost everything looked like stainless steal. Now her eyes were looking at wood, cloth, and other colorful things. She almost lost her breath as she looked around.

"It's beautiful." Becka said.

"It's home." Bubba added. "I love it here."

"Oh I do too." Becka said as she continued to look around.

Bubba made some coffee and then went into his bedroom and

got the other four magazines for his rifle. After loading them he set them on his end table beside the couch.

"You want some coffee?" Bubba asked Becka.

"I've never had it."

Bubba made Becka a mug of coffee and added sweetener and milk. It was how he drank his coffee. Becka took a sip and made a funny face.

"It's bitter." she said.

After adding more sweetener to Becka's coffee he asked what may have happened to David. She had no idea but hoped that the Stylus transported him out of the ship. It was quickly filling with water when they left.

"You'll be safe here until we can get you back to the Stylus." Bubba advised Becka.

"I don't want to go back." she told him. "I want to stay right here ... with you."

"You can do that if they will let you."

"They probably will but ... why even let the Stylus know that I am here?"

"You don't want them to know."

"The Zims might find out and they kill all Stylus hybrids." Bubba could see that she was scared.

"Just stay in the house and you should be safe." Bubba advised her. "I'll call Rick. He and his wife will help you get some human clothes."

"Who is this Rick?"

"A real good friend of mine. Like David ... he is a good friend."

Bubba called Rick and asked him and his wife to come over. He told Rick that it was very important. Rick agreed but did not know why Bubba wanted them both. It was enough that his friend needed them both.

About forty five minutes later Rick and his wife drove up to Bubba's home. Becka went into Bubba's bedroom to wait until he called her. Bubba opened the front door and let in his two friends. Rick and his wife, Beth, sat on the couch. Bubba rolled the chair from his desk and sat down in front of the couch.

"This is very important Rick."

"Okay. What's wrong?"

"How much does Beth know about what is going on?" Bubba asked.

"Everything I know but I don't know much."

"Okay ... just listen to what I have to say and then I will prove it."

Bubba told Rick and Beth what had been going on since Rick was there last. He told them about David who might be dead as far as he knew. Then he asked them both what they thought.

"Remember that I have seen the UFO so what you just said ... I guess could be true." Rick said.

"You said that you had proof." Beth added.

"What you are about to see ... you can't tell anyone. She needs your help."

"Who does?" Beth asked.

"Becka." Bubba called out. Seconds later Becka walked out of the bedroom and stood beside Bubba.

"She's an alien?" Beth asked.

"I'm actually a hybrid ... half Stylus and half human." Becka told them.

Rick took in a deep breath and let it out. "So what do you need?"

"Actually she needs Beth's help." Bubba advised them. "She wants to stay here but she needs to look more human. She needs human clothes and she cannot go shopping."

"Of course." Beth said. "I'd be happy to help her."

Beth and Becka went into an area of the den where there was room to move around. Then Beth took a measuring tape and took measurements of Becka so she would know what size of clothes to buy.

"Rick." Bubba said taking advantage of being alone. "We are involved in a war between two different species and Earth knows nothing about it. We can't call the military or the cops. I have to deal with this myself but I really need your help. Bubba's conversation was cut short with someone knocking on the front door.

Bubba went to the front door as Beth and Becka went into the bedroom. He opened the door and found David standing there. He was wet but otherwise in good shape. Bubba let his friend come in and moved him to the back bathroom. Then he went and got David some dry clothes.

"I have a surprise for you when you get some dry clothes on." Bubba told David.

"What is it?" David asked as he took off his wet clothes.

"Remember when I walked up to you on the Stylus ship? You were laying there unable to move."

"Yeah. Don't think I'll ever forget that."

"Remember that hybrid that stood beside me?"

"Yes I do."

"That was Becka and she is here."

"Let me get dressed. I want to see her."

"Just remember that they were not the ones that hurt you. They were the ones that patched you up while you slept."

"Oh yeah." David remembered. "Then I need to thank her."

As David got dressed Bubba walked back into the den. Beth had finished her measuring and was ready to get some clothes for Becka. Bubba gave her his credit card and asked her to not spend all of his money. Then she and Rick left to get Becka's human clothes.

That was when David walked out of the back bathroom. Instantly he walked up to Becka and just looked at her.

"Thanks for helping me but mostly for knocking me out before patching me up." he said to her. "Those other ones were cruel."

"They are the Zims. They don't care about human pain, just their work."

Once Bubba was satisfied that David was not going to hit Becka he sat on the couch. Becka sat beside him and slid as close to him as she could. David sat in the chair facing the couch.

"So there are two different aliens?" David asked.

45

"Yes." Becka said. "The first ones that picked you up are the Zims. They look like the Stylus but they do not care if you scream while they work on you. Then the Stylus rescued you and brought you to their ship where you met Bubba and me."

David had many questions and Becka was more than happy to answer them all. For almost two hours she answered his questions until there was a knock on the front door. Bubba answered the door to find Rick and Beth standing there with their arms full of clothing.

"We knew that we could get her some good clothes at the Damaged Goods store in town so we went there." Beth said. "I also picked her up some makeup." Beth looked at Bubba and added; "She will not look the same when I am finished."

Oh God." Bubba said. "What is it with women and their makeup?" Bubba preferred his women wearing no makeup at all.

Becka fallowed Beth into Bubba's bedroom and closed the door behind her. Bubba, David, and Rick looked at each other and then went out on the porch. Then they sat down. This was when Bubba told the other two men about the Stylus wanting him and Becka to mate. Rick and David thought that it was funny and laughed. However; their laughing stopped when Becka stepped out on the porch.

Beth stepped out on the porch first but Becka was right behind her. Becka wore a long green skirt with a green long sleeve blouse. She had been wearing her coal black hair up in a bun but now it hung down below her shoulders. She was even more beautiful than before.

"She almost looks human doesn't she?" Beth mentioned. "She could stay here as … maybe your sister."

"Or maybe his girlfriend." Becka added as she looked down hoping for some response from Bubba.

For a while no one said a thing. The others were waiting for Bubba to say something and Bubba waited to see if anyone else might say something. Finally he said; "I guess I could." leaving everyone still not knowing what he would call her.

Becka was silent. She liked Bubba more than she told him. But she did tell Beth when they were in the bedroom. Beth looked at Bubba and insisted on him making a decision. "Is she going to be your sister or girlfriend?"

"My girlfriend." Bubba answered. Then he added "I guess."

Becka turned and started crying. She walked into Bubba's bedroom and closed he door.

"Are you an animal?" Beth yelled. "That woman may not be human but she is still a woman. She likes you very much and all you do is hurt her."

Bubba looked at Rick. "What did I do ... or say ... or what ever?"

"We need to go." Beth told Rick as she went into the bedroom and told Becka. Seconds later she returned and grabbed Rick's arm. Then she stormed her way out of the front door with Rick in tow.

"I think you need to go apologize to Becka." David said.

"But what for?" Bubba asked. "I still don't know."

"Just go to her and apologize. Don't say what for. They don't care. It is just enough that you apologize."

"Why can't woman act human?" Bubba asked.

"She isn't human."

"Oh yeah." Bubba said as he turned and went into the bedroom. After closing the door he lay beside Becka and told her that he was sorry. She rolled over to face him.

"I forgive you." Becka said with a big smile.

Two hours later Bubba walked out of the bedroom and found David still sitting on the couch watching Fox News on the TV.

"With almost ten thousand people from the first caravan at the California border another caravan of over two thousand is approaching them. The Mexican president said that he cannot control them."

Bubba sat on the couch and said nothing.

"You apologize?" David asked.

"Yap."

"You get some?"

"Yap"

"Was it nice?"

"David." Bubba said. "Don't let her know I told you."

"Of course not." David replied.

The two men sat on the couch for a while watching the TV. After about thirty minutes Becka came out and sat beside Bubba. Then she scooted closer to him and lay her head on his shoulder.

"She got some." David said. "I've never seen her smiling that big before."

"Do what?" Becka asked.

"Oh I was talking about that woman on the TV." A quick glance into Bubba's eyes told him to shut up.

"Well I got'a go." David said as he shook Bubba's hand. Then he stepped over to Becka and kissed her hand. "You two have fun now." he said as he stepped outside and closed the door.

Becka spent the rest of the day right there on the couch, beside Bubba, and in his arms.

Chapter 5

Struggle to Survive

Becka spent that night with her head resting on Bubba's shoulder. Bubba was the first to get up the next morning. He was sitting out on the porch when Becka got up. She got herself a mug of coffee and joined him on the porch.

It was a cool morning but not cold. The sun would not be up for another two hours. As they sat there Bubba asked if she was scared that the Zims might find her.

"They have no way of tracking me or finding me. They might have the frequency of your tracking deice though."

"Why do you say that?" Bubba asked.

"How did they grab you the other day?"

"I think they just hovered over me while I was hunting and grabbed me in the woods.

"They grabbed you during the day also." Becka said. "That's not like them or the Stylus."

Bubba and Becka talked about his being grabbed by the Zims for a while. Then they saw a truck coming up the driveway. Becka got ready to run into the house but Bubba said that it was Rick. When the truck pulled up to the house Rick and Beth got out. Beth was still upset with Bubba and walked right past him and fallowed Becka into the house.

Rick sat down with Bubba and they talked about hunting; something that they had not done in over a week. The women were involved in what happened the night before. Becka teased Beth for a while and would not tell her but finally admitted that she hoped that she was pregnant.

"So you two did it?" Beth asked.

"Only once but it was what Bubba called foreplay that I liked the most."

As the women talked Rick and Bubba did some of their own talking. "So what brings you two over here before daylight."

"I was hoping to maybe see the UFO." Rick admitted. "Do you think it is looking for you two?"

"I don't know." Bubba replied. "Maybe you should go hunting while you are here." Bubba advised.

"I brought my hunting rifle to do just that." Rick said.

The two men got up and went into the house. Rick sat on the couch with Beth and Becka. Bubba took the chair from his desk but before he could sit Becka asked him to sit on the couch. When Bubba sat on the couch Becka sat in his lap.

Suddenly five Stylus stood in the den and around the couch. Bubba started to get up but none of them could move.

"They are Zims." Becka warned. "They're gon'a kill me Bubba." Becka was scared and crying. Seeing her fear and her tears Bubba's fear turned to extreme anger. The leader of the Zims looked into Bubba's eyes. For the first time in his life fear entered his heart. This was a look he had never seen in a human. Then he did something that none of them expected. He spoke.

"Human." he said to Bubba. "Fear us not." His English was broken but he made his thoughts known.

"You touch her and I'll kill you." Bubba told him.

"My name ... Bok. You understand?"

"Do you understand what I told you?" Bubba asked.

Another Zim that was behind Becka held something in his hand. Suddenly he looked up at Bok. Using telepathy he told Bok something.

Bok looked at Becka and said; "You're pregnant."

Becka broke down crying. Then Bok lay his hand on her shoulder and said; "You will not be harmed." He looked at Bubba and asked; "Who is the father?"

"I guess I am but we only did it one time last night. How can you already know that she is pregnant?"

"Our devices are father advanced than anything you might have on this planet." Bok said. "None of you will be harmed. Many on our planet do not like harming humans."

50

"How do we know that we can trust you?" Bubba asked.

Bok looked at one of the other Zims and suddenly Bubba could move. The first thing that he did was go to Becka. Then Bok had the other Zim release Becka. Instantly Becka threw her arms around Bubba.

"Because humans are so violent the rest of you will be released when we leave." Bok promised. Then he turned his attention to Becka and said; "Please tell the Stylus that we are not their enemy. Other Zim ships are though."

"Why are you different?" Bubba asked.

"We just are." Bok said. "Like I said earlier ... our people ... some do not like being so savage to humans." Then he turned to Bubba and added; "If we could find you then so can the other Zims. You must have that tracking device removed. We know the frequency."

Bok turned back to Becka. "Oh ... some of the others from your ship are on our ship ... for safety. Eleven died when the ship flooded. We will return them here when we leave.

"Who attacked them?"

"One of our other ships." Bok said. When I saw them do that I ordered my ship out of the area. Now we are being hunted by the other two ships. We must go now but we will be seeing you again."

Suddenly the Zims were gone as quickly as they arrived. Rick and Beth could move again. All four of them said nothing for a while. Then Rick spoke.

"Do you believe him?" Rick asked.

"No." Becka quickly said. "They want my baby."

"You mean our baby." Bubba added as he held onto Becka tightly.

Bubba stood and asked Rick to join him out on the porch. When they were gone the women started talking.

"Ooooooo!" Beth said. "Did you see how mad Bubba got at Bok?"

"I thought that he was going to come out of that chair." Becka said.

"That man loves you."

"Not yet." Becka replied. "He's only known me for a few weeks."

"But Bok said that you were pregnant and that's all it takes." Beth advised her.

"It's just the baby." Becka told Beth. "He would not have acted like that if Bok had not mentioned that I was pregnant."

"I don't know." Beth said with a big smile. Just watch how he acts around you and you'll see that I'm right."

On the porch the men were talking when David drove up. When he got up on the porch Rick and Bubba told him what happened. When the three men went back into the house they found six Stylus standing in front of Becka. Using telepathy she was telling them not to worry and that these humans were friendly.

When the Stylus saw Bubba they walked over to him and shook his hand. Shaking hands was a custom that was quickly becoming popular with the Stylus. To be more at their level and to help them to feel better Bubba got down on one knee to shake their hands.

Paulm was the Commander of the Stylus ship that sunk to the bottom of the lake. As Bubba walked towards Becka Paulm told him "Thanks" by use of telepathy. Bubba quickly stopped and turned. Paulm smiled wondering if Bubba heard him. Bubba tried using his mind and said; "You're welcome." Paulm heard him. From then on Paulm helped Bubba on using his mind to speak to them.

The problem with telepathy was that everyone close by heard what you were saying to one of them. But that was the same when speaking out loud anyway so it did not bother him. He sat beside Becka and heard her thinking something. He looked into her eyes and heard her say that she loved him. She was shocked when she heard him say that he loved her too." All of the Stylus were looking at Bubba and Becka. There was no whispering with telepathy.

Becka scooted right up against Bubba. It was the only thing

52

she wanted to do at that time; and anytime she was close to him.

Bubba looked at Paulm and said; "Somehow; we need to get this tracking device out of my head. Bok said that the Zims knew the frequency."

"But we cannot do that until another Stylus ship gets here. Becka said. "And Paulm said that they did not have time to contact Stylus Command about their ship going down."

"Until we get this thing out of my head none of us are safe." Bubba told everyone. "So what do we do?"

"We all have guns. Mine are in my truck." David said. "Make this a fortress that even they cannot get into."

"All they have to do is transport any one of us out as they wish." Becka reminded everyone. "It doesn't matter what we do we can't stop them."

"We can carry our weapons and if they come here we can shot them." Rick suggested.

"But how would we know if those that showed up were Stylus or Zims?" Bubba asked. "And what about Bok and his crew? I don't trust him but is he friend or foe?"

"I never met Bok before today but I do not trust him." Becka said. "He is still a Zim."

Becka and the other Stylus there all looked at one of the Stylus. Then Becka told the others what he said. "He just said that there is nothing we can do to keep the Zims from just taking one of us."

"How do you take us but leave our rifles where we were?" Bubba asked.

"We can select what to leave behind." Becka advised. "We could leave all of your clothing as well if we wanted to."

"There's something to think about." Beth commented.

Everyone except the Stylus laughed. Becka got up and made some oatmeal for the Stylus. It was not Muka but it came close. After adding sugar they loved it. Then she got blankets and made pallets in the third bedroom for them to sleep on. Then she came back into the den and told the Stylus what she had done for them. After eating they all went into the third bedroom and lay down.

"Well at least Bok kept his word and gave us the Stylus that lived." Beth said.

"Why would he do that if he could just take Becka anyway?" Rick asked.

"I don't know but I just don't trust him." Bubba admitted. "There is just something about him."

"I think I'll just stay here for a while if you don't mind Bubba." David said. "My rifle is in my truck. At least I can be one more rifle in case you need one."

Over the next three days nothing happened. With the oxygen being to high the Stylus could not sleep well. They were active and staying inside the home was hard for them.

Then one night another Stylus appeared right in front of David. He almost shot the creature that was just suddenly there. The Stylus wore the usual big head and eyes hood so he could breath easier. He tried speaking to David using telepathy but Dave could not hear him. He raised his hands hoping to not get shot. Finally Becka came out of the bedroom and stopped David.

"David." Becka said. "He is from a Stylus rescue ship."

Bubba came out of the bedroom. "What's going on?" he said as he yawned.

"This is a Stylus from a rescue ship." Becka said. "He said that a Zims ship contacted them and told them what happened to Becka's ship. They came to get the others."

At that time the other six Stylus walked out of the third bedroom. They stood together in front of the one that just came from the rescue ship. Suddenly all six of them vanished. Then the Stylus that still wore the hood stood in front of Becka. After a few seconds he also vanished leaving Becka there.

Becka turned to Bubba and smiled. "Three Stylus ships will watch over us and keep us safe from the Zims." Then she hugged Bubba tightly.

After a pot of coffee was made Bubba, Rick, and David filled their mugs and walked out on the porch. The sky in the east was barely turning blue. It was going to be a beautiful day.

The three men just sat there for a while with none of them

saying a thing. The air was cool with a slight breeze blowing. Finally Rick spoke up.

"Wow!" he said. "So much has happened the past few days."

"Are we safe now?" David asked.

"I think so." Bubba said. "There's three Stylus ships watching over us now."

"Watching all of us or just Becka?" Rick asked.

While the men sat outside talking Beth and Becka were inside discussing a few things of their own. They were talking about important things like using makeup, jewelry, and shoes. Surely these things had something to do with surviving the situation. Finally they got to talking about what they would cook that evening. At least they no longer had to cook any more oatmeal. They were almost out anyway.

Feeling safe for the first time in a while the men talked about going hunting and bringing some fresh meat into the home. Then Rick and David admitted that they had things at their own homes to tend to. As David walked out to his truck Rick went into the home and got Beth. A few minutes later they also left.

For the first time in a while Bubba and Becka were alone. Bubba looked at Becka and asked; "Can you handle a gun?"

"Never had to." she admitted.

"Well by noon you're going to be a crack shot." Bubba told her.

Bubba went into his bedroom and came out with his Ruger 10/22 rifle. Becka fallowed him outside to where he had a rifle range set up. He walked down the one hundred yard mark and stapled a target to the board. Then he walked back to Becka and started explaining the use of a rifle, it's safety and how to use the sights. Seconds later Becka was taking her first shot.

Becka pulled the trigger and the rifle fired. Using his binoculars Bubba looked at the target. Becka's first shot was only a bit to the right of the bulls eye. She took another shot and the bullet hit closer. Then she took in a deep breath and let it out. This time she hit the bulls eye.

"Damn girl." Bubba said with a big smile. "You're a natural.

Becka fired the rest of the rounds in the magazine with every shot hitting the bulls eye. "That's your rifle from now on." Bubba told her. Then he took the rifle back in the bedroom and came back outside with a High Point nine millimeter pistol and a box of shells.

After covering the holes on the target with masking tape he came back to Becka and talked to her about the pistol. This time she was much closer to the target; about fifty feet from it. Again he explained the safe way to handle it, how to load the magazine, and how to fire it. When she fired her first shot the bullet hit the target just to the left of the bulls eye. The second shot hit the bulls eye. Then she emptied the magazine hitting the bulls eye with every shot.

"That's your pistol from now on." Bubba told Becka.

The two went back into the house where Bubba set her up with a web belt and holster for her new pistol. Before long he had her looking like a soldier ready for war.

Just as Becka was taking her web belt off she heard Bubba talking to someone in the den. She looked out the bedroom door and saw that he was talking to a Stylus. Then suddenly two more Stylus appeared. When they grabbed Bubba's arms Becka knew that they were not the Stylus. They were Zims. Grabbing her pistol she stepped out of the bedroom and pointed the it at the head Zim. Flipping the safety to off she pulled the trigger but, nothing happened.

Startled that he was not shot the Zim that stood in front of Bubba turned to face Becka. Instantly Bubba broke free and started swinging at anything that moved. Then he picked up a small statue of an American eagle and started using it as a weapon. In only a few seconds three Zims lay dead on the floor. Bubba had been hit in the forehead and was bleeding a little.

"This is why you always keep your firearms loaded." Bubba told Becka.

Becka went back into the bedroom and loaded the magazine of her pistol and placed it back in the pistol. Then she pulled the slide back and let it go. Now her pistol was loaded and ready to go. Before placing her pistol in the holster she flipped the safety on.

"Good girl." Bubba said from the bedroom doorway.

Becka smiled and walked over to Bubba as if she was going to hug him. Then she turned and walked into the den.

"Oh!" Bubba said with a big smile. "You're a bad girl now. You must be punished."

As the two laughed two Stylus appeared. Bubba almost hit one of them with the eagle statue when Becka stopped him.

"This is Paulm." Becka warned Bubba. "He was the Commander of my ship."

Paulm informed Becka that the Zim ship had been chased away. She and Bubba were safe again. Then he looked at the three dead Zims on the floor. With a smile he ordered the ship to transport the three to the ship. Then he and Becka talked a while using telepathy but this time Bubba could not hear them.

Bubba went into the bathroom and got the First Aid Kit. He cleaned the wound on his forehead and then put a large band-aid on it. He turned to find Becka standing there.

"You okay Baby." she asked.

Bubba smiled. "That's the first time you ever called me by a pet name."

"Beth is teaching me many things and suggested that I start calling you something other than your name."

Bubba continued to smile. "I love you." he admitted.

"I know." she replied. "I love you too."

Bubba and Becka walked out into the den. He noticed that when the three dead Zims were transported out of his home even the blood on the floor was gone.

"Good!" he replied. "Nothing to clean up."

Bubba and Becka were sitting on the couch a few minutes later when Paulm appeared again.

"It's Paulm again." Becka quickly said. "What can we do for you now?" she asked Paulm.

Paulm stood in front of Becka as they communicated. Again Bubba could not hear what they were saying. Then he wondered if his being hit in the head might have changed things. Maybe that was why their voices were being blocked.

Suddenly Paulm vanished. Becka turned and told Bubba that the Stylus wanted her to go with them back to the planet Stylus. Then she said that she would only go back if he was allowed to go with her. They just wanted to keep her safe from the Zims and it was not safe there at Bubba's home.

"What did they say about me going as well?" Bubba asked.

"They agreed but, remember that the air is thinner there." she reminded him. "You would get tired easily."

"How long would we be gone?"

"Just a little while." she told him. "If I went alone they would want me to stay there but with you going … they know that you would not be able to breath well. They just want me to be safe."

"Why the sudden care for you?" Bubba asked.

"I have in me the first human hybrid baby." she told him. "The Zims want me because of that so now the Stylus are interested."

Would we have any say so on when we could come back?"

"Not really but as soon as the Zims discover that we are no longer here they will leave. We also need to get that tracking device out of your head so that when we do come back the Zims cannot find you."

"Do you want to go?"

"Neither of us are safe here right now." she admitted. "We would be safe on Stylus and we would not be there long."

Chapter 6

The Trip

Bubba called Rick and told him what was going on. He asked Rick to check in on his dog Odie. "We'll be back as soon as the Zims stopped coming around."

After being assured that Rick would check in on Odie he went into the bedroom and started to pack a bag of clothes. "You won't need to take any clothing." Becka said. "That will be provided for you."

"What about my CAR-15 rifle?" Bubba asked jokingly.

"You won't need it either." Becka assured him.

Finally Bubba and Becka stood side by side in the den. Seconds later they were standing in the transport room of the Stylus ship.

"I thought that transporting made us pass out." Bubba inquired.

"That's a different transporter system that we use on humans only."

Bubba looked around and then said; "Okay."

Bubba and Becka were taken to a room that had been set up for just the two of them. "Just step up close to the door and it will open." Becka advised Bubba.

The room was furnished with a desk and bunk beds. Looking at the bunk beds Bubba said; "Guess they don't think we ... love each other."

"It's only a three day trip." Becka said. "I think you'll be okay."

"Exactly where is Stylus?" Bubba asked.

"Almost on the other side of the galaxy." Becka answered. "It only takes three days to get there."

Bubba had a million questions and Becka tried to answer all

of them. They were allowed to walk around the ship except in two places where guards were set up at the doors. Behind those two doors were the weapons room and the bridge. Although Becka was allowed on the bridge Bubba was not. Some of the Stylus on that ship were from Becka's ship that sank and they knew Bubba. The others did not.

The name of the Stylus commander of the ship was Ail. He tried to talk with Bubba when he could using Becka as a translator. Ail wanted to learn more about humans but he was more interested in Bubba's life; how he lived. They did not hunt or fish on Stylus and this concept fascinated him. Eating meat was something that no Stylus was used to.

Still one day from the planet Stylus the ship shook violently. Two Zim ships were attacking the one Stylus ship. The Stylus ship increased speed beyond the danger point but the two Zim ships fallowed. As the three ships fought it out in space the Stylus ship called for help. Luckily two other Stylus ships were not far away. They were on their way to Earth.

When the two Stylus ships arrived the two Zim ships took off. One of them was disabled and the other one left it and it's crew. The two Stylus ships captured the disabled Zim ship and it's crew.

The crew from the captured Zim ship were transported to the same ship that Bubba and a Becka were on and placed in the brig. The brig was not large enough to hold them all so the other two ships had to take a few. The two ships had to change their plans and fallow the other ship back to Stylus to drop off their prisoners. Then they would continue their trip to Earth.

At one time Bubba walked to the brig to see the captured Zims. A Stylus guard stopped him from getting to close to the bars but he was still able to see them. The prisoners looked at Bubba. They had never seen a human in space before. Some had never even seen a human before.

As the Zims looked at Bubba one of them stepped closer to the bars. "Bubba?" he asked.

Bubba was startled to hear a Zim speak English. The only

other Zim that he heard speak his language was Bok. "Bok?" he asked.

"Yes ... my friend." Bok said.

"Why did you attack us?" Bubba asked.

"My ship was with the other ship when they attacked this ship." Bok insisted. "Is Becka here also?"

"Yes." he told Bok. "The Stylus are taking us to their planet so she would be safe from your kind."

"Please tell the commander of this ship that I and my crew are not your enemy." Bok begged.

"I'll tell him about you."

"Thank you ... my friend." Bok said with a bowed head. He was playing the game for all he could but Bubba was not fooled.

"But stop calling me your friend." Bubba insisted. "I still don't trust you."

"Proving myself to you will take time." Bok suggested. "Just give me that time."

Bubba went back to his and Becka's room where she was just getting up. "I figured I would find you in the lunch room easting more muka." she said.

Bubba smiled. "I do like the stuff but I was looking at the prisoners. Bok is there."

Becka quickly looked up at Bubba. "You sure?"

"Yeah. We talked for a while."

"What did he have to say?" Becka asked.

"He wants me to talk to the ship's commander about how nice he was to us. He wants me to tell the commander that he and his crew are not our enemy. He also said that the other ship attacked us not his ship."

"Sorry my love but, both ships attacked us."

"You sure both ships did?" Bubba asked.

"Yes." I heard he commander talking to others about it."

"Then that proves my distrust in him."

"I told you that you cannot trust him." Becka insisted.

"I don't trust him but I thought that you just didn't trust him because he was a Zim."

"No." Becka said. "We speak using telepathy. We hear each other's thoughts. Bok thinks loudly."

"So what does he want?" Bubba asked.

"Our baby … and nothing else."

"I'll kill him first."

Becka stepped close to Bubba and put her arms around her man. With a tight squeeze she said; "I know you would … and I love you too." The two lay down together for a short while; to talk.

There was something about holding Becka that Bubba loved. It was as if she gave off a slight vibration when he held her tightly. She felt good in his arms. He talked to her about this because holding her felt strange but good. She explained it using a cat as an example. If you hold a cat they purr causing you to feel good.

"The Stylus and Zims purr but ever so slightly." she informed him. I can try to stop it if you want but it will be hard."

"No." he insisted. "I like it. I just did not know you did that."

Becka held Bubba tight and added; "It means that I am enjoying being with you." Bubba smiled and the two stayed in bed longer; just talking.

Later that day Bubba and Becka went to see Bok. She was not happy to see him but she was a good actor. Unlike Bok she could hide her thoughts from him.

"You still do not trust me?" Bok asked Becka.

"You can hear my thoughts?" Becka asked.

"No." he said. "But his thoughts are loud."

Bubba looked at Becka." I still can't hear his thoughts … or yours."

"Bok spoke out loud saying; "I thought you could."

"I was just starting to be able to hear your language when some Zims attacked me and hit me in the head." Bubba mentioned. "Now I can't hear any of you."

"I'm sorry Bubba." Bok replied. "Maybe the Stylus can help you with that. I know we could."

Becka pulled Bubba's arm and they left the area. "He was

lying to you about … they could help you." Becka insisted.

"They can't help me to hear your voices again?" Bubba asked.

"Oh I don't now but neither does he." she said. "He was trying to make us look bad to you hoping that you might change to their side."

"You sure?"

"Like I said earlier. He thinks loudly." Becka said. "Bok thinks that he is hiding his thoughts from me but he isn't. He's arrogant and he thinks he is fooling you."

Bubba and Becka went to the lunch room. As Bubba stepped up to the food dispenser a Stylus stepped up to him and handed him large bowl. Bubba took the large bowl in hand and looked at the Stylus. Then suddenly all of the Stylus in the lunch room started laughing out loud. Laughing was something that Stylus never did but for the first time they were laughing.

Bubba knew that this was a joke about him easting so much of the muka at one sitting but he decided to use the bowl. Filling it half way with the muka he sat down with Becka who had already got her muka and sat down. After sitting down Bubba held up the large bowl and thanked the Stylus there. They raised their bowls in turn.

"You made a few friends here today." Becka said with a big smile. "Stylus don't joke around like … making a large bowl as a joke. They don't laugh either and you had them almost rolling on the floor. You are having a great effect on the Stylus. They like you."

"And I like them too." Bubba said as he dug into the muka.

"They know." Becka said. "You may not be able to hear their thoughts but they can hear yours."

As Bubba ate his muka a Stylus walked up to Becka. Seconds later he walked away. Becka said that they were ready to take the tracking device out of his head after he finished eating. This was good news.

When they finished eating Becka took Bubba to the examination room. He lay on one of the tables and the sleeping device was placed on his forehead. Bubba instantly passed out and the Stylus began removing the tracking device. The tracking device had been placed in his head through the right nostrils and left behind the eyes in his sinuses. Placing it there kept humans from removing it.

About thirty minutes later the sleeping device was removed from Bubba's forehead and he woke up. He had a bad headache and was very dizzy but that was all. He lay there for a while because his dizziness was so bad that he could not walk. After a while he got up and Becka helped him back to their room. He laid down and fell asleep again.

The Stylus that took the tracking device out of Bubba's head told Becka that it had been damaged when he was hit in the forehead. It was not even working. Because of it being damaged removing it would cause Bubba some pain for a while. The pain would go away but his dizziness would return from time to time. For the rest of his life he would have dizzy spells.

The word about Bubba quickly got around to the Stylus crew. They felt for their new friend. More and more as they met him in the hallway they would stop and shake his hand.

"They don't hide against the wall anymore." Becka told him. "You have become ... one of them."

"That's got to be some kind of honor." Bubba suggested.

"They have never done it before now so I guess so."

The battle in space with the two Zim ships caused the Stylus to be running late. On the morning of the forth day the three ships orbited the planet Stylus and awaited permission to land. Finally they were cleared and the three ships descended.

As the ships got ready to land Bubba and Becka got ready to be received by Stylus Command. They cleaned up and changed their clothes. Stylus did not grow facial hair so they had not provided a way for Bubba to shave. He had a five days growth but could do nothing about it.

When the ship landed Bubba and Becka stood ready to exit the ship. They stood behind the ship's Commander and a few others. When the door opened Bubba was surprised to see how large the crowd was. They were all there to see him; the killer of three Zims.

When they exited the ship the crowd cheered. Not many of them would have been there if it had not been for Bubba and Becka. The government of stylus was making a big thing out of Bubba killing three Zims with just his hands. The fact that he used a statue of an Earth bird was never mentioned.

The females of Stylus were looking forward to meeting the Human Stylus hybrid that was pregnant from a human. It was a women's thing.

Bubba and Becka were lead up on a platform where higher ranking Stylus were waiting. They all shook hands with Bubba and Becka and then everyone sat in chairs. The Chider; leader of the planet stepped up to podium and just stood there for a long time. Using telepathy he spoke and from time to time Bubba heard him. With the tracking device removed he was starting to hear their thought again.

Then Bubba was asked to say a few words with Becka translating using telepathy. He stepped up to the podium and looked over the crowd. Then he spoke.

"I was not ready for this." He looked over the crowd again. "It is so much of an honor to be among you ... the first human to do this. I have many Stylus friends and I hope that you would consider me a friend as well."

Suddenly Bubba's head began to hurt. He could hear the thousands of voices cheering him. As he walked back to his seat Becka told him that the crowd was happy.

"I know." he told her. "I can hear them."

"You can hear them again?" she asked.

"To many of them." Bubba said. "My head hurts." Bubba passed out from the pain. He woke up later on a padded bed in a room. Becka sat in a chair beside him and held his hand. She was talking to other Stylus. Then she realized that he was awake.

"You're going to be okay Baby." she eased him.

"Who are they?" Bubba asked.

"On Earth you have many newspapers." Becka smiled. "Well

we do too and these are reporters for some of those newspapers."

The reporters tried to ask Bubba questions but he could not process all of them at one time. Becka stepped in and helped as a translator. Bubba spent the next fifteen minutes answering their questions and then he had, had enough. He needed rest. All of the Stylus shook Bubba's hand before leaving and then finally it was just him and Becka in the room.

"You okay Baby?"

"You tell me." he answered as he laughed.

"This is a hospital but not like the ones on Earth. The doctor left just before you woke up and said he would be right back."

"Why did I pass out?"

"The doctor does not know yet. He does not know your anatomy." Becka admitted. "He is calling in a specialist."

A few minutes later the doctor came in with the human specialist. They talked with Becka and then left. Becka told Bubba that they would have to operate again. When the tracking device was removed a tiny piece was left in his head. The operation would take place the next morning.

Later Bubba was given a sedative and he fell asleep. All night Becka sat in the chair beside him holding his hand. Around midnight a nurse came in and to Becka's surprise she spoke some English.

"You ... love him?" the nurse asked.

"You speak his language?" Becka asked.

"I ... trained for travel ... to Earth but ... not go." she said and then asked again; "You love him?"

"Oh yes." she said as she looked at him. "I am pregnant with his baby."

"I know." she said and then added; "My name ... Bamma."

Becka shook Bamma's hand; a custom that those on Stylus had not learned yet. "My name is Becka."

"We all ... know you ... and ... Bubba here." Bamma said. "You speak his ... language well."

Bubba almost woke up so Bamma whispered good-by to

Becka and left. For about thirty minutes she held Bubba's hand and just looked at him. Finally she fell asleep.

The next morning a female Stylus came into the room and asked what she should make for Bubba's breakfast. All they had was muka. Becka laughed and told her that he loved Muka. "Bring him a big bowl of it. He eats more than we do."

About an hour later the female came back with five small bowls of muka. "We only ... small bowls." she said.

"This is fine." Becka assured her.

When the female left Becka woke Bubba up so he could eat. His operation would be soon. Bubba gobbled down the muka and even wanted more but that was it. About an hour later they came to get him for the operation. He was wheeled down the hall and into a room that looked much like an operating room on Earth. Something was placed on his forehead and he was out.

About an hour later Bubba woke up and looked around. He was back in his room with Becka sitting beside him. No one else was there.

"Babe." Bubba uttered. "Babe."

Becka was asleep but woke up to his calling her. "Ha Baby."

"My head hurts." he let her know.

"Come to find out there was not just one piece of the tracking device left in your head." Becka said. "It was a cluster of metal shavings. It took a while to get it all out."

"So I'm gon'a be okay then."

"Oh yes." she assured him. "The doctor said that you would be sore for a while but you would be okay."

Becka stepped out into the hall when Bamma came to the door and called for her. Bubba took advantage of being alone and prayed.

"I need help Lord. Please be with me and keep me ... and Becka and the baby safe. Thank you for protecting us in space when the Zims attacked our ship. You watched over us then. You will watch over us now. Thank you for always being there when we need you."

67

Bamma and Becka talked in the hallway. She warned Becka that there were Zim spies in the hospital and she needed to be careful. Becka told Bamma that she needed to get Bubba out of the hospital but there was nothing that she could do. What Becka did not know was that the Zims were not interested in Bubba. They wanted her and her baby. Actually they did not even want Becka; just the baby. Unfortunately; Becka and her baby were a package deal.

Becka stepped back into the room and walked over to Bubba. She told him what Bamma said about the Zim spies. He knew that the Zims did not want him. They wanted Becka and the baby.

Later the doctor came in and talked with Becka. When he left Becka told Bubba what he said. Bubba could leave the hospital. Four local police would be there soon to escort them to their cottage. What the Stylus called a cottage was really just an apartment. Bubba and Becka would be under constant protection while they were on Stylus. Bubba got dressed but had to wait for their escorts. Finally; about an hour later the police escorts came into the room.

On their way to the cottage one of the escorts told Becka that they would be going to a dinner where they would meet the planet's ruler Yunnan. Bubba went straight to bed to get some more rest. This time they had a large bed to sleep in. Becka lay beside him and they both quickly fell asleep together.

Chapter 7

Home Sweet Home

Two evenings after Bubba's operation was the evening where they were invited to dinner with the Stylus leader Yunnan. The police escorts took them to the Leader's Hall. Just inside and towards the back the Hall was a large dining area. As Yunnan and his wife walked in with Bubba and Becka behind them the crowd cheered and clapped heir hands. They were lead upon a platform with a table facing the crowd. When all four of them stood in their places they sat down together as one. This signified that they were working on things together.

As much as Bubba liked the muka he was hoping to eat something else. He was very much a carnivore and needed some meat. To his surprise that was exactly what was brought out.

As food was brought out and laid in the middle of the table Becka told Bubba what it was. It was customary that after prayer those at the table simply reached out and either cut off or tore off meat that they wanted and placed it on their plate. However; with this being a special event with the leader of the planet Stylus, help cut the meat they wanted and placed it on their plate.

There were also a few vegetables. One large bowl had muka root that had been baked like a potato. Being baked it had more of a roasted garlic taste. Two different types of beans were also there. And of course there was bread that looked more like tiny rolls. Although most of he food looked strange it was the best meal that Bubba had, had in a while. Everything tasted great.

Yunnan stood and a horn blew. This got everyone quiet so he could speak. Bubba could catch a word every now and then; enough to know what Yunnan was saying. Then Yunnan gave Bubba another chance to say something.

Bubba looked at Becka. "What do I say?"

69

"You did great last time." Becka said. "I don't think they care what you say as long as you say something."

Bubba stood and a microphone was moved in front of him. Then he looked over the crowd as he did before. "Yes it's true. I killed three Zims with my bare hands and I did it with pride." The crowd went crazy as they stood and yelled. "I may be from Earth but a part of me will always be … Stylus."

That last remark was all it took. Any Stylus hearts that he had not won; he won there that day. Bubba's status in the area escalated to the point that he could run for a political office and would probably win.

As Bubba sat back down Becka hugged his arm. She was so proud of her man. The rest of the night was spent eating and drinking. Their glasses were kept full all night. Finally Bubba realized that he was getting drunk. The clear liquid that they were drinking was a wine made from the muka root. Having a great deal of sugar in it the muka root made a great wine and distilled alcohol.

"Finally Bubba got so drunk that Becka had to ask the guards to help them get back to their cottage. On Earth this would have been an embarrassing thing; getting drunk in public. However; on Stylus this was an expected thing to happen. The person of honor was expected to enjoy their party even if they got drunk. Yunnan was even proud. He threw a party in which the honored guest, Bubba, enjoyed himself to the point of getting drunk. It was quite the compliment to Yunnan.

Bubba slept all night. Becka stripped his clothes off and placed him in the bed. Then she got ready for bed and lay beside him. She pulled out his arm so that she could lay her head on it. Then she lay there and looked at him until she fell asleep. She loved the father of her child so much.

During the next month Bubba and Becka spoke at different occasions. Bubba was asked to speak to the men of Stylus while Becka spoke mostly to the women. Most of the females asked questions about her being pregnant, the baby, and her loving a human.

Bubba spoke at men's clubs where the main conversation was about hunting. Hunting was not a popular sport on Stylus but he was about to start changing that. Regular men's clubs started changing to hunting clubs. Men on Stylus were getting together and buying large areas of woods that they used only for hunting. The most popular rifle used was a replica of a Hawkins 50 caliber black powder rifle. Bubba described the rifle to the Stylus men and they built it.

Bubba and Becka were changing many things in the area and their influence was spreading quickly. Having a thin frame Becka started showing her pregnancy at only two and a half months. It was mid January on Earth; winter at Bubba's home. Bubba and Becka were close to the equator on Stylus and it was always warm there. The weather on Stylus was much like that on Earth. But the thin air on Stylus weighed heavily on Bubba's lungs.

Bubba was getting weaker and weaker. Finally the doctor that took care of him admitted that he had to return to Earth or die. His body could not handle the constant thin air. Yunnan made plans to send Bubba and Becka back to Earth. He would send two other hybrids to dress and look like humans. They would take care of Bubba and Becka including being their security.

Rommin and Tesh were the names of the two that would be going back with Bubba and Becka. Just before leaving for Earth Rommin and Tesh came by to see Bubba and Becka. They walked into the cottage and sat down. They wanted to get to know Bubba and Becka.

As Rommin and Tesh told Bubba and Becka about themselves Rommin said something that got Bubba's attention. Bubba had two hybrid sons and Rommin was one of them. For a while Bubba could not speak. Rommin looked at his father realizing that what he had said shocked Bubba.

"I'm sorry Sir." Rommin said. "I thought that you knew."

Bubba took in a deep breath and let it out. "Becka told me that I had two hybrid sons but I never thought that I would ever meet one of you."

Rommin smiled. "I was asked if I would like to do this and I agreed instantly. I wanted to meet my Earth father."

Bubba looked down. "I hope I don't disappoint you."

"You disappoint me?" Rommin said as he laughed. "The Zim killer of Earth. No way."

"Thank you Rommin." Bubba said.

"Tesh and I are honored to be the two that will take care of you two … and the baby when it is born." Rommin replied.

"I was not told that you were the one … the human from Earth." Tesh said. "I am also honored to do what I can for you two."

"Over one hundred Stylus and hybrids were considered for this job." Rommin said. "We were chosen from them."

Rommin and Tesh stayed for dinner and stayed late into the night. They would have to be on the ship a few hours after daylight but they did not want to part. Rommin and Tesh had to get ready for the trip. They would all meet again on the ship.

Having just met one of his hybrid sons Bubba could not sleep that night. He had mixed emotions. He knew that he had two hybrid sons but meeting one of them was exciting and also shocking. Rommin looked nothing like him but maybe being half Stylus had something to do with it.

The five Stylus guards came early the next morning. Bubba and Becka's leaving the planet was a secret. Neither Yunnan nor Stylus Command wanted the Zims to know that they were going back to Earth. In fact two hybrids were given the task of being look-a-likes for Bubba and Becka. It would be their jobs to travel the planet under guard making the Zims think that it was Bubba and Becka traveling the planet.

On Earth Bubba and Becka would be protected by Rommin and Tesh. Looking like humans would make it easier to do that job. There was one more thing that might assure their safety.

A party from Stylus had made contact with government officials in the United States. The government had recovered the ship at the bottom of the lake along with the dead that were left inside by the Zims. As part of an ongoing deal the government would also have military out in the woods on Bubba's property to help protect Bubba and Becka. A gate was set up at the entrance of the driveway and two military guards stood duty there at all times.

Bubba could not understand why he was getting so much attention. None of it made any since. The Stylus must have been giving the government something good in trade for their protection. Just before leaving for Earth Yunnan met with Bubba and Becka. Bubba asked what they gave the United States government for him to get such good security.

"Oh we gave them a shield that, when installed, will protect your country from any missile attack." he said with a smile. "They were willing to do anything for that technology and you two are very important to us ... the people of Stylus."

When Bubba and Becka got on board Bubba realized that his entire conversation with Yunnan was done by telepathy. Neither of them spoke out loud. He and Becka also learned that the ship Commander was Ail. This was the same ship that brought them to Stylus.

Bubba and Becka even got their old room back. They were shocked to see that the bunk beds had been replaced with a larger bed. The room was small so the desk had to be removed but neither of them cared. Being able to sleep as he held her was more important than a desk that they never used.

The ship ever so gently shook. "What was that?" Bubba asked Becka.

"We're lifting off." she replied.

Bubba lay down on the bed. The thin air on Stylus had him doing that a great deal. He would be okay soon after returning to Earth.

This time the Zims left the ship alone. Having three other ships flying as an escort may have had something to do with it. This time they arrived on the back side of the moon three days after leaving Stylus. After waiting until dark the ship went down and hovered above Bubba's home. Seconds later Bubba, Becka, Rommin, and Tesh were standing him his den.

Becka instantly took Rommin and Tesh to the two back rooms. They put away some clothing and other gear that they brought to help them do their jobs.

The first thing that Bubba did was make a pot of coffee. Then he went into the bedroom and got his CAR-15. After getting a mug of the coffee he took it and his rifle out on the porch. Then he lay the rifle across the table and sat down. It was still dark but he did not care. He was home and that was all that mattered. He was also breathing better.

Becka walked into the bedroom and could not find Bubba. She looked up at his gun rack and noticed that his CAR-15 was missing. Then she smelt the coffee and knew where he was. He was so predictable.

When Rommin and Tesh came into the kitchen where Becka was she showed them the coffee. "You can find your father out on the porch with his rifle and a mug of coffee. He loves both of them." Becka told Rommin.

Rommin got himself a small cup of the coffee and then went out on the porch. He sat in the chair beside Bubba and for a while said nothing. He was trying to take in the smells of the hill top. Then he took a sip of the coffee.

"Oh man." Rommin said. "This stuff is nasty."

Bubba laughed and asked him; "Did you add any sugar to it?"

Rommin got up and went into the house where Becka showed him the sugar.

Becka suggested that he also add some powdered milk as well. "Taste better?" she asked.

"Some but it is still bitter." Rommin replied.
About a minute later he came out on the porch and sat down again.

Father and son sat there talking until the sun started to come up. They both went back inside and refilled their mugs and then went back out on the porch. By then the sun was up enough that they could see the lake.

"It's beautiful out here." Rommin said. "And the air is so

74

fresh and clean."

"It's ... home." Bubba said with a big smile. "And I can breath again."

Rommin knew nothing about firearms and started asking his father about the CAR-15 on the table. Before long they were on the rifle range with Bubba showing Rommin how to aim the rifle. When he fired his first shot Bubba realized that his son was a natural; just like Becka. Then Bubba went back into the home and came back with a Ruger Mini 14 rifle. Rommin fired seven rounds and hit the bulls eye with every shot.

"This is your rifle from now on." Bubba told Rommin. Then he explained how the Mini 14 worked and how to load a magazine.

Bubba talked with Rommin about going hog hunting some night. Rommin did not like the idea of killing an animal.

"Then how do you expect to defend Becka and me?" Bubba asked Rommin.

"I would do what ever I had to do." Rommin replied.

"And if that meant killing a Zim ... could you do it?"

"Of course. Protecting you two is my job."

"When we shoot a wild hog we eat that hog." Bubba insisted. "You see Rommin ... hunting is a combination of putting food on the table and a sport of going against another animal. With wild hogs that sport is a dangerous one. The main thing is that it puts food on the table.

"Can't you buy the meat in the store?" Rommin asked.

"Yes but ... hunting a hog or any other animal is free food." Bubba explained. "It only cost the price of a shell."

"Some Stylus hunt but it is considered shameful to kill an animal." Rommin said. "But you changed that with many of the men on Stylus."

"I taught them to eat the animals they killed."

"You say that hunting wild hogs is dangerous?" Rommin asked.

"I said it could be dangerous." Bubba informed his son. "They can rip your legs up with their tusks."

Rommin smiled and agreed to go out with his father and Rick. Bubba had already called Rick to let him and Beth know that he and Becka were home. They were suppose to come over the next day.

The sun had not yet risen but it was daylight enough to see around. A jeep came up to the house so Rommin went into the house. A Sergeant and Colonel got out of the jeep and walked upon the porch.

"I'm Colonel Dotter ... the CO of those protecting you." He stuck out his hand and shook Bubba's hand. "This is Sergeant Giffen. He will be over all ten of my soldiers here." He sat in a third chair and continued. "I have been briefed and I do know that there are two aliens here. Is there anything else you want me to know?"

"I don't think so Colonel." Bubba said. "You want to meet one of those aliens?"

The Colonel smiled and agreed to meet with the alien. Bubba called out to his son. Rommin opened the door and slowly stepped out. Then he slowly walked to his father.

"My sperm was taken a few years back without my knowing. This is Rommin ... my hybrid son. A female hybrid is inside."

The Colonel shook hands with Rommin but never stood. "He almost looks human."

"Well ... I am half human." Rommin said.

Rommin looked at Sergeant Giffen. Giffen stood ready to pounce if he had to. He held his M-4 rifle with his finger on the trigger. "You can relax Giffen. You're also protecting me ... remember?"

"Something wrong Sergeant?" the Colonel asked.

"No Sir." the Sergeant replied. "Just never met an alien before."

"You will meet others son. Now take your finger off of that trigger and make sure it is on safety."

At that time Becka and Tesh stepped out of the house. Only after they were outside did they see the Colonel and Sergeant. The Sergeant quickly brought up his M-4 and pointed it at the

76

women.

"Lower your rifle Sergeant." the Colonel yelled. "Now if you cannot handle this job then I'll give it to someone else."

"I'm okay Sir." the Sergeant advised the Colonel. Then he looked up at Becka and Tesh who were walking by him. "I'm sorry ladies." That was when he realized that Becka was also an alien. He took a deep breath and let it out. "Okay!"

"Well if there is nothing else then we need to go." the Colonel said. "I will have men walking your property and around your home at times. Please don't shoot them."

"Do you know what the enemy looks like?" Bubba asked the Colonel.

The Colonel did not know so Bubba described the Grays but let him know that only the Zims were the enemy. "Although the Zims and Stylus are from two different planets they looked alike." he added.

"Then how will my men know when to open fire?"

"I don't know Colonel but the Stylus will only appear inside my home. If you see a Gray out here … just have fun. It probably will not be our friends … the Stylus."

"So if these … Zims show up they will not be up to any good?" the Colonel asked.

"You will not see the friendly Stylus out here so kill any aliens you see." Bubba advised.

"Will do Sir." the Colonel said as he stood. Ten he turned his attention to Rommin and said; "It was such a pleasure to have met you."

The Colonel and Rommin shook hands as Rommin said; "The pleasure was mine Sir."

The Colonel and Sergeant left the porch and got into the jeep. As the Sergeant drove off the Colonel waved. Everyone on the porch waved back. Bubba told everyone what all the Colonel said. Then he turned to Rommin and told him that they would not be doing any hunting.

"That's okay Dad." Rommin said. Bubba was still getting used to being called Dad. "I'm not so sure that I would get into killing an animal anyway."

Bubba and Rommin stood and fallowed the women back into the house where they found three Stylus standing in the den. It was Paulm and two others. Paulm had been given command of another ship. He had word from the planet Stylus. Bok had escaped. He and his crew stole a ship but no one knows where he went. It is believed that Bok went back to his planet.

Paulm went on to tell them other news from Stylus. The women were happy that some women's groups were popping up and spreading around the planet thanks to Becka. Bubba was happy to hear that hunting clubs were popping up all over the place as well. The most popular rifle used was still the replica of the Hawkins 50 caliber black powder rifle.

Bubba walked into his bedroom and came out with his Hawkins 50 caliber, black powder rifle. "Take this back to them and show them what the Hawkins rifle looks like. "Maybe they can make improvements."

"Thank you Bubba." Paulm said. "I am in one of those hunting clubs so I will hand this over to our club president."

"Paulm." Bubba said. "Does Yunnan hunt?"

"Oh yes. He loves it."

"Then please give this Hawkins to him." Bubba said. "Tell him it is a gift from me to him but, ask him to allow others to copy how it is made."

"I will do that." Paulm said with a big smile. "He is going to love this."

"Also let him know that their black powder needs to be refined or made better." Bubba added. "They need to work on making it better."

The planet Stylus had plenty of Potassium nitrate, coal, and sulfur so they could make black powder. They just needed to make it better.

Paulm and the other two Stylus left vanishing into thin air. Just as they did there was a knock at the front door. Bubba answered the door and found Sergeant Giffen there.

"Do know a Rick and Beth Sir?" the Sergeant asked pointing

at Rick's truck.

"Oh yes." Bubba admitted. "They are good friends."

"With your permission we will allow them past the gate from now on." the Sergeant added.

"Please do." Bubba replied as the Sergeant waved for them to get out of their truck.

"Thank you Sir." the Sergeant replied being very professional.

"What the hell was that all about?" Rick asked.

"Come on inside and I will tell you all about it." Bubba said with a big smile. "Come on in."

Chapter 8

Security

Rick and Beth sat on the couch. At that time Becka and Tesh walked out of the kitchen. Rick looked at Tesh and Rommin realizing that they were hybrids like Becka.

"This is Rommin and Tesh." Bubba told them. "They have been sent to protect us."

"And how did you get the military to help in that?" Rick asked.

"Oh that was a deal made between the planet Stylus and our government." Becka said. "Your government was willing to do anything for the anti-missile shield around your country."

Bubba and Becka told Rick and Beth other things that had been going on while they were gone. The one thing that hurt Rick the most was that there would be no more hog hunting. Rommin and Tesh added something to the conversation every now and then. Then Rommin shocked Rick and Beth when he called Bubba, Dad.

"Why did he call you Dad?" Beth asked Bubba.

"Many years ago the Stylus took my sperm and impregnated a female Stylus." Bubba told Rick and Beth. Rommin here is one of my two sons."

This gave the group something else to talk about for a while. Bubba explained that he had been taken by the Stylus for over twenty years and that Becka had known him all that time. Then the question came up about Becka's age.

"Well I would never get involved in a woman much younger than me so ..." Bubba said as he looked at Becka.

"You didn't answer the question." Rick mentioned. Then he turned to Becka and asked; "Think you could tell us?"

Becka smiled real big and said; "I think ... I am ... about

nineteen." she said toying with Rick's mind.

"Oh come on." Rick said loudly. "Something tells me that I'm the only one here that does not know."

"Why do you think we are playing with you so much?" Bubba asked.

Rick was not getting mad but he was getting very upset. Bubba knew that his friend was reaching his limit on this but he wanted to push Rick's limit's a little more anyway. Finally Becka spoke up.

"I'm ninety six years old Rick." Becka told him. "I'm just a little older than Bubba is."

"For one thing you're not ninety six years old." Rick insisted. "You're closer to twenty and that reminds me of another question. What do you want with a man that is about forty years older than you?"

Everyone but Rick and Beth were laughing. Then Rommin told them that hybrids live to be about three hundred years old. Then he added; "She really is ninety six."

"Maybe you should be giving me makeup tips." Beth said.

"Yeah ... she was wearing to much but ... she cut back on it for me." Bubba said. "I don't like a woman wearing so much shit on her face hat I can't kiss her."

"She looks almost all human now." Rick mentioned.

"From a distance you can't tell that she isn't human." Bubba said. "This morning she and Tesh walked right past the Sergeant with him thinking that they were both human women."

Beth and Becka agreed to help Rommin and Tesh look more human. Again Beth measured them both and then took Bubba's credit card and went into town. She came back a couple of hours later with plenty of clothes for them both.

First Beth worked on Rommin. He came out of the bedroom an hour later and looked good in what she got him. Then with Rommin wearing one set of new clothes Beth and Becka started working on Tesh.

Rommin sat on the couch and joined in on the conversation that Bubba and Rick were having on wild hog hunting. "I don't agree with hunting … just killing an animal." he said.

"We do eat the hogs you know." Rick said with a smile.

"I know but …"

"Aren't you here to protect your father?" Rick asked not giving Rommin time to answer before he asked; "How can you kill any enemy if you can't kill an animal?"

"It's hard to explain … I guess." Rommin responded. "With an enemy I am protecting my father or myself but with an animal I am shooting a defenseless animal."

"Hunting wild hogs … you would not be killing a defenseless animal." Rick admitted. Then he turned to Bubba and added; "Jump in here anytime."

"Why should I?" Bubba asked him. "You seem to be having so much fun."

"He's your son not mine." Rick insisted.

"And he is a man too … a man that can do what he wants." Bubba defended his son.

Rick stopped arguing with Rommin and just sat there saying nothing more. He knew that Bubba was a hunter; a man that lived hunting and yet he defended Rommin. He could not understand a man not wanting to put free meat on the dinner table but that is not how Rommin saw it. The two men had two different ideas about hunting and there was no changing either of their minds.

"It doesn't matter anyway with the military walking the wood." Bubba admitted. "They will just keep the hogs off of the property."

At about that time another truck drove up behind the jeep again. This time the Sergeant was alone.

"Do you know this man Sir?" the Sergeant asked Bubba.

"Yes." Bubba quickly admitted. "He is also a close friend."

"Then we will let him come on in from now on if you wish … Sir."

"Yes … please do that." Bubba said as he walked over to the steps. The Sergeant left as David met Bubba.

"What the hell was all of that about?" David asked.

"That's what Rick said his last time here." Bubba said as he shook their hands. "Becka and Tesh is in the house."

"It's getting colder so I'm going inside too." David said.

A cold front was coming in and it was about to rain anyway so Bubba, Rick, and Rommin also went inside. With 7 people in the house chairs from the dinner table had to be brought into the den. Bubba took the rolling chair from his desk. It was padded and perfect for an old man's butt.

Bubba had not seen David since he and Becka came back to Earth. He had to catch David up on all of the news. After about an hour and with the help of the others David learned everything that had happened.

"So Bok escaped and even stole a ship to fly home in?" David asked.

"He and his whole crew escaped." Bubba said. Then he turned his attention to everyone there.

"Now everyone remember." Bubba said as he pointed at David, Rick, and Beth. "I guess this is just to you three. No one can know that anything different is going on here. There are no aliens here and if something happens … it never happened." Bubba looked at everyone and then back at the three. "If anyone asks you about the security just say that I came into some money and I hired a security company. Don't talk to anyone about anything going on, on my property."

Then Rick mentioned the one thing that bothered him the most. "And there will be no more hunting either."

"Not being able to go hunting is really bothering you isn't it?" Rommin asked.

"Well …" Rick thought about it. "Yes … it does."

Bubba walked over to Rommin and put his arm around his son's neck. "Rick will always be Rick. Like me … he loves to hunt."

Rommin smiled and looked at Rick. Then he turned and walked into the kitchen. Tesh fallowed him.

"Being on Earth is making me feel funny." Tesh mentioned.

"In what way?" Rommin asked.

"It's in my stomach … an uneasy feeling but … only when I am around you." she admitted as Becka walked into the kitchen.

"You only feel that way when you are around Rommin?" Becka asked.

"Yes." Tesh agreed. "Am I catching something from him?"

Becka smiled and then said;" In a way … yes."

"Is it fatal?" Tesh was getting scared.

"Some would say that it is but it's not." Becka said still smiling. "You're starting to like Rommin. You must like being around him."

"But we hybrids are not allowed to show our feelings and we are not suppose to like another hybrid." Tesh said as she was afraid of breaking a law.

"You're on Earth now Tesh." Becka assured her. "Here you are allowed to have feelings for anyone you want … except for my Bubba."

Becka left the kitchen and the two alone. She was not sure how Rommin felt about Tesh but he stayed in the kitchen and talked with her. Becka came back with her glass full of water and sat beside Bubba. Then she leaned over and whispered in his ear. "I think Tesh and your son might have something going soon."

"Why do you say that?" Bubba asked.

"Look in the kitchen and see for yourself." Becka asked.

Bubba looked into the kitchen and saw his son and Tesh holding hands. They were talking and smiling. Bubba looked away from Becka and smiled.

"I still saw you smiling." Becka told Bubba.

"You're crazy." Bubba told her and tried to hide his smile.

Before long everyone had noticed the two in the kitchen. Finally they came out and pulled Becka aside. They had a few questions for her. Becka took Rommin and Tesh in the main bedroom for some privacy. Bubba got up and fallowed. When he got in the bedroom he found Becka telling them about love.

"However; you should never have sex before you are married." Bubba told his son and Tesh.

"But you and Becka did." Rommin said. "You even got her

pregnant and you're not married."

Bubba looked down at the floor. "I know and we were wrong." Then he looked up at Becka and said; "I have been thinking about this. I don't want our child being a bastard." He looked deep into Becka's eyes and asked; "Will you marry me?"

Becka leaped into Bubba's arms and yelled; "Yes ... yes ... of course I will."

Becka ran out into the den yelling that Bubba finally asked her to marry him. Tesh fallowed her leaving Bubba and Rommin in the bedroom wondering what happened. With all of the women in the den screaming Bubba and Rommin walked into the den and then outside.

Rick and David walked outside behind Bubba and Rommin. The women were still screaming but it was a bit more tolerable out on the porch.

"Why do women have to scream like that?" Rommin asked.

"I don't know." Bubba said. "I don't think God knows."

"So you two are finally tying the knot?" David asked.

"You know that knot will be around your throat ... don't you?" Rick added.

"You guys are terrible." Bubba commented. "And I'm gon'a tell Beth what you said."

With it now almost silent in the house Bubba turned and went inside. The other men fallowed. As soon as Becka saw Bubba she ran to him again and jumped into his arms. Becka was one happy woman.

Everyone stayed and talked until late in the night. David left first as he had worked most of the night before and still had not been to bed. About an hour later Rick and Beth left but promised to be back the next day. They would help Bubba and Becka plan the wedding. Rommin and Tesh went to their own bedrooms leaving Bubba and Becka to go to their bedroom.

Bubba and Becka knew that they could not have a regular wedding. No marriage licenses could be used. They did agree that the marriage should be right in the eyes of God.

The people of Stylus and Zim worshiped the same god that

those on Earth worshiped. Of course they called him by a different name but it proved that one god made the entire universe. How else could beings on three different planets worship the same god? So this is why Becka agreed to a wedding that was good in God's eyes.

Bubba took a bath and then went to bed. He quickly fell asleep while Becka took her bath. She came out of the bathroom and had to move his arm out so she could lay her head on it. Once she slid close to her man and lay her head on his arm she also fell asleep.

That night around three in the morning everyone in the house woke up to gunshots outside. Bubba, Rommin, and Becka grabbed their rifles and ran out on the porch.

"Actually … you two shouldn't have come out here." Rommin insisted. "Tesh and I … and all of your government soldiers are trying to protect you two. We can't do that if you're both running out into the gunfire."

Bubba looked at Becka. "He's right you know but … looking at you standing there with that rifle in your hands … you are turning me on so much right now."

"You're a monster." Becka said. "All you think about is taking me to bed and … talking." She was starting to like that joke.

Rommin laughed until someone came around the corner of the house. It was one of the soldiers. Then a jeep flew up to the house and slid to a stop. Another soldier that Bubba did not know got out of the jeep and met with the other soldier.

"What's going on?" Bubba asked.

The two soldiers ignored Bubba and did not even look up at him. Then he and Rommin walked over to the steps. Looking down at the two soldiers that were only about five feet away Bubba repeated himself.

"What's going on out here?" Again there was no answer as the two soldiers continued to talk.

"Get back over to the table and get ready to shoot if you have to." Bubba whispered to Rommin. Seconds later Bubba raised his

CAR-15 and fired three quick shots into the air. He got their attention that time.

Both soldiers had their M-4 rifles pointed at Bubba who was just standing there smiling. "I wouldn't do that if I were you." he said as he pointed at Rommin. Rommin was pointing his Mini-14 rifle at them.

"I highly suggest that you two lower your rifles." Bubba said. "You see ... Rommin there is a hybrid ... half alien and half human. Now that alien side of him is very unstable. To tell you the truth ... he's a real nut case. And you see ..."

"Dad ... Dad. Rommin yelled out.

"What." Bubba snapped at Rommin.

"They lowered their rifles about thirty minutes ago."

"Oh!" Bubba said as he looked at the soldiers. There's a lesson to be learned here today but ... I'll be damn if I know what it is." With that comment and a load of embarrassment he turned and walked into the house.

"Sorry gentlemen but he does not like being ignored." Rommin informed them. "And you need to know that ... neither do I. Now I'm going to ask only one time before I lower my rifle and start shooting. What's going on out here with the gunshots a few minutes ago?"

"I shot two aliens at the back of your home." one of the soldiers said. "Three others just vanished in front of me."

"They can do that." Rommin informed them. "Their technology is farther advanced than anything you have here on Earth."

"But the other man said that you were an alien but you look nothing like the two I shot." the first soldier mentioned.

"I am one of the good guys ... a human alien hybrid." he told them. Another female hybrid is in the house. She and I are working inside the house to protect them. You guys work out here to protect them and it looks like you're doing a great job." Rommin turned and started back to the front door. "Thank you guys." he added before walking inside.

"Well ... did they tell you what happened out there?" Bubba

asked Rommin.

"Of course ... after you told them about that twitch I had from the alien side of me."

Everyone looked at Bubba and Rommin laughed. Then he started telling them about the two Zims that were shot and the three that got away. He also told them that the two Zim bodies would be taken away by the military. Suddenly Becka got up.

"That was not the agreement that Yunnan made with your government." Then she walked into the main bedroom and came out with a tiny device in her right hand. It was a way to communicate directly to Yunnan. She went out on the porch and called to the planet Stylus.

The communication device was slow to the Stylus point of view. It took almost twenty minutes to get a message back. They were getting Yunnan at that time. Bubba and Rommin came out on the porch but Becka asked Rommin to please go back inside. She allowed Bubba to stay but he had to be quiet. A few minutes later Rommin came outside with two large mugs of hot cocoa. Then he went back inside with the others.

Rommin asked the others to please leave Becka to her job. He made sure that they all knew that she needed to be alone. He was not sure exactly what her job was but it was easy to see that she was fallowing orders from Yunnan.

About thirty minutes after being told that Yunnan was being called to their communications center Becka got another call. It was Yunnan. Becka told him that two Zims had been killed and the military was taking the bodies. It took another thirty minutes to get an answer back from Yunnan.

In their agreement with the United States government they were allowed to keep any dead Zim but not if they were dead Stylus.

"Forgive me Sir." Becka said. "I misunderstood. The two dead were in fact Zims."

"I thought that the Stylus did not speak." Bubba asked. "You used telepathy."

"Our telepathy is only good for about a mile at best. After

that we must use communications like this"

"So that was Yunnan that I heard?" Bubba asked.

"That was him."

Then something came to Bubba's mind. "Were you put here for this?"

"No!" she replied. I came here to be with you. But while we were on Stylus Yunnan asked me to stay in communications with him about anything that might have gone wrong. Basically I am watching your government to make sure they keep their word."

"I have no problem with that." Bubba replied.

"Did you think that I just came here to do this?" Becka asked. "I really do love you Baby. That is why I am here … to be with you … the father of our child."

Bubba leaned over and gave Becka a hug. "I love you too Babe."

After Becka got the final message from Yunnan telling her that there was no problem she and Bubba walked back into the house. They sat down on the couch and noticed that everyone was looking at them.

"Well …" Rommin said.

"Oh Yunnan just said that your government was allowed to keep any dead Zims but not any Stylus." Becka said.

"How can you tell the difference between the two?" Rick asked.

"I can tell and if your government takes a Stylus … dead or alive … I will be letting Yunnan know.

Chapter 9

Temper Tantrums

The Zims were not seen again for over a month. Everyone was relaxing some but they knew that more Zims could return at any time.

Becka was now four months pregnant. Because she was half human everyone assumed that she would carry the baby for nine months but the Stylus females carried their unborn child for about seven months. They are much smaller and have no need to carry the baby any longer. However; Becka looked to be about five months pregnant according to human women.

Becka was also sucking up all of the attention that Bubba was giving her. He was always rubbing her stomach and talking to the baby inside her. He even went into town one day and came back with a Ruger 10/22 rifle for the baby.

"But you don't even know if the baby is a boy or girl." Becka told Bubba.

"Does it matter?" he replied.

"She will be part your child so I am sure that she will love guns too."

"She ... hmmmm!" Bubba said with a smile. "Now how do you know it's a girl?"

"I just think it is." Becka said. "It's just a feeling."

"Well he or she ... they will still be our child and with the baby being part me ... it will be beautiful."

"Yes dear." Becka commented.

From there they did discuss medical care for Becka and the baby. She had, had no care at all and neither liked it. They decided to pray about it.

"Father ... Becka needs doctor care but we can't take her to a

doctor in town and I don't want the government involved. Please send us someone to take care of her medical needs."

A few days later Paulm showed up with two guards. They appeared in the den as Bubba and Becka were watching the TV.

At first Bubba started to jump up but Becka stopped him. "It's Paulm." she told him.

"Sorry Paulm." Bubba said. "You all look alike to me."

"That's okay Bubba." Paulm said using telepathy. Bubba was receiving him but still spoke using his mouth.

"I came by to check up on you two." Paulm said. Then he noticed how much Becka was showing. "That's right. You're about five months pregnant?"

"Four months." Becka corrected him.

"Would you like my medical team to look you over?" Paulm suggested.

"I would like that." Becka admitted.

Paulm talked on his communicator on his wrist and asked for the medical team. About a minute later three Stylus appeared in the den.

"This is Doctor Stimmis. He is my doctor and these are his medical team." Paulm told Becka.

The medical team took Becka into the main bedroom while Paulm talked with Bubba. "You can hear my thoughts?"

"Yes Sir but I am still not good at using telepathy back." Bubba replied.

"That's okay." Paulm said. "As long as you can hear me then you go ahead and speak out loud."

"Okay." Bubba agreed.

Paulm asked Bubba many questions. Mostly he was concerned with how Rommin and Tesh were doing. Bubba had nothing but praise for them both. Then Paulm's questions turned to the military guards outside. He could not answer most of the question. Paulm just wanted to make sure that everything was okay. Then Bubba mentioned the two dead Zims and Paulm got upset.

"I know that two were killed but three escaped." Paulm said. "There are no Zim ships in or around this solar system so you're safe."

"Thank you Paulm." Bubba replied.

Finally Becka and the medical team came out of the bedroom. "She's doing great." Stimmis said using telepathy.

Paulm thought for a moment. Then he told Bubba; "I have a hybrid female that is training to be on the medical team. She has been training for over a year and she's smart. Her training is in the human anatomy so she would be perfect here. Would you like me to leave her here for Becka?"

"If she wants to." Bubba said.

Paulm laughed. "It does not matter what a hybrid wants. They simply fallow orders."

"So they are your slaves?"

Paulm thought about his answer before speaking. "They are our workers and that is all but ... we are now discovering that they are pretty smart. That is why I have had Mobay training as part of the medical team.

"Please leave her here for Becka." Bubba agreed. "That would make us both feel better."

A few minutes later Mobay appeared in the den. This gave Bubba and Becka a problem. Where would she sleep? Bubba had a few cots and set one up for her in the den for a while.

Before leaving Paulm said that he left a crate of dehydrated muka in the kitchen. "I know how much you like it." he said as he vanished. While Bubba checked on the crate of muka in the kitchen Becka helped Mobay settle in.

Mobay was another beautiful hybrid female. She had been trained for over a year in the human body for some reason that Bubba did not know. But she was the closest thing to a doctor that he could get for Becka. Finally he walked over to Mobay and introduced himself.

Before Bubba could say a thing Mobay stuck out her hand to shake his. "It is such a pleasure to work for the human Zim killer."

"That's okay Mobay." Bubba said with a smile. "That story grows every time it is told."

Rommin and Tesh were already there and had introduced themselves. With Becka, Rommin, and Tesh being the only other hybrids in the home Mobay stuck with them. After a while Becka, Rommin, and Tesh explained to Mobay that she was no longer a working tool or slave for the Stylus. She was free. It was something that her mind could not grasp but she would understand in time.

The next morning Bubba got up early as he always did. As he walked into the kitchen to make a pot of coffee he noticed that Mobay was sitting on the couch.

"Are you okay Mobay?" he asked her from the kitchen.

"Oh yes Sir." she replied. "I'm just nervous."

Tesh heard them talking and got up. After getting dressed she walked into the den. "Good morning everyone." Tesh said.

"Good morning." Bubba said. "Mobay isn't feeling well. She is nervous about being here."

"Oh no Sir." Mobay insisted. "I am just nervous but I don't know why."

"You heard those stories about Bubba didn't you?" Tesh asked.

"What stories?" Bubba asked. He had not been told about some of the stories that some Stylus are passing around.

"Yes ... I have."

"What stories." Bubba asked. "I thought that all Stylus liked me."

"Actually ... there are some that do not think much of you." Tesh told him. "They see you and other humans as test animals and that is all. Then when you came to Stylus so many of the population liked you very much. So those that did not like you started many stories about you ... lies ... all lies."

"Just because I am human?" Bubba asked.

"Not really." Tesh said. "Because you are a test animal that became more popular than them."

"Jealousy." Bubba commented.

"That's it. Tesh replied.

For a while Mobay told Bubba the stories that she had heard about him. One story she was told that he raped all hybrids; male and female. Not being gay Bubba got upset over this lie. He allowed Tesh to continue telling her what she had learned while she was there.

Bubba was a good man; a Christian although he sometimes did not talk like it. He loved Becka and was very faithful to her. They were even planning their marriage so their child would not be born without a last name. This was even a big thing on Stylus.

As the days went on Mobay learned more and more about living on Earth. She loved going out on the porch but was afraid to be alone out there. The military guards scared her. Then one day David came by.

Everyone at Bubba's home had someone else but not Mobay. When David came over she stared at him as he walked up on the porch. Everyone else was on the porch as well. Mobay sat on the far side of the table. As Bubba introduced David to Mobay she stood and stuck out her hand. She was expecting David to shake her hand but instead he gently held her hand and kissed it.

The look in David's eyes was the same look that Bubba gave Becka when they met. Finally David whispered; "You're a hybrid?"

This scared Mobay as she thought that he would have nothing to do with her. But she was wrong. As she slid her hand out of his and started to walk into the house David stopped her. Grabbing her shoulders and turning her to face him he looked into her eyes.

"What I meant was … that … you're beautiful."

"Take a breath David." Bubba yelled out to David but he did not budge.

David continued to look into Mobay's eyes until he snapped back into reality. "I'm sorry. I didn't mean to stare at you."

Mobay smiled. "That's okay." she said with her smile ripping at David's heart.

"You two want to join us over here?" Bubba asked.

94

David was embarrassed at how he was acting. Placing his hand on Mobay's shoulder they walked over to the others. Only Becka and David noticed it but as he and Mobay walked she slid her hand down and around his hand. Mobay had never had anyone before. It was illegal on Stylus for hybrids to get emotionally involved with another hybrid. But now she was on Earth and she was free.

Suddenly there was a gunshot out in the woods. "In the house." Rommin yelled. It was a code meaning that Bubba, Becka, and Mobay were to get in the house. Tesh went inside to protect them. Rommin ran into his bedroom and came back out with his Mini-14 rifle.

"We almost got another one." a soldier said to Rommin. "He and two others got away. They just vanished."

Rommin went back into the house and told the others what the soldier said. "That means they're back."

"They can just take anyone they want right?" David asked with a pistol his hand. With all that was going on he got his Texas Concealed Handgun Licenses and now carried a model 1911.

"That's right." Becka said. "So why are they walking around outside?"

"I have a confession to make." Tesh said. " In my room I have a dampening field generator. It stops anyone from being able to come in or go out by use of a transporter."

But how did Paulm come in here with two others … and with Mobay?" David asked.

"We were wearing interrupters on our wrist." Mobay said as she held up her hand to show hers. "The Interrupters have to be set at the exact frequency as the transporter or even we cannot come or go."

"So all the Zims have to do is find the right frequency." David mentioned.

"There are millions of frequencies that we could be using." Tesh said. "They would never find the exact frequency."

About that time Rick and Beth drove up. Bubba went outside to meet them and found that everyone else had fallowed him.

"Boy is there a lot to tell you." Bubba told Rick as he shook his hand. It was a cold afternoon so the women went back into the house. The men stayed out on the porch.

"What is it?" Rick asked as he sat in a chair. "What on Earth has you so excited?"

All of the men started talking at once. Finally they stopped and laughed about it. Then one by one they took turns telling Rick all that was going on.

"And David has a girlfriend too." Bubba said picking on his friend.

"I do not." David insisted as the other men laughed. "Mobay is not my girlfriend."

"Who's Mobay?" Rick asked.

"She is another hybrid that Paulm dropped off to take care of Becka." Bubba said. "I have to admit that she is cute … isn't she David?"

"Oh shut up." David said as he turned and walked into the house. The other men fallowed him.

Everyone had been invited to a bar-b-q on Bubba's porch. Being colder than it was suppose to be Bubba had to run out to the pit and turn the meat every now and then. Finally the meat was cooked and he brought it all in for all to eat.

Becka had made her first potato salad but it was great. Beth brought a large bowl of macaroni salad. Mobay and Tesh turned out to be quite the cookie bakers. Everyone ate their fill that evening.

As Rommin bit chunks off of a piece of meat Bubba reminded him that the meat he was eating was wild pork. "It's good." Rommin replied. "I never said that I would not eat it. I just will not kill it."

The other men laughed. "I'm sorry to laugh at you Rommin." Rick said. "Before there were stores to go to … if you did not kill something to eat you didn't eat."

"But you have stores now." Rommin argued. "There's no need to kill animals."

"Rommin." Rick said. "Beth and I are poor people and meat

96

is expensive in the stores. I not only hunt because I like hunting but I do it so she and I can eat. If I did not hunt then sometimes we would not be eating. Do you understand?"

"I do understand hunting if you need to but my father has some money. He doesn't need to hunt."

"Many humans do not like us hunters either." Bubba admitted. What do you say that … you do not try to stop me from hunting and I will leave you alone for not wanting to?"

"I guess I can work with that." Rommin agreed. "You can't go hunting as long as the soldiers are out there anyway."

That last remark along with the smirk on Rommin's face ripped into Bubba's heart.

Becka saw the anger in Bubba's eyes. "Baby." Becka said ever so quietly. "It's okay. You'll be hunting again soon."

"Maybe we should go back to Stylus." Bubba suggested. "There's a lot of Stylus there that will let me hunt on their hunting reserves."

Of course Bubba did not really want to go back to Stylus but he made a point and had the last word with Rommin. It was quiet for a few minutes as everyone thought that Bubba was really considering going back to Stylus. Then the silence was broken and everyone started talking again.

When Bubba finished his meal he stepped out on the porch. At the bottom of the steps he saw Sergeant Giffen talking with three soldiers. He walked over to the steps and waited for Giffen to finish talking to the soldiers.

"Yes Sir." Giffen said as he looked up at Rommin on the porch.

"I need to let you know about something." Bubba told him. One of the hybrids inside has a dampening field around this home. None of the Zims or Stylus can transport into the home or transport anyone out. The Stylus have what they call interrupters that they wear so they can get though. The Stylus are the good aliens. Only they can get through. That is why you keep finding aliens … the Zims out here."

"Thanks for letting me know this." Giffen said. "I was

worried about killing one of the good aliens."

"Also ... we have another hybrid in the house." Rommin added. She is part of a medical team. Her job is to take care of Becka."

"No problem Sir." Giffen said. "We will not be shooting anyone on the porch."

"The hybrids want to start coming out on the porch without one of us with them." Rommin commented.

"I know that the hybrids are friendly but still make sure they stay on the porch." Giffen added.

"Will do." Rommin said as he turned and went back into the house.

When he got back inside he found everyone talking about Bubba's and Becka's marriage.

"I hope you all allow me to throw in a few ideas every now and then." Bubba mentioned.

Becka walked over and gave Bubba a tight hug. "I'll let you say a few things."

"Yeah!" Rick said. "She'll let you say all you want and then do what she wants anyway."

"Just remember this." David said. "There is a reason a man wears black to his wedding. He knows that his life is over."

"To all of his friends he is dead." David added.

The women let go of any hands that they were holding moments earlier. They even got up and walked into the main bedroom. After shutting the door David spoke.

"Was it something that I said?"

The men started laughing knowing that their women would be back in their arms that night. However; that was not going to happen. The women were planning a revolt.

After everyone went home Bubba went into the bedroom. He took a bath and then lay on the bed. Becka wore her sexiest nightgown. Then she walked over to the bed and saw Bubba's arm stretched out.

"Please move your arm." she said ever so softly.

"But you always sleep on my arm." Bubba reminded her.

"But not tonight." she added through her teeth.

Bubba moved his arm and rolled over with his back to Becka. He knew that she and the other women were angry with what the men were saying about marriage but it would pass. However; this was the first time that she had gone to sleep without her head on his arm. That still bothered him.

Bubba woke up during the night and found Becka laying close to him with her head on his arm. He smiled knowing that this anger she had would not have lasted long. But did she lay her head on his arm out of habit or did she do it because she wanted to? He would know the answer to that question in the morning when they got up. And if she was still angry then he would make sure that she knew that she still slept with her head on his arm.

When Bubba woke up a few hours later he found that Becka had moved off of his arm. She probably hoped that he did not know that her head was on his arm but he would make sure that she did. He got up and started to brew some coffee but the coffee pot did not work. The light came on but it would not get hot. This is when he thanked God for instant cocoa mix.

Bubba sat down on the couch with his mug of hot cocoa and tried not to wake up Mobay. However; she was already awake. She turned over and told Bubba that the coffee pot did not work.

"I know but I'll go into town today and get another one. We have hot cocoa in there."

"What is that?" Mobay asked.

Mobay got up and Bubba showed her the instant cocoa mix. Running the water until it got hot he filled a mug for her. After mixing in a package of the cocoa mix she took a sip. From then on Mobay was addicted to hot cocoa.

They both came back in the den where they set at opposite ends of the couch. Bubba always sat on the right end where he had a holster wired to the right end of the coffee table. In the holster he had his Ruger P-95, 9 millimeter pistol. He always kept it close by.

For the next two hours the two sat and watched Fox-and-Friends on the TV. Mobay was started to get very interested in the different governing powers of the country. From time to time Bubba had to explain something so that she did not turn into a liberal communist. If she did that then she would have to leave. Bubba did not want any communist in his home and Rommin was starting to lean that way.

Chapter 10

Try and Try Again

Rommin walked into the den rubbing his eyes. "The TV is to loud. You woke me up."

"I'm sorry Rommin." Bubba said. "I'll keep it down tomorrow."

"That's okay Dad." Rommin commented. "I needed to get up anyway."

"The coffee pot is broken." Bubba said. "I'll get another one today. In the meantime there is some cocoa mix in there."

As Rommin walked in to the kitchen Mobay jumped up to get herself another mug of the hot cocoa. "I love this stuff." she told Rommin.

Right at that time Tesh walked into the den and looked at Rommin and Mobay talking. She thought that Mobay was hitting on Rommin and got upset. She walked into the kitchen and looked right into Tesh's eyes and hissed with an angry look on her face.

"What the hell was that?" Bubba asked. He heard her hissing all the way in the den.

"Tesh." Rommin said. "There's nothing going on here Dad." Then he walked into the den and sat on the couch.

"Did Tesh just hiss at Mobay?" Bubba asked Rommin.

"Yes Sir." Rommin replied. "Hybrid females do that when they feel threatened."

"What threat?" Bubba asked.

"Tesh likes me and ... I like her too." Rommin explained. "I guess Tesh thought that Mobay was trying to get to close to me."

But I thought that Mobay liked David."

"She does. It's a female thing."

Bubba looked into the kitchen and caught Mobay and Tesh

walking into the den smiling. What ever was going on it was over now.

Before long everyone in the house was up. With everyone drinking hot cocoa they quickly ran out.

"When I go into town today I'll pick up a coffee pot and a lot more cocoa."

"I don't like you leaving the house Dad." Rommin said. "You're only safe under the dampening field around this house."

"I don't think the Zim would try to grab me in broad daylight."

"They might." Becka said.

"What's the range on one of those transporters anyway?" Bubba asked.

"Just under half a mile." Mobay said. "Closer to a quarter of a mile."

"Then they would have to come out in the daylight where everyone would see them and get that close before they could grab me." Bubba argued.

"Who's to stop them?" Becka asked. "If they grabbed you then do you really think your military jets would catch up with them and get you back?"

"Good point but why would they even want me?" Bubba argued more. "They want Becka and the baby."

"They may grab you to trade for Becka and the baby." Rommin said. "She loves you and you know she would do anything for you."

"And the Zim know that too Baby." Becka said ever so softly as she hugged his arm tighter.

"Bubba let out a heavy sigh. "I know your right. I'll have someone else get what we need."

Becka hugged Bubba's arm even tighter. "Thank you Baby." Remembering that Becka slept on his arm the night before he said; "As long as you keep sleeping on my arm ... like you did last night."

Instantly Becka pushed Bubba's arm away. "You are a monster. Cook your own breakfast."

I'm not hungry." he told her with a soft voice.

There was nothing else that Becka could do but pout which was something she did well. But before long she moved her arm back around her man's arm. Angry or not she still loved him and that came first.

Later that morning Rick and Beth came over. Bubba asked if they would use his credit card and buy things they needed. They agreed. They also agreed that the Zims might try grabbing him to use as a hostage or bargaining chip to get Becka and the baby.

Bubba had not realized how vulnerable they were; how useful he would be to the Zims. He always thought of himself as not being that threatened but he now knew what the Zims could do. From this point on he asked everyone to carry a firearm with them at all times when outside. Then he thought about something else.

Turning to Rommin and Tesh he asked; "How are you suppose to protect Becka and me with no weapons?"

"Oh we have weapons." Tesh responded. "What do you think this is on my wrist?"

"I thought that it was a communications device like what Mobay has."

"She does have a communication device but Tesh and I have weapons on our wrist." Rommin told his dad. "How else would we be able to do our job of protecting you two?"

Bubba got up and tripped over Mobay's cot. "Oh I'm sorry Sir." Mobay said. "I should have moved that when I got up."

It's okay." Bubba said easing her mind.

"I've been meaning to talk to you about that." Rommin said. "She can have my room."

"Where are you going to sleep?" Bubba asked.

Rommin put his arms around Tesh and said; "With her."

"You two sure about this?" Bubba asked them.

"Yes Sir." the both said in agreement.

"Then move your things out so Mobay can move in."

Rommin and Tesh went into his bedroom and moved his

things into her room. Then Mobay moved her things into her new bedroom. Bubba folded up the cot and put it back in it's bag and stowed it away in the hall closet.

"Have you two set a date to get married yet?" Beth asked knowing that they had not.

"We do not even have anyone to marry us." Bubba said.

"I could do it." Rick mentioned. "You want a ceremony that would be right in the eyes of God right?"

Bubba and Becka both agreed.

"Then I would open the ceremony in prayer, let you two say your own vows, and then close the ceremony in prayer. That should please God."

Bubba and Becka thought for a moment. "Marriage licenses was started in the 1940's as just another way to tax people anyway." Bubba mentioned.

"That's right." Beth said. "Before that people still got married."

Bubba and Becka agreed and set the date for the first Sunday in May. This gave them just over a month to set things up.

The women started their screaming again so the men went out on the porch. For at least an hour the women would scream and then stop only to start screaming again minutes later. After realizing that they would be out there for a while Rick left to go get the coffee pot and cocoa.

Bubba built a fire in his cast iron stove that he had set up on the porch so he and the others could stay warm. Before long he had the stove almost red hot. The men cuddled around the stove and talked about the wedding.

"Like it matters what we decide." Bubba said. "The women make all of the wedding plans."

"Isn't there one thing that you want?" Rommin asked.

"I would like everyone to be dressed in camouflaged clothing." he replied. "I want a camouflaged wedding."

"Then march in there and tell her." Rommin said not really expecting his father to do it. He was starting to get into this.

Bubba got up and walked into the den. After closing the door the women looked at him. "I want a camouflaged wedding where everyone wears camouflaged clothing."

"I thought you might so we already decided to do it." Becka told him. "But I am still wearing a white dress."

Bubba smiled. "You are perfect."

When Bubba returned to the men and told them what Becka had already decided. They saw it as something that the women came up with and Bubba still needed to put his ideas in the wedding. But Bubba backed down from the idea.

"I got what I wanted and that's all that matters." Bubba told them. Then the conversation turned to hunting, fishing, and guns.

About that time David drove up to the house and got out of his truck. His first words were; "Where's Mobay."

The other men laughed and told him that she was in the house planning a wedding." Right at that time the women screamed again.

"OH … I think I'll stay out here." he said.

"Good idea." Rommin said. "There's more of them in there than us out here." Then as a joke Rommin grabbed his father's arm and said; "I'm scared Daddy. Help me."

The others laughed as Bubba pushed Rommin away. About that time Rick came back with the coffee pot and cocoa mix. He and Bubba went into the house and got a pot of coffee brewing. When Bubba told the women that there was more cocoa mix the women got up and flooded the kitchen. Bubba and Rick barely got out of the kitchen with empty mugs.

By time the women got their hot cocoa the coffee was almost finished brewing. When it did finish the two men got their coffee and went back outside. As they sat down they reminded the other men that the coffee was made.

Bubba got an old coffee pot for brewing coffee over a fire. He filled it with water, put coffee grounds in the holder and set it on the cast iron stove. A few minutes later they had more coffee.

It seemed to be getting colder but the sun had been up for a few hours. Then it started to snow. That half of the porch had a roof so the men stayed dry. Then Bubba thought about something.

"If the snow is making it through the dampening field ... or shield ... then why can the Zims not come through?"

"Only biological things cannot get through." Rommin advised. It goes around the home and this porch to about seven feet from the ground. That is how the soldiers are walking so close to the house."

"If the soldiers can walk under it then can't Zims?" Bubba asked.

"Yes but they would have to come in through a door or window." Rommin told him. "Then we would get them."

"Can they take one of us from under the shield?"

"No." Rommin added. "You could be standing right under the edge of the shield and they would not be able to take you. But stay on the porch anyway."

"No problem." Bubba replied.

The next morning Bubba woke up early and performed his usual duties. He made a pot of coffee, sat on the couch, placed his pistol in the holster, and then watched Fox News on the TV. It was not much but at his age, by time he sat on the couch, he was tired again.

By time Bubba sat on the couch Rommin and Tesh were walking into the den.

"Good morning Pappy." Rommin said as he laughed.

"You can call me Dad or father or even late for a catfish dinner but never call me Pappy again." Bubba said with a serious look on his face.

As Rommin quietly walked into the kitchen Bubba looked up and Tesh and smiled. She smiled back and said nothing to Rommin.

After they got their coffee Rommin and Tesh came back into the den and sat on the couch. Seconds later Becka joined them. Bubba stood and started walking towards the kitchen to refill his mug. Mobay fallowed to get more of the hot cocoa.

Suddenly three Stylus appeared but not all the way. For

three seconds they looked to be out of phase. They were shifting from being there and not being there in split second intervals. Then they were gone.

Did everyone see that?" Bubba asked.

"They were Zim." Rommin said. "They were wearing the large alien head hoods. The Stylus would not have done that."

Bubba went into his bedroom and grabbed his CAR-15 rifle. Becka fallowed and grabbed her Ruger 10/22 rifle. By time they came back into the den Rommin stood there with his Mini-14 rifle.

But how could the Zims get through the shield?" Becka asked.

"They can't unless they had onc of the Interrupters." Mobay mentioned. "The only Interrupters that I know of are all on Paulm's ship."

"The Zims have been getting very aggressive lately." Bubba added. "Bok and his crew not only escaped but stole a Stylus ship. Could any of these Interrupters be on that ship he stole?"

"The only way that a Zim could come here like they just did was if they had Interrupters but did not know the exact frequency." Mobay told them.

Then suddenly another Zim appeared alone but he was out of phase like the three before him. Rommin quickly fired three rounds but the bullets passed right through the out of phase Zim without harming him. Within a couple of seconds the Zim was gone.

Bubba walked into the kitchen to checked out what Rommin shot. The refrigerator had two holes in it but it still worked. Duct tape would fix it for a while. The third bullet passed through the front of the microwave. With the glass door shattered it was ruined.

"Sorry Dad." Rommin said.

"That's okay Rommin." Bubba said. "It was more important to kill the Zim. You had no way of knowing that the bullets would just pass through him." Bubba thought for a moment and added; "Now that you have killed a microwave you might as well

107

go hog hunting."

Bubba sat back down beside Becka and put his arm around her. She scooted closer to him and hugged him tightly. She was scared. Never before had the Zim come so close to getting her and her baby. As she cried Bubba held onto her knowing that there was really nothing that he would be able to do to stop the Zim. The rifles were of no use against them because they could grab anyone and vanish in a split second. They only helped he men to feel better as if they had some hint of control. The truth was that they had no control and that was so frustrating.

Two hours went by with no more Zims flashing in and back out. Bubba and Becka agreed to remain seated on the couch making it harder for a Zim to grab them. Rommin continued to move around so if the Zims came back they would not know where he was. Being seated Bubba knew that his rifle would be to hard to use so he lay his rifle on the coffee table. Then he pulled his pistol from it's holster and lay it in his lap.

Mobay had an idea and went into her room. As she changed the frequency of the Dampening Field Generator she heard some screaming in the den. Not knowing what had happened she ran into the den to see that another Zim had tried to transport through the shield. When Mobay changed the frequency the generator trapped the Zim in place but still out of phase. This killed the Zim who finally appeared on the floor. His body smoked.

Mobay went back into her room and finished the process of changing the frequency on the generator. Then she returned to the den finding the men moving the dead Zim outside. His smoking body put a stench in the air that was making everyone sick.

Seeing a soldier Bubba called for him. When the soldier walked up to Bubba they shook hands.

"Please inform your sergeant that we have another dead Zim for him."

"Yes Sir." the soldier said as he made a call on his cell phone.

About twenty minutes later a Humvee backed up to the steps.

108

Four soldiers got out and loaded the dead Zim in it. Then they left as quickly as they came.

"Don't talk much do they?" Bubba asked the soldier.

"No Sir." The soldier was very respectful. Bubba still had a feeling that the soldier did not care much for any aliens including the hybrids.

"This Zim got killed trying to get past the shield over the house." Bubba informed he soldier. "Please tell your friends to kill any aliens they see out here but not hybrids on the porch."

"I've only met one ... I think a male hybrid." the soldier mentioned. "He was nice to talk to."

"Thank you." Bubba said before thinking about what he was about to say. "That was Rommin ... my son."

"Your son Sir?"

Realizing what he had done Bubba now had to explain it all to the soldier. "My sperm was taken many years ago. Rommin is half human from me and half alien. Now he is here to protect Becka and me."

"Who is Becka?" the soldier asked.

"She is another hybrid inside ... my future wife." Bubba commented.

"Is she the one that is pregnant from a human?"

"Yes and ... I'm that human."

"Keeping it in the family right?" the soldier said realizing that it sounded insulting. "I'm sorry Sir. I joke around to much."

"That's okay. It was funny." Bubba assured the soldier. "I'm the same way."

"Tell your son that I enjoy talking to him." the soldier said. "He seems to be pretty smart."

"Are you allowed to come inside for a moment?" Bubba asked.

"I don't know Sir."

As the soldier stepped up on the porch he said that he was Private Marcus Benson. Everyone got quiet inside when Bubba opened the door and allowed Marcus inside. He introduced Marcus to everyone there.

"Please forgive me for staring but ... are all hybrid females this pretty?"

""We are all good looking according to human standards." Rommin said. "It has something to do with the human DNA."

"Oh yes." Marcus said as he stepped closer to Rommin. "You're his son ... Rommin is it?"

"Yes I am."

Marcus enjoyed being among the hybrids but he had to get back outside. He was still on duty. As he walked out of the door everyone told him good-by.

About an hour later three Zims appeared wearing their large head hoods. This time they were not out of phase. Two of them grabbed Bubba and then all three of the Zim and Bubba vanished.

Everyone in the house jumped to their feet. Rommin ran outside and looked up into the sky. Just above the house was a Stylus ship that was quickly leaving. Rommin ran back inside.

"It was the Zims." Rommin yelled. He looked around the room. "Where's Becka?"

The others explained that as he ran outside two Zims reappeared and grabbed Becka. They now had Bubba, Becka, and the baby. Mobay walked out on the porch and contacted Stylus Command on the planet Stylus.

Minutes later Stylus Command called back and told Mobay that the Zim had captured a Stylus ship. Bok used the Stylus ship that he stole in capturing the other Stylus ship. It was Paulm's ship that was captured.

Mobay came back in the house and told everyone what she learned about Bok. The problem was that there was nothing that they could do.

"But why would they grab Bubba first?" Tesh asked. "Why would they grab him at all?"

None of them had any answers but there was one thing for sure. Bubba's and Becka's lives were about to change and not for the good.

Chapter 11

The Twins

As soon as Bubba appeared on the ship he was grabbed and thrown to the floor. At the age of sixty-four he was not getting up quickly. Seconds later Becka appeared. She was thrown to the floor beside him.

"Father ... please help us." Bubba quickly prayed. *"Please give me the strength I need."*

It may have taken Bubba a while to get up but when he was up the fight was on. This was something that the Zims had not planned on. By time a large hybrid knocked him back onto the floor he had badly hurt six Zims and killed another one.

Becka quickly kneeled by her man. Then she hissed like Tesh had done earlier.

"Now, now little one." the Zim hybrid said as he walked towards Becka.

"You touch her and I'll kill you, you son of a whore." Bubba warned as he stood.

The Zim hybrid continued to walk towards Becka paying no mind to the old human man on his right. Suddenly Bubba quickly reached out with both hands and grabbed the hybrid's head. A quick twist later and the hybrid fell to the floor dead.

Bubba looked at Becka and said; "Well ... I warned him."

Then Bok walked into the room. "Bubba." he said with a big smile.

Bubba lunged at Bok but suddenly felt his whole body stinging. The next thing that he knew was that he was waking up on the floor of a small cell. He stood and yelled for Becka but there was no answer. He yelled again and felt his body stinging again.

"The first time you felt that it knocked you out." Bok said as he walked around the corner. "And don't worry about Becka. We aren't going to hurt her … or that baby."

"What do you want with Becka and my baby?" Bubba asked.

"Actually it's just the baby that we want." Bok said. "Your baby is more than you know." Then he smiled and looked right into Bubba's eyes and added; "Becka knows." The truth was that Becka did not know.

"What about my baby and where is Becka?" Bubba yelled.

"You need to understand something Bubba." Bok said. "You're a waste of space on this ship. If you cause me to much trouble then I'll just have you ejected out into space. Do you understand?"

"If I'm such a waste of space then why did your men grab me first?"

"They were suppose to have grabbed Becka but when they appeared they grabbed you by mistake." Bok informed him. "You were not suppose to be here."

"Then why do you keep me here?"

"Because I like you Bubba." Bok said. "I don't know why but I like you. Maybe it's just that all humans are scared of us but not you. You never were."

"I know that the Stylus have been picking me up for about twenty five years but have you?"

"Not me but other Zims have grabbed you … I think twice many years ago." Bok said with a smile. "If I read the report right you were not worth it to continue picking you up."

"The Stylus thought I was worth it for about twenty-five years." Bubba argued.

"The Stylus are stupid." Bok argued back. "Did you ever wonder how that the Stylus and Zim look alike although we come from two different planets light-years apart?"

"Yeah I have." Bubba admitted.

"About seven hundred years ago our planet had a civil war and many of the Zim took off and moved to the planet that is now called Stylus." Bok told Bubba. "The Stylus are only Zims that lost the war and moved away."

"No one ever told me."

"That means that Becka is half Zim." Bok added as an insult. "In a way ... if you two got married then you and I would almost be brothers."

"No you son of a whore." Bubba insulted Bok. "The Zim do not care about the humans they grab but the Stylus do."

"They are week Bubba." Bok said as he walked away. "And you are just a test animal for us to test drugs and diseases on."

There was no bed or even a toilet in the cell. It was small; made for a Stylus which only stood about four feet high. Bubba sat in one of the corners not knowing where Becka was or what might happen to him or her. Because of this he prayed again.

"Father I really need you right now. Please be with Becka ... where ever she is. We really need your help Father." He began to cry but quickly stopped. He did not want his eyes to be red when Bok came back. It would look bad and he had to look strong. *"I have no idea what you're going to do but I trust you to do something. Becka and our baby are in your hands."*

Bubba looked outside his cell at the wall in the hallway. It looked like stainless steal. All of the shinny steal was enough to drive a man mad. The Stylus ships had other things in them like wood and what looked like plastic. They used colors but the Zim did not. The Zim ship had the boring steal everyplace. The Stylus might have come from the Zim but they were not Zim. The two races were nothing alike.

Later a Zim came by and looked at Bubba. He had a bowl of muka but, just before sliding it under the bars he spat in it. Bubba quickly picked up the bowl and threw it at the Zim. Muka cover the Zim as well as the walls and floor of the hallway.

The Zim started to unlock the bar door but Bok walked up and asked what he was doing. The Zim told him that for no reason Bubba threw the bowl of muka all over him. When the

Zim left Bok asked Bubba what happened.

"Just before sliding it under the bars he spat in it so I gave it back to him." Bubba told Bok. "I love muka. God I love it but not if someone spits in it."

"I'll have another bowl brought to you" Bok said. He looked angry either at Bubba or at the Zim that spat in the bowl of muka.

"Bok." Bubba said softly. "I'm trying to cooperate with you. Could I see Becka?"

Bok thought for a moment. "Becka is in a room with a locked door. I'll have you moved there but do not cause my crew any more problems."

"And if they spit in my muka again?" Bubba asked.

"Then don't eat it and tell me about it."

"Good enough." Bubba said. "Then I will not give your crew any problems."

"Then we have an agreement." Bok commented.

"Our first agreement." Bubba said.

Bok smiled. "I think you're right."

Bok left and a few minutes later four Zim stood in front of the bared door. One of them opened the bar door and waved for Bubba to fallow him. The other three Zim fallowed behind Bubba.

As Bubba walked down the hall to where Becka was they passed a room where he noticed something that he knew about. He stopped and looked at the setup for an alcohol still. He asked if he could look at the still but the Zim did not know what he was saying. At the end of that hall they stopped and the door was opened.

Inside the room was Becka sitting on her bed crying. Before Bubba could even walk in the room she jumped up and leaped into his arms. The door was shut behind him and locked.

"Are you okay Babe?" Bubba asked but Becka could not stop crying. She hung onto Bubba as if her life depended on it.

"Don't let them take my baby." Becka begged.

"I think they want it to be born naturally and you still have

114

about five months to go." Bubba tried to assure her.

For the first time Bubba could do nothing to easy Becka's fears. He could only hold her and hope that it was enough. As he held her he prayed again.

"Father. Here we are needing you again. There's not a whole bunch that we can do. I have no weapons and if I fight back again they may eject me into space. Please help us Lord."

Suddenly the door opened and a bowl of muka was set on the floor. "You hungry?" Bubba asked Becka.

"I ate a few minutes before you got here." Becka replied.

"Then that's mine ... replacing the one I threw at the Zim."

"You what?" Becka asked.

"A Zim brought me some muka earlier and spat in it so ... I threw it all over him." Bubba said with a smile. "He thought that he was going to come into my cell all by himself and do something about it but, Bok came by and stopped him."

"Can you stay out of trouble ... just for a little while?" Becka asked Bubba.

Bubba looked at he for a moment and then replied; "I'm not to good at that."

By time Bubba finished his muka Bok came by with two guards in case he was jumped. "You two feeling better now that you're together?" he asked.

"Thank you Bok." Bubba said.

"Well I have got to keep her happy." Bok replied. "See. You're good for something Bubba."

"Where are we headed?" Bubba asked.

"To our planet ... Zim."

"I couldn't talk you out of that could I?" Bubba asked.

"That's it." Bok said. "That's why I like you so much. You keep me laughing."

By the way Bok ... I noticed that you have an alcohol still just down the hall."

"Yes we do." Bok replied. "We make our alcohol from Muka.

Some of it is for medical use but some is for drinking."

"I have a small still on Earth and I saw that your still could use another part."

"What part is that?" Bok asked.

"If you add a thumper between the still and the cooler your alcohol would taste better. The thumper takes out any impurities." "

Bubba went on to describe what a thumper looked like and how it worked. Bok was intrigued enough to ask Bubba to make this thumper. Bok took Bubba to the room with the still and watched as he built the thumper. Using a large jar he drilled two holes in the lid. Then he placed some of the tubing in the holes at different levels. The Zim stood back as Bubba added the thumper to the still. The Zims started brewing the alcohol again. A little later Bok tasted the alcohol and loved it.

Bubba was returned to the room where Becka waited for him. Later that day a Zim brought Bubba a small jar of the Muka alcohol which they called Balma. When the Zim left Bubba tried the Balma but did not like it. It was to sweet but drinkable. He still preferred his Rye whisky that he made on Earth.

Bubba had made some goody points with Bok but it was just part of a plan. He only acted nice to Bok to gain his respect and maybe sympathy. It was all he had.

Then suddenly the ship shook as if they were being attacked. Then it shook two more times. Alarms were going off and Zims were running every which way. Bubba stood ready in case the Zim came in to kill either him or Becka just to keep the Stylus from getting them.

When the door to the room opened Bubba grabbed the Zim opening it and snapped his neck. "God I enjoyed that." he said as he stood back and waited for another.

Becka no longer cried. She stood beside Bubba ready to attack anyone coming into the room. For a long time no one came into the room. Fighting could be heard in the hallway.

"The Stylus are here ... on board." Becka told Bubba.

Then the door flew open and Bubba grabbed the Zim and

116

was about to snap his neck when Becka stopped him. "He's a Stylus."

Another Stylus entered the room. One grabbed Bubba by the arm and the other one grabbed Becka's arm. Then one of them spoke into a communicator on his wrist. Another second later Bubba and Becka stood on a Stylus ship with the two Stylus that got them.

"Bubba ... Becka ... fallow me." It was Ail and this was his ship. Bubba and Becka were rushed into a room where a dampening field had been set up to keep the Zim from taking them back.

One armed Stylus stayed with them in case a Zim showed up. Fighting was heard in the hallway so Bubba and Becka knew that there were Zim on that ship. However; the Zim did not stand a chance. It was three Stylus ships against the single Zim ship. Finally it got quiet in the hallway.

The Stylus guard opened the door and found many Zims dead in the hallway. Bok had sent them all to grab Becka again but the dampening field stopped them. Although all of his crew were killed or captured Bok escaped in an escape pod. Bok had ejected all of the escape pods to cover his escape. By doing this he had abandoned his crew and left them to die or be captured.

When things calmed down Ail came back to see Bubba and Becka. He told them that Paulm had been killed when Bok captured his ship. This did not set well with Bubba who now hated Bok more than ever.

Ail also told them that they would be taken to Stylus for a short time while they searched for Bok. The planet Zim was heavily defended so the Stylus would not be attacking their planet. Finding Bok on the planet Zim would be left to the many spies Stylus had on their planet.

The next day Ail's ship landed on Stylus. This time no one knew that Bubba and Becka were on board except for Yunnan and maybe two or three others. They landed at night and kept Bubba and Becka in the shadows until they were safely in Yunnan's Palace. The planet Stylus also had plenty of Zim spies on it so Yunnan wanted to keep Bubba and Becka hidden and safe.

Once in the palace Bubba and Becka were rushed to a room that had been set up just for them. Minutes later Yunnan came into the room and instantly shook their hands.

"Now you will be known as the human that has killed five Zims and one Zim hybrid." Yunnan said to Bubba. Then he continued to tell them that at least for a little while they needed to stay in the room. An armed guard would be outside the door at all times. "I am so happy that we were able to get both of you back." Yunnan said before leaving.

The ruler of the entire planet of Stylus personally greeting them was an honor that no one had ever received. Yunnan was even taking it upon himself to see to their security and care while they were there. Later a Stylus came into the room and gave them news from Earth.

Her name was Micus. She was the head of security for Yunnan's palace. Using telepathy she spoke to them.

"Your friends on Earth have been told that you were safe and that you would be home soon. You will be here for a few days while we search for Bok. As long as he is alive then you two will never be safe." she told them. Then she looked at Bubba and added; "So you killed two more Zims and a Zim hybrid?"

"Yes Ma'am." he responded.

"Well … your being here is a secret but Yunnan wants the entire planet to know what you did."

"No problem here." Bubba let her know.

Micus left. Bubba and Becka went to bed but, with Bok still out there neither of them slept well. Five or ten minutes of sleep here and there was all they got. The next morning a large breakfast was brought to their room. It was much more than they could eat. Coffee was becoming popular on Stylus and they even had a pot of coffee with their breakfast.

Unable to leave the room for three days almost drove Bubba and Becka crazy. Early on the morning of the forth day armed Stylus guards escorted Bubba and Becka back to Ail's ship. At the entrance of the ship Yunnan waited to see his two friends off.

"Thank you Yunnan for all of the help you have given us." Bubba said as he shook Yunnan's hand. "You're a good friend."

Suddenly shaking hands was not enough. Yunnan gave Bubba and big hug. Then he turned to Becka and hugged her as well. "I'll be seeing you two again just before the baby is born."

"Why would you do that?" Bubba asked.

Yunnan looked puzzled. "I just thought that you would want to have the baby here in our hospital. All you have back on Earth is a hybrid with some medical training."

"Sounds good to me if that is okay with you Babe." Bubba asked Becka.

Bubba and Becka continued to get on board and went straight to their room. Minutes later the ship lifted off. It would take three days to get to Earth so they settled in and made the best of it.

That evening Ail dropped by to see Bubba and Becka after finally finding the free time. As they talked Bubba asked him why their baby was so important. Ail let out a heavy sigh and answered his question.

"As you know Earth, Stylus, and Zim worship the same god who had a son. You call him Jesus but we call him Muchee. But what I am about to tell you is not religious but political." Ail told them as he sat down.

Just after we broke away from Zim and came to Stylus it was prophesied that two children, a boy and a girl would be born as a hybrid. These twins would free the Stylus from the Zim. But now we know that the translation was wrong. The twins would not be born as a hybrid but of a hybrid." Ail stood and continued. "You are pregnant with twins … a boy and a girl. Your children are the prophecy.

"And their names would be Johm for the boy and Meshet for the girl.

"So it has nothing to do with God but politics?" Bubba asked.

"This is why Bok is trying so hard to get Becka to his

planet." Ail advised. "Then he could raise them and brainwash them into thinking that they are Zim. These twins will be very powerful. We just don't know in what way they will be powerful."

"Why has no one told us about this prophecy before now?" Becka asked.

"Like I already said …" Ail replied. "We only recently learned the true translation of the prophecy."

Before leaving Ail shook their hands. Then he left for his room to get some badly needed sleep.

Bubba and Becka sat on the side of their bed for a long time saying nothing. They were taking some time to let it all sink into their brains. Just an hour earlier their baby was just another unborn baby. Now they were having twins that would lead the Stylus into freedom from the Zim. So much was happening so fast but at least now they knew why there was so much interest in their child; their children.

Chapter 12

Little Odie

Bubba and Becka stood ready to be transported into his home. In his home their friends waited to see them again. Ail talked to Bubba and Becka one last time before they left.

"Do you have room in your home for one more Stylus?" Ail asked Bubba.

"Not really but … I guess they could sleep in the den." Bubba confessed. "Why?"

"I need to send one of my Stylus to set up a better Dampening Field Generator than the one Mobay has." Ail said. "Then Mobay can operate it. Tem would only be there to set it up and then he would come back here."

"No problem." Bubba said.

"Tem and his generator will transport down in a few minutes." Ail said as he quickly left.

Bubba and Becka looked at each other and smiled. Suddenly they were standing in his den. Everyone that lived in Bubba's home walked over to greet them. David, Rick, and Beth were also there. As they all talked Tem transported into the den along with the Dampening Field Generator.

Tem asked Bubba where he might want the generator placed. Bubba simply told him to scoot it against the wall. "It will be out of our way there."

While Tem worked on the generator other parts to the generator would suddenly appear in the den from time to time. It took two days for Tem to finish building the generator. So many parts were transported that Bubba thought that the generator would be big and bulky. When Tem finished the generator was almost unnoticeable behind the recliner.

"Now you will be protected better." Tem told Bubba. Then

he turned to Mobay and told her a few things. After that he gathered his tools together and stood in the den. With a wave of his hand to Bubba and Becka he vanished.

"You two came close to never coming back again." David said.

"I know … I know. Bubba agreed. "But this bigger Dampening Field Generator is suppose to be better.

"It's much better than my small one." Mobay replied. "Even the stolen Interrupters that Bok has will not help him anymore."

"How is that?" Rick asked.

"Now it takes a different type of Interrupter to get through." Mobay advised everyone. "This Dampening Field Generator can detect weapons of any type … even bladed weapons. It can be set to leave the weapons behind or I can set it to allow them through."

"But when they grabbed these two they did not use weapons." Rick said. "They just grabbed you and vanished before we could do anything."

"I can set this generator to hold anyone that is transporting through it for up to ten seconds." Mobay said. "During that time we can see who it is and grab them as soon as I let them through."

"Well that should do it." Beth mentioned.

"This generator does one more things." Mobay mentioned. "Anytime anyone tries to transport through the shield Ail's ship is contacted. They are at the bottom of the lake just waiting in case we need them."

It was quiet in Bubba's den. Then David had one more question. "Who has these Interrupters for this generator?"

"Ail has four … the only four for this generator." Mobay said with a big smile.

With all of the excitement Becka was tired. She stood and went into the bedroom to lay down. Bubba lay beside her with her head on his arm. "I love you Babe." he told her.

"I love you too Baby."

"Ha Rommin." David asked. "You carry your dad's Mini-14 rifle but you have a weapon on your wrist. Why do you carry

122

both?"

"I just like the Mini-14 rifle. The weapon on my wrist is like having a pistol."

"How does it work?"

"I just point it at someone I want to shoot and press the button with my other hand."

"If it takes two hands to operate then ... why use it?"

"It's what they gave us to use here." Rommin commented. It emit's a sound wave at a frequency far above your ear's ability to hear it but it makes you sting all over. There are three setting on it. The first setting will quickly get your attention. The second setting will knock you out. The third setting will kill."

"By the way everyone." Mobay said. "Tesh will be taking over the Dampening Field Generator responsibilities so I can get back to just taking care of Becka."

"Being trained in the medical field ... why were you also trained in this ... generator?" David asked.

"I was trained to operating the generator first. Learning it was simple." Mobay said. "Then I was trained in the medical field to see if I was smart enough. The Stylus always thought that we hybrids were not very smart. Now they have learned that most of us are smarter than them."

"That's like the people around here. Rick said. "Everyone thinks I'm goofy."

"No Baby Doll." Beth mentioned. "You're big and strong but you're also goofy all over."

Everyone laughed not realizing that they were making him feel bad. Rick said nothing as his friends continued to laugh at him.

"Goofy or not you're still my friend." Rommin said.

Then the others agreed with Rommin and let Rick know that he was still their friends. Most humans would not hurt a friend's feeling but sometimes do it without realizing it. We only see that we have done it after doing it. Then it is a time for apologies and reassuring the friendship.

When it started getting late David, Rick, and Beth went

home. Everyone in Bubba's home stayed up a while as Fox News was talking about military training around the same lake that Bubba's home overlooked. After going to bed everyone in the house could hear helicopters flying over all night.

Rommin and Tesh walked out on the porch. Tesh had the communicator that Mobay had earlier. While Mobay concerned herself only with Becka's health Tesh would be taking care of any communications with the Stylus ships and their home planet. Tesh called Stylus Command on the planet Stylus to let them know what the United States military was doing just in case it was something against them.

An hour went by with no word from Stylus Command. Then Tesh was contacted by Yunnan himself. What was going on was that the US government was getting ready for a visit by Yunnan. Conditions between the Stylus and the US government was so good that Yunnan was visiting the US president himself. That meeting between the two leaders would take place someplace around where Bubba's home was. That was the true reason for the military being there. There was no training but no one was to know the truth.

Yunnan went on to advise Tesh about three ships being on the bottom of the lake. At that time she saw two Stylus ships suddenly appear above the lake only to lower themselves to the lake and below the surface. She told Yunnan about the two ships. Yunnan advised her that Ail's ship was already on the lake floor.

By this time Everyone else was already up as well. Bubba and Becka waked out on the porch. Bubba had his CAR-15 rifle in hand. Tesh explained to them what was really going on. By time the sun was coming up everyone in the house was out on the porch.

It had only been daylight for about an hour when a Humvee drove up to the house. Three officers got out along with the driver, Sergeant Giffen.

"Is it safe for us to come up on your porch Sir?" Giffen asked half way joking. He and Colonel Dotter knew that they were safe but the other two officers didn't.

"Of course." Bubba admitted. "You're all safe here."

As the men walked up on the porch Sergeant Giffen introduced the officers. "You know Colonel Dotter. He is the CO over all operations on your property. This is 2 Star General Moore. He is the CO over all military forces in the area. And this is 4 Star General Norman. The President placed him in charge of all things involving the Stylus and Zims."

Then it was Bubba's turn to introduce everyone there. "This is Becka ... soon to be my wife. This is Rommin my son and this is Tesh. They will be the ones killing you if you lie to me about what is going on." Bubba could see the fear in their faces so he decided to back off some. "I was just joking about that but still ... don't lie to me." Then he turned to Mobay and said; "This is Mobay. She has been trained in human anatomy and is Becka's ... doctor."

"We have doctors that could take care of her. General Moore said.

"And at what point would you take her away and dissect her and my baby for your own interest?" Bubba got angry. "You have me confused with someone that trust you. I love my country but I do not trust my government. I ..."

"Baby." Becka quickly stopped him. "Please forgive him General. He loves me very much ... as you can see but we have seen to many times where your government will grab someone for what ever reason and no one sees that person again. The Zim are animals but at least they do return who they take ... back to where they were taken. That makes you more of an animal than them.

General Moore and Norman stepped back. Then General Norman said; "I like your honesty and I am sorry that you feel that way." He looked around at three of the soldiers walking around the home. "Do you trust these soldiers?"

"I do because I have met and talked with them."

"So they earned your trust over time?" General Norman asked.

"Yes."

"All I ask is that you give me time to prove myself as well."

Becka thought for a moment. "I guess I can do that but you might consider steering clear of … my man here … for a while anyway."

Bubba's eyebrows were still lowered. "I didn't trust these men either at first … but I do now. I will give you time too. But you still fallow orders from others that do not care about us. Just remember that I am a great shot with this thing." he added as he held up his CAR-15 rifle."

General Norman took a step back and looked at Becka. "I think you're in great hands right here." he said as he pointed at Bubba.

"Before leaving we do have a few questions … if you don't mind." General Moore mentioned.

"If you want." Bubba said.

"Actually I was talking to the … hybrids is it?"

Becka, Rommin, Tesh, and Mobay looked at each other and agreed.

The Colonel and two Generals sat down and asked their questions. Bubba asked Sergeant Giffen if he would like to come inside. He agreed.

"You can relax in here Giffen." Bubba said. What do you know about these two Generals?"

Bubba and Giffen were in the kitchen getting some coffee. "I don't know much about them Sir. I'm sorry."

"If you did learn something that I needed to know would you tell me?" Bubba asked. "On which side do you place your loyalty?"

"And if I choose to be more loyal to you and I am caught at it I could be executed."

"Just fallow your heart Giffen." Bubba said. "God will guide you."

The two men talked a while longer but when Giffen's mug was empty he said he had to go. Before walking out the door and onto the porch he turned to Bubba and said; "You all have been very nice to me." He thought for a moment and added; "My

126

loyalty is with you."

"Thank you Giffen."

"It's Ted ... Sir. My first name is Ted."

"Then I guess it's ... Thank you Ted."

Ted opened the door and stepped out on the porch with Bubba. They found the officers still asking questions. Of course the hybrids only told what they wanted the human officers to know.

As the officers stood Becka walked over and put her arms around Bubba. General Norman stuck out his hand to shake Bubba's hand. "Well at least Becka got to know us a little. But I have to admit that you probably will never see me again."

"Why not?" Bubba asked.

"My job keeps me in Washington DC ... in the Pentagon." You will probably see General Moore from time to time though."

Bubba moved to shake General Moore's Hand and then Colonel Dotter's hand. Finally he shook Ted's hand and said; Hope to see you again soon ... Sergeant Giffen." Bubba did not want to let the officers know that he and Giffen had got so friendly that they were using first names. This might make Ted look bad.

When the Sergeant and officers were gone those on the porch compared notes. Come to find out the officers continued to ask questions about the Stylus weapons but the hybrids pretended to know nothing about the weapons. The officers were more concerned about obtaining advanced technology than anything else.

Rommin did admit that they asked him a few questions about Bubba being his father. There was nothing to hide there so he explained everything he knew to them. The officers did take written notes so the hybrids were very careful at what they said.

Bubba, Becka and Mobay walked back into the kitchen where Bubba got another mug of coffee. Becka and Mobay got their usual mug of hot cocoa. Then they went back to the couch and watch the local news to learn what the government was telling the people.

The people of the area were being told that all of the military was not there for training but for a movie being filmed there. It was a one year project that might take a bit over a year to film. All citizens were asked to act normal and they might catch themselves in the movie. They were also told that if they saw any "flying saucers" they were not to call the police. These were American aircraft from the Space Force that President Trump had started. The flying ships were real but they were part of the America's Space Force. Of course the United States Space Force had nothing like these ships flying around but it made a good cover story for anyone spotting a Stylus or Zim ship.

Those in the den watching the TV laughed at the story the government was telling everyone. The reporter was so convincing that if those in Bubba's den did not know the truth they might have believed the story as well. The government story was so convincing that the reporter believed what she was telling everyone. Basically the story was; calm down everyone. It's just a movie being filmed.

Just as Bubba turned the TV back to Fox News there was a knock on the door. Rommin answered the door to find General Moore standing there. Rommin stepped back and allowed the General to come in. He started telling everyone the story about a movie being filmed when they all started laughing.

"You want us to believe that story too?" Bubba asked.

General Moore was silent for a moment and then realized that they probably thought that he was trying to tell them that story. "Oh no." he said. "That's just what we are telling the public. I'm just here to let you know that it is our cover up story. That way if anyone sees an alien spaceship then we have already told them it is just part of the filmed movie. We do not want to public to panic or start shooting at the alien ships."

"I did not think about that." Bubba admitted. "I guess some will shoot at the ships but they aren't going to hurt them."

"I'm sure they won't." General Moore stated. "But those bullets will still come down someplace and maybe hit someone."

"That's true. They always come back down."

The General left leaving those in Bubba's home to laugh some more. It was quiet the rest of the day with Bubba's TV glued to Fox News. They did talk a little about the movie being filmed in that area but they mentioned nothing else about it.

Bubba continued to watch Fox News until they started repeating the news for those that just tuned in. He searched the stations for a good movie and found one about conspiracies of the American government.

"Oh this is perfect." Bubba mentioned but the movie was low budget and not good at all. Taking his rifle and big glass of ice tea with him he went out on the porch. Rommin got his own glass of tea and joined his father. Bubba had not been paying much attention to his dog Odie so Becka let him out as well.

Odie was a faithful dog that loved Bubba very much. He went straight to Bubba and lay at his feet. Bubba looked at his buddy and smiled.

"He's getting old isn't he." Rommin mentioned.

"Yeah. He doesn't have much time left." Bubba sadly admitted.

Suddenly two Zims appeared on the porch just eight feet from Bubba. One of them stunned Bubba with the device on his wrist. When Bubba fell to the deck Rommin fired his Mini-14 and killed the one that stunned his father. Then he noticed that Odie was attacking the other Zim chewing on his ankle. Being in pain the Zim fired his weapon at Odie stunning him. By time the Zim looked up Rommin was firing three shots at him. The second Zim fell dead.

The women ran out on the porch wondering what was going on. Becka instantly kneeled beside Bubba but he was only stunned. Then she checked Odie laying beside him. Although the device on the Zim's wrist was set to stun only, it was still to powerful for the small dog. Odie was dead.

Mobay instantly looked Bubba over while two of the military guards ran up on the porch. The two guards watched the area from the porch while the others quickly got Bubba back in the house.

While Bubba slowly recovered from being stunned the others started asking how the two Zims got through the shield. Mobay and Tesh looked over the Dampening Field Generator.

Inside the generator Mobay and Tesh found a timer set to lessen the area that was covered. The generator had been set to cover a few feet beyond just the home and porch. The timer was set for midnight the previous night and to cut back the coverage area to no longer cover the porch. Mobay and Tesh quickly removed the timer and increased the coverage back to just beyond the porch.

When Bubba recovered he sat on the couch. Odie was placed in his lap. Bubba could not hold back the tears. He had, had Odie for many years. The little dog was not a pet but his little boy. Becka sat beside him trying to be of some comfort to him. Then he stood and rapped Odie in a towel. After that he went outside to bury his little boy.

As they passed the two Zims on the deck Bubba noticed that one of them was still alive. The one that was shot first was moving. "Rommin." Bubba said. "Hold this piece of shit here."

"I will." Rommin answered.

Bubba continued to carry his dead dog down the steps. Then he turned sharply to the right and lay Odie on the ground. He grabbed the shovel and started digging a hole beside the steps. When the hole was big enough he lay the shovel down and placed Odie in the hole. Then he spoke out loud thanking Odie for being the best friend he ever had. He filled the small grave and gently stepped on it to press the dirt down.

Still crying Bubba carried the shovel up on the porch and handed it to Rommin. "Stay out of my way for a while."

The Zim looked up at Bubba. For a moment he and Bubba just looked at each other. Then Bubba grabbed the Zim and started beating on him. From time to time he threw the Zim against the house. The Zim screamed from the pain but no mercy was in Bubba's heart that day. He continued to beat the four and a half foot tall creature. Even when the Zim no longer moved Bubba continued to kick him. Then suddenly Rommin stopped his father.

"He's dead Dad. He's dead."

"Give him to the soldiers."

Bubba walked into the main bedroom and on into the bathroom. Becka fallowed. Bubba started to clean his hands which were covered with Zim blood but also some of his own. His fist were full of cuts and in one spot the skin had pulled back three inches. The rage in his heart was still there numbing any pain in his hands. Becka gently washed his hands and bandaged them up. When the bleeding stopped she would have Mobay take over.

"If I will do that for killing my dog ... can you imagine what I will do if they hurt you?" Bubba uttered to Becka.

"I love you Baby." Becka told him.

"Love you too." Bubba added as he started to cry again.

Bubba looked like he was in his own little world. He just stood there but moved when Becka said something. She walked him to the couch and sat her man down. Then she got him a cup of coffee and brought it to him. Mobay was looking him over.

"Is he okay?" Becka asked Mobay.

"He will be okay." Mobay said. "I guess he loved that little dog more than we thought."

Chapter 13

Cloaked

After burying Odie Bubba sat on the couch beside Becka. For many hours he just sat there saying nothing. Then Rommin noticed a change in the look on his face. The hallow, empty look was no longer there and the old Bubba seemed to be coming back. By time Becka walked him to bed he still had not changed much.

That night Becka changed the way they had slept for so long. This time she slept with her chest against his back. He slept on her arm that night as Becka held onto him as tightly as she could. This time he needed her andshe was going to be there for him; all night.

The next morning Becka woke up and realized that Bubba was not in bed. Only wearing her nightgown she ran into the den and found him sitting on the couch watch the TV. He had already made coffee and had a mug on the end table beside him.

"You okay Babe?" Bubba asked.

"Are you okay?" Becka asked as she walked up to him.

"I am now Babe."

Becka went into the kitchen and got her usual mug of hot cocoa. Hearing Bubba's voice everyone in the house also got up to check on him. Before long everyone was seated and holding their mug of coffee or hot cocoa.

"Tesh." Bubba said finally breaking the silence. "Contact Ail and let him know that Tem set that timer in the DFG."

"You sure he did it?" Tesh asked.

"You and Mobay are the only ones that know anything about that thing and neither of you had it taken apart. Tem must have placed it in there when he put it together. He's a Zim spy."

Tesh instantly went out on the porch and called Ail's ship.

132

Two minutes later Ail came back to her. She told him what Bubba said and what all happened. Ail thanked Tesh and signed off.

Ail sent three Stylus to put Tem in the brig. When the three had Tem locked up Ail called Tesh back and told her. Then he told her that later he would come see them about what Tem had done.

Tesh had the Dampening Field Generator or, DFG as they started calling it, set for holding the person transporting for seven seconds. Just before noon someone tried transporting through the shield. It was easy to see that it was Ail so nothing was done. In seven seconds he materialized in the den.

Ail held what almost appeared to be an informal court. It was easy to see that he was in charge. As Ail spoke someone else tried transporting through the shield. It was Tem and three guards. When they materialized everyone could see that Tem had his hands bound in front of him. For two hours almost everyone gave their testimony and answered questions. Tem was even given time to ask his line of questions. Then all of the questions came to a halt when someone drove up to the house.

Bubba was still not one hundred percent so Rommin went outside to see who it was. Out of the Humvee came Sergeant Giffen and Colonel Dotter. They met Rommin on the porch but he did not want to let them in without Ail's permission. Rommin came into the house and told Ail who was on the porch and said that they wanted to come in and see the trial. Ail was very strict. They could come in and observe the trial but they had to remain quiet.

Rommin explained Ail's rules and the two outside agreed. All of the chairs were taken so Ted and Dotter stood in the corner. Ail was irritated a little but understood Colonel Dotter's interest in the trial which could finally continue.

The Colonel and Sergeant missed out on much of the trial as Ail spoke using telepathy. Most of the time the hybrids also spoke using telepathy but used their mouths when they realized that some of those there could not hear anyone using telepathy.

133

Finally after a good three hours Ail had heard enough. Tem had even admitted that he was the only one that could have placed the timer in the DFG but insisted that he did not do it. Suddenly there was gunfire outside. Tem was forced to the floor of the den while the guards held him down. One even sat on him. Ail stood his ground but Tesh stood with him. Mobay stayed with Becka while Bubba and Rommin went outside with their rifles.

The military guards on Bubba's property were firing into the woods behind the house. No gunfire was seen coming from the woods but every now and then a soldier would fall; either wounded or dead.

Then finally an enemy was seen. Zim soldiers could not able to transport through the shield so they were trying to break through the line of military soldiers and then just walk up on the porch. This was the only way to get past the shield; by going under it. However; Stylus Command never considered this when they developed the DFG.

Bubba fired a single round at one of the Zims but missed. The next three rounds did not. Before that Zim could hit the ground three others stepped out of the bushes. A soldier on the ground fired hitting one of them. As the three Zims started to fire at the soldier Bubba and Rommin opened fire on them. Three more Zims fell dead. At this point the soldiers started pushing into the woods behind Bubba's home. After Rommin insisted that Bubba go back inside but they both did.

The gunfire continued outside. Ail had already contacted his ship but did not want to ask for reinforcements. The soldiers outside would not know the Stylus from the Zims. He did ask for Bubba and Becka to transport back to his ship with him for their safety. They agreed. First Tem and the three guards with him transported back to Ail's ship. Then a few seconds later Ail, Bubba, and Becka transported to Ail's ship. Bubba and Becka would be safer on Ail's ship as it sat on the bottom of the lake with two other Stylus ships.

Back at Bubba's home more Zims were transported to the surface on Bubba's property not knowing that Bubba and Becka were no longer there. Colonel Dotter went out to the Humvee and got on the radio and called for reinforcements. Just seconds later two helicopters flew over but no Zim ships were found. Suddenly the two helicopters dropped out of the air and crashed into the lake close to Bubba's land. A minute later soldiers flooded Bubba's land and the surrounding area. Finally the Zims were transported back to their ships and the fighting stopped.

"Do the Zims have a cloaking device on their ships?" Bubba asked Ail.

"Both the Zim and Stylus have been working on cloaking our ships but we could never get it to work." Ail said. "Maybe they did."

"I saw to many Zlm soldiers for them to have come from just one ship."

"They must have cloaked ships." Ail commented. "We cannot find them."

The five Zim ships escaped into space in case the Stylus had some way of finding them. From where they were, they could see the Stylus mother ship on the back side of the moon. They decided to attack the mother ship.

A Zim ship could transport soldiers even while it was cloaked but it could not use it's weapons while cloaked. Not wanting to be seen the Zim ships transported their soldiers right into the Stylus mother ship. They caught the mother ship off guard. Many of the Stylus were killed but they still had more personnel on board the mother ship than the combined five Zim ships. The attack failed.

Twenty six Zims were captured and another thirty seven were killed. The Zims transported a few of their captured soldiers off of the Stylus mother ship but the Stylus stopped the transports. All five Zim ships had to run home with skeleton crews.

This attack on the mother ship was proof that the Zims now had cloaked ships. Now the Stylus had to find a way to detect cloaked ships. The technicians on Stylus started working on this as soon as they learned about the cloaked Zim ships.

After everything had calmed down for a while Bubba and

Becka transported back to the house. It was already dark but everyone there were still up waiting to see them. The Sergeant and Colonel left many hours earlier. Now the US government knew about the Zim ships being cloaked.

Everyone hugged Bubba and Becka but hugging Becka was becoming harder. She was now almost five months pregnant and no one wanted to hug her tightly out of fear of harming the babies.

David came there just after Bubba and Becka left for Ail's ship and supplied another rifle. Just after they came back Rick and Beth drove up.

"You mean we missed all of the action?" Rick asked.

"Looks like it." Bubba replied. "This time we had a lot of action."

"I heard you killed another Zim ... beat him to death David told me." Rick said with a smile. That makes you six doesn't it ... plus a Zim hybrid."

"Plus he shot one of the three Zims on the ground." Rommin added.

"That must have been what the military was taking away as we got out of the truck." Beth mentioned.

"They can have all of the dead Zim they want." Rommin reminded them.

The problem is that now the Zim ships are cloaked." Mobay said. "We can't see them."

"Cloaked?" David asked. "A Cloak is nothing but a cover over something to keep you from seeing it."

"We know that." Tesh said.

"Then what do they use to cover the ships?"

"It's called a cloaking device." Rommin replied.

"No ... I mean ... what does this device emit that cloaks the ship. Is it sound or electrical pulses or maybe a radio wave?"

"Stylus and Zim have both been working on cloaking our ships but we do not know what they are using." Mobay said. "We were working with sound waves but we were getting no place with it."

136

You know … I have all kinds of instruments for measuring sound, radio waves, and even electrical currents." David said. "I could set them up here and then just stick back and wait for them to come back." Mobay gave David a hug.

"Yeah I think Mobay might like that too." Rommin mentioned. Everyone laughed but shy little Mobay removed her arm from around David's waist.

Mobay was not as tall as the other hybrids. They were all close to six feet tall but Mobay barely reached five feet, one inch. She was told that her father was a very short man.

David left to go home and bring back the instruments he had mentioned. Because of security around the area he was stopped at the gate and one more time before getting home. After loading the truck he had to go back through the checkpoint and Bubba's gate again. After leaving Bubba's home it took three hours to get back.

Bubba and Rommin helped David to move his instruments into the house. The only place that had any room for it was in Mobay's room. After moving a folding table into the bedroom David started moving his instruments into the room and putting it all together on the folding table. Bubba, Rick, and Rommin just stood back out of the way watching David plug in electrical cords, twisting wires and doing other things that none of them could understand. Then when he finished he still had to sit in a chair and calibrate everything. By time he had finished the other three men had lost interest and left. The only one that was still there was Mobay.

With no one looking Mobay stepped up to David and put her arms around him. For a short while they just hugged. After a quick kiss they went into the den where everyone else was.

"You know … you two have forgotten about something else." Beth mentioned. "What about your wedding?"

Becka looked at Bubba and said; "I am not going to get my white dress and you're not going to get your camouflaged wedding. There is so much going on. What do you say that we just do it tomorrow. Please baby."

Bubba smiled. "That sounds great."

The women got together to plan the wedding and the men got together to plan the feast after the wedding. Beth went into town to buy things needed to make deviled eggs, macaroni salad, and potato salad. When she got back the women started making their specialties. When they finished it all went into the refrigerator. There was only one rule in the house that night. No one was allowed in the refrigerator. Getting milk for coffee the next morning was the only exception.

After not getting much sleep that night the men got together around three in the morning and started cooking the meat. Rick even brought his gas grill over to help with all of the meat that was being cooked.

Sergeant Giffen, Colonel Dotter, General More, and General Norman were invited to the wedding. General Norman could not make the long trip from Washington DC. Ail was also invited.

Before leaving home around 2:30 in the morning Rick grabbed a half gallon of moonshine that he had made. Before the men even started cooking the meat they started drinking. Another rule popped up from the women. No one was allowed to get drunk until after the wedding. The women really did not want any drinking at all until after the wedding but with the men being men accidents happened. Every once in a while the jug of moonshine fell over and spilt some of the moonshine down a man's throat. Accidents happen.

Finally the time came and all of the men came inside. Rich took his place beside the TV and Bubba stood in front of him. There was no music so the women hummed the wedding march as Becka walked out of the bedroom. As Becka stepped up beside Bubba he said; "God you're beautiful."

"Let us open this wedding in prayer." Rick said. "Father … we are here today to join these two in holy matrimony … in every way that we can to be pleasing in your eyes. Please bless this couple that stands before you Lord."

Rick looked at Bubba and Becka. "You may hold hands and say the vows that you have prepared. Bubba. You first."

"Oh God. I forgot to prepare any vows so this is from my heart." He looked into Becka's eyes. "I love you so much. I will protect you with all that is in me. I'll be with you when ever you need me. I will worship you … as my wife. And finally … I am sorry I did not write any vows down and make this better."

"Now you Becka." Rick said.

"I love you too Baby. I will be with you whenever you need me. I will wash your wounds and hold you to keep you warm. I will do whatever it takes to make you the perfect wife. And I did write this down." Everyone laughed.

"Do you have a ring?" Rick asked.

Bubba pulled one of his rings out of his pocket. Becka understood that he could not leave the cover of the DFG to get her a ring from town but she did not care. They were finally getting married and that was the important thing.

Then Rick closed the wedding in prayer. "Father these two now stand in your shadow as one. Please bless them both as one."

"By the power invested in me as a Christian and by God I pronounce you two husband and wife." Bubba took to long to move so Rick added. "If you don't kiss her I'm going to."

Bubba and Becka kissed and the wedding was over. Instantly they were hugged by everyone there. They were finally husband and wife. It bothered Bubba that he could not go into town and get her a good wedding ring. But he knew that she understood.

Suddenly there was more gunfire outside. All of the men ran outside with rifles in hand. The Zims were attacking again. This time the Zims retreated and left. The fight left three Zims dead and one captured. None of the soldiers were killed but two were wounded. But on the porch Rommin and Bubba had been hit. In this attack the Zims were using projectile weapons.

Bubba and Rommin were brought in the house where Mobay instantly started working on Bubba. He had been shot in the left shoulder and insisted that Mobay take care of Rommin first. Rommin had been shot in the stomach and that was never good. With both men laying on the floor Ail insisted that they be transported to his ship. Mobay agreed. Of course Becka went along. Tesh wanted to be with Rommin but she was needed there at the house.

While Rommin and Bubba transported to Ail's ship, still at the bottom of the lake, David checked his instruments. He looked over all of the recorded information and came up with what he thought the Zims could be using to cloak their ships.

David came out into the den and said; "They are using an electro-magnetic field as a cloak or at least in the cloaking itself."

"I think you're wrong David." Tesh said. "The ships float in the air by using an electro-magnetic field as propulsion. This is what you picked up."

"Okay then." David said. "Thank you and I'm back to work." He went back into Mobay's room and looked over his instruments again. *Maybe it was something that I did not record. Maybe it is something that I am not looking for.* David could not figure it out and that bothered him. He always considered himself a genius when it came to things like this. Rick walked into the room and looked at his friend.

"Sometimes I cannot figure something out so I stop and come back to it later." Rick advised his friend. "Sometimes we cannot see the answer because it is right in front of us."

David looked at Rick. "That just does not make any since." Then he thought about what Rick said. He got up and went into the kitchen. After getting a mug of coffee he went back into the room and sat down. Looking his instruments over again he found nothing. Then he noticed something. He had also recorded the electrical field from the DFG but part of the signal was not coming from the generator. It was coming from outside. After coming up with a few math problems he started seeing how their cloak worked.

David walked into the den and asked Tesh; "How much do you know about how the DFG works."

"I know everything about it." Tesh said. "Why?"

"I think I know how their cloaking works."

"Show me what you found out." Tesh said.

David took Tesh into the bedroom and showed her what he

found. By time they came out of the room she believed that David found the answer. To prove it they would manipulate the DFG and try to cloak the house. Rick walked out onto the driveway to where he could just still see the house. He had a hand held radio. On the other radio David asked Rick if he was ready for the test. Tesh crossed two wires that overloaded the DFG but it did not trip the breakers to the house.

"Rick." David said. "Can you still see the house?"

It took a few seconds but Rick finally came back. "What house?"

"Can you see the house?" David asked Rick again.

"I see the steps and a little bit of the porch but that is all." Rick admitted.

Tesh uncrossed the two wires and David asked Rich what he saw then.

"I see the whole house now." Rick said. "What did you two do?"

David asked Rick to come back in the house where he would be safe. Then he and Tesh agreed to not cloak the house again. If the Zims saw the house vanish then they would know that the Stylus had the cloak figured out. Everyone in the house cheered for what David had discovered. Tesh needed to let Ail know about the discovery but she did not want to tell him by use of communications. So she got permission for her and David to come to his ship.

A few minutes later David and Tesh vanished from the den and appeared on board Ail's ship. They were taken to the bridge where Ail sat in his chair waiting for them. David was in shock seeing all of the Stylus working on the bridge. It was just so much to take in at one time.

Tesh started speaking using telepathy while David continued to look around the bridge. Then Ail started asking David questions by speech. David answered his questions and told Ail how he came to his conclusions. Then he told Ail about the experiment and making the house vanish under a cloak generated from the DFG.

141

The Stylus ships had shields that could be raised to protect them from any Zim attacks. David and Tesh were allowed to manipulate the ship's shields to see if they could cloak the ship. The ship's shields were basely the same as what the DFG did so it should work.

Ail had one of the other ships on the bottom of the lake watch his ship. About thirty minutes later one of the other ships reported to Ail that his ship was no longer there. Tesh reversed any action they did and his ship was seen by the other ship again. Ail had a cloaked ship now but it took two people to operate it.

One of the Stylus were trained by David and Tesh in how to cloak the ship using their shields. Then they went to the other ships and made the adjustments and trained Stylus on those ships. The problem was that they could not see each other or the Zim ships. Air collisions were very possible.

Ail called Stylus Command and had three ships come to Earth to replace the ones there. Then they would fly to Stylus and have the adjustments made permanent. They would not be back for at least a week.

Chapter 14

The Prophecy

Three months went by with not one Zim nor any of their ships being found anyplace close to Earth. It seemed that the Zim had given up on trying to get Becka's babies. Becka was now eight months pregnant.

Tem was found guilty of being a spy for the Zim and was executed. He was placed in the transporter and transported from Ail's ship to Bubba's home. Mobay had the DFG set to stop anyone from coming through. It was a painful and horrorable way to die but in about fifteen seconds Tem appeared on Bubba's den flood dead.

All of the Stylus ships were now cloaked and they even figured out a way to detect other cloaked ships. Only one Stylus ship sat on the bottom of the lake now and it was Ail's ship. He and his crew kept a close eye on Bubba and Becka.

Then one day the Zims came back and the fight was on again. Without warning a Zim ship attacked the house itself. They knew that Bubba and Becka slept at the northern end of the home so they attacked the southern end.

It was just after midnight when a cloaked Zim ship appeared about half a mile above Bubba's home. The Zim ship fired two shots into the southern end of the home almost totally destroying that end of the home. Rommin, Tesh, and Mobay came running out of their rooms and into the den. Rommin continued out on the porch with his rifle. Seconds later Bubba stood beside him.

Suddenly seven Zims appeared on the ground and tried running up the steps but thy were cut down by Bubba and Rommin. About eight more ran out of the woods from behind Bubba's home but the soldiers fired at them dropping four. The others retreated.

143

The Zim ship had hoped that firing on the house would drive Becka out making it easier for them to grab her with their transporter but, they failed. As the Zim on the ground were being transported back to the ship the ships Commander had the ship fire two more rounds at the front gate killing eight soldiers that were running up the driveway.

The entire attack only lasted one minute. By time Ail's ship found out what was going on and they came up to the surface of the lake the Zim ship was gone. Ail had his ship hover just above the lake's surface the rest of the night. Being cloaked he did not worry about being seen.

Bubba went back in his home and looked at the damage. Only then did Becka, Tesh, and Mobay come out of the master bedroom. With soldiers covering the grounds outside Rommin joined Bubba inside.

"Well they tried to kill someone." Rommin said.

"I don't think so." Bubba replied. "It looks bad but for some reason they only hit this end of the home. Now why would they do that?"

"Maybe they somehow knew that you and Becka were at the other end of the home and they just wanted to drive you two out from under the shield." Rommin said.

Bubba looked at Rommin. "You know ... you could be right." he admitted. "Good thing I never left the porch and she never came out."

"Dad." Rommin said. "I think you two need to go back to Stylus for a while."

Bubba took in a deep breath and let it out. "I think so too."

Rick, David, and Rommin agreed to have the home repaired while Bubba and Becka were gone but, Bubba did not want to go. Finally Becka agreed to go to Stylus while Bubba stayed and had the home repaired. Mobay would go with Becka to take care of her.

Early the next morning Becka and Mobay transported to Ail's ship. With the cloak engaged they left for Stylus. With the babies due in just four weeks Bubba did not want to see Becka

144

leaving his side but, he knew that she would be safer on Stylus. The question then was should they let the Zims know that she was gone or still there?

The next day Bubba contacted contractors and took bids on his home being repaired. By time Becka and Mobay got to stylus Bubba had decided on one contractor. However the contractor would not be able to start for another week. In the meantime they did come out and cover that end of the home with a tarp in case it rained.

One day David came and got all of his equipment and took it home. Then he came back to help in any way he could. He had a business to run so he had to get back to that the next day.

Rick came every now and then to check up on the progress of the home but that was all. For the most part Bubba and Rommin stood alone. Bubba had the contractor's workers place a plastic wall between the damaged part of the home and the rest of it. He used the excuse of keeping the wind and dust out of the rest of the home. The truth was the plastic kept the workers from seeing the hybrids there. The hybrids would be allowed to come into the den and enjoy the TV and kitchen. With their rooms being repaired they would be living in the den.

One morning there was a knock on the front door. Thinking that it was the contractor Bubba answered it.

"Hello Sir." a young woman said. "I am Peggy Dotter, a reporter for the City Currier newspaper."

"Yes Ma'am." Bubba said not sure what to do. "What can I help you with?"

"I heard that your home was accidentally hot by some military explosives while filming." Peggy said. "I would like to hear your side of the story."

Bubba thought about what she said about the military's story so he agreed to talk with her on the porch. "Just sit at that table and I'll be right out."

About a minute later Bubba walked out of the house with a glass of ice tea in one hand and his CAR-15 rifle in the other. After laying the rifle on the table he sat down across the table from Peggy.

"Is the gun necessary?" Peggy asked.

"Yes ma'am." Bubba quickly replied with a big smile. "There's a lot of wolves out here."

Peggy had a sad look on her face. "I don't like guns."

"Oh!" Bubba said smiling even bigger. "You must be one of those young liberal communist I've been hearing about."

"I'm not a communist." Peggy quickly replied.

"Are you a liberal Democrat?"

"Yes ... but I am not a communist."

"If you're a liberal then you're a communist." Bubba insisted. "The communist want to destroy this country. You greasy liberals want the same things starting with taking my guns." By this time Bubba was getting loud.

"Sir." Peggy said interrupting Bubba. "Could we get back to me doing my job ... interviewing you?"

Bubba calmed down. "Yes ma'am."

Peggy asked Bubba many questions and did a great job even after being insulted. Bubba only said what he thought the government would want him to say. When Peggy finished she stood and told Bubba good-by. Using a kind voice Bubba still could not hold back an insult and asked that she never come back.

"You're a nice woman and good reporter but ... you're still a communist. I don't like communist."

Peggy's smile turned to a frown. "Okay Sir. I don't like people that think they have to carry a gun around. That is what the police are for."

"But you commies hate the police too." Bubba said raising his voice again.

A Humvee drove up. As Sergeant Giffen and Colonel Dotter got out Bubba yelled to them. "Get this communist whore out'a here or I will ..." Bubba said grabbing his rifle. "With this."

"Wait a minute." Tom said as he ran up on the porch. "You don't want to shoot her."

"She's a communist whore." Bubba yelled as he got even

more angry.

Colonel Dotter grabbed Peggy's arm and said; "You need to leave Baby Doll."

"You know her?" Bubba asked but Dotter and Peggy continued to walk away.

"Yes Sir … he does know her." Tom informed Bubba. "She is his daughter."

Peggy drove away and Dotter came back up on the porch. "Sorry about that. She is a bit headstrong."

"No I'm sorry." Bubba said. "I just learned that she is your daughter but she came onto me about carrying this rifle."

"She is a strong liberal … that's true but she is a nice girl." Dotter said. "Those damn colleges only teach the students how to hate America. Her mother and I cannot change her mind."

"Well … keep her away from me." Bubba advised. "When this country finally falls apart because of the liberal communist I will be shooting every one of them that I can find. Keep her away from me."

"I'll do what I can but she has her own mind."

"Your guards at the gate can stop her." Bubba advised.

"Yes they can but …"

"But nothing." Bubba insisted. "Just do it."

Tom whispered in Dotter's ear and asked him to drive back by himself. "I can walk back after calming Bubba down some."

"Good idea." Dotter whispered. Then he turned and walked back to the Humvee and drove away.

"Sorry about that Bubba." Tom said. "She is a liberal all the way."

Bubba and Tom went into the house and got themselves a mug of coffee. Then they came back outside and sat at the table on the porch. For a while neither of them said a thing. Then a truck drove up. It was the owner of the construction company that was going to repair Bubba's home.

"Are you Bubba?" the man asked as he stepped up on the porch.

Bubba stuck out his hand to shake the man's hand. "Yes sir."

147

he said looking at the man's truck. There was no doubt that this was the truck of a man that worked construction. Tool boxes sat on top it the sides of the bed and a rack on top held two ladders.

"I'm James Pollie of Pollie's Construction."

After shaking Bubba's hand James looked over Bubba's home and then came back to tell Bubba what it would take to repair the home.

"It will take a bit but I can get your home back to normal in two months." James said. "I see my men came in and put up the plastic you asked for."

"I thank you for that." Bubba said. "Just to let you know I had them double the thickness of the plastic because I have a cousin inside that cannot be breathing that dust."

"No problem Sir. I'll give you what ever you want."

"Sounds good." Bubba agreed. "I had one company that came through and promised things that he never delivered. Because of that you now have the job."

"Well let's make sure I deliver." James said. "We will be out here tomorrow morning. First I need to see what all we need which means taking this part of your home apart. Only then can we start fixing it."

"I understand." Bubba admitted. "See you tomorrow."

Bubba watched as James got into his truck and drove away. His thoughts turned to Becka. He knew that she was safe on Stylus but he still felt that she would be safer with him. He knew that he was wrong in thinking that but it was a man's thing. A man is suppose to protect his family. How could he protect his new wife if she was not there? hen again; he did not protect her well when she was there earlier.

The next morning Bubba was sitting in the den watching the local weather on his TV when he heard noise outside. Stepping out on the porch with his pistol he saw James directing men to their jobs. It was just 6:00 a.m. and the sun was not even up yet but they were already at work.

Seeing Bubba on the porch James joined him. "I hope you do not mind us starting this early."

148

"I am always up very early anyway." Bubba replied.

Only then did James notice the pistol in Bubba's hand. "Not going to shoot us are you?" he asked with a smile.

Bubba smiled. "No but ... tell your men to get used to us carrying firearms out here." he advised. "And one more thing. My son likes to join me out here from time to time but he is a bit deformed in the face." Bubba mentioned about Rommin. "Please ask the men not to stare at him."

"I always talk to them at noon when they break for lunch." James advised. "I'll mention it then so they all know."

"And we do come out here in the early morning with our rifles to drink our coffee. Don't worry."

"All of my men are country boys that grew up with guns. I'm sure they'll understand."

James went back to his work and Bubba went back in to the home. Bubba told Rommin what he told James about him being deformed. That hurt Rommin's feelings until Bubba explained that he would be able to continue drinking his coffee on the porch now. Drinking his coffee on the porch in the early morning was something that Rommin loved to do so he excepted the story.

Bubba and Rommin got their mugs of coffee and, of course Rommin grabbed his rifle too, and went out on the porch and sat at the table. One time James walked up on the porch and talked with Bubba about something and then got back to his job. Rommin was nervous about his coming so close but felt much better when James left. From then on he did not worry about the workers looking at him.

Tesh on the other hand did not like going outside much. Staying inside and unseen was just fine for her. While the construction was going on she would do any contacting Stylus Command at night.

*   *   *   *   *

On the planet Stylus Becka was getting ready to give birth. Yunnan took a personal interest and visited Becka almost every

149

day. She wanted so much for Bubba to be there when the babies were born but she understood that he needed to be at home. She was staying busy with giving speeches at women's groups. However; she was causing problems with her support of the hybrids wanting more freedom.

The hybrids had been created for the purpose of being workers. They were bigger and stronger than the Stylus and Zim. Now the Stylus were discovering that they were also smarter. The hybrids were claiming that they were not created but born into the Stylus race. They were half Stylus. A human sperm was always implanted into a Stylus female citizen. With their mothers, who they never knew, being Stylus citizens they also wanted to be considered Stylus citizens.

As Becka became very popular with the Stylus hybrids and many of the Stylus females she was becoming unpopular with the Stylus government. Before long even Yunnan stopped coming to see her. He was getting heat from those in the government that did not like Becka nor his visiting her so much. It looked like he supported her views on hybrid rights.

As Becka got closer to giving birth she was advised to stop the hybrid rights issue. With the government taking care of her and her unborn children she needed to lean more to their side in this hybrid's rights issue.

One morning Becka woke up with pains in her stomach. She feared that it was time to give birth and called for Mobay. Mobay had Becka sent to the local hospital where she was taken straight to the maternity ward. About an hour later it was decided that this was a false alarm. Becka was not giving birth yet. However; the doctor still wanted to keep her in the hospital over night and set her up an a private room. Security around the room was high with one armed Stylus guard in the room, another one outside the door, and another one walking the hallway.

A female Stylus working at Yunnan's Palace was given a promotion and placed in charge of Becka's personal security. Her name was Mecka. While most officers in the security force only wore their uniforms when they had to Mecka wore her uniform anytime she was on duty. She was a by-the-book Stylus that took great bride in her job. This was the reason she got the promotion and placement as Becka's personal security.

"With no complications over night Becka was released to go back to her cottage the next morning. Mecka had Becka's cottage check for anything unusual before moving her there. When the cottage was cleared Mecka had Becka transported home. Then a guard stayed with Becka at all times. Other guards walked outside stopping anyone wanting to visit.

On the evening that Becka came back to her cottage the guards stopped someone wanting to visit her. As soon as the guards saw that it was Yunnan with only two guards they allowed him through. When Mobay opened the door Yunnan came in and walked over to Becka. Leaving over he gave her a hug and then stood up.

"How have you been doing?" Yunnan asked.

"Just fine Sir." Becka replied. "I do miss my husband though."

"Why did he not come with you?"

"The Zims blew up one end of our home hoping that I might run out so they could grab me." Becka replied. "Bubba stayed to make sure the repairs on our home was done right."

Yunnan smiled. "I like Bubba." he said. "He makes me laugh a lot."

"He does that to everyone." Becka agreed.

Suddenly Becka had more pains and called for Mobay again. As Mobay checked Becka she stood back. Without any warning Becka's water broke. Yunnan had never seen a child's birth and jumped up quickly backing away. Mobay called for Mecka and Becka was back at the hospital within thirty minutes.

As Becka lay on the gurney in the maternity ward the doctor got her ready to give birth. One look and he told her that it was going to happen this time. Becka smiled as she thought about her husband back on Earth. She wished so much that he was there. She did not see him as just making sure that the home was repaired properly. She saw her husband as staying on Earth to fight the evil Zims. In her eyes he was her hero and almost a god.

Suddenly there was fighting heard out in the hallway. Mecka came in the delivery room and advised the doctor to continue. Zim spies were trying to break in to grab Becka and her two children. The Zim saw this as their last chance and were putting everything into this attack.

Firearms could be heard being used in the hallway. Finally the door opened and Mecka was shot. Falling to the floor she tried to fire one shot but was kicked in the face knocking her out.

Then the Zim turned and looked at Becka. It was Bok.

Bok stepped up to Becka who was at that time giving birth to the first child. As the doctor deliver the first child and popped it on the back to help it start breathing Bok looked into Becka's face.

"Don't worry Becka. We will take care of your children."

Becka felt along her right side where she had a Ruger LC, 9 millimeter pistol in a holster. She smiled as she pulled the pistol and flipped the safety off. Bok looked back at her.

"Why are you smiling?" Bok asked her.

"Because sometimes Muchee, God, takes care of our enemies himself and sometimes he delivers our enemies into our hands so that we may deal with them." At that time Becka pulled the trigger three times. Two of the bullets entered Bok's head and the third passed through his neck severing his spinal column. He was dead before he hit the floor.

Mobay had awaken and fired at the two Zims standing beside her. They fell to the floor. More fighting was heard in the hallway as Stylus reinforcements started pushing their way towards the delivery room. Three Zims backed into the delivery room as they fired at the Stylus reinforcements. Mecka instantly shot two of them as Becka fired three times. All three Zims fell dead.

Becka fell back. With the pistol still in her hand she gave birth to the second child. By this time Stylus security had regained control of the entire hospital. Seventeen guards stood in the hallway outside the delivery room. That many guards were not needed but most of them wanted to see the two children prophesied hundreds of years earlier.

Both children were taken into another room where they were cleaned and checked. Then they were rapped in tiny blankets and brought to Becka. As the doctor worked on Becka to stop the bleeding she gazed on her twins.

"As according to prophecy ... your names will be Johm and Meshet." Becka looked at the boy and said; "You are Johm." She looked at the girl and added; "You are Meshet."

Johm and Meshet were taken into the hallway. The nurses held them up and said their names. "Johm and Meshet." the nurses yelled out for all to hear.

Later Becka lay in her private room again while Johm and Meshet lay in their small beds not far away. A nurse stood by keeping the twins safe and secure. The hospital was so covered with security that Mecka did not worry about any more Zim attempts to grab the twins.

"Thank you Father for watching over my children." Becka prayed as she looked at Johm and Meshet. *"Please keep all three of us safe and I will bring them up knowing and worshiping you. This I promise."*

Chapter 15

Bok's Kids

Bubba watched the work being done on his home but John seemed to be doing a great job. Tom and Dotter came by one day and talked to Bubba about him allowing the government to add a few things to his home. Bubba not being one to trust the government asked about what Dotter wanted to add to his home.

"I told Peggy that she was not coming out here again." Dotter said. "She said that she would do what ever her boss told her to do so … I talked to her boss."

"What happened there?" Bubba asked.

"Oh not much." Dotter said. "I just asked how he liked his newspaper business being audited every year." Dotter looked at Bubba with a big smile. "He agreed."

Bubba, Rommin, and Dotter all laughed. Dotter went on to tell what he wanted added to Bubba's home. It was mainly sensors of different types. Bubba insisted that no weapons be added to his home but agreed on the sensors.

With evergreen trees and bushes covering the area it was rare to be able to see through them. However; when the Zim attacked the front gate those two rounds cleared a few trees. The area around the gate could now be easily seen from the porch. One morning when Bubba and Rommin were sitting out on the porch drinking their coffee Bubba looked down at the gate area. It was nothing unusual to see heavy guns or tanks moving around but he saw three heavy guns being set up as emplacements.

"I wanted no big guns on my property so they set them up just outside my gate." Bubba mentioned to Rommin.

"Well he did do as you asked." Rommin replied with a smile.

Tesh walked just outside the door so that none of the workers would see her. "I got a call from Stylus Command." she advised

Bubba and Rommin.

Tesh got the message and then replied to it knowing that there would be at least a twenty minute wait.

"What did they say?" Rommin asked.

With much excitement in her voice Tesh said; "Johm and Meshet have been born." Then she looked right at Bubba and added; "You're a Daddy now."

Bubba looked at Rommin. "Already?"

"She is due about now." Rommin answered. "She's been gone almost a month now."

"My God ... it has been that long." Bubba said as he realized how time had flown by.

By this time Becka was wanting to come home so her husband could see the twins. However; the Stylus government did not want the prophecy twins to leave the planet. Becka worried about this because she knew that she could not just get up and walk home. She had to win the Stylus government over and that meant winning Yunnan over. She invited Yunnan to an evening meal and there she convinced him to allow her and the twins to come home.

It was late in the evening and the workers were getting ready to go home for the day. Bubba sat on the couch watching the TV when three Stylus appeared in his den. Instantly he jumped up but a familiar voice was heard. It was Ail. Bubba lay down his pistol and walked over to Ail and shook his hand.

"I have good news." Ail told Bubba. "Someone came to see you."

A few feet away Becka and two nurses appeared. The nurses held the twins. For a moment Bubba just stood there looking at the twins. Then he stepped over to Becka and gave her a big hug.

"Behold Bubba." one of the nurses said. "Your prophecy twins."

As Bubba gently stroked Johm's head he said; "They look almost ... full human."

"Well they are three quarters human you know." Becka said as she put her arm around Bubba's waist.

Bubba and Becka sat on the couch and the twins were handed to them. Bubba held Johm while Becka held Meshet. As they sat there Becka told her husband about a few rules that they both had to go by. Becka had to agree to these rules before she would be brought back with the children.

Because the twins were prophesied hundreds of year earlier and because they were to be the saviors of the planet Stylus they would have to be raised on Stylus while they were being taught to be leaders. Bubba did not like this but he also understood.

"How often would I get to see them?" Bubba asked.

"Yunnan said that you could come see them anytime you wanted." Becka advised. "He is even considering sending the twins here from time to time for some of their training so that you could spend time with them."

"Considering who our children are ... I guess I can work with that." Bubba admitted. He still did not like it but the twins were not just your every day humans. They were part of a prophecy; future leaders of the planet Stylus. That demanded special treatment, training, and education.

"One more thing." Becka said.

"Oh God. What now?" Bubba got ready for another rule.

"The twins and I will have constant guards around us." Becka advised her husband. "Mecka is the head of security over me and the two kids. She will be here soon. They came on the same ship we did.

There was a knock on the door so Rommin answered it. Dotter came in with Tom behind him. At that time everyone was shocked when Mecka and her security team transported into the den.

"It's okay Mecka." Becka told Mecka who was staring at Dotter and Tom. She went on to tell Mecka who Dotter and Tom were. Only then did she and her team relax. The security team spread out to cover the home. They used devices of some type to check for anything that was not suppose to be there such as tracking or listening devices. Minutes later Mecka and one of her team members walked out of Bubba and Becka's bedroom with something in their hands.

They had found a camera and a recording device. "These are not Zim or Stylus." Mecka said. "They are from this planet."

Bubba looked at Dotter. "You got anything to say?"

"I don't know anything about those." Dotter insisted.

"Rommin." Bubba said as he looked down at Johm. "Please take the Colonel and Sergeant outside and asked them to leave."

"And if they won't leave?" Rommin asked.

Without looking up Bubba replied; "Then kill the Colonel but not Tom. I no longer trust the Colonel but I like Tom." He looked up at the Colonel and added; "Tom doesn't lie to me."

"I need to talk to you about all of these aliens around here and the need for the government rebuilding your home." Dotter said.

"So you can fill the home with more of your listening devices and cameras?" Bubba whispered not wanting to wake up the twins. "How many times have you filmed Becka and me in bed?"

"None." Dotter insisted. "But to clear my name I will find out who did."

"And you will tell me?"

"If I can." Dotter said.

"No." Bubba argued. "Until you give me a name and proof that they did it I will continue to blame you."

Dotter thought for a moment. "Good enough." he replied. Then he and Tom left the home.

Just as the Humvee drove away Rick and Beth drove up. When they came in the home Beth instantly saw the twins and ran to them. Doing her job Mecka ran and stopped Beth.

"Don't touch the children." Mecka insisted as four others in her team stepped in closer.

"Sorry Beth but this is her job." Becka said. Then she turned to Mecka and added; "These are very close friends. They would never hurt the twins."

With that Mecka and her team stepped back. Beth sat beside Becka and took Meshet in her arms.

"Oh she's so pretty." Beth replied. Then she wanted to hold

Johm but without giving up Meshet. The nurses passed Johm over to her and stood by as she held both babies. "Oh Becka ..."

With the women melting over the children Bubba, Rommin, and Rick stepped outside. It was already getting dark outside. Bubba looked up into the skies at all of the stars. "Not to long ago I looked at those stars and wondered if we were alone. And now I am part of something bigger than the universe itself."

"That you are a Daddy." Rommin said. "A year ago you had no children and now you have five."

"I wish I could find my other two hybrid children." Bubba mentioned.

"You will some day." Rommin said. He did not want Bubba to know but his other two hybrid children were being searched for at the time. He wanted to surprise his father when they were found.

Mecka came out on the porch and looked up at the stars. "I know something that Becka does not want you to know but ... I think you would like to know." Mecka looked at Bubba. "She was quite the hero while giving birth."

"What happened?" Bubba asked her.

"You see this bandage on my arm?"

"I noticed it." Bubba replied.

"While Becka was giving birth the Zim tried one more time to take the twins in a massive attack on the hospital. I got shot and then kicked in the face ... by Bok."

"He was there?" Bubba asked.

"Oh yes ... but let me finish." Mecka pleaded. "As Bok broke into the delivery room Becka pulled that Earth pistol that she carries on her right side. She shot Bok in the head twice and in the neck once. All three shots were kill shots all by themselves."

"That's my Babe." Bubba said with a big smile.

"Then three Zims broke into the delivery room and she and I opened fire killing them." Mecka looked at Bubba and added; "She did all of this while giving birth to two children."

"Why did she not tell me?"

"She did not want you to worry." Mecka answered.

"What is there to worry about?' Bubba replied. "It's already happened."

Bubba turned and went back in the home where he sat on the couch beside Becka. By this time she was holding Meshet again and handed her over to her father. Beth was taking pictures with her cell phone so Bubba took both children in his arms. Suddenly there was an explosion outside.

Becka and Beth quickly took the babies from Bubba's arms. Then Bubba jumped up and ran into the bedroom and grabbed his CAR-15 rifle. By time he was at the front doors Rommin was there with his rifle. Bubba and Rommin met Rick out on the porch. Another explosion caused them to look up into the sky.

Two more explosions could be seen about a mile above the Earth but what was exploding could not be seen. It had to be Zim and Stylus ships fighting as they were cloaked. Suddenly something large hit the lake close to Bubba's land and skidded onto the bank but what it was could not be seen.

The soldiers that were watching Bubba's land as part of an agreement with the Stylus rushed to the crash site. Later other soldiers rushed in the gate and down to the site.

Bubba, Rommin, and Rick stood on the porch and watched what was going on down below. As hard as the soldiers tried they could find no way inside the Zim ship. But while the soldiers worked to find a way inside Ail's ship was transporting the Zim prisoners from their crashed ship to his own.

The three men went back inside the home. Bubba leaned his rifle against the arm of the couch and sat back down beside Becka. A nurse handed Meshet to him. As he looked into his daughter's face he smiled.

"I thought that with their birth this would be over but it isn't." he told anyone listening. "I hope it is a Zim ship that crashed below. It's resting on the lakeshore below the house."

At that time three Stylus started to appear in the den. The DFG held them in place for seven seconds; long enough for those there to see that it was Ail and two of his men. When they finally materialized Ail looked at Bubba and smiled.

"We got one of them Bubba." Ail said. "But two others got away."

"So it is a Zim ship resting on my lake bank below the house." Bubba replied.

"Of course." Ail said still smiling. "We also captured most of the crew but some were transported to one of the other Zim ships before it left. I think five got away including the ship's Commander."

"At least you got one ship but how many are left?" Bubba asked.

"Many Sir." Ail admitted. "They have many places on their planet where they are building more and more ships."

"Then shouldn't Stylus be attacking those places?"

"We try but their defenses cover the areas around these places." Ail argued. "Only now is Yunnan having other sites built where we can build more ships."

Ail left Bubba's home to go back to Stylus. He had many prisoners to take back. But Ail had not been gone long when there was a knock at the front door. Rommin answered the door. It was Tom and Dotter.

"Good morning to you all." Dotter said. Then he turned his attention to Bubba. "I need to talk to you about something."

"Go ahead." Bubba said.

"For one thing I still do not know who placed that camera and listening device in your bedroom but I am still looking." Dotter admitted.

"What else do you need?" Bubba asked.

"The military will have to bulldoze a road down to the crash site so we can get a truck down there to bring the space ship out."

"So after placing a camera in my bedroom so you can watch me and my wife have sex you want to rip my property to pieces." Bubba was getting angry.

"I told you that I didn't do that. Dotter insisted.

"Well who else could have?" Bubba asked through his teeth. "It was either you or someone under you."

"Neither I nor anyone under me has been past this den."

160

Bubba thought for a moment. "That's right … as far as I know."

Dotter sighed heavily. "I just wanted to let you know that the boll dozers will be here in the morning."

"And what if I say no?"

"That spaceship down there belongs to the government." Dotter insisted.

"That's right … the Stylus government." Bubba replied.

"The dozers will be here in the morning." Dotter's voice was firm.

Rommin raised his rifle and pointed it at Dotter." Are you really sure you want to start a war with us?"

"The government will pay you for any damage done to your land but … we will take that ship out of here tomorrow." Dotter said as he turned and walked to the door.

"Don't come back here Dotter." Bubba said as he handed Meshet to Becka and stood. Then he grabbed his rifle and added; "You might not be walking out next time."

"You want to lay some laws down so I will as well." Dotter said with a raised voice. "This home and everyone in it are restricted to the home. Anyone visiting must leave now and no one will be allowed back in."

"And what about the workers rebuilding my home?" Bubba asked.

"Maybe I don't care." Dotter said just before a loud boom was heard.

Having enough of the Colonel's yelling at his father Rommin took a stand and fired his rifle hitting Dotter in the thigh.

After falling to the floor Dotter said; "You shot me."

"Oh no." Rommin said. "The gun shot you. The liberal communist in your country say that guns kill not people kill. Therefore my gun shot you not me. And that's another thing. If guns kill then why do the people holding those guns go to prison? Since guns kill then shouldn't the guns go to prison?"

"That's my boy." Bubba said as he laughed.

With Tom's help Dotter stood and walked outside. From the

open door he yelled; "You'll pay for this."

About two minutes later the Humvee was heard driving away. Bubba laughed but advised Rick and Beth to leave while they could. They refused. Instead Rick went out to his truck and brought back rifles and ammunition for him and Beth.

"We'll make our stand with you." Beth said taking her rifle from Rick's hands.

As a show of defiance the men went to the refrigerator on the porch and got out a deer ham and a wild hog ham. They were thawing out the meat for a feast anyway. Now they had a reason to have that feast.

That evening everyone at Bubba and Becka's home ate well. The women had only a few potatoes to make potato salad and they could not go into town so they did what they could. Beth knew that if she went into town for more food that she would not be allowed back in the gate.

When it was dark enough Tesh went out on the porch and contacted Stylus Command. She told them what had happened and informed them that Bubba's home was now under siege by the American government. Then she sat back in a chair and waited for their response.

Minutes later someone tried transporting into the den. No one knew who it was but they held their fire. It was no one they knew. When the figure materialized the figure said that he was Stylus and the ship Commander at the bottom of the lake. His name was Boost.

Boost overheard Tesh's call to Stylus Command and was wondering if he could help. He looked at Bubba and admitted that he had seven Stylus soldiers that were ready to defend them and the twins with them. Bubba said that he did not need more mouths to feed in his home but asked Boost to stand by in case he did need them. Boost agreed and then transported back to his ship. Later a crate of muka transported into the den. Boost had heard how that Bubba loved the muka.

The next morning Bubba, Rommin, Rick and Beth stood on the porch with rifles in hand as a large bull dozer backed off of

162

a trailer. It came up the driveway and stopped right beside Rick's truck. Dotter stood beside the boll dozer. Bubba waved for Dotter to come to him.

As Dotter walked up on the porch Bubba said; "I know our government needs this ship so ... take it. But the government will pay me for the damage done to my property."

Dotter agreed and even allowed James and his crew to finish working on Bubba's home. Bubba knew that he was fighting a loosing battle and had to give in to Dotter but his distrust of the American government got worse. Giving in to Colonel Dotter cut Bubba deeply. It was something that he would never forget of forgive Dotter for.

Later while the men were back in the home Boost appeared again. He walked over to Bubba and Becka and looked at the prophecy twins as they were being called on Stylus. Then he stood straight and looked at Bubba.

"We have learned a few things that you need to know." Boost said. "After Becka killed Bok his three children were given command of three Zim ships. His two sons were the ones that we attacked last night. They both got away and their sister commands a ship that was just finished being built."

"Great." Bubba said looking down at his daughter Meshet. "Now we have three Boks to deal with.

Pollie's Construction finished the repairs on Bubba and Becka's home. Rommin and Tesh moved back into their room and Mobay moved into hers. Everything started looking better. However; the three children of Bok had other plans. Avenging their father's death was all they thought about.

"Father." Bubba said as he prayed. *"Thank you for bringing my children home to me. But now we are being faced with another threat ... Bok's three children. Please watch over all of us as we go on to fight this new threat. Please give me the wisdom I need to be a good father and husband. Now Lord ... my own government is against me so I now have two home fronts to fight. Thank you Father for everything you do for us and I can rest assure that you*

are watching over us. I know this because you said you would. Amen."

Other Publications of

Vernon Gillen

Below is a list of my other novels and books that have been published.

Novels

1. "Texas Under Sicge 1."
   Tale of a Survival Group Leader.
   After a man is voted as the leader of his survival group in Texas a self proclaimed Marxist president asked the United Nations troops to come in and settle down the civil unrest. The civil unrest was really nothing but Americans that complained about how he ran the country.

2. "Texas Under Siege 2."
   The Coming Storms.
   The young group leader continues to fight when the countries that made up the United Nations troops in the United States decided to take over parts of the country for their own country's to control.

3. "Texas Under Siege 3."
   The Necro Mortises Virus.
   As the group leader continues to fight the UN he learns that an old organization really controlled everything. They were known as the Bilderbergs. Tired of the resistance in Texas they release the Necro Mortises virus also known as the zombie virus.

4. "Texas Under Siege 4."
   250 Years Later.

This novel jumps 250 years into the future where the Bilderbergs are still living with modern technology while the other people have been reduced to living like the American Indians of the early 1800's. One of these young man stands up and fights the Bilderbergs with simple spears and arrows.

5. The Mountain Ghost 2."
    The Legend Continues.
    The Mountain Ghost continues to fight the Chinese and North Koreans soldiers that have invaded the entire southern half of the United States.

6. "The Mountain Ghost 4."
    The Ghost Warriors.
    After Russ and June have twin girls they grow up and move back south to fight the Chinese and North Koreans as the Ghost Twins. Before long they grow in numbers and call themselves the Ghost Warriors.

7. "Neanderthal 1."
    As a child he was injected with alien DNA. While in the Navy he was injected with Neanderthal DNA. Now because of these two injection without his knowing young Michael Gibbins changes into a six and a half foot tall Neanderthal from time to time. He grew up being bullied in school and wished that he could change into a monster so he could get back at them. Now he wishes he could take that wish back.

8. " Neanderthal 2."
    Little Mary Ann, the daughter of Michael and Evie grows to the age of thirteen. As she grows she learns that he has many of the same abilities that her father had; and more. The problem is that she has a hard time controlling them and her anger. This causes problems for everyone watching over and trying to hide her.

9. "My Alien Connections 1."

After learning that he has been abducted many times over the years sixty-four year old Bubba is asked to be a part in an alien experiment. He ends up falling in love with an alien hybrid that has known through all of his abductions.

But the Aliens, the Stylus are at war with another planet, the Zims. As their war continues the Zim try to take the twins born to Bubba and his alien hybrid wife who have been prophesied hundreds of years earlier. Do the Zim win or does Bubba win?

Other Books

1. "Carnivores of Modern Day Texas."

A study of the animals in Texas that will not only kill you but in most cases will eat you.

2. "Zombies; According to Bubba"

After studying the Necro Mortises virus for my novel *Texas Under Siege 3*, I realized that I had a great deal of information on it. After finishing the novel I wrote this book leaving the reader to make their own decision.

Unpublished

A great deal goes into publishing a novel or book that takes time. After I write a novel I have someone proofread it. Then I have to find an artist to draw the cover picture which is hard to do. Actually finding an artist is easy but finding one that I can afford is not so easy. Then the novel or book has to be approved by the publishing company. Only then is it published. Then you have kindle and that opens another can of worms.

The fallowing novels are unpublished as I write this but will be published soon. Keep checking Amazom.com for any new novels that I have published.

1. "The Mountain Ghost 1."
   The Legend of Russell Blake.
   After the Chinese and North Koreans attack the southern United States two young brothers, Brandon and Russell Blake go after the invading enemy. After Brandon is killed Russell smears a white past allover his exposed skin and earns the name Mountain Ghost.

3. "The Mountain Ghost 3."
   The Ghost Soldiers.
   After the death of Russell Black his son, Russ, continues as to bring death and destruction to the enemy as the new Mountain Ghost.

5. "The Glassy War."
   Three thousand years in the future and three galaxies away the United Planet Counsel fight and enemy that is trying to control every galaxy they come to. After both star ships crash into the planet the survivors continue to fight.

6. "The Fire Dancers."
   I stopped writing this novel to start writing the Mountain Ghost series but I will be getting back to it.

I hope that you have enjoyed this novel. Please help me by sending your comments on what you thought about this novel or book by contact me through my web site at http://cabubba7.wexsite.com/bubbasbooks . By doing this you will let me know what you, the public, are looking for in these types of novels and books. I have a very creative mind, a bit warped some say but, still creative but, I still need to know what you are looking for. I thank you for your assistance in this.

Vernon Gillen

Shoulder pressed against the ever-cooling window, face hidden but attention obviously on the world outside or the book in her lap, and her feet curled up on the seat next to her, her chubby limbs and bags taking up as much space on the ripped vinyl as possible. Her best defense had always been staying as still and quiet as possible. Kind of like a possum playing dead.

Don't talk. Don't move. Never make eye contact. She had repeated the commands in her head since childhood and, more often than not, they had turned out to be sound advice. Sometimes, she wasn't so lucky.

Like right now.

When the woman had gotten on last night, she had looked around the near-empty carriage and decided that she just had to sit on the seat across the aisle from Ruby. *It's polite to keep some distance if possible,* Ruby had longed to mention. *Like in cinemas or bathrooms.* But she hadn't been able to get the words out, and the woman hadn't taken the hint. Since then, every so often, the woman would sneak glances at Ruby. Or stare. It was hard for her to tell when she could only see the woman from the corner of her eye. But Ruby could *feel* her watching. With dull, lifeless eyes that were the color of frosted ice. Each time she noticed the emotionless face turning in her direction, Ruby would purposefully fix her gaze outside the window. Or use her book as a shield. It didn't help. At some points, it just made it worse. Not being able to see the living doll made it easier for her brain to convince her that it had moved closer.

She, Ruby would chastise herself instantly. *Not a doll. A person. She.*

Logically, she knew it was her own fault. Or, more precisely, the fault of her malfunctioning brain. But no matter how many times Ruby reminded herself that the person across from her was living and breathing, and probably very pleasant, it didn't change the fact that she just didn't seem human. Not completely.

Finally, the days and hours drained away, and Ruby's final stop was in sight. She sank deeper into her seat as the train ambled along the track, slowing to an excruciating crawl. The closer they got, the louder the conversations around her became. Dozens of them at once, the words overlapping as the tones rose and fell. She could hear the shifts, but they all meant nothing to her. From the very edge of her vision, she saw the woman had turned to face her again. The features of her face created peaks and valleys under her tanned skin. Her eyes, flat and dull, stared at Ruby. The glare only breaking when with the woman blinked. Suppressing a shudder, Ruby turned her full attention to the window.

Don't talk. Don't move. Never make eye contact.

They had left the barren stone and snow drenched slopes behind that morning and had continued down into a valley. Nestled within the belly of the mountain range and protected on all sides, the valley had managed to clutch onto the last traces of autumn. The rise in temperature had hit her first. Although the air still seemed like ice, it had somehow discovered how to change into a gas. There was considerably less snow. The thin layer that was still there melted in the sunlight, withering into slush or seeping into the earth and creating large puddles of mud. Only tiny patches of sleet managed to cling to the forest of evergreens, but the other plants testified to the change of seasons. Leaves of crimson and orange speckled across the thick wall of trees while bare branches clawed out of the foliage like dead grasping hands.

The lazy arch of the sun was another sign of the changing seasons. This far north, the sun never truly set during the summer and barely rose throughout the winter months. It was strange to see it already so low even though she had prepared for the sight. Her new employers had warned her repeatedly about the short days in their emails. It had come up so many times that Ruby was convinced that the hours of prolonged darkness had been a problem for those who had held the position before her. They had also mentioned, at length, that the sense of isolation could be a much larger problem. After reading about how she would be alone for what felt like the hundredth time, it had been a struggle not to reply that the promised isolation was what had attracted her in the first place. For the first time in her life, she was free to seek an escape from other people. From all the stress and pressure of being forced to interact with the endless array of pseudo-humans. But, since it was all too hard to explain over emails, she had kept that to herself.

The train gave a final jolt, jarring her from her thoughts. As she came back to herself, she saw that there was still nothing but untouched wilderness on her side of the train. *Did we have to stop for another freight train?* she wondered. The freights had the right of way on these tracks. And since they were often fifty to a hundred carriages long, it always took a while for them to pass. She had just settled in to wait when she noticed that the people around her were getting up. Blinking in surprise, she looked across the train to see that they had, in fact, arrived.

The further they travelled from any major city, the smaller the train stations had become. For the last few stops, the stations tended to be small and easily missed. This one wasn't an exception to the rule. It seemed that the entire building could be seen from where she sat, each end fitting neatly within the line of windows that ran the length of the carriage. With a new coat of honey-lemon paint and the sun glistening off of the paneled windows, the building did have a certain cozy feel. But the attempt at care and presentation couldn't hide the battering harsh weather that time had given it. Under the cheerful paint, the wood was chipped and warped. And as she stood, she could see the thin cracks that were working their way through the slab of concrete that served as the platform.

Since she wasn't that tall, Ruby didn't have to worry about bumping into the overhead storage as she stretched out her spine. Her legs throbbed as blood flowed back into them. Leaning against the window, the chill quickly worked through the layers of her clothes, she rolled each of her ankles in an attempt to speed up the process. Unfortunately, a storm of pins and needles followed the throb. In her little corner, she shook her legs and waited for the limited crowd to leave. The woman across the aisle stood up, the movement drawing Ruby's gaze. Before she could realize her mistake, Ruby had made eye contact.

Don't talk. Don't move. Her mantra didn't help her this time and she couldn't resist. It didn't matter that she quickly snapped her eyes back down to the floor or that she did her best impersonation of a statue. She had the woman's attention. Feet shuffled across the thin carpet and crept into her field of vision. The woman was barely a foot away, staring at her, waiting for Ruby to acknowledge her presence. *Don't move. Don't look.*

"Are you okay?"

Ruby kept her eyes on the floor as she nodded. For the last three days, the only person she had been forced to talk to was the person manning the dining cart. And even then, she had managed to get away with mostly pointing. No shower. No real privacy. No fresh air or decent food, and still these few days had been the most relaxing of her life. She had known that the peace wouldn't last. But she hadn't been prepared to be thrown back into it this quickly.

Swallowing thickly, she glanced at the woman. The hope that her nod would have been the end of it crumbled away as the woman cocked her head to the side. *What did I do wrong? How wasn't that a decent answer? What does she want from me?* Before she could spiral down into her thoughts, Ruby forced a smile and thanked the woman for her concern. She used the tone people liked the most. Happy and carefree, and oh so sweet. It was a tone she could maintain even as her gut twisted up with dread. The woman bared her teeth; her brightly painted lips peeling back as her cheeks stretched. Her dull eyes didn't move off of Ruby's face. And she was still standing at the end of Ruby's row of seats. The small crowd was dwindling fast, and the woman continued to block Ruby's only exit.

With a twist of panic, Ruby quickly took stock of her surroundings. Most of everyone had left, and the few who remained were moving swiftly to the doors without the slightest glance in her direction. The glass felt like a sheet of ice as she pushed herself back against it. *Should have left first. Stupid girl. Don't panic. Don't talk. Just breathe.* Each of her knuckles pressed against her skin as she subconsciously balled her fists. The pins and needles had subsided, leaving her legs

8

feeling at least stable, if not secure. Her cheeks hurt as she forced her smile to stay in place, and her heartbeat began to pick up. *It's okay,* Ruby tried to convince herself. *This is a public place. She's not going to do anything.* The words rang hollow even to herself, beaten down by a flood of memories to the contrary. While her father's favorite saying might not have carried any weight, her mother's had been proven time and again. *Some people are born with a bull's eye on their foreheads that they can never rub off.* The words repeated in her head. It was a small comfort to at least be aware that she was one of them.

It seemed like each muscle in her body contracted at once as the woman peeled her lips back further, flashing the spikes of white that emerged from her ruddy strips of her gums. The skin of the woman's face twisted and bunched and Ruby watched the whole display with that fake smile fixed into place. It took all the concentration she had not to slump with relief when the woman collected her bags and scattered off to the side, leaving Ruby with a slight wave and a farewell. When the woman was gone, she gave into the urge and sagged against the closest seat.

The train was empty now. Without the clatter of footsteps against metal and the flutter of words, the carriage was cast into a heavy silence. Distantly, she could still hear the people on the platform and the hiss of the train as it settled, but all of it seemed to prove the silence around her instead of breaking it. Closing her eyes, she took in a few steadying breaths. *Just a little longer. You're almost there,* she told herself. Maybe a few more hours at most and she'd be all alone. With only the woodland creatures and a few dogs for company. The image that appeared within her mind was enough to slow her heartbeat. The train jolted, and she stumbled slightly. Worried that the train might be preparing to go, she snatched up her bag and winter coat and jogged to the door.

The platform had obviously been built to accommodate a different style of train, one that was supposedly lower and wider, and the discrepancy left a gap just large enough to be awkward. She staggered upon landing and threw her weight forward to keep from tipping back over the rim of the platform. An extra bit of embarrassment came with the maneuver as she bit back a curse. She knew it was going to be cold, but the train's heating had shielded her from the worst of it. The second she left it behind, an arctic chill rose up to surround her. Shivering and bopping on her feet to keep some warmth, Ruby dropped her bag long enough to shove her arms into her jacket. Already, the cold had gathered against the inner material and it took a while for her body heat to fend it off.

Rubbing her bare hands together, she looked around, trying to figure out where she was supposed to go next. Apparently, the building served a dual purpose, train station and grocery store. She hadn't anticipated that. Or the number of people that would be milling around. While it was nowhere near the size of the crowds she had fled the city to escape, it was far more than she had intended to search through to find her new employers. So, she stood there, shivering and bouncing, the hissing train pushing puffs of warm air against her back, and waited for the crowd to thin.

"Ruby Dawson?"

She jumped at the question and turned to see a couple edging closer to her. A man and woman. The lines on their faces spoke of age and outdoor work, while the bright colors of their thick clothes hinted at a flare for the dramatic as much as they did a taste for the practical. The man's hair was far darker and longer than his wife's was, but they were both starting to gray.

"Mr. and Mrs. Cobalt?"

The man flashed his teeth and Ruby braced her feet.

"Mr. and Mrs. Cobalt? How official."

Ruby blinked at him but said nothing.

She watched as the couple exchanged a glance. The man leaned forward and whispered, "I'm just joking with you."

"Oh," Ruby said before smiling brightly and forcing a laugh.

Again, the pair before her looked at each other. *Wrong move,* she thought as she snatched up the strap of her bag and tightened her hands around it. *They're still showing their teeth. Is that a good sign? Smile or sneer?* Shaking her head to stop the drizzle of thoughts from becoming a rampaging storm, she forced an apologetic smile and shrugged.

"I did mention in my last email that I have a form of social-emotional agnosia. Did you get that one?"

"I did," the man said, the two words coming out at a slightly slower pace than the others before them. The shift didn't last as he continued. "And I had full intentions of looking that up, but the only place that has the internet around here is the library and I'm kind of dodging the staff at the moment. There was an incident with one of their books and a cup of coffee."

His wife swatted his arm. "You're a grown man. Take the book back."

"I will. I have a plan. I'm going to drop it off before their opening hours on the day we leave." Before Mrs. Cobalt could give a response, he turned his attention back to Ruby and flashed his teeth again. "So, what exactly does that mean?"

"I can't read body language," she swallowed thickly, giving them time to respond before adding. "Facial and verbal cues are lost on me, too."

Mrs. Cobalt leaned forward slightly. Ruby's fingers clutched at her bag strap.

"I'm sorry. What does that mean exactly?"

This was a conversation Ruby had faced a thousand times before. And still, she was unable to find a decent way of explaining it. Or, at the very least, one that didn't lead down a path of far more questions than she had answers.

"I can't tell when people are joking. Or any emotion really."

"You don't feel emotion?" Mr. Cobalt said.

"No, I do. Just as well as anyone else. I just can't see the cues to tell me what other people are thinking and feeling. If you want me to know, you'll have to tell me directly, or I won't get it."

"So, you can't see when people smile?" Mrs. Cobalt asked.

"I see it. The muscle movement. But my brain can't apply any meaning to it."

"Well, when people smile then they're happy, dear."

Ruby blinked at the woman. It was a familiar statement, one that always seemed to pop up in some form or another during these conversations, and while she couldn't stop the response from popping into her head, she had learnt to keep it from tumbling out of her mouth. *Gee, thank you for that. This piece of information completely fixes the broken synapses in my brain. I wish it hadn't taken seventeen years for someone to tell me.* Clearing her throat, she smiled slightly.

"People understand better when I use a scream as an example," Ruby said with well-practiced patience. "I can hear it just fine. The ears work. But there are a lot of reasons why someone might raise their voice. Excitement, rage, happiness, fear. My brain can't tell the difference between any of them."

"Can't you tell by looking at them?" the man asked.

"That would be facial cues," Ruby said. "And I can't read them. I see the basic movement but, again, I can't attach any meaning to it. It's kind of like every day is Halloween. You know, with everyone in masks."

Ruby rarely tried to lighten the mood with a joke, mostly because she rarely knew if she stuck the landing. Still, she had learned that people liked the analogy that reminded them of candy better than her life-size humanoid doll descriptions.

"That must be very confusing," the woman said.

And stressful. Agonizing. Irritating. Terrifying. "It can be awkward," Ruby said instead. "You'll just have to be direct with me. And please, don't use sarcasm. I will not understand it."

"Right, well. I'm Aaron, this is Betsy, and we're both honestly pleased that you're here." Aaron over pronounced each word as if dictation was the true issue.

Ruby thanked him for his kindness and her fake smile became just a little bit more real.

Betsy clapped her hands together, the sharp sound cracking across the now quiet platform. Once she had their attention, she led the way into the building with a flash of teeth and a wave. That was another typical response to the revelation of her condition. Lots and lots of exuberant body language. It was actually kind of funny, how people's reaction to learning she didn't understand subtlety was to become the

12

living equivalent of the inflatable flailing men that were outside of car dealerships. But funny or not, the attempt to communicate in a way she could understand wasn't lost on her. At the very least, it made them seem like real people, despite appearances.

Heated, humid air washed over Ruby as she followed the Cobalts into the building. While it wasn't a wide structure, it was long, and a bit over half of the structure was devoted to the town's supermarket. To her right, behind the stand-alone bundles of fresh produce, a parade of freezers ran the length of the wall. Rows of shelves filled the area closest to the door she had just entered, and people pushed shopping carts around those collecting their suitcases. A cold wind crept in on her left, as one of the station workers kept the door open while he unloaded the luggage next to the sales bin.

Ruby had always idolized those who could travel light. Each time she was planning a holiday, she had this fantasy that she would finally be one of those people that only needed a single carry-on. The reality, however, always fell short. But all those times before were nothing compared to this. The promise of living months on end in a cabin in the middle of nowhere had resulted in her bringing far more than she ever had before. They had to wait a little while for the workers to hurl her three overstuffed suitcases out of the guts of the train. Each one was dropped onto the floor with a loud thud and groan.

Aaron grabbed one of the bags and made the same noise as he struggled to lift it. "What did you pack in here?"

"That one has my books. You said I should bring some."

Betsy chuckled under her breath, the sound leaving Ruby to wonder if she had said something amusing or was currently being mocked.

"Well, that's good," Betsy said. "We'll also get you set up at the library before we leave. You'll be surprised how quickly you can get through a good book up here."

Ruby nodded and thanked Betsy as she took one of the remaining suitcases. The concrete floor didn't have a smooth finish, but she was grateful for it all the same as she tugged the last bag along. In one lurching group, they crossed the room and exited out into the parking lot. While they hadn't spent all that long indoors, it had been more than enough for Ruby's thick winter coat to make her sweat. The wind ravaged the little droplets the first chance it got, freezing them against her skin and making her shiver. The sun might not have been high, but the glare it created made her eyes ache and reduced the world into strips of shapeless color. With her bags to contend with, they had barely made it to the ramp before her eyes had finished adjusting.

A lot of care had been taken to maintain the town of Hidden Valley's rustic aesthetics. It was old-fashioned and quaint in a way that only tourist towns were. After all, no one traveled this far into the heart of the Yukon to see something modern. They wanted adventure in the great white North. To feel as if they were stepping back in time to the height of the gold rush. To be comfortable while they lived out the idolized version of pioneer life. At least, that's what she had hoped for, and Hidden Valley hadn't disappointed. Sure, a bit of it seemed fake around the edges, but it was unique, quiet, and had room enough to breathe.

The locals' homes were clustered just off the main street, hidden behind hotels and gift shops that were crafted to look like old saloons. They were right on Main Street, and the limited assortment of restaurants all vied for space on it. The streets were clean, and the air held delightful scents of baking bread, spices, and pine. In all, the town wasn't that large; it seemed that she could see most of it from where she stood, the buildings themselves appearing to huddle for warmth. Or at least to distance themselves from the endless forest that spread out around them, and continued uninterrupted in each direction until the mountains rose too high for the trees to follow.

Betsy led the way to a van. It looked well used but serviceable and had the logo of their dog sled company plastered on the side. With a sharp tug, the unlocked sliding door gaped open. An instant later, Ruby found herself flat on her back, the unforgiving concrete pressing its chill into her bones, while a few pounds of an overexcited sled dog and slobber, strained to reach her face. Neither Betsy nor Aaron

14

seemed to be in much of a rush to pull the dog off of her. Ruby supposed that might have been because she couldn't stop laughing. Between dodging its tongue, she noticed that its fur was a flawless white and puffed out around its neck and jaw like muttonchops. Its paws were huge, almost as large as her entire hand, and its eyes shone a brilliant icy blue.

"Bannock," Betsy snapped as the dog yelped and lurched for Ruby's face again. Once more she managed to squirm out of the way, although that didn't deter it from trying again. "Off."

At the command, Bannock backed up a few steps, just enough to place its massive paws on either side of Ruby's hips. The order to keep his distance didn't stop the dog from stretching his tongue out in an endless attempt to lick Ruby's face. His tail swished so hard that his hind legs staggered back and forth.

"Sorry about that. He's just excitable," Aaron said as he rubbed his hand into Bannock's scruff. "He knows you're the one who's looking after him for the next five months and he's trying to suck up."

"He's still really a pup. But once he settles down, he'll follow your commands well enough," Betsy said.

Sliding back to avoid Bannock's affections, Ruby sat up. She couldn't resist sneaking a quick pat before getting to her feet. Bannock's fur somehow managed to be even softer than it looked. And while the tips held the nip of the cold air, the lower layers were thick enough to hold in his warmth. He pressed into her touch as he stomped one paw, trying to loop his long limb around her arm and pull her closer.

"Well, hey there, Bannock," she laughed. "Aren't you gorgeous?"

"Can you read dogs?" Aaron waited for Ruby to look up to him before he continued with a flurry of hand movements she didn't understand. "I mean, they don't really have facial expressions, but they have basic body language."

"They're a lot easier to read than people. Mostly because of the one for one correspondence. One emotion, one motion." she said as she got to her feet.

Aaron nodded as he began to load the bags. With a yelp, Bannock lumbered over to Betsy's side. On all fours, his back still almost reached the woman's hip. The colossal dog bumped his weight against Betsy's leg until she agreed to pat him.

"Bannock's our bear dog," Betsy said.

"I'm sorry, I don't know what that means."

Aaron loaded the last bag and slid the door shut. At the same time he crouched slightly, the motion instantly grabbing Bannock's attention.

His words came out at a fast pace. "What do you do if you see a bear?"

Bannock threw his head back and barked at the sky, his enthusiasm drawing him up onto his hind legs, making him lurch and leap. His reward was some praise and a dog treat Aaron pulled from the pocket of his khakis.

"Remember to take him along if you go walking beyond the main area of the dog yard," Betsy said. "He'll raise the alarm as soon as he catches a stray scent. Keep you from crossing paths with a wolf or bear. You can also keep him in the cabin with you, if you want. The others are fine to take in, but Bannock's a giant lumbering baby He's grown used to the privilege and will whine all night if you leave him out. Come on, then. Let's get the errands out of the way. Aaron, grab that book of yours."

Ruby didn't know what surprised her more, that the library was next door to the train station, although it shared some space with a hardware store, or that dogs were allowed inside. Bannock wasn't the only one that was trotting around the shelves. One was currently using the line waiting at the counter to scout for someone to rope into a game of fetch.

While Aaron and Betsy joined the cue, Ruby was left to drift around the store. The rows of shelves were stuffed thick with novels. Some of them looked new, others with spines that had been broken a thousand times over, but all of them were in remarkable condition. It all spoke of a town that took care of the one sure form of entertainment they had to get them through the long winters. She brushed her hands over their spines as she sought out the sci-fi and fantasy sections. Her suitcase was filled with the books she had put off reading because of her final exams, and the desperate search for some kind of employment after leaving school. It seemed like a lofty goal to make it through all of them. But she had a feeling that five months of nothing to do would turn out to be far more time than she had been anticipating.

Rounding one of the shelves, she caught her first glimpse of the far wall and the rows of black framed pictures that covered it. Sunlight slipped through the window to flare over their glass centers, and the flare seemed to draw her near. Vaguely, she was aware of Bannock by her side, his nails clipping against the bare wood floors. As she drew closer, the figures in the old photographs became clearer. Judging by clothing style, they seemed to have been taken during the gold rush, back when the town and surrounding areas were first being settled by the hopeful and desperate. Each one had a small patch of writing nestled at the bottom. Her attention brushed over the names of those pictured with little interest. Below each one, there was a strip of red writing, the ink faded with time. She had to squint to read the short lines; a place and date.

A last known location? They had gone missing? She studied the rugged men of the picture with more interest before another strip of red caught her attention. Then another. And another. Walking along the walls, she found a dozen more frames that marked the people pictured as missing. Some had been noted as lost. Others as murdered. And the numbers kept growing. Some of the pictures were of small parties, made up of just a few miners that could have been lost in a single landslide. But some of the others were whole families. Or groups of dozens. Reaching the far end of the wall, she paused and glanced back over the display. *How can such a small town see so much death?* Bannock nuzzled at her hand and she reflectively reached to scratch his ear.

"That's a lot of people," she told him.

"It was a harsher time," a voice said.

She wasn't expecting a response and almost yelped at hearing one.

Spinning around, Ruby found herself being watched by a woman with large eyes and straight brown hair. The woman stepped closer to the wall but kept her eyes on Ruby.

"Many people came out here seeking a fortune. Very few of them had any actual idea of how to survive in such an environment. Some learned quickly. Others, well, not quickly enough."

"Why were so many of them murdered?" Ruby asked.

"Cabin fever," the woman said. "Shove a bunch of people into a small cabin in the middle of nowhere, leave them for months on end with the cold, the dark, the silence. Under conditions like that, people find out that they weren't as sane as they assumed themselves to be."

"They killed each other?"

"Most likely. In some cases, members of the party would band together and kick others out of their camp or cabin, let them freeze to death. If the animals didn't get to them first."

It didn't matter how much Ruby searched the woman's features, how hard she listened, there was nothing for her to gather. No way to tell why the woman was offering her this information. Ruby tensed a little as the woman turned her dark eyes onto her.

"The Yukon isn't like other places. It's not forgiving of weakness. Of body or of mind."

Not knowing what to say, Ruby fell back onto her standard response. She nodded and slightly turned her head. It let people know that she was listening but also gave off a nonthreatening, submissive vibe. This time, the move allowed her to study the wall of photographs again.

"There aren't many places around here that don't have a dark history. The cabin you'll be staying at is very close to where those people went missing. And near where they were murdered."

With her stomach twisting up in knots, Ruby turned to see the woman pointing to a spot about halfway down the wall. There was no way to tell which picture she was actually pointing to, and the woman didn't seem keen to clarify her statement. *Does she tell everyone this sort of stuff? Like a weird ice-breaker? Maybe she's the local historian?* Ruby didn't want to contemplate the other option, the one that suggested that anyone without the shackles of her condition would be seeing blazing red flags right now. Still, it bubbled up into her head as she pulled the large dog closer to her side. *Is she threatening me?*

"There you are," Betsy said as she came around the aisle. After a moment, she caught sight of Ruby as well. "Good, you're here, too. Ruby, this is Esther. She runs the hardware store and is a good friend of ours. She'll be staying in town while we're gone. If you need anything, you just come right here and ask her."

Ruby nodded her understanding. "Okay. It's nice to meet you."

"Nicer than you think," Aaron said as he came into view. Bannock instantly trotted over to him, tail wagging and head high. "Her house is two doors down, the one with the pink front door, and she's also agreed to let you use her washer and dryer. And her shower. That might not sound like much now, but when it's twenty below you'll appreciate it."

"That's really kind," Ruby said, remembering to add a 'thank you' a second later.

While her resolve might break as the winter came in, Ruby knew she wasn't going to be quick to take Esther up on the offer. Still unable to tell what the woman had been trying to achieve with their previous conversation, Ruby was hesitant to even be around her. In fact, going into her home, alone, seemed like far too big of a risk. That was a rule people with her condition lived by. Never go anywhere you don't feel completely safe, because you'll never know you're not. Not until it's too late.

Esther didn't say much more, just the normal pleasantries, and Ruby found herself watching the woman's joints more than her face. She might not be able to tell when someone had it out for her, but she could definitely see when someone was about to take a swing at her. She doubted the older woman would. But life was full of surprises.

"We have your library card all sorted," Betsy said. "Let's go introduce you to the dogs."

Ruby nodded and followed the two out of the store. Esther's final words chased after her, and Ruby's shoulders flinched at hearing it.
"Good luck."

keen to face off with one. With quick little glances, she tried to take in the area and listen to their long list of information at the same time. When there was a pause, she asked the first thing that was bothering her.

"I thought you said the place was fenced."

"It is," Aaron said as he pointed to the wooden rails that formed a box around the dogs.

They had used fallen logs and hadn't done much to disguise the fact. The 'fence' consisted of two rails, with plenty of open space below both lengths of wood for even her to squeeze through. There were two main openings, one on the far side and one much closer. A curving dirt track ran the length between the two, separating the dogs into clusters, and she figured that the path was for them to run the sled through.

"Wouldn't the wolves just go in?" she asked.

"Like Betsy said, they're smart. They don't like getting blindsided. It wouldn't stop them if they really wanted in, sure, but it's enough to give them pause. And really, that's all you need."

Ruby looked up at him as she helped pull her bags free. "It is?"

"Sure," he said with a flash of teeth. "Wolves are just like any other predator. You don't always have to defeat them. You just have to prove you're too much effort for not enough payoff." He slid the door of the van shut, his teeth still showing, pearly white in the sunlight. "Predators always go for the easiest prey."

Ruby nodded her understanding. It wasn't exactly a foreign concept. In fact, she had seen it in action more than once. People often mistook her inability to tell when someone was lying for gullibility. Or stupidity. Freaks, weirdos, and creeps would all bypass her friends for a chance to take advantage of her in one way or another. She had learned how effective even the disguise of defenses could be.

The tour was quick, the instructions even quicker. With only a few hours sleep over the entirety of her three-day train ride, Ruby couldn't quite remember anything they said, no matter how hard she tried. She kept repeating the instructions in her head, hoping for some of it to stick. *The generator's in the shed and she had to make sure to flip a switch before pulling the rip-cord to start it. Petrol is stored behind the shed, shielded by a little alcove. Use dry kindling to start a fire and add the sturdier wood once the flames have grown. Don't confuse the red tipped poppers for the real bullets. Never shoot behind the animal or it will charge forward.* It all jumbled into a mess of words in her head and that was before she was finally able to meet the dogs. By the time she made it through, her pants were covered with slobber and loose fur.

It barely seemed like they had arrived and already she was being led back to the van. They were going to drive her back to get supplies and drop them off. After that, she would be on her own.

"Don't look so worried," Betsy said. "I've made up a folder with all the information and instructions you need. You'll be fine."

"And we'll pop back in tomorrow morning before we leave town," Aaron said. "This way might be a bit daunting, but it's the most efficient way to see what you haven't figured out yet."

Ruby nodded and forced a confident smile that she hoped looked somewhat convincing. Despite her little bubble of panic, it was comforting to have Bannock nibbling at her fingers, insisting on another scratch. As they neared the van, she noticed for the first time that they weren't at the end of the road. It curled around, the forest swallowing it up and giving the illusion of a dead end.

"What's down there?"

Betsy's shoulders jumped. "Not much. Peter Martin's place is about three miles down. Another dog yard. He might drop in and check on you from time to time."

"Do I have any other neighbors?"

The question made both of them laugh as they climbed into the front van seats. Ruby supposed that served well enough as a 'no'.

***

The night didn't fall. It rose.

Creeping first amongst the tree trunks, it swirled and gathered across the ground before climbing higher. Unfamiliar with the roads, it took her twice as long to make the trip back to the dog yard. Ruby had grossly misjudged how quickly the darkness would come, or how thick it would get. She had just enough time to park the van, stack her suitcases by the cabin door, and put the groceries on the step before the sun began to sink behind the treetops. Fumbling with the generator, it took her almost twenty minutes to turn the floodlights on. The harsh white glow made the yard look surreal as she set about feeding the dogs.

There were seventeen dogs if you counted Bannock, and each one of them had a personalized ratio of kibble to water. She was relieved to see that each doghouse had a name plaque. It made it a lot easier to follow the feeding instructions. This too took longer than she had expected, and there was an ache brewing in her joints when she finished. The next task on her to-do list was to clean the yard. She was grateful that the process included a shovel and wheelbarrow rather than plastic bags and hands. After days of sitting still, the exercise felt as good as it did painful, but she was glad when the task was done.

Sweat glistened across her brow, freezing just as quickly as her body produced it. And while she roasted under her jacket, her fingers and toes had steadily been reduced to ice. Flipping through the pages of the binder, she found that there was only one task left for the night. She had to move two of the dogs to the playpen. It wasn't just a fully fenced in paddock; this one was made of actual metal links. Aaron had explained that it gave the dogs a chance to stretch their legs and socialize. The Cobalts had worked out the roster for the coming months, and Ruby checked it three times as she tried to find the corresponding dogs, Snow and Fire. Snow, as her name suggested, was pure white like Bannock, except she was a giant puffball with legs. Fire was black, with a white face and belly. Ruby figured out why he had been given that name when she had filled his bowl. The dog had one hell of a temper. Not vicious, exactly, but quick to growl, not too happy to see her coming close, and seemed to like trying to trip her with his chain.

As she waited for the dogs to finish up, she stretched out her back and glanced up at the sky. It was impossible to see much of anything beyond the glare of the lights. So it was only as she looked around her that she saw how completely the night had swallowed the world. It was as if the floodlights had clawed out a stop of reality from the black nothingness. Everything beyond that razor fine line was gone. Glancing over her shoulder, she found that she could only see the side of the visitor's tent closest to her. The other half had disappeared into the night and she couldn't even see the shadow of the cabin beyond that, even though it was only a few feet away.

Suddenly, she felt the cold. It ravaged the sweat she had worked up and made her fingers ache. There was a calm to the night that she wasn't accustomed to. No traffic or alarms. Nothing to stir it but the wet sounds of the dogs eating. Every so often, she thought she could hear a twig snap. Or dead leaves crunching as something moved through the undergrowth. But the sound was always lost under the noise of the dogs before she could pinpoint where it came from.

"It's just rabbits," she told herself. "Maybe a bird."

Hearing her voice helped to steady her, but it didn't stop the quiver at the bottom of her gut. She couldn't shake the knowledge that something could be watching her from beyond the ring of light, and she would never know it. Shaking her head, she decided that it was time to finish off her nightly chores and go indoors. She just needed one night to settle in, that's all. This new sense of paranoia would disappear once when she was familiar with the area.

When the dogs finished eating, she made one last check of the binder. She was definitely supposed to move Fire and Snow. Aaron had shown her how to handle the dogs when moving them from one place to another. How to grip their collars and pull them up, so only their hind legs were on the ground. She had thought it looked cruel, but he had assured her that it didn't hurt them, and that since they were working dogs, she'd soon lose control of them if they were on all fours.

For all his gusto, Fire let her unclip him easily enough. Her air numbed fingers curled tightly around his thick collar and she pulled him up. Fire grunted, the sound becoming choked off and hissed. Guilt sliced through her and she let him down, allowing him to practically drag her towards the playpen. It was undignified but quick and worked well enough in the end. He was pushing hard against her leg and she opened the chain-link door. When there was just enough space for him to squeeze through, he did so, almost forcing her off her feet in the process. Quickly closing the door, Ruby dusted her hands off, breathed some hot air onto them, and went in search of Snow.

The living puffball sprang from the muddy earth to the top of her doghouse and back down. Over and over, taunting Bannock as he raced around her. Getting her off the leash was simple enough and once again, she didn't have the heart to lift the dog onto her hind legs. With an excited yelp and surge of pure muscle, Snow leaped forward. Ruby was yanked off her feet. Her fingers slipped free of Snow's collar as she slammed against the cool earth. The night broke out into a chorus of crazed snaps and yelps, drowning out any trace of silence as Bannock's paws narrowly missed stomping her head. Ruby snapped her head up in time to see Snow springing off into the unbreakable darkness, Bannock close on her heels.

Panicked, Ruby hurled herself onto her feet and sprinted across the yard. The well-trodden ground gave way to patches of grass as she passed between the outhouse and the playpen. Then saplings barely bigger than twigs that surrendered the ground and gnarled bushes with needle-like barbs slashed across her thighs as she pushed past. She was a good few yards beyond the ring of light when she realized what she was doing. Staggering to a stop, she glanced around, straining to see into the darkness that had rushed to meet her.

In places, the foliage of the forest opened up enough to allow the glow of the floodlights to follow her. It lit up small patches, creating outlines of tree trunks and creeping branches, catching the small traces of moisture that lingered in the air and creating a hazy fog that loomed around the canopy. The moonlight managed to weave around some of the

29

more barren branches, but even their combined efforts could not fight off the shadows. Night clung to the forest floor, hiding the details of the world from her sight. It played tricks on her mind, creating shapes that crouched in the corners of her vision but disappeared when she turned to see them. In the distance, the dogs still bellowed and howled, their sound the only point of reference she had. If they were to go silent, she wouldn't be able to find her way back.

But while it grounded her, the noise hid the sound of anything nearby. As she stood there, the chill of the air working through her layers of protection to find her bones, she could swear that she heard something move through the underbrush. Not constant. Just a crunch of dead leaves every so often. Creeping around her. Coming closer.

Ruby swallowed, her throat suddenly dry. "Bannock! Snow!"

The dogs continued to bark, any one of which could be her fugitives. Something shifted through a bush just beyond her sight and her body froze. All the possibilities of what could be lurking unseen flooded into her head. Slowly, she inched her foot back.

"Bannock!" she called again, louder than before.

Her heel had just hit the earth, completing her first step backwards, when the world went silent. The baying of the pack didn't pitter out as they lost interest. It stopped with a cluster of yelps and left her alone in the crushing silence. Never in her life had Ruby heard silence like that. Consuming. Stifling. Like a tangible thing that bore down upon her and filled her with every breath.

Ruby's knees locked into place and she froze. There was a voice in the back of her mind that was convinced she would lose all sense of direction if she were to turn now. That without the dogs to guide her, she would end up going the wrong way. With staggered breaths, she tried to calm herself. But the more she soothed the wild thought that she would get lost, the more room there was for a new feeling.

She was being watched.

The shadows suddenly seemed filled with eyes as a million unseen creatures. As the silence continued to stretch out, unbroken by even the chirping of an insect, she couldn't shake the feeling that it wasn't just things within the woods that were watching her. It was the woods itself.

"Ruby."

It was spoken as a sigh, a breath, and her eyes widened to hear it. *It's just the wind,* she told herself. But the leaves didn't rattle and there wasn't the slightest gust upon her skin.

"Ruby."

A twig snapped, the distance from her impossible to tell. She took another step back, still unable to believe what she was hearing. Cool sweat prickled along the base of her neck as she scanned the forest around her. The shadows and trunks played tricks on her eyes. Everything within her peripheral vision seemed to creep forward only to still once more when she fixed her gaze upon them.

"Ruby."

While the voice was still barely more than a whisper, it was clearer now, and distinctly childlike. Working on reflex, she opened her mouth, ready to call out to the child that was lost somewhere within the bushes. Another twig snapped and the words choked off in her throat. The sound came from barely a few feet to her side, but the forest held its secrets. Everything remained silent. Still. The sensation of being watched grew stronger and more menacing.

Panting harshly, she slowly inched her foot back. A cold wind swept up her spine. As it reached her neck, the sensation changed, spreading out and solidifying. Soon, it enclosed around the back of her neck, as firm and solid and real as a human hand. It squeezed.

Twisting around on her heel, Ruby found the area as empty as it had been, with just the ghostly light of the dog yard playing in the gathering darkness. She bolted for them. Her boots thundered against the leaves and muck, crunching and sloshing, the wet earth sucking at the soles of her shoes as if to trip her. Thorns slashed at her as she raced through the brush, gouging at her clothes and streaking across the backs of her hands. Too numb with both cold and fear to feel the pain, she barreled, forcing her legs faster and away from the demonic

31

twists of shadows closing in upon her. Smothering her.
Trapping her.

With a staggered cry and weak legs, she stumbled free
from the tree line. The floodlights blinded her and she lifted
one arm to shield her eyes from the glare. She didn't stop
running until she was back within the brilliantly lit yard,
surrounded by the dog houses. The silence remained, broken
now only by her panted breaths and for one moment, she was
sure all of the dogs were gone. Her eyes adjusted and she
blinked out over the area. A clink of chains drew her attention
and one of the dogs poked his head out from the open door of
his dog house. Raising its nose up, it sniffed at the air once and
then drew back inside, leaving her once again alone in the
silence.

Ruby's ribs ached as her heart thundered against them.
Her hands felt empty and her back exposed. Opening and
closing her fists, she studied the tree line. The impenetrable
darkness offered little in return. Just possibilities, deathly
silences, and the unwavering certainty that someone was
watching her.

A scream ripped out of her as the forest burst forth, leaves
exploding up into a cloud of debris while a blur of light
barreled towards her. Ruby staggered back as she flung her
arms up to protect her face. Bannock barked, the sharp sound
drawing the other creatures back into life. The insects chirped.
The wind rustled the leaves. And the dog yard was once more
home to a flurry of sound and movement. The dogs squirmed
free of their houses, their chains rattling and tails wagging.
Bannock bounded around them, riling them up with every
pass until he came to stand by Ruby's feet.

Dropping to her knees, she bundled the dog into a tight
hug. The sensation of his soft fur slipping through her fingers,
of his radiating warmth and pounding heartbeat, helped her
mind to settle reality from fantasy. In time, he protested the
treatment and tried to squirm free. A scratch behind the ears
kept him close as Ruby let her heartbeat settle and her pain
ebb away. She had never been in the woods before, let alone at
night. There was sure to be a lot of normal occurrences that
left her reeling.

Maybe there had been a wolf, she thought. A predator scoping out the area would explain why the dogs had gone into hiding. *Or should they have been louder?* She couldn't fairly remember what Aaron and Betsy had told her, and she supposed that it didn't matter now. She still had to find Snow.

With one last hug, which Bannock gallantly if not begrudgingly accepted, Ruby got to her feet. Bathed in the off-white glow of the floodlights, it was easier to be calm. To feel centered and protected. The sounds of the dogs also helped to ease her nerves.

Let's do this again, she thought. *Only this time like you actually have a functioning brain. Okay, so, light. And a shotgun. Where did Betsy say she kept the flashlights again?*

It didn't matter much when she turned her attention over the paddock. An insistent whimper drew her attention and she found Snow circling in front of the playpen. On each pass, she would grumble and rise onto her hind legs, her front paws scratching at the latch like she was trying to open it herself. Ruby crossed the yard. With each step, the dogs closest to her would rush out and nuzzle at her hands. When she passed, they would retreat once more. They didn't go into their dog houses, but they never strayed too far from the entrance.

Bannock was at her side when she finally reached Snow. Her concerns that he would rile her up again proved to be pointless. Snow completely ignored him. It was the latch that had the dog's full attention and she scratched at it with more conviction as Ruby drew near. The metal of the gate was like ice as she pulled at the latch. It clunked up. Before the door had time to swing wide, Snow nuzzled her way in. Fire rushed to meet her and the two dogs curled around each other in the middle of the gated area.

"I guess you don't like her running off either, huh, Fire?" Ruby said.

Fire barely spared her a passing glance and he shuffled more tightly around the fluffy dog beside him. Once they settled, they looked like a single mound of fur. Ruby closed the latch and her eyes drifted up to the far side of the playpen. To the forest that pressed in against the fence, a few stray branches poking through the metal mesh like searching fingers. The darkness gave few secrets away and the feeling of being watched crept over her skin once more.

"Bannock," she whispered as she blindly reached for the dog, "stay close, okay?"

A cold wet nose nuzzled against her palm in answer. Finally tearing her eyes away from the shadows, Ruby set out across the yard at a quick pace. The cabin stood in the far corner of the clearing. Everything would seem better once she had a full stomach and a warm blanket, with Bannock by her side and a fire driving the shadows away.

Chapter 3

Ruby opened the cabin door and was greeted by a flood of icy air. By the glow of the floodlights, she groped for the light switch. She vaguely remembered Aaron telling her that the cabin was also wired to the generator, although it was best not to run the yard lights and the internal lights together for hours on end. It wasted too much gas. Her numb fingertips found the protruding switch, and making sure to squint first, she flicked it on. She needn't have gone to the trouble to protect her eyes. The single bulb that flickered to life was barely brighter than the light of a few candles.

Bannock slipped past her legs and padded into the cabin. Narrow and short, the wood walls offered a limited space. Most of it was taken up by the bed. Pressed against the far corner, just below a window, the queen-sized bed was made up with two pillows and a thick sleeping bag. A table, hardly big enough to accommodate the two seats tucked around it, lay just beyond the threshold. She only had to pull one chair out half an inch to keep the door flattened against the wall. To her right, there was what could pass for a kitchenette. A sink, a few cupboards, and a little bit of bench space. Beyond it, tucked into the corner but still only a few feet away from the end of the bed, was a cast iron fireplace. The belly of it was round and plump, the top flat and big enough to rest a saucepan.

Kindling, she reminded herself as she searched around the fireplace. The dim light didn't allow much to go by, but she managed to uncover a stack of wood and a box of scrunched up newspaper. Creating a little mound of paper, she carefully formed a teepee of sticks. It was easy to remember how it had looked when Aaron had done it. And a lot harder to get her frozen fingers to recreate it. Eventually, the pyre was formed and the crumpled paper took on the flame from the small pack of matches that had been left on the corner of the wood pile.

It didn't take long for the fire to grow. It greedily swallowed up the larger pieces of wood that she fed it. A golden light spilled out from the open iron door of the fireplace. It claimed every corner quickly. The warmth that followed took far longer. Crouching down, she checked the large container under the sink. There wasn't much water in it, but there was some, more than enough for a cup of coffee. The handle of the saucepan felt like dry ice against her bare skin. The pump of the sink wasn't much better. As she pressed and pulled, the pipes released a groan that both rattled and slurped, the water gushing free in broken bursts.

Setting the saucepan to boil, Ruby fed the fire once more and then left to bring her suitcases inside. The fly screen door thumped back into place with a loud crack each time she passed through. It was odd how comforting she found that. The woods were still alive with sound, bugs and owls, and small creatures that scurried through the undergrowth. But none of it seemed reliable. It could disappear again just like it had before. The slam of the screen door came without fail.

She ended up having to pile her suitcases, one on top of the other, in the corner next to the bed. They still ate up the space, but at least there was room to move. Bannock claimed another hunk of her floor. Curled up before the fire, he refused to move, forcing her to step over him to get from the fire to the sink and back.

"You literally have a fur coat," she grumbled at the dog.

He lifted his eyes to her but didn't bother to raise his head. Looking through the cupboards and bags, she managed to find a mug and one of the instant coffee packets she had taken from the train. A pleasant scent filled the cabin as she combined them and set the mug aside to cool. There was enough water remaining that Ruby decided a sponge bath was in order. She hadn't even spent a full night out here yet and already the idea felt decadent. Steam rose from the cloth that she dabbed into the water and heat flooded her skin at its touch. The hard part wasn't getting clean. It was getting back into her clothes fast enough so that she didn't lose all the warmth she had gained.

Switching over her shirt for her fleece pajama top had been a disaster. Still cursing the cold and shivering, she decided that a much faster pace was needed for switching over her pants. The second she lowered them, exposing her once protected skin to the air, the decision was made to go one leg at a time. She wiped the warm damp cloth over her right leg.

An owl hooted. Bugs called to one another. The fire crackled. And, just outside her window, a twig snapped.

Ruby bolted upright, her hands clenching tightly around the different cloths. She held her breath. Strained to hear. But there were only the common, repetitive sounds of the night. Still, her stomach churned, and the paranoid feeling of being watched settled into her chest once again. In the distance, she could hear the dogs padding around, their chains tinkling slightly. Slowly, she returned to her task. Her pace was far faster than before and she finished off her left leg in a few quick swipes. The elastic of her pants had barely touched her waist when a branch moved, its leaves and twigs scraping against the window behind her.

The floodlights didn't reach behind the cabin. So when she spun and looked out of the back window, all she could see were layers of shadows shifting against one another. Her heart lurched in her throat as she froze in place and stared at the glass.

It's so dark, she thought. *Someone could be standing right there and I'll never see them.*

The thought entered her mind, bringing with it a flood of paranoia and ideas. She could almost feel the gaze of someone upon her, watching her, tracking her every movement with crazed eyes. Swallowing thickly, she tried to push it all aside. But the mental images lingered and fed her imagination.

People went missing here before.

Barely a muscle in her body moved. The war she raged was all in her head and in getting her mind to obey her and reason. She had almost managed to calm herself down when another rustle of movement caught her. A footstep. Just outside the door.

She whipped around, almost tripping over her feet in her haste, a cold lump forming within the pit of her stomach. There was no window at the front of the cabin and somehow that just made it worse. She stepped back, ready to chastise herself once more for being a silly little coward. Bannock's growl stopped her. It was low and menacing, and his eyes locked on the slender door of the cabin. Something shuffled on the other side of the wood and Bannock shot up onto his feet.

The scruff of his neck bristled as he lowered his head. Still growling. Still staring at the door.

Ruby stared too, her attention fixed on the little latch that served as a lock. With limbs full of stone and fear rebounding around her chest, she inched her foot forward. Bannock's snarl grew steadily louder. His lips pulled back, the tips of his fangs glistening in the firelight. There was a crunch outside and Ruby flung herself against the door. Holding it in place with her eyes, she slid the lock into place and staggered back. Three solid knocks made the wood quake within its frame.

Where is the gun? The thought came unbidden to her mind as Bannock braced his forelegs and released a guttural growl. She caught sight of the shotgun by the door, tucked away on a specially built shelf. Her hands were numb, along with the rest of her, as she reached out for it.

"Ruby Dawson, you in there?" The voice was rough and gravelly and while she strained against her brain to find any hint of meaning to it, she was sure she didn't recognize it. The door rattled again. "Ruby? I'm Peter Martin, your neighbor. I heard the dogs get up in a fuss and thought you might need some help."

Don't move. Don't speak. The mantra had kept her well out of harm's way over the years, even if it did lead to some awkward situations. It was refreshing to have someone else's judgment to fall back on. Even if it was just the judgment of a dog. Turning her eyes from the door, she glanced over to Bannock. He still seemed interested in their visitor, but his hair had smoothed and he was no longer panting, his tongue dangling from the side of his snout. *Well, if he's not growling, it should be okay. Right?*

"You okay in there?" Peter said.

"Just getting changed," Ruby stammered as she cast her eyes over to Bannock again, watching his reaction as she took a step closer to the door.

He lumbered up onto his elongated legs and trotted a step closer. Either he was interested in greeting Peter or he had plans to bolt again. It was hard to tell. But, for all appearances, he had an opinion, which was more than she had, so she decided to follow his lead for now.

Peter remained silent as Ruby approached the door. Bannock trotted closer and became a warm weight against her leg as she opened the door a crack. A hand instantly smacked against the wood and tried to force it back some more. Ruby instantly shoved back, but it was her foot that kept it in place. Biting back a hiss, she could feel the first trickles of blood seeping into her sock.

"Aren't you going to invite me in?" Peter said.

Ruby's stomach dropped into the heels of her feet. Squeezing her eyes shut and bracing herself against the door, she rolled the words over and over in her head. It didn't make any difference. Any hint of threat the words might have held were just as lost on her as any playful teasing. In that moment, she felt the distance between her and the town. Felt each mile of isolation. Peter shoved again, widening the gap enough that Bannock could shove his head through, and Ruby braced her shoulder to keep it from moving any more.

"Is something wrong with the door? This place is falling apart. I can have a look at it for you if you want. Just let me in."

"I don't want Bannock to get out," Ruby said in a rush. "He was acting up earlier."

"I get it."

There was a soft chuckle. *Is he laughing with me or at me?*

"Hey, why don't you get into the gap so we can at least meet face to face? I feel kind of rude like this."

It was impossible to slip into sight and keep her weight against the door. Her stomach twisted into knots as she checked again with Bannock. All she could see was mild curiosity in the animal's behavior, so she shuffled slightly and peeked around the edge. The floodlights pressed against Peter's back, shrouding his face in shadows but making his size startlingly clear. He was a giant of a man. Robust and wide and tall enough that he would have to stoop to fit through the doorway. His jaw was covered in a thick beard, the mat of wiry hair concealing his features and hanging down his neck. She was so caught off guard by his appearance that it took her a moment to notice the rifle in his hands.

"Well, there you are. Aren't you a pretty little thing?"

Ruby saw a flash of teeth within the thick bush of mattered hair. She chanced a glance behind him, only daring to look away for a split second.

"I didn't hear your car," she said.

"Didn't bring one."

That made her swallow hard and her fingers tightened her grip on the door. "Aaron and Betsy told me that your place is pretty far off."

Why would you be here without a car? Why would you be here at all? Was it you who was watching me in the woods? The flurry of questions was shoved to the back of her mind as one took pride of place. *Was that you behind the cabin?*

"I was running some of my dogs," he said. His colossal torso shifted as he pointed to the far side of the yard, one thick finger signaling out a bush on the very edge of the light. "The entrance to the path is just on the other side of that hedge. I don't use it so much in winter, what with the lake frozen and all, but right now we still have to go the long way around."

She flicked her eyes between the man, the gun, and the place he pointed to. "Where are your dogs?"

"I left them a bit up the track. They tend to rile up these guys. Anyway, I heard the fussing and I thought you might need a hand. It's just you up here, right?"

Ruby's hand drifted down to Bannock. Even as she felt him straining against her leg to get out, she wanted to reassure herself that he was there.

"Snow got out for a bit," Ruby confessed. "But she's back now. Everything is good."

"That's good."

Shifting her weight again, Ruby asked weakly, "Why are you out so late? And with a gun?"

Peter laughed. Ruby couldn't decide if she liked the sound.

"It's only just past six. And as for this guy," he lifted the heavy looking shotgun with one hand, the metal surface catching the light. "No one should go into these woods without one. They did tell you *not* to go roaming around these woods by yourself, right? You just stay in that cabin and keep those lights on. The woods are full of predators you don't want to run into at night."

Ruby nodded quickly and promised that she would.

"You going to have Bannock in there with you all the time?"

"Yes."

The answer slipped out easily. She still couldn't quite tell what to make of Peter, but she was sure that she didn't want him to think she was here alone. At the same time as she spoke, however, he slipped his hand through the door and ruffed up Bannock's fur. The dog took the pat and the snack that Peter offered a moment later. The uneasiness that she had felt vanished as Bannock munched on the unseen morsel.

"That's good. He's a good dog. Well, it seems like you have it all under control. If you need anything, I'm just down that road. Give me a yell."

"I thought you were a few miles away."

Peter laughed again. "Sound has a way of travelling around here. You'll learn that you can't really judge distance. Things that sound close can be pretty far off. It works the other way, too. You'll be surprised what can creep up on you."

He nodded at her once, the ends of his hair bobbing with the movement, and turned to go.

"Peter," she asked in a rush. "Were you behind the cabin? I heard something moving back there."

"Wasn't me," he said. She couldn't tell if he was lying. "I'm sure it was just a rabbit. They tend to hang around back there."

With one more nod, he headed off down the dirt road. She couldn't see his sled dogs and soon lost track of him within the shadows. But every so often, the light would catch against the barrel of his shotgun. A quick flare that helped to pinpoint his progress. The dogs continued to bay and yelp as she watched until even that flickering light faded away.

Shivering in the encroaching chill, she made sure to lock both doors and pulled the curtains tight.

Chapter 4

The cozy confines of the cabin seemed to be exempt from mundane things like time. Without a clock, there was no way to judge if minutes or hours had passed, so they soon began to feel interchangeable. The fire crackled as it emitted a glorious glow and equally welcomed heat. The wind picked up, growing into a muffled howl that whispered through the cracks around the windows. Every so often, Bannock broke the serenity with a sleepy huff, but he never left the patch of floor by the fireplace that he had claimed as his own. Ruby didn't mind the loss of his body heat. The sleeping bags that she had unzipped to form a bedding did an excellent job at keeping her comfortable. Laying on her stomach, a novel in one hand and a cup of steaming coffee in the other, Ruby settled into the unstable serenity.

She knew that, at any moment, Peter could return and the idea left a sour taste in the back of her throat. Perhaps he was actually kind. There was every chance that she had misjudged him. That it wasn't his behavior but her disorder that had made him seem threatening. But she couldn't shake the feeling that someone had been stalking around the cabin, and he was the only 'someone' out here. With simmering paranoia, she made sure to face the door as she read. But, as the pages passed, it became easier to believe that he wouldn't be coming back.

She was so comfortable that she didn't want her body to ruin it. Unfortunately, as time dragged on, the pressure in the pit of her stomach grew too much to bear. There was no getting around it. She needed to make a trip to the outhouse. Reluctantly, she struggled out from under her blankets and gasped. The air wasn't as warm as she had thought. Piling into her knee-length snow jacket and opting for her snow boots over her regular sneakers, she readied herself to leave the comfort of the cabin behind. All her preparation didn't matter much when she finally opened the cabin door. An icy draft swept past her and covered her from head to toe as it swelled to fill the room. The sudden blast dropped the temperature enough to make Bannock lift his head with an annoyed growl.

The noise died off when he saw what she was doing. At that, he lurched to his feet and trotted past her into the night.

While the floodlights illuminated most of the yard, there were still a few feet of darkness separating the cabin from the reassuring glare. Bannock was barely more than a shadow, aimlessly wandering with his nose low to the ground. She lost sight of him altogether when she closed the door behind her to keep in the warmth. It was at that moment when the silence caught up with her. Without the walls to smother it or the sounds of the fire to cover it, the wind took on a ghastly undertone as it slithered through the surrounding forest. The floodlights had reduced the trees to towering figures that loomed over her, shifting as if they were edging ever closer. The cold pressed down upon her like a physical weight as it squirmed under the edges of her clothes.

Ruby zipped her coat higher up her neck, shoved her hands into her pockets, and jogged across the dividing space. The sounds and shadows didn't seem as bad when she entered the ring of light, so she slowed into a walk and watched her breath puff out in smoky clouds. A few of the dogs had curled up, their noses tucked under the protection of their fluffy tails to fend off the cold. The others had gone into their houses, cramming themselves into the small space and leaving only their twisted chains visible. The few dogs that were interested in her movements did little more than lift their heads or thump their tails against the dirt. And even that seemed like too much effort when they realized she wasn't going to feed them.

A breath of arctic wind pushed against her back, carrying with it the faint cry of an owl and the promise of a sharper cold yet to come. Beyond the steady drone of the generator, the world was populated with only the faintest of sounds. The snorts and rustling of the dog. The crunch of the leaves under her boots. Her thin and feathery breathing as her lungs struggled to adjust to the chill that filled them. If the air alone was this bad, she wasn't looking forward to sitting on the outhouse toilet seat.

Hunching her shoulders, she rounded the visitor's tent, shaving a few seconds off of her journey by cutting across the edge of the garden. She made sure not to destroy any of the plants as she jumped over the row of boundary rocks. Nestled behind the visitor's tent and surrounded by trees, the outhouse sat just beyond the ring of light. It was small, flimsy, and filled with shadows.

The hinges of the outhouse groaned and rattled as she forced the door open. There was barely any room within the tiny space, and the air somehow seemed even colder than outside. As she crammed the door shut, her lack of a flashlight became painfully apparent. The only light was the gleam of the floodlights that blazed through the cracks between the blanks. It looked almost as if a spaceship were landing outside. She smiled slightly at the thought as she waited for her eyes to adjust. The best she could do was make out the vague outline of a roll of toilet paper and a bottle of sanitizer perched on a small shelf.

Somehow, the actuality of warm skin coming into contact with the wood was worse than what she had been imagining. With a sharp gasp, Ruby resolved to make the whole process as quick as possible. She needed to get back to the cabin before she lost every last trace of warmth from her bones. The hand sanitizer was just as bad as the wood had been.

Then, with one solid thump, the lights died.

Cast into an unbroken darkness, Ruby froze. Fear sizzled through her veins, filling every muscle until she could barely breathe around it. A single thought bounded against her skull in time with her throbbing heartbeat; *Peter's come back.* Her ears rang at the intense silence that bore down upon her. But, as the moments dragged, her mind started to work again and she remembered that she had left the cabin light on. The bulb was so weak that the firelight had quickly outshone it, so she had forgotten to turn it off and it had been taxing the generator ever since. The gas must have run out.

Groaning in frustration, she fixed her clothes to better defend against the wind and ran over the options in her head. It seemed a simple enough task to collect a flashlight and fill the generator. But the reality made her hesitate. Juggling a gallon of gas and a flashlight in the pitch black, with a wolf infested forest at her back, didn't seem like the brightest idea.

She had no idea what time it was, but it had to be late. It was possible that dawn wasn't that far off. Instead, she could just pass the night in the cabin and deal with this in the morning. If she kept the fire going, the smoke should deter any lingering animals. It seemed like the far superior option.

Resolved, she reached forward, searching through the ebony abyss for the door. She found the rough wood and was just about to push when she heard the bushes behind her rustle. Footsteps pounded over the underbrush and sprinted around the front of the outhouse. Snapping her hand back, Ruby stared at the door, her heart hammering within her chest. *That couldn't be what I thought it was,* she told herself. She repeated the words within her skull, but she couldn't convince herself that it was true. They were footsteps. Human footsteps. *Maybe it was Peter?* She tried to reason. *But why would he be running around her outhouse in the middle of the night?* A voice in the back of her head told her to stop that line of thought because there was no way to get to an answer that would be in any way comforting.

Biting her lip, Ruby froze in place and strained to hear the slightest sound, trying to pinpoint where the person was now. She could hear the wind blowing, rustling the dying leaves that still clung to the trees. There were no other sounds. Her blood turned to ice as she realized that everything else had faded away. Just like before, when she had ventured into the wood after Snow and the world had evaporated around her. No birds, no bugs, no dogs grumbling as they sought out a more comfortable position. It was as if nothing existed beyond the frail walls around her. She blinked rapidly, trying to force her eyes to adjust to the dark, desperate to see even the slightest shadows. It was no use. She was blind. And she hadn't locked the door.

Her lungs felt too small for her chest as she reached out with a trembling hand. The unfinished wood scraped against her fingertips. It flaked and splintered, threatening to drive shards into her skin as she searched over the surface. *There has to be a lock,* she told herself. But no matter how hard she tried, she couldn't remember if there was one. The leaves crackled again. She couldn't pinpoint where it had come from.

Within the same moment, they would appear to be in a dozen places at once. As if she were surrounded. There was no way to tell how big it was. But there was no mistaking that it was close. *It might just be Peter,* she told herself again.

There was no comfort in the thought.

Her nail brushed against a thin slip of metal. It clunked against the wood, a tiny sound, but one that was instantly followed by another footstep. Ruby pressed her hand over it to keep it silent and held her breath. *Had they heard? Do they know I'm here? Are they looking for me?* The thoughts crowded into her mind as the frost covered hook pressed against her palm. With her other hand, she searched for the latch.

The leaves crackled under a flurry of footsteps. A wave of cold air rushed through the cracks in the wood as the stranger raced past. Surging forward, she fumbled the flimsy hook into place and staggered away. The back of her legs collided with the seat and her knees almost dropped her onto it. Each step drew closer to the door. They were slow. Measured. There was no doubt anymore. Someone was on the other side, and they were beginning to circle the outhouse.

Ruby held her breath until her lungs became infernos behind her ribs. Still, the only sound was of the person's footsteps as they methodically walked around the tiny structure. In the crippling darkness, it was all too easy to imagine that the stranger could see her, sense her, like a shark circling its prey. She squinted, trying to force the shadows into some discernable shape by sheer force of will. The world around her remained a blank slate.

There has to be a reason, she thought. *Something logical. Something simple.* But she couldn't think of what that might be. The town was miles away. The night was freezing and promised only to get colder. And the silence of whoever was out there drove away any thought that it might just be a lost hiker looking for a safe place. *They're looking for me.* The awareness drove into her chest like an iron spike. *The fire is still burning in the cabin. Anyone passing would see it.* As she began to tremble, she struggled to squash down that line of thought. All of her attempts amounted to nothing. But her mind snapped still when the footsteps stopped.

The wind stirred once more, strong enough now to bring with it the traces of wet earth and pine. On shaking legs, she inched forward. The steps didn't come closer. They didn't leave. There was only a stifling hush that almost felt painful. Ruby could almost feel someone watching her. In her mind's eye, she could picture the stranger pressed up against the wall, staring at her through one of the cracks, waiting for her to feel safe enough to come out.

Time continued on and the winter chill took its toll. Her hands ached as the air ravaged them. Too scared to leave herself vulnerable, she refused to shove them into her pockets. A fine tremor shook her. *If I run, could I get back to the cabin before they catch me? Would they chase me? Should I risk it?* The thoughts pounded in her mind as much as her heartbeat.

Biting down on her lip until she could taste the faintest traces of blood, she used the pain to help center herself. *It's probably Peter. He probably saw the lights click off and came to check if everything was okay. It can't be anything bad. If it were, the dogs would be barking.*

The dogs.

Her spine straightened as she held her breath once again, exploring the silence to try and catch any hint of movement. If Bannock was nearby, she might be able to get him to come with her back to the cabin. The race through the unknown, completely blind, didn't seem as daunting if she could have the massive dog by her side.

Feeling slightly emboldened, she arranged herself into a crouch and pressed her ear against the wall. Each gust of wind spilled over her skin as though the night itself were breathing. Nothing stirred. She pressed a little closer. The leaves crackled just inches from her ear. Jerking back, she clamped one hand over her mouth to stifle her startled scream. The other grabbed the lock, keeping it firmly in place. Gathering what remained of her courage, she shot to her feet, pressing her hand over the latch in an iron grip.

The structure suddenly felt insignificant. Fragile. Ruby could hear it straining now, battling against the soft wind to

47

remain upright. It was alive with creaks and groans. Like a thousand whispering voices, each promising that the next second would be the last. That one more gust and it would all crumble down around her. But the door didn't break open and the roof didn't fall. The moments stretched out into nothingness, all suspended within the strange silence. Anticipation crawled over her skin as she stood there. Shivering. Waiting.

Bit by bit, tension twisted her up like spools of barbed wire. Every inch of her ached. The wind was only growing stronger. It pressed against the side of the outhouse until she could hear the slats of wood shuttering against each other. More than anything else, it was that sickening sound that steeled her resolve. Forcing herself to keep her breathing deep, she slowly edged towards the door. For every inch she took, a million images filled her mind of what could be waiting for her. They morphed from a well-meaning neighbor to an axe-wielding madman to a creature that had clawed its way from the darkest recesses of her mind.

Closing her eyes made no difference to what she saw. But the warmth of her lids proved how swiftly the temperature was dropping. Her fingers couldn't shiver anymore. It was as if they had been encased in blocks of ice, barely leaving her enough mobility to pull the hook free. When only the tip of the hook remained in place, she opened her eyes and allowed herself one more second of indecision. Then she flipped the latch, hurled the door open, and bolted out into the night.

Clouds had gathered, the thick blanket choking off the little light that the moon would have provided. Working by memory alone, she tried to round the visitor's tent but misjudged the distance. Her shin slammed into something solid. Pain sliced up her leg at the impact, and a bolt of blinding pain sent her toppling to the ground. Her shoulder collided with the small stones that lined the garden. A jolt of burning pain sliced along her, but the position kept her head from hitting the earth full force. Her panted breath stirred the particles of unfrozen dirt, bringing it up to sting her eyes as she struggled to keep down her pained sobs.

A twig snapped from somewhere behind her and her breath stuck in her throat. Then there was another crack. And another. Each one coming closer at a rapid pace. Jaws latched onto her arm and yanked with determination. She screamed and thrashed, her mind screaming *wolf* with a hurricane force. The approaching steps filled her with enough fear to make her realize that the fangs on her arm weren't tearing at her. Instead, they were holding and pulling, dragging her forward.

"Bannock?"

Holding onto the thought, Ruby lurched to her feet and followed whichever way the animal pulled. The steps sounded only a few feet behind as she limped into a sprint. Suddenly, they passed the edge of the visitor's tent and the firelight of the cabin blazed to life in the corner of her eyes. It was dim. Just a meager slip of gold that escaped around the edges of the curtains and door. She barreled towards it, pain forgotten, Bannock yelping at her side.

The screen door squealed as she yanked it open. It swung back to drive against her side as she threw her weight against the wooden door, the strike creating a new burst of agony as she worked the knob. Bannock leaped inside the moment she was able to open the door. She followed, slamming the door shut without looking back. Her fingers could barely move as she fumbled with the little sliding lock. Still captured by panic, she grabbed one of the chairs from the nearby table and jammed the back of it under the hand. A few swift kicks to the legs and she crammed it in tight enough to keep the door in place.

It was as she limped away from the door that her adrenaline left her. Without it, the pain in her leg soon overshadowed most of everything else. Still watching the door, she blindly reached for the bed, her legs crumbling as she sunk onto the mattress. The sleeping bag slipped and she dropped heavily onto the floor. A pitiful sob broke from her throat. *Had that been real?* The question boiled in her head. She had heard it. With every step she had taken back to the cabin, there hadn't been a shadow of a doubt that someone, or something, had been following her. But now that she was surrounded by the warmth and glow of the fire, she wasn't so sure. The memories repeated in her head. And, with each rendition, she doubted herself a little more.

Her sole piece of evidence was Bannock. Forsaking his spot before the fireplace, he curled up beside her and whimpered as he sought out her attention. With one more broken sob, she wrapped her arms around his neck and buried her face into his fur. He leaned into the touch, nuzzling her knee as he continued to whimper. While she couldn't wrap her mind around what had just happened, she knew she wasn't going to leave the cabin again tonight. And she wasn't going to let the fire burn out.

Chapter 5

Ruby stirred as the air slipped under the rim of her sleeping bag to caress her with an icy hand. That and the slight tinge of smoke that tinted her every breath made it clear that the fire had died out. Blinking her eyes open, she made the mistake of moving her legs. While the sleeping bag radiated with warmth where she lay, it was frigid just an inch beyond it. Shivering, she retreated to her original position and tried to go back to sleep. Unfortunately, she overshot and ended up kicking Bannock's side with her heel. With a snort, he lifted his head and turned to face her. Dog or not, there was no mistaking that kind of resentful glare.

Grumbling slightly, he dropped down onto the ground and began to stretch out his spine. Figuring that this was a sign that her sleep-in was limited, Ruby forced herself to sit up. She gave up the second the frozen air touched her bed-warm shoulders and pulled the sleeping bag over her head. It took a few moments for her to gather the courage to venture out again. Wrapping the sleeping bag tightly around herself, she shuffled over to the fireplace. Even though she only had very limited practice in starting fires, she still found it far easier than her first time to get the flames lapping at the wood once more. Heat poured out towards her and she warmed her hands. It was then that she noticed that her breath was misting. She watched it churn and dissipate into the air. Her brow furrowed. *It shouldn't be this cold yet.*

Still shielded by the sleeping bag, she shuffled to the window. As she demanded more from her leg, the small ache in her shin began to blossom into a dull throb that echoed the length of the bone. It was a painful reminder of last night. It didn't matter how long she had turned it over in her mind, she still hadn't been able to figure out what had been chasing her. But nothing else had happened and her exhaustion had pulled her into a restless sleep.

Reaching over the table, she cautiously pulled up one edge of the curtain and blinked into the early morning light. Snow drifted down like lazy rain, the flakes catching the light as they flipped and toppled. There must have been quite a downpour last night because the world was covered with about half an inch of fine powder. The sight made her smile and she turned to Bannock.

"Look how pretty it is."

The dog yawned and re-stretched his legs until they trembled.

She tilted her head. "Still one of the best conversations I've had lately."

She had a growing suspicion that she would be talking to all of the dogs by the end of the season. At Bannock's growing impatience, Ruby decided that she better get changed quickly or be prepared to clean up a mess. Searching into the deeper recesses of her suitcase, she found the clothes she hadn't thought she'd have to use this early in the season. Thermals, thick socks, and a fake fur-lined hat that had flaps she could secure over her ears. Ruby had never changed so fast in her life, but she still lost a good chunk of her body heat. Because of this, she decided to let the fire burn while she started her chorus. Anything to fend off the chill. She pulled the water jug out from under the sink and rattled it around. Empty. Sighing, she retrieved her thick wool gloves. It would have been nice to come back to a nice hot drink.

"I'll have to learn to keep an eye on the water level, huh, boy?"

Instead of responding to her voice, he crowded towards the door and scratched at the legs of the chair that still barricaded it. She hesitantly approached it and quickly snuck another glance out of the window. The yard was peaceful and quiet, brought to a new level of beauty by the still falling snow. Nothing looked out of place. In the light, all the things that had looked so daunting were now simply trees.

Even with this reassurance, sludge still bubbled within the pit of her stomach as she began to dislodge the chair. She couldn't help sneaking another quick glance out the window before pulling the chair free. Its legs scraped over the floor and she winced at the sound. Now there was only the tiny lock keeping the door in place, and she felt a new wave of trepidation. Something in her core told her not to go out there. But Bannock grew restless and reared up to scratch at the handle with both paws. She bit her lip, reached up, and quickly flicked open the lock. Nothing came barging in. Slowly, she opened the door. Bannock slipped through the first chance he got and raced across the open area.

The jug bounced against her shin as she struggled through the doorway and bit back a pained hiss. In her haste to get warm, she hadn't spared the time to properly look at the wound. But she only needed a passing glance to know the damage. A vast portion of her skin was now taken up by a purpling bruise that spread out from the point of impact like a rash. Making a mental note to clean it up when she had some hot water, she tried her best to ignore it.

Grabbing a couple of jugs that were stored by the fence, she decided to walk down to the lake, not wanting to destroy the tranquility with the roar of a car engine. Bannock seemed happy enough by her choice and jumped around her legs before racing off with an excited bark. She was cold, hungry, and completely at peace. Last night seemed like a distant memory, and all that lay before her was a day full of playing with dogs and finally getting through her novel.

The lake might not have felt all that far off if it hadn't been for the ache in her shin. As it was, she continued at a slow but steady pace and breathed deeply of the pine-scented air. She couldn't tell how long it took and she wasn't trying to keep track of it. Bannock knew the way. He darted from one side of the road to the other, sniffing at everything before bouncing down the embankment like a jackrabbit. Ruby followed at a far slower pace, careful of any dips or loose soil that the snow could already be hiding.

Despite her care, her foot hit a slick patch of earth and sent her sliding. Dumped onto her butt, the jugs toppled from her hands and bounced down the rest of the way to end up in the lake. Ruby planted her feet and brought herself to a sharp stop within inches of the water's edge. Quickly shifting onto her knees, she reached for the jugs that were drifting slowly away, her gloved fingers slipping over the plastic sides. Bannock seemed to find the whole thing amusing and began to leap and dart around her, kicking up the water, mud, and snow. Ignoring him as best she could, she leaned over a little further, straining not to fall into the water.

Bannock slammed his weight against her back and flung her forward. The arctic water rushed up to meet her, engulfing her like a thousand icy knives. The air rushed from her lungs in a painful gasp and her mind scattered to a stop. She scrambled back up onto the bank, the water gushing from her to melt the frost covered mud. The soaked wool of her gloves numbed her fingers as they found an unnatural groove. Trembling violently, she hurled herself onto all fours and looked down at her hands.

A footprint. A human footprint. Her brows furrowed as she followed the trail with her eyes. It curved along the rim of the lake before traveling it to climb up the embankment and disappear under the cover of the plants. Her stomach cramped when she realized that the trail headed back towards her cabin.

The blare of a car horn made her snap her head up. Each muscle in her body squeezed and trembled, making it a struggle to get back onto her feet. With an agonizing amount of effort, she lifted her head to see Aaron rushing down the embankment towards her.

"Ruby, we thought that was you. Are you okay?" The soles of his boots cracked through the hardened mud as he reached the shoreline and held out his hand.

She took him up on his offer and allowed him to drag her the rest of the way onto her feet. Her waterlogged pants clung to her like sheets of ice, numbing her legs and gushing down to fill her boots. Already her teeth were chattering. Aaron urged her to move with one hand pressing at her back.

"What are you doing getting wet in weather like this? Come on, now. Hurry up."

"Wait," Ruby said. "Look what I found."

Struggling to keep her balance, she tightened her grip on Aaron's hand and pointed at the trail of footsteps. They barely managed to hold his attention for a moment.

"I'm not sure why that's worth noticing."

"Someone was walking around the camp last night," she said, her air clouding before her.

"You mean Peter? He was supposed to come by yesterday and introduce himself."

"I don't think it was Peter–"

"He didn't come by?"

"No, he did, but this was late at night."

Aaron laughed and Ruby was forced to wait with a growing sense of dread to see what kind of laugh it was.

"You city kids are all the same."

"What?"

"It was probably just a rabbit."

She shook her head. "No, this sounded like footsteps."

Gently, he began to push her towards the incline.

"There are a few rabbits that like to nest around the area. They can get surprisingly territorial. One probably just chased you a bit." He laughed again and Ruby was almost certain that he was openly mocking her. "It can sound pretty intimidating for someone who's not used to it."

"So," she stammered, trying to follow his line of thought as her brain numbed, "you think Peter left these?"

"No, they're far too small for him. They're probably left over from when his nephew visited." Aaron paused and looked her over carefully. "Are you okay? I mean, if you don't think that you can do this job, now is the time to say it."

She opened her mouth slightly but couldn't think of what to say. *Had it really just been a rabbit and a trick of the mind?* This time, as she mulled over the question, the answer seemed incredibly simple. And regardless, one awkward night wasn't enough for her to throw aside not only her job but also her home for the next six months. She had nowhere else to go. So she shrugged one shoulder and forced a smile.

"I'm alright," she said. "I think you're right. Strange place with strange sounds and my mind ran away with me."

Still, Ruby couldn't keep her eyes from drifting back to the footprints as she crawled her way up to Betsy and the waiting car.

Chapter 6

With all three of them present, it didn't take long for them to clean the yard and feed the now ravenous dogs. Aaron taught Ruby the best ways to spread the straw within the doghouses for maximum insulation. An easy task in principle, but far harder in reality as the dogs made a game of pulling it back out the second she turned her back. They worked their way through the doghouses as Betsy went into the visitor's tent to take care of a few last-minute things.

By the time the jobs were done, Ruby felt like there was an inch of snow piled up in every crease of her jacket, mixing with layers of dog fur and slobber. She tried to clean herself off, absently following Aaron as he moved towards the playpen.

"Was Snow hard to handle?" Aaron asked.

The dog in question was currently brimming with both excitement and energy, alternating between leaping against the fence and running around in circles.

Giving up on her gloves ever being clean again, Ruby shrugged. "She made a little run for it. But it was fine in the end."

After Aaron's reaction to her story about being chased by phantom sounds, she wasn't about to tell him how she had been scared in the woods. Looking back on it now, her fear seemed childish, and certainly nothing to risk losing her job over.

"She'll do that," he said. "Actually, they all do."

He turned and watched her silently for a moment. Hesitantly, she smiled.

"That was a joke, right?" she asked.

"Yes, it was."

Ruby chuckled and he flashed his teeth in what she assumed was a pleasant smile.

"Just remember to keep a good grip on them. Even if one does scurry off somewhere, they'll always come back for dinner."

Aaron brought Fire and Snow out, leaving her to put in the next two on the roster. Luckily for her, the next two dogs to go into the playpen were barely more than pups and had yet to grow into their strength, allowing her to display a little bit of competence. Securing the golden furred Nugget and the shaggy Echo was easy, and Aaron flashed his teeth at her again. She took it as a good sign.

On their way to the visitor's tent, Aaron noticed that some of the garden stones were dislodged from their usual places. Ruby wrung her hands as she waited for him to ask her about it, but he never did. He just absently pushed them back into place with the toe of his boot and continued on his way. Her leg ached just a little bit more as she followed.

The moment Ruby passed the threshold, it struck her as strange that she hadn't looked inside before. It was larger than she would have thought, but just as cold. The gathering snow created splotchy shadows across the heavy canvas roof, and paintings, photographs, and postcards of the pack decorated the space. Hooks ran the length of the opposite wall, sled dog harnesses dangling off each one, ready for the next season. A barrel stove that was similar to the one in the cabin took up the closest corner, and old but comfortable looking sofas had been shoved back against the far wall. Beyond that, it was just open space that served as the perfect storage area for the boxes they had brought in.

Betsy straightened up from the boxes she was packing and dusted her hands off on her thighs. "All done here," she said. "How are you two going?"

"The pack is set. I don't think they're going to miss us at all," Aaron said.

"Good," Betsy said with a flash of her teeth. "Well, if you don't have any questions for us, Ruby, we need to get on our way. The train leaves in about an hour."

The question brought into stark clarity that Ruby was going to be well and truly on her own. Last night, the thought that someone was coming in the morning had seemed like a well-needed safety net. She wouldn't have that tonight. *No one would be coming for me,* she thought. *No one would be expecting me. A lot could happen before anyone could even think to look.* Ruby shivered at the thought but quickly tried to cover it up as a symptom of the encroaching cold. Wrapping her arms around herself, she made a show of rubbing away the chill.

"I'll be fine," Ruby smiled. "Enjoy your trip."

"Don't worry so much," Betsy said. "Just make sure to keep the water jugs in with you. Oh, and restock the cabin's firewood. They're forecasting a snowstorm tonight. Nothing too serious but you don't want to be caught out in it."

"I will," Ruby assured. "If it gets really bad, should I bring the dogs in?"

Aaron was the one to answer, "I don't think that will be necessary. Not with the new straw. You'll only ever have to bring them in once it starts dropping to around twenty degrees below."

"And watch your liquids," Betsy added in a light tone. "Using the outhouse during a storm isn't exactly pleasant."

Aaron laughed as he slipped around Ruby and headed for the door. He seemed intent on getting out of here as quickly as possible. Ruby assumed that it had been a while since the couple's last vacation. There were a few more parting words, some warnings and reassurances, but Ruby barely heard any of it. Her mind kept returning to the fact that she would be alone. For some reason, the certainty of isolation made it harder to keep her mind from straying back to the footprints she had found.

Aaron's explanations made sense. She couldn't refute them and didn't have any of her own to offer. But there was just something about them that struck deep into her brain and lodged there. Standing in the tent's doorframe, she watched their car pull out of the yard. The dogs broke into a flurry of barks and she found comfort in the noise. *At least they'll be here,* Ruby thought with a little smile. *So, not completely alone.*

The rumble of the engine lingered long after she had lost sight of the car within the forest. Gradually, the dogs calmed down and went back to playing with the straw. Ruby stayed where she was, holding herself tightly, and watched the snow as it gently hovered on the slight breeze. The peacefulness that enclosed the scene filled her with every breath, and she leaned against the doorframe, settling it to better delight in it.

Something shifted. She couldn't place what, or where, but it was impossible to deny that something was different. Her skin crawled. Pulling herself to full height, she searched the yard in quick glances. Nothing was missing, at least as far as she could tell, but the uneasy feeling continued to grow within her chest. A chill slipped up along her spine like a skeletal finger and she spun around, her breath caught in her throat. The back of the visitor's tent was just as empty as it had been before, the shadows too weak to hide anyone or anything. But she couldn't shake the feeling that she was being watched.

Swallowing thickly, Ruby backed out of the threshold and firmly closed the door. She was still staring at the wood when Bannock ambled up to sit at her feet. His presence eased the strange sensation and brought a smile to her face. Crouching down, she scratched behind both of his ears at once. But instead of crowding into her, demanding more attention, he stood rigid, his gaze locked on a patch of trees beyond the other side of the road. A slow, deep growl worked its way up from his throat as his ears flattened. Ruby searched the area with a renewed sense of dread. Dozens of shadows lurked within the towering trees, each with the potential to keep a thousand secrets, but she couldn't pinpoint whatever it was that held Bannock's focus.

"What is it?" Ruby asked as she rubbed the rising scruff of his neck.

A new tendril of fear curled around her heart when Bannock bared his fangs. The sensation of being watched returned, and she crowded a little closer into the dog's side.

"That lady at the library, Esther," Ruby said aloud to break the unsettling silence. "She told me that people go missing in these woods all the time."

Bannock shifted his weight back and forth. His growl died but his focus remained. Ruby slowly got to her feet, still unable to pinpoint what was setting him off. The feeling of eyes upon her intensified until she expected to feel someone breathing against her neck.

"Maybe we should go ask a few more questions."

The first step away from the possible safety of the tent was the hardest. Her pride wasn't enough to keep her at a steady pace. She ran to the cabin and snatched up the van keys and her wallet. Just before leaving, she remembered to make herself somewhat presentable.

The fire-warm air of the cabin was a relief to her numb fingers as she brushed her hair. *Wool knit was a horrible idea,* she thought ruefully. A small voice whispered in the back of her head that it might not be the only mistake she made.

Quickly brushing her teeth, she changed into a clean pair of sweatpants and wiped down her jacket. It wasn't the best she had ever looked, but she was beyond caring. Pulling her hood up over her hair, she double-checked that nothing was close to the fireplace and ducked out of the cabin. It was strange to not lock up a place when leaving it. Stranger still not to even have the option. But Bannock's sudden impatience was a good distraction.

She had to jog to catch up with him before he scratched the paintjob trying to get into the van. He barely moved out of the way as she yanked the driver's door open. In an impressive feat of agility, he scrambled and leaped until he managed to get up into the high-set seat. Pulling herself in after him, it took her a few moments to organize her knee-length snow coat. It was a lot more material than she was used to dealing with. Tossing her wallet onto the dashboard, she slipped the key into the ignition and reached out to pat Bannock. But he wasn't sitting with pride on the passenger seat. Instead, he had crammed himself into the limited leg area before it. Curled up tight, he propped his head on the console and watched her with pleading eyes.

His agitation was infectious. Her gut twisted as she glanced around the yard again. Sealed within the car, the already soft noises of the area muffled by steel and glass, left her with a strange feeling of disconnection. It was as if she could see or feel reality but not have both at the same time. One hand pressed against her stomach. She pushed until the quivering, churning sensation settled. *Nothing is there,* she assured herself. *The dogs would bark if something was out there.* Still, her free hand subconsciously crept up the side of the door until she found the lock. She flicked it. The sound of each door latching into place helped her feel a little less queasy.

Ruby was still scanning the area as she turned the key. The engine rattled and snarled, shaking the van before it sputtered out. She turned the key again, swallowing hard like that would somehow force down her rising panic. The van groaned again. *It's the cold.* The realization battled in her mind. *Betsy had said that it wouldn't work in the cold. But how cold is cold?*

Fear rose like bile in the back of her throat as she continued to crack the key. *Please work,* she begged. *I'm not ready to be stuck here.* She lost track of how many times she tried, only to listen helplessly to grinding metal. Finally, with a violent shutter, the van relented. Ruby melted against her seat as a sigh of relief slipped past her lips. Winter was arriving quicker than she had anticipated. *If it is the cold affecting the van, how long do I have left before it's useless?*

She didn't want to think about it. But still, the question lingered in her mind as she drove into town. For the first time, she felt every inch of the distance.

***

Ruby sunk her teeth into the stick of jerky as she absently flipped through the pages with her free hand. As the town's self-appointed historian, Esther had dedicated a whole section of the library to local history. Ruby had only needed to ask about local disappearances to be left with a stack of books almost as tall as Bannock. She had spared a moment in town to buy a new pair of gloves. Fur-lined and long enough to reach her elbows. It was strange how simply having warm hands made her feel like she was in control of her life. Barely more than an hour had passed before the company of the town grew to be too much and she had retreated to the yard.

She spent the day playing with the dogs, taking a few of them at a time for long walks down the road. But the clouds had grown thick and the wind had transformed into a constant force, and she had been forced inside. Learning from past mistakes, she boiled some water and had her sponge bath early. With nowhere to be, Ruby changed into her pajamas, snuggled under the sleeping bag, and devoted herself to searching through the books.

The wind became a wail. It pounded against the side of the cabin as the air thickened and turned gray. Secured in the warmth inside, Ruby had marked the time by how often she had to restock the fire or get something to eat. The few times she used the bathroom, she hadn't been able to bring herself to close the door. She could endure feeling exposed. It was not being able to see that she couldn't stand.

Absently chewing the dried, salty meat, Ruby glanced at another photograph of missing people. Most were the same as the ones that hung on the library wall. Black and white images of a time that seemed long ago. While Esther had hinted about more recent disappearances, mostly tourists that locals assumed had lost their way in the seemingly endless forest, the books didn't address them. Most of them didn't mention anything outside of the gold rush era.

Turning another page, she was instantly drawn to an array of photographs that spilled from one page to the next. They were all of the same brittle little cabin. At the bottom of the page, there was a brief statement. Skim reading the paragraph, she found that the cabin pictured had once belonged to a family; a married couple, and their three young children. They had all vanished one summer. No sign of attack. Nothing missing.

That makes eight, Ruby thought as she rechecked the names and dates. *Eight different families in three years. How can that be normal?*

In the far, right-hand corner, there was a small photograph of a poem found carved into the wall of the abandoned cabin. According to the tagline, it was believed to have been put there by one of the children.

"They knock three times," she read aloud. "Don't open the door. Once they come in, God sees you no more."

Ruby stared at the photograph as the lines of the simple poem rolled around in her thoughts. There was something about it that seemed both familiar and alien at the same time. And the longer the answer eluded her, the more significant it felt. Shaking her head, Ruby flipped the page and tried to dismiss the stray thought. But she couldn't. Reluctantly, she turned back to the poem, wanting to read more about the missing family. Bannock's cold, wet nose pressed against the bed-warmed skin of her arm and made her jump.

"You did that on purpose," she mumbled as she pushed him back.

Bannock nipped at her fingers. She snapped her hand back quickly, but his slobber still covered her skin. With a grimace, she wiped her hand off of the end of the bed. Bannock trotted around so he was closer and tried to chew on her again.

"What is with you?" she said before realizing how bright the fire had become.

Crawling off of the bed, she gently pushed him aside so she could look out of the window. The sky was darkening rapidly. Wind licked past the glass, carrying the snow until it looked like albino tentacles reaching out from an unseen monster. The walls rattled and groaned. And it was almost impossible to see the road anymore in the grayish fog. She had barely an hour left before night would swallow the world. *I really need to get a watch,* she thought as she snatched up her snowsuit and yanked it on over her pajamas. It was thick and cumbersome, and when everything was zipped into place, she couldn't lift her arms over her head and her stride was reduced to a swaying waddle. Struggling against the material, she pulled her hat into place, tied down the earflaps, and used her only scarf to cover any other bit of bare skin she could.

Despite all this, the first gust of wind ripped the air from her body. She barely made it a foot from the threshold before she was panting. With every blink, she could feel the moisture on her eyes begin to freeze over. Bannock followed, although resentfully, and his white fur was soon lost amongst the barreling snow.

Each exposed inch of skin froze and cracked, but the space protected by her suit began to swelter. Sweat beaded against her skin as she dragged the heavy jugs about to feed the dogs their evening meal. The sensation was in stark contrast to the few patches of unprotected skin that were brutally ravaged by the cold. Huddled in their houses, none of the dogs ventured out to meet her. As she packed the last items away, it occurred to her that she hadn't refilled the generator yet.

The snow attacked her skin like hail as she lumbered around to the side of the visitor's tent. The storm reduced it to barely more than a shadow against the gray. Shielding her eyes with one gloved hand, Ruby spotted the forest. She froze. The generator was only a few feet away, the wind lashed at her clothes, and her lungs were screaming but she couldn't bring herself to move. Before her, the trees lurked in the swirling fog. There, but not. And she didn't want to go anywhere near it. She could *feel* something within the haze. It was watching her. Waiting for her.

Leave, Ruby told herself. *Get back in the cabin.* But the thought of enduring the night without the floodlights pushed her forward. The hutch that housed the generator was small, and a snowdrift had already formed along the door. The pile looked insignificant but kept the door lodged in place as she tried to yank it open.

The sensation of being watched was back. Ruby snapped around, yet there was nothing to see but ice and snow. She yanked harder. The door remained in place, but she felt the phantom draw closer. The wind drove into her back hard enough to rock her forward. With every blink, she spotted something moving far off, playing through the shadows, creeping towards her. Falling to her knees, Ruby racked her hands into the snowdrift, clearing the space to shove the door wide.

Groping blindly in the space between the bulky generator and the hatch wall, she found the tank of gas and pulled it free, fumbling her gloved hand over the cap. A dark shadow streaked behind her. With a startled cry, she lurched to her feet and plastered her back to the wall of the tent. The tank slipped from her hand.

Gas bubbled out to drench the snow. *Shit,* Ruby dropped down. *No, no, no.* More of the precious liquid sloshed out as she fumbled with the tank. The generator, the van, the snowmobile; this was all she had to run them on until her next trip into town, and it was soaking into the snow at her feet. By the time she had the tank in her hands again, half of the gas was gone.

Her hands trembled with more than the cold as she lined up the nozzles and poured the remaining gas into the generator. It gargled down every drop and Ruby felt the empty weight of the gas can with a dizzying dismay. *Please, last the night,* she thought as she shook out the few remaining drops. The wind roared past her ears, working with the chill to make them ache. *How does it turn on?* Every part of her ached and throbbed, making it near impossible to think. Each time the answer loomed on the edge of her awareness, another shadow moved. Ruby jabbed at the button, driven on by growing need. *Pull the crank.* Her hand moved to follow the order. It had just touched the plastic when the streak passed her again. Something unseen slammed into the wall of the tent, creating a loud crack that could be heard over the wind. She screamed and lurched back. Sucking down each breath, she searched for what was out there with her. There was only white.

Her skin crawled, her heart hammered against her ribs, and the lack of a decent breath was making her dizzy. She yanked on the cord again, dragging it out with the force of her desperation. The machine shook, and grumbled for a moment and then became silent. All the while, the demons from her mind were returning. The cold made her sluggish and awkward as she yanked again. And again. Each time the generator promised to come to life and each time it failed. *Come on,* she begged. *Please, just turn over!*

The pressure at the back of her mind was too much to endure. The sound of material shredding cut through the gathering night. *Something's on the roof.* The thought struck her and her head snapped up. As she watched, a dark shape emerged over the edge of the building. Ruby lurched back. Her feet slipped out from under her and she fell hard against the snow, still clutching the crank handle. The generator roared and whined like a waking beast. Ruby didn't take her eyes off of the looming shape, didn't blink, but still lost sight of it as the floodlights turned on and bathed the area in a discolored glow. She tossed the can back inside, slammed the hatch door shut, and bolted for the safety of the cabin. Every step kicked up the powder-like snow. It caught on the wind and froze against her legs, slowing her even more. She didn't dare look behind her.

Bannock greeted her as she lumbered to the cabin door. Huge hunks of snow covered his fur as he hung his head low, his tail tucked between his legs, a deep growl rumbling up from his chest. He was staring at the roof of the tent. Reaching over him, Ruby pulled the screen door open. Bannock didn't break his gaze until the metal edge tapped his side. Then he whirled around and frantically clawed at the wood with both paws. Ruby's gloved hand smacked down on the handle. The second there was the slightest gap, Bannock slammed his body weight against it and shoved himself through.

Ruby threw herself in behind him, tripping in her haste and toppling onto the cabin floor. Warmth coiled around her, seeming to strip the last bit of energy from her bones. Dragging in deep breaths, she finally felt her lungs respond as the ice that encased them cracked. Curling in on herself, she sucked in the dry air, desperate for her head to stop spinning. The snow that clung to her began to melt. It dripped from her hat, ran in tiny streams down her legs, soaked into the layers of her scarf until it was impossible to breathe through the soggy material. Chest heaving and exhausted, she pushed herself up just enough to unwrap herself and toss her scarf, hat, and gloves to the side.

Steadily, warmth began to seep back into her bones and her thoughts took shape. *What was that thing?* Out of the hazy recesses of her mind, the poem came back to her. Reason wouldn't push it aside and she finally looked over her shoulder at the screen door. *They knock three times,* she recalled. Her eyes searched every inch of the screen until she admitted it to herself; it didn't have a lock. Her fingers felt thick and useless as she clawed at the shoelaces of her boot. Under a layer of snow, the material had stiffened up and her nails nearly snapped before she could rip them free.

Without it, the boot flopped against her foot as she rushed back to the door. Her fingers were beginning to go numb by the time she finished looping one end around the handle of the screen door. Quickly, she pulled the wood door closed and used the free end to do the same thing in turn. One final tug and the two were securely tethered. Since the screen door opened out and the wood door in, the shoelace insured that opening one would keep the other closed.

Feeling slightly less crazed, Ruby shut the door. She slid the flimsy lock into place and jammed the chair back under the handle. It didn't help shake the image of the figure watching her. She yanked the curtains tightly closed. But it was Bannock that finally dimmed her crackling panic. He was lounging by the fire, too lazy to lift his head as he watched her move about. Ruby felt empty as she stripped off her suit, restocked the fire, and turned off the overhead light. *I'm not worried*, she told herself repeatedly. *But I'm not going out there again.*

Chapter 7

Three sharp knocks jerked Ruby awake. She blinked, her mind as sluggish and slow as her eyelids. As she stared at the far wall, the world gradually sunk back into awareness. The fire had burnt out from its previous blaze into simmering embers. If it weren't for the numerous cracks and drafts, the room would have been stifling. Ruby remembered her desperation to shake off the memory of the figure she had seen. So she had put the history books aside for the night and returned her attention to her novel. She could remember reading, her eyelids growing heavy. Warmth and a full stomach and Bannock snoozing by the fire. Somewhere along the way, she must have fallen asleep. Her mind snapped into focus when she heard it again. Three hard strikes. Someone was knocking on the door.

Ruby bolted upright. In the dim light, the door seemed far larger than it ever had before. Something dark and monstrous. Dread sloshed in her stomach. She couldn't pinpoint why she felt so exposed until she noticed the bottomless abyss beyond the curtain. And the silence. The steady hum of the generator was gone. *Why are the floodlights off?* The thought screamed inside her skull and held her frozen in place. The knocking came again.

Tap.

Tap.

Tap.

Each one separated from the others by a long pause. She flinched with every blow. Then there was nothing. Nothing beyond the howl of the wind and the groan of the shivering trees. *Someone's knocking on the door.* It sounded so simple when she thought the words. But it made no sense. Not here. Not now. This time it made her heart squeeze.

Slowly, she loosened her feet free of the sleeping bags and stood up. Teeth nipped at her ankle. With a choked yelp, she lunged back up, the mattress bouncing and the box springs creaking. On all fours, she inched forward and peered over the edge. Bannock's head poked out from under the bed. He blinked up at her, ears flat, head low. A pitiful whimper worked its way out of his throat before he wiggled back out of sight. Ruby was struck with the sudden, intense urge to follow him. She couldn't place why, and that confusion left her still until a voice called to her.

"Excuse me, miss." It was soft and unassuming. Smooth like polished stone. And hearing it made her stomach twist up so tightly that she almost gagged. "We need to use the bathroom. Can we come in?"

Ruby started at the door, unable to reply even if she had wanted to. The request was too surreal. And it took her a moment to realize what was wrong with it. It didn't rise and fall as it should. There wasn't any inflection. Just a single, unchanged monotone that sent a cluster of spiders skittering down her back.

"Miss?"

"There isn't a bathroom in here," she forced herself to reply.

The effort left her breathless, as if every last molecule of oxygen had been stripped from the room within an instant. Her hands clenched at the bed sheets and she sucked at the air, trying to get her lungs to work once more. There was only silence as she strained against her body. Then, as if she had never spoken, the voice came again.

"Excuse me, miss. We need to use the phone. Can we come in?"

Her jaw clenched shut until her teeth ached. She didn't know who was standing outside her door. She didn't know why. But she knew with unwavering certainty that she didn't want them inside. Nor did she want them to know that she didn't have a way to contact the outside world. Still, a reply boiled up inside her, rolling like sludge up her throat to press behind her teeth. She bit her lip to keep it back. Droplets of blood swelled across her tongue, but she kept her silence.

All the while, however, her body had been moving. Her skin felt clammy and cold as she inched her way off of the bed. She shivered against the sensation as her foot pressed down on the floor. Without thought, without permission, her legs began to carry her across the room. Dragging her closer to the door even as she longed to cower away. The emerging flutters of panic that filled her chest cavity were made all the stronger as Bannock began to whimper behind her. She managed to glance over her shoulder, trying to catch sight of him again. But he remained in his hiding spot, far out of view, with only his sniveling mewls to let her know he was there at all. It was fear in that sound that made her pause.

"Excuse me, miss. We need to use the phone. Can we come in?"

The repetition came in that same tranquil monotone that somehow still managed to rise, crisp and clear, over the growling storm. Despite her mind screaming for her to do the exact opposite, Ruby took the last few steps. She stood there, staring at the chair that held the door in place. *Don't touch it. Don't answer. Don't open the door!* Still, she found herself reaching out with trembling hands. The chair legs scraped across the floor as she slid it free. Bannock whimpered, his high-pitched protests marked by his nails skittering against the floorboards. He was pushing himself further back under the bed. She could hear him cowering into the far corner. Still, she couldn't stop herself, her fingertips from rising. The latch was cool to the touch as she slowly slid it open. *Don't let them in!* Ice pressed out from her core, melting against her now overheated skin to create a sensation that left her dizzy.

The door handle didn't feel real as she cradled it in her palm. The sharp clack of the metal latch working jarred her from her thoughts. Slowly, she inched open the door. Snowflakes poured inside, carried on a rampaging wind that pushed back her hair, ravaged her neck, and slithered through the gaps in her knitted socks. Then the door pulled against her grip and the screen door rattled. She had forgotten about the shoelace. With its slack used up, the screen door pulled against its frame and the wooden door was kept in place, open only a few inches. It was more than enough for the arctic breeze to slap her in the face. Startled, she sucked in a full, rich breath and blinked out into the darkness.

Ruby's lungs squeezed tight at the sight of the child standing on the doorstep. Firelight spilled through the gap to drench the stranger's feet and creep up his legs. But it never rose high enough to illuminate his head fully. Light gray shadows covered his shoulders and the lower half of his downturned face. But, with the hood of his sweater pulled up, everything beyond the tip of his nose hid under a cluster of impenetrable darkness. Ruby's stomach twisted and churned, the contents becoming as thick as tar. She swallowed, working down the lump as it lurched its way up.

It took her a moment to place even one reason why the child's presence would provoke such a strong reaction. All she could come up with was his clothes. A loose hooded sweater, a thin pair of jeans, a worn pair of sneakers. None of it could offer him any kind of protection against the elements, yet it didn't seem to affect him at all. The little boy, who could barely pass for being any older than eleven, just stood there as if the wind and snow barely touched him. Then she noticed his skin.

Pale and pallid, and didn't carry a single line, smooth as plastic. More like a mask coating his features than like living flesh. The boy didn't move. Not so much as a flinch or a shiver. Ruby found herself watching his chest, waiting for the rise and fall of his breathing. She stared. She waited. But she could never tell if he was actually breathing.

"Excuse me, miss."

Her attention snapped to the boy's face. She watched it move. Observed as each sound passed his lips. Never once did his lips, or his skin, or any single feature of his face move like they should.

"We need to use the phone. Can we come in?"

The same words. The same monotone. And it was as if her mind was slowly shutting down. Her fingers shifted against the handle. They caught on the shoelace tied between the doors, making the wood door sway and the screen shutter. The sound rattled between them. The little boy didn't move.

"Can we come in?"

As if this was a signal they had been waiting for, two figures took a step towards the cabin door to emerge from the murky depths of the night. Just like the boy, they both stood with their faces turned to the floor. And like him, neither of them was dressed for the cold. Ruby could only use their size to guess at their ages. The one on the boy's right looked to be a girl and couldn't have been any older than four. She too had a thin hoodie, this one a faded pink. Long curls of platinum white hair slipped out around her neck. It was upon noticing that her bare toes were the same flawless shade as the rest of her, that Ruby realized they didn't have hues or tones. Every bit of their skin that she could see was the exact same shade. *Like living dolls.* The thought passed through her head as she shifted her gaze to the girl on the boy's left.

She looked to be around seven, perhaps a little older. The beanie she wore had two long tassels that drifted in the wind. Her hair was arranged into one neat braid and her arms, exposed under the short sleeves of her t-shirt, remained stone still at her sides as the snow gathered against them. From the little she could see of their faces, both shared the boy's unnatural humanity.

Ruby was blindsided with the sudden urge to fling the door wide open and bundle the children up from the cold. As if sensing her reaction, all three of the children took another step closer. It brought the boy further into the light while the two girls remained obscured by the shadows. The proximity made her stumble back, a profound sense of primal dread burrowing down into her bone marrow. An electric snap of red-hot fear sliced Ruby in two when she noticed that their new position also barred the door. She was trapped. *Don't let them come in,* a voice whispered in the back of her mind. *Close the door, now!*

"Where did you come from?" The question had trembled from Ruby's lips before she realized that she had spoken.

Without lifting their faces to look at her, all three children raised their left arms and pointed with bare fingers to some far off point. Ruby's eyes flicked to the side, but there was nothing to see in the encroaching darkness. She turned back to the children. Her jaw clenched around a startled cry when she found that they had edged closer again. The little boy was now only a breath away from the decrepit screen door. It seemed as if all he had to do was touch it and it would crumble away.

"Are you Peter's nephew?" she asked.

All three lowered their arms and kept their eyes fixed onto the ground. They remained silent.

"Where are your parents?"

It was the little boy that answered. "Excuse me, miss. We need to use the phone. Can we come in?"

Ruby let out a shaky breath. "What are your names?"

Once again, only the boy answered. "We need to use the phone. Can we come in?"

"It's late and cold. You should go home."

"We need to use the phone," the boy replied, his voice louder than it had been before. "Can we come in?"

"You can all tell Peter that this was a good prank. You really scared me. But you need to go home now. And tell him to turn the floodlights back on, please."

It was all she could think to say. Without the lights, it was possible for her neighbor to park his car even within a few inches from the cabin and she would never see it. And this wouldn't be the first time she had been the butt of someone's joke. There was only one glaring problem with her theory. And that was the children. They weren't natural. She could feel it, pressing on the back of her mind, screaming through her veins and vibrating through her bones. There was something very wrong with these children.

When the boy repeated his line, she found her fingers squeezing the door handle. Every bit of her urged to slam the door closed, and she tried to do it. Her arm trembled with the strain, her knuckles turned white and throbbed with her heartbeat, but she couldn't do it. She couldn't move. Unable to move her eyes off of the little boy, she could still hear Bannock's growl. It was both terrified and savage at the same time. Her heart thundered and hot tears burned the corners of her eyes. *Don't let them in! Don't let them in! Don't let them in!* The thought filled her head to drown out the boy's voice.

"No."

"Miss–"

"You can't come in," her voice cracked around each word. It hurt to speak. "Go home."

She threw every ounce of her concentration into closing the door. Finally, her body listened. The children noticed the movement. They snapped their heads up in unison. Ruby froze, her hand fumbling from the door as she stumbled back. Their eyes were pools of liquid onyx. No whites. No rings of color. Just a sheet of slick obsidian set within their artificial faces.

"You have to let us in," the boy said firmly.

His eyes consumed her mind. They swam through her head and chased off all other thoughts before they had time to form. There was a vague twinge of pain from her battered shin as she stepped forward. She felt the material of her pajama shirt slide against her shoulder as she lifted her hand. The cool metal bit against her sweat-slicked palm as she closed her fingers around it. Ruby felt it all but none of it had any meaning. Black eyes held her captive as she pressed down on the handle. A soft click sounded and the children pushed forward expectantly.

Shifting closer, Ruby's side caught the shoestring. The screen door smacked against its frame while the wood door slammed into her back. A spike of pain snapped out across her hips as the handle collided against her spine. Flinching, the moment of pain cleared Ruby's mind of the ebony fog. She hurled herself back, her body moving more like a marionette. *He did that,* her mind screamed. *He made me do that. How did he do that?* She pattered against the door and pulled out to the side. Catching herself before she fell, Ruby clutched the door with both hands and pulled back to keep the screen in place.

"What are you?" she choked, her eyes flickering between the three creatures before her.

They remained silent. Watching her with unblinking, hideous eyes.

"What are you?!"

They stared at her, trying to catch her gaze. She could feel their presence pulling and slashing at the edges of her mind, trying to claw their way back in.

"Go away."

"You have to let us in," the boy's voice was louder. Stronger.

Ruby shook her head, eyes on the floor.

"You have to let us in!"

Her mind was starting to crack under their assault. Bit by bit, they were seeping inside and her hand began to lift once again, drawing closer to the door handle. With the last ounces of her mental strength, she resisted the magnetic pull long enough to grab the edge of the interior door. Ruby slammed it closed. Without their eyes upon her, it was easier to think.

The boy screamed, his voice rising to a shrill, ear-splitting noise. He pounded on the door, demanding she let them in, the same words taking on a more piercing tone with each rendition. It drove into her skull like molten spikes and her knees buckled under the strain. Snatching up the chair, she crammed it back under the handle and lodged it in place.

"Leave me alone!" Ruby screamed. "You're not allowed in!"

Within a split second, it all stopped. The endless pounding. The shrieking demands. There were only the wind and her sobbed breaths to break the silence. Falling to her knees, Ruby pulled herself over to the fireplace. She restocked it, adding log after log until the blazing glow destroyed the shadows within the cabin. With her back to the fire, she hugged her knees to her chest, her eyes darting from the door to the window. They were the only two points of entry. *Which one would they come through?*

A panicked yelp cracked from her as light suddenly streamed in through the curtains. She started at it. Waiting. Breathless. It took a long moment for her to realize that a soft hum had added itself to the night. The light wasn't a threat but the floodlights coming back on were. Curiosity pulled her to her feet and she crept closer to the window. She pulled up the very edge of the curtain and peeked out. The storm raged on, filling the air with tiny specks of white. She couldn't see anything beyond that.

With the light pouring inside, the doors locked, and the flames burning away the chill, her adrenaline slowly ebbed away. Exhaustion pressed down on her until she could almost feel her bones crushing under the weight. She had never felt so tired. So completely and utterly drained.

Curling up on her bed, Ruby tried to make some kind of sense out of what had just happened. There had to be an explanation, an avenue, an excuse that would offer her some comfort. But she could only find two points that made her breathe easy, and she didn't know if they should even do that. The first was that the dogs were barking. Every so often, she could hear a sleep mumble or a lazy yap, but they were there, and they weren't afraid. The second came when Bannock pulled himself free from under the bed. With a little whine, he crawled up onto the mattress and pressed up against her side. She drew him into a tight hug and stared at the wall until the sun rose.

Chapter 8

A lifetime passed before the sun inched above the horizon. Ruby watched as light seeped around the edges of the curtains and painted the walls with a pinkish hue. The encounter with the children hadn't left her mind for a second. But with repetition came doubts. She questioned everything she had seen and felt. It all swelled within her mind, the sharp edges of fear dulling as she ground it against logic and reason. By the time the light hit the floor, she had convinced herself that it must have all been a prank. *What the hell is Peter's problem?* she asked the question over and over until anger simmered under her skin.

Throwing the sleeping bag off of her, she pulled herself into her snowsuit and washed her face, a plan forming in her mind. The moment she had finished her morning chores, she would go confront Peter and tell him to keep his relatives out of the yard. Her bravado wavered as she removed her chair barricade, but she clenched her teeth against it and held tight to her frustration.

The blistering cold smacked her in the face as she trudged out into the half foot of snow that blanketed the earth. Rounding the corner of the tent, she was almost among the dogs before she saw it. The gaping hole in the wire mesh of the playpen fence. Running as fast as the snow and suit would allow, she searched the pen, the yard and forest beyond, but she couldn't catch a glimpse of either Nugget or Echo. She hesitated when she reached the gaping hole and spotted the blood that tipped the broken wire. Taking care not to touch the sharp barbs, she slipped through the space and hurried towards the doghouse, calling for the two pups with growing desperation. Blood spattered the ground, discolored and dulled under the layers of snow. There was so much blood. And each breath of wind stirred the snow to expose more. But there was no sign of the dogs.

"Nugget!"

Her breath misted before her as she spun in tight circles, scanning every inch of the frozen land around her.

"Echo!"

The other dogs skulked in their houses and refused to move beyond poking their heads out. Without them, a crushing, unnatural silence hung over the world. Not knowing what else to do, Ruby called for the dogs again. Her voice echoed off the trees and rolled unanswered into oblivion. *Wolves.* The thought came into her mind, followed by the full force of reason, but she couldn't bring herself to believe it. *The kids.* Her blood thickened into ice with the certainty that came with the notion. She had worked hard to convince herself that it had all been a prank. That they had simply been having some harmless fun at her expense. But harmless children don't brutalize puppies.

Focus, Ruby told herself as her brain scattered into a thousand thoughts at once. *Feed the dogs. Then go to Peter. Tell him what's going on. He'll help you find Nugget and Echo.* With a course to follow, she felt on firmer ground and rushed to feed the rest of the pack. She checked each one of them carefully as she went. They were all scared but uninjured.

Grappling for excuses, she told herself that it was possible Nugget and Echo had caught a rabbit or some other small creature. Maybe that was where the blood had come from. It was possible the children had only cut the wire. She didn't believe a word of it, but it was easier to deal with than the other ideas that filled her mind. Bannock huddled with some of the others, watching her closely but not daring to follow her around like he had the day before. It was that change that scared Ruby the most. When she grabbed the van keys, she made sure to get the gun as well. It felt heavy. A lot heavier than it had been just a few days ago. Forcing herself to go slowly, carefully, she loaded the poppers into the barrel, the way Aaron had taught her. After a moment of hesitation, she shoved a few real slugs into one of her outer pockets and left the cabin.

Keeping the barrel trained on the ground, she hurried to the van. Ice had accumulated around the edges overnight and it cracked as she pried the door open. It was colder inside than out. She was barely in the driver's seat when she turned the key. The engine didn't make a sound.

"No," she begged on a whisper as she tried again. Nothing. No matter how many times she cranked the keys or pleaded, the engine wouldn't turn over. Slipping out of the car, Ruby bit her lips and tried to think.

"The snowmobile!"

Finding it was easy, but turning it on proved impossible. Ruby rambled and muttered under her breath as she struggled to understand what she was doing wrong. Her heart was slamming around her chest when she finally located the problem. The gas tank was empty. On a broken shutter, the last traces of warmth left her body. The gas. She had used some of it and wasted the rest. She was stranded. She wouldn't have the lights tonight.

Think, she commanded herself as she clawed at her head with one hand, the other tight around the butt of the shotgun. *Calm down and think. Peter. He'll help find the dogs. He has a car. Maybe gas too. And he owes you for his little joke. So start walking.*

The miles ahead felt like an insurmountable distance, but she didn't have a choice. She needed help and it was the only way to get it. Gripping the shotgun with both hands, she headed back out into the yard, feeling like each step was increasing the distance she had left to go. Pausing at the gate, the forest still and the clouds gathering, she checked her weapon again. The shotgun felt clunky and strange in her hand but she wasn't going to let go of it. Her voice cracked as she called Bannock to come with her. He hesitated but obeyed. *Just get to Peter,* she told herself as the once energetic dog kept close to her side. *Just keep walking and everything will be fine.*

***

Hours passed but she never seemed to get any closer. She kept to the middle of the road. Partly because the higher peak helped her avoid the deeper pitfalls of the snow, but mostly because she wanted to be able to see anything creeping up on her. Over time, however, even walking through the thinner layer of snow grew difficult and painful. Ruby kept trudging forward, her muscles tight and her feet throbbing. The whole time, Bannock had never strayed far from her side. His eyes never stopped searching the thick forest that crowded in on either side of them. Every so often, he would hesitate, nose lifting to sniff at the stray scents in the air. It didn't matter how many times he did it; her heart stopped each time. Even with the sun high, dark shadows still lurked amongst the tree trunks. In those moments, it didn't matter how much space there was around her. She still couldn't breathe. But then Bannock would lower his head and look at her as if pleading to go home. She would tighten her grip on the shotgun and force them forward.

The gun was getting unbearably heavy and the cold had invaded her every cell by the time she finally caught a glimpse of Peter's cabin. It was all the motivation she needed to pick up her pace again, ignoring the stings and protests of her body. But as they neared, the air shifted and the noises of the wildlife fell away. The now familiar sensation of nothingness made her freeze midstride. With wide eyes, she looked around. Just like all the times before, she couldn't find what had scared the animals into silence. Ruby pried one hand off the shotgun and reached down, allowing Bannock to nestle his nose against her gloved palm. The reassurance was enough to make her continue. Slowly. Carefully. Her eyes darting around with every step.

The towering trees pulled back, opening into a little meadow that hugged a large dark wood cabin and dog yard. Just like her own pack, the dogs had gone into hiding. They cowered within their tiny boxes, their chains softly rattling as she passed. Bannock whimpered and shifted closer until his fur brushed against her leg. Her breath misted, obscuring her vision as she followed the stone lined path to the front door, the pristine snow crunching under the soles of her shoes with every step.

"Peter?" she called, her voice crackling with the nerves that budded against her chest. "Are you here?"

The cabin steps groaned under her weight as she climbed up on the porch. The front door was ajar.

"Peter?"

Bannock whined as he lowered his head, the scruff of his neck rising as his tail slipped between his legs. Ruby swallowed thickly before calling for Peter again. Just like before, it went unanswered. Barely able to bring herself to do it, she reached up with one hand and pressed it against the door. That was all it took to force it open. In the hush, the slight gasp of the hinges sounded louder than a scream. She flinched back.

As the gap widened, she could see directly into his darkened living room. The sunlight crept in and gleamed off of the small pools of blood. Trembling, Ruby went down the stairs, her eyes locked on the crimson liquid that streaked across the floorboards and splashed the walls. The wind shifted and the faintest traces of rot drifted out of the depths of the house. Gasping for air, Ruby jerked around, sure that something was rushing up to grab her. But only the empty air met her.

Sunlight glistened off the windshield of his truck. The sharp glare hit her eyes and snapped her thoughts into action. *Find Peter. Get the keys. Get help.* Flimsy plan in place, she shifted her grip on the shotgun and slipped across the threshold, Bannock reluctantly at her heels. The floorboards creaked as she moved. While the cold slowed the effects of decay, the walls had trapped the stench enough to make it roll her stomach. Bile burned the back of her throat as she crept deeper into the living room.

"Peter? Are you okay?"

Shut up! her mind screamed at her. *What if they're still here?* The lie she had forced herself to believe was destroyed, leaving her with only the certainty she had felt last night. While they looked like children, they were anything but human.

Three steps more and the hunks of flesh became impossible to miss. They were scattered everywhere, little moist chunks clinging to the floor and furniture, each radiating out from a place beyond the edge of the couch. Ruby shifted one trembling leg forward, careful to avoid the pools of fluid, and pushed up onto her toes to look over the high back. A corpse was sprawled out across the floor rug, limbs severed from the torso, ribs bone pale and bared by the mangled meat of its chest.

Screaming uncontrollably, Ruby threw herself back. Her foot hit one of the puddles of slop and she toppled onto her back. The shotgun crashed against her hips but she refused to let it go. Bannock scattered around her, his barks savage and wild. She scrambled to her feet, unable to breathe beyond her whimpers. *Keys, keys, keys.* The word screamed in her head and she clung to it as her last point of sanity. She needed to get out. Get away. Just run.

Barreling into the kitchen, she searched the counters. Nothing. She ran to the door, frantically shoving her hands into the pockets of the hanging jackets. Tears boiled against her eyes only to freeze as they hit the air. *Keys. Keys. Keys. The children are here. They killed him. Run!* In her panic, Ruby couldn't remember when or where she found the keys to the truck. They were just suddenly in her hand, sharp points gouging her palm as she clutched them tightly. *Run!*

Only a short distance separated the door from the truck, but sweat still beaded against her skin as she hurled the door open. She dragged herself inside, waiting the heartbeat it took for Bannock to follow before she slammed the door shut and locked it.

"Please start," she sobbed as her trembling hands turned the key.

The engine roared to life, growling steadily as the metal frame rattled around her. Throwing it into gear, she smashed her foot on the pedal, refusing to let up as the truck skidded around the curves of the road. They bucked, lurched, and left the road more than once, but she didn't pay any attention. Not until they hit an unseen pothole and something heavy thudded against her legs.

Glancing down, she met the cold dead gaze of Peter's severed head.

Chapter 9

"His head was in the car!" Ruby screamed at the police officer standing before her. "That isn't the work of an animal. It was those kids!"

The officer held up his hand. The gesture told her more than all of the twists and scrunches of his face could. She slumped and tried to catch her breath. In her mind, she was telling the story from start to finish in a clear and precise manner. But it didn't matter what it sounded like in her head when everything that came out of her mouth was a hysterical shriek.

"Where is his head?"

She closed her eyes. "I tossed it out the window. I was terrified. I've never seen a dead body before. I wasn't thinking straight."

Again, he lifted his hand and she bit her lips to stop her babbling. The hospital lights were too bright. They burned her eyes as she sat on the examination table, her paper gown crinkling each time she moved. Peter's blood had been all over the back of her jacket and pants and they had been collected as evidence. A nurse was quickly scraping Ruby's nails in search for more.

"Tell me about these kids again."

"They killed him! They took Nugget and Echo! What else is there to tell?"

His voice was a slow, crisp drawl. Ruby remembered people telling her that it was supposed to be calming. Right now, it only added to the tension that twisted like snakes under her skin.

"Take a breath. We're going to sort all of this out," the officer said.

That was a statement he repeated a lot. By now, she knew he wasn't going to continue unless she took an exaggerated breath. Pressing her heels against the side of the examination table, she heaved her shoulders.

"Good. Now, I am going to help you, but I need you to answer my questions first, okay?"

"Okay," she mumbled. For once, the sound of her voice matched the tone in her head.

"Now, you said there were three children?"

She nodded. "A boy and two girls."

"And what time did they arrive at the cabin?"

"I don't know. Late. Or really early. It was during the storm if that helps."

The man paused and tapped his pen against the top of his notepad. She flinched at every thud. Neither of them spoke again until the nurse left the room.

"You left three children alone, in the woods, during a snowstorm?"

Ruby stammered, "They weren't really kids."

"What were they?"

"How am I supposed to know that?" she snapped before she could stop herself.

"You said they were kids."

"Well, I meant that they *looked* like kids."

"But they weren't?"

"No."

He arched an eyebrow and tapped his pen again. "What were they then?"

"I don't know," she spat each word. "Demons, maybe? Ghosts? Enough people have gone missing out there that even the grass is probably haunted."

"Ghosts?" he said slowly.

"Their eyes were black. Completely black. How is that possible?"

"A trick of the light? You said it was dark."

"No," she shook her head. "I know what I saw."

"Three children alone in the middle of the night."

Ruby stared at him for a long moment, fruitlessly studying his face. "You don't believe me, do you?"

"I believe that you think you saw something."

"Think?" she said. "They ripped Peter's head off!"

"If it were the kids," he said, the pace of his voice slowing again. "That means that they left you alone, traveled for miles in a blizzard, and attacked someone twice their size and strength. That doesn't make sense, does it?"

"Murdering someone doesn't make any sense to me," she said. Tensing her fingers around the edge of the examination table, she released a long, strained sigh. Her next thought made her straighten again. "I didn't invite them in."

"Yes, you mentioned that."

"They kept asking me to invite them in. I refused. But maybe Peter didn't."

"He was a good man."

Catching the officer's eyes, she silently pleaded for him to understand. "Maybe they can't come in without permission."

"Like a vampire?"

She rolled the question over in her head even as she knew it was no use. There was no way for her to tell if he was mocking her or asking for clarification.

"Maybe," she stammered meekly. "They did try and force me into it."

"It's not consent if they trick you into it."

"Haven't you ever watched T.V? Like the ghost hunter shows? They always have cases of people getting possessed because demons tricked them into it."

"You believe those shows are real?"

Her mouth dropped open, but the words didn't come out until a heartbeat later. "I know this is real. Those *things* that visited me last night were real. And they killed Peter."

"And went through all the trouble to put his head in his truck?"

With that question, she was sure that he was mocking her. It didn't matter. Her brain was already making the connections. The shadows that had scared her last night. That hadn't been an accident or a trick of her mind. They wanted her to waste the gas. So she couldn't run the generator. So she couldn't use the snowmobile that was supposed to be full but wasn't. They had limited her options until she had to go to Peter.

"Oh, my God," she whispered. "I told them to go to Peter. I told them that he was there."

"They're children, Ruby. You understand that, right?" the officer snapped. "You left children to die in the woods because you watch too much T.V."

"No!"

"Yes. We've got a search party out and you best start praying they find those kids alive. Because if they don't, I'm holding you personally responsible."

She balled her hands into fists and clenched her jaw. "And what about Peter? Are you blaming me for that, too?"

"We're still trying to sort all of this out. But I told you. Odds are it was a hungry wolf."

Ruby lowered her gaze in defeat. "Can you help me look for Nugget and Echo?"

"The dogs? Three kids are out there possibly suffering from hypothermia and you're worried about the dogs?"

"Those kids," she struggled around the word, "took them. If we find the dogs, we might find them."

Ruby stared at his pen as it tapped against the notepad. His breath came heavily through his nose, like a snorting bull.

"Right now, you need to stay here," he said slowly.

"I'm not hurt."

"But you're evidence," he said. "We're searching your cabin too. You can stay in a hotel tonight."

"What? No. I can't leave the dogs. They'll kill them."

He snorted again.

"Please. I can't let them get hurt," she added quickly.

"An officer will be out there. In case the kids come back."

Ruby clenched her jaw as she held the man's eyes. "You better tell them not to answer the door."

Chapter 10

The replacement clothes they had given her were in good condition but were useless against the biting cold. They had let her leave the hospital room but not the building itself. The furthest she was allowed to go was a bench just inside the sliding glass door. To keep her calm, they had allowed Bannock in that far. Hour after hour, she had buried her hands in his fur. The thick tuffs slipped through her fingers but it couldn't remove the physical memory of Peter's head against her palm. Even now, it felt like she was holding the dead weight.

Police officers came and went, all asking her questions but none of them believing the answers she gave. As far as she could tell, they had reached the conclusion that she was a weak little girl who was a long way from home and had made a very foolish decision. She couldn't argue with any of it, although she knew her 'foolish decision' was different from what they were thinking. Those monsters had gone to Peter because of her. Because she told them to. She should have shot them.

As the sun began to set, the first officer she had talked to, Mark, came to see her again. She could feel his disgust radiating from him in waves. In his eyes, she had, intentionally or not, murdered three children. She sobbed with relief when he told her that she was no longer a suspect in Peter's death. He went on to explain why. Something about the state of the vehicles in the yard, the snow piled around them, and Peter's time of death. Ruby understood the general idea, she lacked the skill set necessary to survive a storm like that on foot, but the rest was lost on her. It didn't matter how hard she tried to focus, all of her thoughts returned to images of Peter's mangled corpse. When he told her she could go back to the yard, she quickly surged to her feet.

"You'll help me get them to town? Can we look for the pups?"

Mark's eyes narrowed. "I'm not helping you do anything. We still haven't found the kids. So, as a Hail Mary, I'm going to light a bonfire and hope they see it."

She didn't try to hide the horror that played across her face. "You're going to lure them back to the dogs?"

"You know, not one of Peter's dogs was injured. Seems more like you hurt the pups, not the scared and abandoned children."

Ruby hugged herself tightly, but it did nothing to fight off the chill in her bones. "They're not kids."

"You know what? You really should stay with me at the yard tonight. It'll be good for you to see that it's just a bunch of trees. You need to accept reality."

She looked up at him. "I don't want to go out there again. I want to bring the dogs here, where it's safe."

Mark gestured to the door. "Too late now. We'll barely get out there before sundown. And I'm not making two trips. So, you can either come with me or spend the night at the local hotel."

Bannock butted against her thigh and the decision was made. She couldn't leave the dogs. Mark didn't speak a single word to her for the length of the trip and Ruby was grateful for it. She stared out the window, her heart hammering within her chest, each beat shuddering through her veins. The shadows were starting to rise again and the pink sunset made the snow glow. Ruby scrambled out the second he brought his truck to a stop. It was only as her feet hit the earth that she remembered.

"I needed gas for the generator."

Mark didn't look at her but lifted a small metal tank out of the bed of his truck. It looked to be just enough to keep the lights on for the night.

"What about my shotgun?"

"I'm not giving you a gun," he said.

"What?"

"I'm not arming a girl that can't tell the difference between reality and T.V."

"What if a wolf comes?" she demanded.

"I have my sidearm." He jabbed a finger at her over the bed of the truck. "You're not going to touch it."

Ruby didn't bother to stay and argue. There was too much to do. Her replacement shoes slid over her feet as she raced around the yard, gathering the dogs one by one, bringing them into the limited space of the cabin.

The sun was kissing the horizon by the time she got the last one inside. Mark had spent his time creating a massive pillar out of long hunks of wood. He lit it as she passed. One spark and a ghastly whoosh, and the flames shot up above her head, crackling embers spitting off to dance across the sky.

Stocking the fire, he watched her carefully as she ran to his van and collected the gas tank. The sensation of being watched clawed at her back as she moved for the generator. She couldn't tell if Mark was enticing the sensation or if it were the others. Without hesitation, she yanked the cord. The generator rattled and the floodlights switched on to drive back the encroaching night. The sun was nothing more than a gilded line stretched out atop the treetops. And it was rapidly fading. Her fingers touched the door handle just as the last rays of daylight died.

Despite the cramped conditions, the dogs clustered together, each one seeking to be as far from the door as possible. The light of the bonfire pressed against the windows and Ruby used it to start one of her own. Only as the heat began to push against her, did she allow herself to acknowledge the agony the cold had drawn from her skin.

The screen door slammed. Ruby snatched up a chunk of wood and held it tight as she whirled to the noise.

"Easy," Mark said. "It's just me."

The flames of his raging fire framed him as he stood in the doorway, the orange glow slashing into the darkness just to be beaten back again. She shuddered.

"Lock the door," she told him. "And keep your gun close."

***

Ruby's head jerked up as a few dogs let out a disgruntled grumble. The traces of her waking nightmare vanished as she watched Mark work his way towards the door.

"Where are you going?" Ruby asked.

Mark didn't bother to look at her as he continued stepping over the dogs. "I need to restock the bonfire."

"You can't go out there," she snapped as she scooted off the edge of the bed.

"There is nothing out there," he said.

"Yet."

He rose one hand to her. "It'll take five minutes. You can stay here. Or maybe use the bathroom. You've been obviously uncomfortable for a while."

Ruby contemplated that for a moment, weighing her options against her mounting need. Most of the night had passed without sight or sound of them. It was possible they were gone. They had their victim. And with the roaring bonfire and an armed officer, the prospect was tempting.

"Okay," she mumbled.

"I promise not to come back in until you're done," he said.

Ruby hesitantly followed him through the doorway, her eyes darting around the shadows. Taking a deep breath, she ran into the snow. Her borrowed boots did so little against the cold that it felt like she was barefoot. The wind whipped against her, cutting through her jacket and slicing to her core. She ignored it as she rounded the tent and found the outhouse.

In record time, she was done and running back to the cabin when the floodlight clicked off. By the light of the bonfire, she spotted Mark, his face upturned as if he was trying to pinpoint the problem by sight.

"Run!" she screamed as she barreled into him.

Her hands clawed at his arm, her momentum making him stumble.

"Get back in the cabin, now!"

Refusing to move, he slipped his arm out of her grip and peered into the shadows.

"It's just the generator. I'll check it out."

"No!"

She latched onto his arm again, tugging and shoving until he was forced to take a step. As he began to stagger forward, she raced ahead, urging him on. The glow of the cabin called to her as she wrenched open the screen door and looked behind her.

"Come on! Hurry!"

Mark took a few more steps before he paused. Brow wrinkling, he looked over his shoulder, back towards the tent.

"Do you hear that?"

"No," she snapped without thought. "Please, Mark. Just get in here."

He held up his hand to silence her and started towards the tent. Drifting behind the bonfire, the flames hid him from view. Ruby waited, bouncing restlessly on numb feet, her eyes locked on the other side of the bonfire. He didn't emerge. The fire crackled. Her breath misted. The dogs behind her whimpered. Still, Mark didn't come back into sight.

A scream shattered the calm. Made of pure fear, it cracked her chest open and gnawed at her heart. Ruby bolted forward, her feet crunching through the snow. It only took her a moment to get to the other side of the bonfire, but Mark was already gone. Panting hard, she glanced around, trying to catch sight of him again. The snow had been disturbed, broken by something being dragged through. She followed the trail to the rim of light. Something stirred within the darkness. The screaming had stopped but bounced off the trees until it sounded as if it was coming from everywhere at once. His hands emerged from the shadows, clutching at handfuls of earth, trying to bring himself forward as he was dragged back.

"Mark!"

A few feet still separated them when a gunshot cracked. Ducking back, she raised her hands to protect her head as the stray bullet drove through the wood above the cabin door. With a thick, wet squish, blood gushed over the pristine snow. Mark's scream died instantly, leaving only the crackling fire to break the silence.

Then footsteps thundered towards her.

Ruby spun on her heel and bolted back towards the cabin. The snow crunched behind her, drawing closer with every second. It didn't matter that they had started with a vast distance between them. The separating space was dwindling as she struggled with her cumbersome snow clothes. As she neared the cabin, she could hear them following only inches behind.

91

Ruby flung herself towards the cabin. Tiny hands latched onto her clothes, the thin material tearing apart as she forced herself over the threshold. Toppling down, she fell onto a few of the dogs that couldn't move out of the way. The screen door slammed back into place and she crawled forward, frantically looking over her shoulder.

The three children stood just beyond the door. Framed by the lapping flames, fresh blood dripping from their tiny fingers. Their eyes were bottomless pits like gaping holes within their skulls. They looked as if they had just climbed out of the bowels of hell. As motionless as stone, they stared down at her, their position the same as they had been the night before. Once again, it was the boy who spoke.

"Excuse me, miss. Can we come inside?"

"No!" She screamed it in her mind, but the word came out of her mouth as a broken whimper.

The children didn't blink.

"Excuse me, miss," the boy began again in his dead tone. "You have to let us inside."

Swallowing thickly, she lurched onto her feet. Her body hunched forward, readying herself for the moment when the children opened the door. But they didn't even look at the handle. Their eyes remained focused solely on her. Straightening to her full height, she towered over the children. It didn't stop her from feeling tiny. Weak and vulnerable. The boy's face barely moved as he spoke to her.

"Let us in. We won't take long."

Ruby darted forward and slammed the door closed, lodging the door in place with the chair as she choked on her dread.

Chapter 11

Ruby's arms trembled as she tightened her grip around her legs. Broken sobs wracked her body. She rocked with every gasp for air, the motion knocking her forehead against her knees. A smoldering lump swelled her throat shut, forcing the fire within her to pour from her eyes in scorching tears.

The event played over in her mind. She searched every second for what she could have done better or faster. There had to have been a moment that could have changed everything. Something she could have done to save him. It was a torture that didn't make any difference. Mark was dead. Just like Peter. And she was alone.

The whimpering of the dogs corrected her. They all huddled together until it was impossible to tell one from the other. She wasn't alone. The children were still out there. Wiping the tears from her eyes, Ruby tried to think of what to do next. She tried to weave her memories together to recall if there had been a radio in Mark's van, one that could contact the police station, but she couldn't get past the image of his hands clawing into the snow. *Had he locked the van? Where were his keys?* Her heart turned cold. *Where was his gun?* The more she thought about it, the more she hoped the children had it and knew how to use it well. Dying instantly from a bullet to the brain was far more merciful than enduring what Peter and Mark had.

An agonized mewl shattered her thoughts and drove her to her feet. It started as a tiny sound, barely audible over the hiss of the fire, but soon became a high-pitched, wordless begging that ripped at her insides. *Mark's still alive?* She stared at the door, unable to move her feet. The dogs around her grew restless, mirroring the sound of the wounded animal outside. There wasn't a window that faced the front of the cabin. The only way to try and see it was to open the door.

They can't come in without an invitation. She felt a certain amount of reassurance the first time she told herself this. It didn't last. By the time she reached for the handle, the repetition had lost its power. But the mewling continued. A painful, helpless whimpering that she couldn't ignore. *Mark might be alive.* She shifted the chair out of the way and slowly opened the door. Just an inch. Barely enough for her to peek out and check the threshold. Ruby had prepared herself to see the children still standing there, still waiting for her. But the area was empty. A cold sweat slicked her palms as her eyes darted around. She couldn't see them. But she still felt their eyes upon her.

They can't come in uninvited. Ruby used the theory as armor, a shield for her mind as she opened the door a little wider. The bonfire still burned, its flames as tall as she was. Without the floodlights, it was impossible to see anything beyond the ring of golden, dancing light it provided. On the far rim, she spotted Mark's hands slumped lifelessly on the stained snow. Fresh powder had begun to fall, muting the bright crimson of his blood into a rusted maroon.

Ruby clamped a hand over her mouth. She didn't know if she wanted to scream or weep hysterically, but she was certain that she didn't want the children to hear her. Over her harsh breathing, the whimpering continued. It wasn't coming from Mark. Blinking back tears, she searched the ring of light. There was movement on the far-right side where the light touched the fronts of the van and truck. The high set of the vehicles and play of shadows offered an innumerable number of hiding places for something as small as a child. She was just about to close the door when something shaggy and mattered with blood dragged itself into the ring of light, mewling as it went.

"Echo!" Ruby screamed before she could stop herself.

Her hind legs were obviously broken and twisted into a horrid angle. It made it impossible for the pup to stand. So, she dragged herself forward with her front paws, drawing herself slowly towards the cabin. Ruby bit back a cry as she watched the helpless animal struggle. *It's a trap!* It didn't matter how much her mind shrieked it. Ruby knew she couldn't just leave the wounded dog with those monsters. Squeezing her eyes shut, she tried to think up a plan. *Be smart. Think.* But then Nugget added his pained screams to Echo's and her already limited plans spiraled into nothingness.

You can't get them both. The cold rationale of her mind whispered. *Not before the kids get you.* Ruby had no illusion that she was stronger than the black-eyed children. Not after seeing Peter's remains and witnessing how quickly they had taken Mark. They had overcome two fully grown men like a wolf pack. *What chance do you have?* So far, it seemed that her only weapon was her speed. She was taller than they were, her legs longer. It was possible they were just toying with her, allowing her to think that she could outrun them as some kind of sick game, but she didn't think so. They hunted in packs. They used traps and surprise. She might be able to outrun them if she wasn't restricted by snow gear. But even if she could, even if she did have this single advantage, she couldn't possibly outpace them while carrying the weight of a wounded husky. Let alone two. But the animals continued to cry, the sounds driving into her skull, her heart breaking as she watched them inch closer to the cabin.

Slamming the door closed, Ruby lunged into the kitchen area and flung open cupboard doors. She dragged out whatever she found and searched through the items across the floor. There was a single knife. It was long, but dull, and she questioned the strength of the steel. There were extra supplies for the outhouse, rolls of toilet paper and sanitizing liquid. Holding her breath, she quickly read the back of the bottle, searching for the warnings she had seen on others before. Highly flammable. She dumped the rolls into a saucepan and doused them with the liquid. Grabbing the unzipped sleeping bag off her bed, she hacked at one end with the knife, tearing a hole in the material until there was a gap just big enough to slip over Bannock's head. It dragged behind him like a massive cloak.

"If you can pull a sled," she said to him as she rubbed his flank, "you can pull a couple of dogs."

He whimpered, and she was left questioning if he would follow her commands. Taking a deep breath, she shed her heavy outer layers, picked up her knife and saucepan and inched to the door.

"Come on, boy."

Bannock didn't move.

95

"Heel."

He took a step back. But as she inched the door open again and the tortured sounds of the pups came in, Bannock pushed forward, alternating between a growl and a whine. Fire shoved closer to the door, his growl deep with a flash of fangs, his shoulders hunched and ready for a fight.

"There's something to be said for pack mentality," Ruby breathed as she gripped the screen door handle.

They're not really children, she reminded herself as she flung the door wide open and bolted into the freezing cold, Fire rushing ahead while Bannock kept pace by her side.

The first child she spotted was the smallest of the three. She came out to block Ruby's path to the wounded dogs. The boy had been hiding behind the van to her right, the older girl in the shadows of the tent to Ruby's left, and they both rushed out to block her retreat. None of them had suspected that she would run for the bonfire instead of the dogs and that bought her a few more seconds.

Fangs glistening in the firelight, Fire hurled his large bulk onto the smallest child. The little girl didn't make a sound as they staggered back. Ruby lost them behind the wall of flames. The older black-eyed girl was only a few feet away when Ruby managed to thrust the saucepan into the bonfire. The sanitizer liquid ignited with a rasp. The girl lunged for Ruby's arm. Whirling around, she crashed the hot pan down on the girl's head. A scream ripped from her tiny lungs as steam bellowed and the metal hissed. With her knife clutched tightly in her fist, Ruby shoved at the girl's chest. The blow made her stumble back. The hunks of wood tripped the demon child's feet and she fell back into the bonfire. The towering flames spewed sparks into the air as they swallowed her up.

The stench of burning flesh filled the air. *They're not really children.* It was hard to believe it until the thrashing girl's scream morphed into an otherworldly shriek. High-pitched, shrill, but bellowing like a drum. The flames had caught on the girl's clothes and her skin boiled as she struggled to put them out.

Ruby turned and the boy was upon her. Flipping the pot in her hand, she dumped the blistering contents over him before thrusting the red-hot metal onto his head. She gagged as he began to boil as well. Clouds of steam burst forth from the pan as he scratched blindly at the metal. Pushing him aside, Ruby raced as fast as she could to the wounded animals. Bannock was already with them, nudging them with his nose to urge them on. He squirmed as Ruby scooped up the heavy dogs and dumped them onto the sleeping bag secured around his neck. Their yelps of pain merged with the unearthly screams, but she didn't have time to care.

"Go!" she shouted the second the dogs were on the sheet, and she pointed to the cabin with every ounce of authority she had.

Mercifully, Bannock chose this moment to be obedient and he sprinted forward, dragging the wounded pups behind him at an astonishing speed. Out of the corner of her eyes, Ruby spotted the little boy. He hurled the pan into the bonfire and ran for her. There wasn't time to get around him and back to the cabin. Turning, she hurled herself around the edge of Mark's truck, praying that he also never felt the need to lock his vehicle. She sobbed with relief when the door popped open under her touch. Hurling herself inside, she reached back to slam the door shut. It crashed her already battered leg between the seat and the door. Pain sizzled along her leg, but she managed to lock it anyway. The boy smacked his hands into the window, leaving smears of Mark's blood across the glass before he ran around towards the driver's door. Ruby lunged for it, her trapped foot held in place, contorting her knee until she yelped. The door lock was just out of her reach. Holding the blade of the knife, the icy metal slicing into her palm, she jabbed at the lock with the thick hilt. It snapped into place just as the boy arrived.

He wasn't out of breath. He wasn't in pain. Standing completely still he stared at her, the firelight dancing across his inky black eyes. Ruby could only stare back, frozen in horror as she realized that the boy hadn't burned. His flesh had liquefied. The skin of his forehead dripped with the consistency of melted wax, warping the shape of his skull like there were no bones underneath. He didn't blink as his skin oozed over his left eyes and gathered along the line of his mouth. Slowly, he lifted his hand and tapped his knuckles against the glass.

Tap. Tap. Tap.

"Excuse me, miss. Can I come in?"

In a streak of fur and fang, Fire raced across the yard, moving too fast for the little girl to keep up. He launched into the air, crashing his weight onto the boy. They both toppled down beyond Ruby's view. Without thought, Ruby threw herself at the door, hand fumbling with the lock. It popped open and she spilled out of the truck bed. Her feet hit the ground and the pain was instant. It crackled in her ankle and lashed across her knee, making her buckle against the side of the van. Fire's growls were as loud as the older girl's screams. She had dragged herself from the flaming pit. Her clothes glowed like embers as they melted against her softening skin. Ruby had lost sight of the smallest child. Locking her eyes on the cabin and readjusting her grip on her knife, Ruby ran for it, each step bringing a new wave of pain.

Bannock was at the cabin door. The rest of the pack clustered around the door, scratching at the screen as they tried to get to the wounded pups. Ruby wrenched the door open and backed it there with her body. Bannock dragged forward but struggled to get the dogs over the heightened threshold and past the others. She dropped to her knees. The blood oozing from her palm seeped into the material as she bunched her hands in it and tried to lift them up. With her muscles freezing and the knife still heavy in one hand, her body wasn't up to the task. Bannock surged forward again. She shoved. And they slipped into the warmth of the cabin.

Fire used her back for a boost as he bounded over her. The sudden blow crushed her against the floor, her skull cracking against it. A blinding white claimed her vision as the world seemed to tilt and heave. Bracing her hands on the floor, she tried to push herself up. The cold had both numbed her and changed her skin into a bed of needles, each one of the thousands driving into her as she moved. Every movement felt as if her bones would rip free. Still, she refused to release her hold on the hilt of her knife.

The screen door dug into her side. Her body was too ravaged and her thoughts too thin for her to meet the challenge of moving it. A hand grabbed her ankle. It drove her limb against the earth as it squeezed. Pain ripped through her as her bones bent under the pressure. Instinct caused her to rear her back, her hand flying wide. There was a moment of resistance. A soft, wet squish. Ruby blinked, her vision cleared, and she found herself staring at the knife. It was now buried to the hilt in the smallest child's eye.

Her frozen fingers refused to release the hilt as she trembled. The fingers on her leg released, allowing Ruby to pull free and scramble back over the threshold. The retreat slowly pulled the blade out of the twitching girl. At last, it slipped free. The black-eyed girl dropped like a rag doll.

Ruby couldn't scream. Each attempt broke apart in her raw throat and became desperate gurgles and clicks. The screen door bumped shut between her and the night. A crunch of snow made her gaze snap up. The motion brought a pain that nearly blinded her again. The other children approached. Their steps measured and unhurried. Snow flickered around them on the growing breeze. The cold didn't concern them, but Ruby's body was wracked with violent shudders. There were only a few points of warmth left on her body, each one hidden under the blood that trickled from her palm and forehead.

The two older children, both melted and deformed, looked down at their little companion. Observing but silent. The corpse twitched and jerked. Wild barks filled the cabin and Ruby scrambled further back, drawing her legs away from the door. A scream rattled from her chest as she watched the dead girl blink. Her eyelids skimmed over the mangled remains of her flesh twice more. Then, like a marionette pulled up by its strings, the girl rose back onto her feet.

Ruby's ribs ached with her heaving breaths. "What are you?"

The boy stepped to the front of the group. Fire's fangs had ripped apart his body, but he didn't bleed. His melted skin dripped from his features. Ruby could hear the droplets hitting the snow as he knocked against the screen frame.

Tap. Tap. Tap.

"Excuse me, miss. You have to let us in. We promise to be quick."

Ruby kicked the internal door shut.

Chapter 12

Waves of pain woke her. Nausea twisted up her stomach as her vision shifted and her head throbbed. Blinking her eyes open, she found herself sprawled over the cabin floor. Blood had pooled under her skull, becoming tacky as she slept. It tugged at her broken skin as she forced herself to sit up. Struck by a dizziness that sparked against the inside of her skull like fireworks, Ruby braced her hands on the floor and tried not to retch. If there had been anything in her stomach, she was sure it would have ended up on the floor.

This is bad. The whisper came from the deepest recesses of her mind. Having never suffered a concussion, Ruby didn't know the sensation. But she was sure that she hadn't laid down to sleep. She had passed out. The untreated wounds of her palm scraped against the wooden floor, making her hiss and snap her hand away. Pangs sizzled down her legs. They started in her knee, travelled along her shin, and splashed out through the joints of her ankle. She whimpered at the thought of putting any weight on it.

Bannock nuzzled against her side; his cool, wet nose bumping against her flushed cheek. Without looking at him, she rubbed at his fur, using the back of her hand to protect her cuts. He struck her with a bit more force. Her stomach heaved as she swayed and forced herself to lift her head. The sleeping bag was still looped around his neck, the pups cradled on the padded train. Pain rattled through her as she forced herself into a sitting position and began to work Bannock free. With that done, she found her knife and slashed off some long, thin strips.

Clean up. Check the dogs. Get the hell out of her before sundown. The water jugs were too heavy to move with one hand. She kicked it over, washed her hand in the water that gushed free, and left the rest to gurgle out for the dogs to drink. It took a few wipes to clear the dried blood and get a decent look at her wound. Puffy and red, she hoped the arctic air would keep it from swelling too much. At least it didn't look infected.

She wrapped a strip of the cloth around her palm, not sure if her makeshift bandage would do more harm than good. As she pulled herself to the pups, she wished she had saved some of the water. But they would have to wait. There was no need for an x-ray to know that their hind legs were broken. The bones pushed against their skin at odd places, and any cuts had been licked clean by the pack. Small growls escaped both of them as she neared. There wasn't much she could do, anyway. And she decided any of her attempts wouldn't be worth the pain.

"Don't worry," she soothed as she patted each of the pups in turn. "I'm getting us out of here."

Forcing herself onto her feet was excruciating. She had to grip the end of the bed with both hands and hurl herself up, the crushing pain leaving her on a broken moan. She paused, waiting for it to ebb away before she dared to tug at her pant leg. Her knee looked far worse than her hand, and she wasn't going to suffer the pain of removing her boot to get a glimpse of her ankle. It wasn't broken. Anything else could be dealt with when she got to the hospital.

Clenching her teeth, she struggled into her jacket and gloves, trying and failing to keep her mind focused on escape. *We'll be gone before sundown*, she reassured herself as the thoughts still bubbled to the surface. *There won't be any need to run*. Still, dread pooled in her stomach. Her best defense was gone. She yanked open the wooden door and a scream ripped from her throat.

In retrospect, she should have known that the black-eyed children would do something with Mark's head. But she hadn't expected them to leave the severed skull on her doorstep. Gripping the doorframe, she barely managed to keep herself upright as she broke apart into hysterical sobs. It was the pain that brought her back. That urged her forward.

As she slipped out, she was careful not to touch him. But it was too close and the screen door tapped against his cheek, making him rattle slightly. It was all for nothing as the dogs surged past her. The door slammed open and his head was sent bouncing over the snow. Ruby squeezed her eyes shut, choked down a breath, and limped forward.

The snow had fallen overnight to cover most of the evidence of what had happened. It blanketed Mark's body and smothered the bonfire embers. But what drew her attention was how high the sun was. *How long was I passed out?* The already short hours of sunlight had dwindled all the more. *Move!* The command made her lurch towards Mark's body as fast as she could. But it wasn't that fast. The layers of snow would have been hard for her to move through normally, but her pronounced limp slowed her process to a crawl. *Keys*, she thought. *He has the truck keys.*

She didn't bother to muffle her screams as she forced herself to kneel down next to his corpse. The pain at least served as a distraction for what she had to do next. His back was ripped to shreds, the blood crystallizing in the cold to look like tiny gems. She tried not to notice the flesh and bone as she checked his pockets. The cold had frozen him solid, making it harder to roll his dead weight onto his back, and each failed attempt brought her focus back to what she was doing. Her stomach twisted. Squeezing her eyes shut, she turned her head and gagged. Given time, her stomach settled.

When she was ready, she patted down the many pockets of his jacket and pants. The keys were gone. Getting up was more torturous than getting down had been. Already drained and aching from the cold, she limped to his truck. She checked every storage place she could think of and still came up with nothing. All she could think was, if they were still here, if the children hadn't taken them, then they must have been dropped in the struggle. Casting her eyes over the thick snow, it occurred to her that she could waste a whole day looking for them. All with no guarantee that the truck would even start. There was no sign of the gun.

Mark was a cop, she told herself. *There is a search party organized for the children. Surely, someone will come out here, eventually.* She checked the sky again. Clouds were gathering fast, dulling the once blinding sun into a spot of light against the gray blanket. Too new to the region, she couldn't make any defined judgment of the time, but it seemed that midday had passed. *Someone should have come by now.*

If they had, it would have taken more than a passing glance for them to notice Mark's body in the snow. Or his head at her door. They wouldn't have just left after something like that. *What if they don't come at all? Or if they don't come until night?* She played with the idea of heading to Peter's again. There was the possibility that there was another car she hadn't seen before. But the throb in her leg promised that she wouldn't make it on foot. *Not before nightfall,* her mind taunted. Maybe if she could find a hose, she could siphon the gas from Mark's truck to the snowmobile. *Would the dogs run beside? What about Echo and Nugget?*

Her head snapped up to the sounds of the dogs growling. Casting her eyes across the yard, she expected to see the children standing amongst the pristine snow. Staring her down with their bottomless eyes. Instead, she found that some of the dogs had taken to pawing and nipping at Mark's corpse.

"Stop it!" she bellowed as she lumbered forward, clapping her hands, and flinging her arms wide.

It was enough to deter them. At least for now. Ruby had to keep a sharp eye on him as she struggled to pull the heavy food bag free. All the while, she couldn't suppress the thought that she was next. *How much will be left when someone finally comes? A hand maybe. A foot. They'd eat my stomach first.* She shoved the thoughts from her mind as she gave up maneuvering the bag. The pain in her leg helped to keep her thoughts at bay as she retrieved the knife. She stabbed open the sack and let the dogs eat their fill where it lay. Watching them gorge themselves, she cast her eyes back to Mark. *You shouldn't move a body at a crime scene,* she told herself. It was followed quickly by a sharper thought. *No one is going to believe me anyway.* Ignoring the pain in her hand, she grabbed his arms and dragged his sizeable bulk towards the tent.

Sweat trailed down her face as she finally got him inside. Setting him on his back, she tried to cross his arms over his chest. His frozen limbs refused to move. Not able to give him even that much dignity, she forced herself to endure collecting his head, and placed it by his body. Fussing with his clothes, she bit back her tears as she tried to make him look somewhat peaceful. *He died because of you.*

"*They* killed him," she snapped aloud. With the last of her convictions, she added. "I'm not dying here."

Hurling herself back onto her feet, she limped to the shed and ripped it apart, searching every corner and hiding place where a hose could be stored. She found nothing. Mark's truck. The van. The cabin. The dogs were still eating when she stormed back into the tent. She tore the boxes apart and flung their contents aside but there was no hose. There was nothing. Broken, she staggered out of the tent.

Her frantic pursuit had taken longer than she thought. Or perhaps the promise of the coming storm was about to be a reality. Either way, when she stepped outside she found that the sky had darkened considerably. *And no one had come*, the bitter voice in her head whispered. *What if the children went into town? What if there was no one left to know or care that she was out here?* She gripped the railing with both hands as she struggled to keep the floodgates of her panic closed. There wasn't enough gas to run the generator for the night. There would be barely enough to keep a fire lit.

The knowledge pressed down on her shoulders and she slumped against the railing. She didn't know what else she could do. Helplessness built in her chest, mixing with her pain and fatigue until she couldn't contain it all. Tears burned her eyes before swiftly freezing against her lashes. *How long would it take to cut wood?* Even as she thought about it, she couldn't decide if it would even be worth it. Perhaps freezing to death was a better way to go. It seemed peaceful when given the alternative.

Angrily wiping her cheek, she forced down her rising panic and self-pity. *I'm not dying here.* She glanced back into the tent, trying to find a spot she might have missed. Then she noticed the harnesses. *They're sled dogs.* Limping back in, she stripped the material from the walls and dumped them in a pile outside of the tent. It was hard to find where they had stored the sleds for the winter, harder still to drag it out into the yard. She had never harnessed a dog, never run a sled, and her inexperience made her process slow. After a few failed attempts with an increasingly impatient Bannock, she headed back into the tent and ripped the pictures off of the wall. Using them as a reference, she mimicked the way the straps looped and secured around the dogs.

The front of the sled had a few dozen ropes and clips that all seemed to lead nowhere. She clipped them onto the dogs. The ropes all twisted up on themselves as the dogs lurched and staggered. She was struggling with Snow when the lead dog yelped. At the command, the attached dogs bolted forward. The sled barreled against her legs, tossing her back and making her tumble over it as it continued on. All the dogs yet to be harnessed raced up to play and taunt the others. In the chaos, Ruby had time to get to her feet and fling herself onto the back of the sled. They raced forward as she struggled to work the reins. At the last moment, the dogs turned at a sharp angle to avoid the fence. The sled skidded out of control and cracked against it. Ruby's spine struck one of the heavy wood planks before she slipped through a gap and was dumped onto the snow.

Chapter 13

Get up.

The thought came through the haze in Ruby's mind and pushed at her senses. She didn't want to. A deep cold had seeped into her bones, dulling the throbbing ache she knew would return the instant she made the slightest shift. Flecks of snow burned against her exposed skin as a wet tongue licked across her cheek. A few strands of her hair covered her face, fluttering softly in the growing breeze. She peeled her eyes open and blinked into the darkened air. With a slight whine, a dog nuzzled her again, forcing her to raise her head.

The movement was slow and small, but it still felt like her skull was splitting in two. She gripped her head with one hand and pressed at her temple. The splitting roar ebbed into constant ringing. Slowly, she took it all in, trying to guess how much time had passed. The thick sheet of clouds contained the sunset, making the sky darken rather than painting it with different colors. Shadows were creeping up with the cold. Night was closing in fast, but she had no idea how long she had left.

Every joint in her spine sparked as she forced herself onto all fours. She couldn't remember anything beyond the moment of impact. But hours must have passed while she was unconscious and the dogs free to run wild. They hadn't roamed too far, each one deciding to keep close to the food bags. Her head was swimming. Before, she had struggled to think straight. Now, regaining consciousness for the second time that day, Ruby's vision blurred every time she blinked.

Using the fence that had wounded her, she dragged herself to her feet. Learning from her mistake, she collected one of the remaining hunks of wood as she limped over to the dogs that were still attached to the sled. This time, she made a point of carefully jamming the wood under the blades, preventing the dogs from moving forward. Or, at the very least, allowing a little bit of warning if they tried to bolt.

Time was precious now. A treasure she was quickly losing. She couldn't spare a second of it wallowing in the pain that rippled through her. It took every ounce of her focus to recall her past failures and successes. She didn't move until she knew what she wanted to do. Her head screamed that it was taking too long, but without having to repeat anything, she soon had the remaining dogs in place. Before, they had been somewhat reluctant. Now, with night stalking them, it was as if they feared being left behind.

The day had turned to dusk, the air around them thickening with tension, when she tentatively placed her feet on the runners. The cuts on her hand screamed as she gripped the woven material of the reins. It was hard to keep her weight balanced with one leg threatening to buckle at any moment. Stiff and shivering, she slipped the wooden block free. In broken lurches, the dogs trotted forward. They wanted to run and it took all her weight and strength to keep them from doing so. Their first voyage consisted of the few feet that separated the yard from the cabin. She barely managed to hang on for even that long.

With a hard yank, she brought them to a stop outside of the cabin door and shoved the plank back into place. Carrying the injured pups, one by one, made her arms ache and her spine shatter, but she didn't have much choice. The soft snow swallowed her feet with every step. There was no way she was going to be able to drag them over it. As gently as she could, she positioned them on the flat area of the sled designed for passengers or supplies. Their anxious whimpers grew sharper and faster as the sun continued to creep below the horizon.

Under the last of the light, she searched the cabin for her winter hat, scarf, and all the flashlights she could find. As a last-minute thought, she grabbed her wallet. If all went well, she wouldn't have to return. If it didn't, at least she wouldn't be seen as just a headless, nameless corpse. Putting it in her breast pocket, she zipped it closed and patted the bulge, then drank the last remains of the water. The few drops were enough to make her feel ill. As her last act before leaving the tent, she lit a fire and stocked it with all the remains of the woodpile. Perhaps, if she had any luck left to her name, the children will think that she was still there. It wouldn't trick them for the whole night. But all she needed was the head start.

She had only been in front of the fire for a few moments, but the shift in temperature was noticeable and hard to abandon. Still, she hurried outside, closing the door tightly behind her. Echo and Nugget were still making pathetic little noises when she neared.

"It's okay." She gave each a pat, the motion soothing them as much as it did her. "It'll all be okay."

It was already getting hard to discern the air from the trees, but she refused to turn on the flashlight yet. The dogs should know the way and she didn't want to draw any attention. Tension rolled through the pack, as if one's fear fed the other, and she took her place at the back. Her breath misted as she kicked the wood block. It spared her from bending over, but even that limited movement hurt.

The second the block scattered away, the dogs broke into a run. Ruby shifted her weight forward, trying to keep her footing and steer at the same time. The frame rattled violently under her, coursing pain through her leg with every jolt. They raced across the yard and out onto the road. It was barely a turn at all but still almost enough to toss her aside again. Not daring to slow them down, she took the long ends of the reins, swung them around her waist, and made them into knots. They were flimsy and loose, but it made her feel better. Thrown or standing, the dogs would take her with them. Her last tug on the knot cracked the reins. The dogs took it as a sign to speed up and worked themselves into a sprint.

The icy wind lashed across her skin, working its way through the thin material of her tattered jacket and the thin gaps of her scarf. The dogs' paws kicked up the snow as they sailed over the bumps and grooves of the weathered road. The piles of snow and ice smoothed the journey, but her battered and raw body ensured that she felt everything. Exposed to the elements, the wind and chill broke her apart. Her vision blurred and her head rolled as the dogs worked themselves into a frantic pace. It was getting harder to keep upright. Harder to take each jolt without a cry of pain. But she bit back the pain, determined to make their escape as silent as possible. It wasn't as if she believed that the children would hear her. It was that her most primal fear told her they already could. They seemed to lurk in every shadow. Their eyes following her wherever she went.

It was too dark now to see much beyond dusky shapes pressed against the grayish sky. Hunching forward, she tightened her grip on the back of the sled and snuck a glance over her shoulder. A part of her expected to see the children following behind. Her attention was caught by the single pinprick of gold that marred the horizon. The cabin. The fire still burned. And they were still close enough to see it.

The freezing air played with the injuries, pushing her closer to unconsciousness as her body heat dwindled. The snow was coming faster now, striking her like hail, and stinging her eyes. Without warning, the dogs lurched forward with new desperation. Ruby forced herself to straighten and search the shadows that draped over her with renewed focus. Her heart rammed against her rib as adrenaline flooded her veins, drawing her further back from the precipice of pain. She couldn't see anything. While she longed to use one of the flashlights, she didn't dare turn one on while the glow of the cabin was still visible.

A new snarl made her change her mind. Fumbling in the pocket where she had left the flashlights, Ruby clutched one of the cylinders and yanked it free. A beam of light cut through the shadows when she clicked it on. She panned the shaft over the side of the road, looking for the noise that seemed so close. It took her a split second to see the flash of movement. The shape was unmistakable.

The wolves had found them.

Spotting one made it easier to see the others. Half a dozen of them were spread out on either side, keeping pace with the dogs as they barreled down the road, slipping through the brush with practiced ease. Ruby reached for the knife, her only weapon to defend herself. Her glove patted across the canvas pocket but found nothing beyond the two spare flashlights. She had left it behind.

Fear gripped her as she cracked the reins and forced the dogs on. No matter how fast they ran, the wolves were always beside them. Then one leaped onto the road, blocking their path, forcing the dogs down the embankment. The sled skidded across the road and she was forced to push her weight down on her injured leg to keep it from tipping over. Snow washed out in waves and her flashlight flung from her hand as the sled careened into the waiting wolf. The large animal snarled and snapped for her head, its fangs snapping next to her ear. Before it could sink its teeth in, the sled jerked forward and followed the sled dogs down the embankment, leaving the growling wolf behind.

With a sharp buck that made her feet slip, the sled hit the bottom of the incline. The crack of ice cut over the rushing wind. The sled fishtailed, throwing her from one side to the next. She could do little more than cling to the sled and trust that the pack knew which way to turn. The sheet of ice gave way under them, shattering into large hunks that rattled under them as icy water sloshed over her feet. If it weren't for the constant pull forward, she would have sunk into the lake.

The fracturing ice made the wolves keep their distance. But it wasn't until they broke up onto the bank once more that she felt sturdy enough to reach into the pocket and pull out a second flashlight, this one heavier in her palm. She flicked it on in time to see one of the massive creatures, one of them launching itself towards her. She swung the flashlight. The glass shattered on impact and the bulb crumbled, leaving the exposed wires to spark and hiss in the darkness. She clicked it off with her thumb but kept the solid weight in her hand. As the forest drew closer, the branches slapping and slashing at her face, Ruby could do little more than hold on and swing blindly at any sound. She hit more branches than animals.

The ground bucked and rattled, tossing her around without any warning. Her injured leg gave up on trying to keep her upright. But shifting her weight made it harder to keep the sled from tipping. With a final, broken lurch, they slammed over a hill and raced out into an opening. After the oppressive darkness, the slither of moonlight was blinding. She could see the shapes and shadows of the retreated tree line as they crossed the open meadow. The wolves flanked them, a row of streaking figures on either side. Locking her attention on them, she hadn't been ready for the next buck. Her knee gave out and her hands slipped their hold. The reins knotted around her tight and dug into her stomach as the slack cut short and she was dragged behind the retreating sled.

Then the dogs stopped.

The sled skidded over the snow, and Ruby was sent topping and rolling until the snow grew thick enough to stop her.

Exhausted, battered, and panting, Ruby tried to sit up only to slump back down again. Her brain swirled within her skull. The best she could do was roll onto her stomach. Through panic alone, she had managed to keep the broken flashlight in her hand. She held it like a club, ready to wield it even as her body refused to move.

Swallowing thickly, she looked up at the clearing. A massive shadow claimed one side of the meadow, but she couldn't see the wolves. The dogs had grown silent. Forcing herself up onto her knees, she tried to undo the knot, but her hands could only fumble over the strap. There was a crunch and her dogs shifted. Ruby lifted her torch and clicked it on.

The bulb sparked, creating a glow in the darkness. In the flickering light, she caught sight of the little boy standing at the very edge of the meadow. With each blast of light, he drew a step closer. Scrambling up onto her knees, Ruby clutched at the sled and cracked the reins. The dogs rushed forward, but she couldn't hold on. For a moment, the reins dragged her behind. Then the material snapped and she rolled to a stop. Pressing up, she lifted the flashlight. The next flicker brought the boy closer. In the one that followed, the eldest girl appeared by his side. Half of her skull was deformed, as if it were folding in on itself. Ruby dragged herself to her feet. Every limp was like walking on glass, but she raced towards the looming shadow, hoping to find a place to hide. Her stomach plummeted when her broken flashlight brought Peter's cabin into view.

Behind her, the children broke into a run. Their footsteps hammered like her heartbeat. The pain in her limbs was unbearable, but she lunged up the stairs, fingers gripping the railings to pull herself up faster. A small hand slipped between the gaps, grasping for her ankle. Ruby had to leap to avoid the searching fingers and a sharp crack sounded as she landed awkwardly on the porch. On hands and knees, she crawled to the door and forced herself inside. She had just enough left in her to slam the door shut before she crumbled against it. Heaving each breath, she listened as the smallest child crawled out from under the porch. Each stair groaned as she calmly walked up them. Ruby's heat stammered and panic swelled within her as the handle above her head turned. *Peter invited them in,* her mind screamed. *They can get in!*

The light still flickered as she sobbed and scrambled up towards the lock. With a metallic click, the door began to open. Ruby threw her weight against it but it was barely enough to keep the door in place. The soles of her boots scraped across the floor as she struggled against the constant force pressing against the other side. Pain burned within her ankle like molten lead. Sweat beaded across her skin and her muscles screamed, but she managed to make the door gradually inch back into its frame.

Keeping it in place was harder. Unwilling to drop the bulky, broken flashlight, the only weapon she had, Ruby fumbled to flick the lock into place. The polished surface slipped through her gloved fingers. The girl didn't relent for a second. Tears burned Ruby's eyes as she choked on her sobs. Bracing her feet, she lunged for the lock once more. Her heart leaped as it clicked into place.

In the resulting silence, it was impossible to miss the groan of the porch. It spurred Ruby into motion and she ran for the couch. The pain in her ankle increased with every step, but her fear was worse. She didn't stop until the couch had been pushed over the limited distance and was lodged in front of the door. The sparking flashlight pressed hard against her palm as she clenched her fingers into the soft arm of the sofa. Silence fell over the frigid insides of the cabin, broken only by her heaved breaths and the rapidly shifting sounds of the dogs. Tension built in her with every passing second and burst from her in a scream as the three knocks rattled the door.

"Let us in," the boy demanded.

"No."

"We don't need permission."

"Why are you doing this to me?" she snapped, her fear mixing with her rage and panic until she didn't know what to feel.

Seconds felt like hours as they refused to reply. Slowly, trying not to make a sound, she pushed herself higher and limped back from the door.

"What are you? What do you want?"

The boy spoke in barely more than a whisper, but it tore her open all the same. "We want to come in."

"No."

The silence was shattered as the children began to pound on the walls. By the flickering light, she caught sight of their heads passing by the windows. They moved from one to the next in the gasps of light. Smacking harder on the glass, screaming at her like wild animals, demanding that she let them in.

Ruby turned the light off, seeking some shadows she could hide within. The light died, but the pale moonlight turned the children into silhouettes. And if she could see them, they could see her. Hunching in on herself, she clutched the flashlight with both hands. *Think. Think. Think.* Glass shattered as the kids broke the windows. Their demands and screams grew, driving her insane as they tried to hurl their tiny frames through the high set windows.

She lumbered as fast as her battered legs would allow, stumbling into the kitchen. On the way, she grabbed everything she could and threw them at the children. They scattered at the impacts but always came back. *Think. There has to be something.* Her hands skimmed over the kitchen counter, her supply of weapons rapidly dwindling. Then she found the stove. She turned it on, allowing the stench of gas to pour into the room with a sharp hiss. Ripping open the cupboards and drawers, she searched each of them. Cutlery rattled together as her gloved hand found a knife, and she shoved it into her coat pocket, the blade slicing into the lining. Tiny hands, their skin pale and fine in the moonlight, hooked around the edge of the slim kitchen window. Shards of glass scattered down over the counter like hail. She tossed everything she found, but they only receded when she drove a barbeque fork deep into its wrist.

Amongst the scattered items, she found a few bottles. Her shoulder ached as she launched one after the other at the children as they appeared. The bottles exploded on impact. Their contents splashed across the walls and dripped from the broken shards of glass still lodged within the window frames like fangs. The children ducked away but always returned. The cabin reeked of gas and scattered alcohol. Then she only had one bottle left.

Yanking off the lid, she took a sniff. The smell of linseed oil burned her nose. Peter must have used it to stain his furniture. A plan formed in her mind, broken and vague. She didn't know what she was doing. But, as the demonic children kept screaming, promising her a death far swifter and more merciful than what they had given to Peter or Mark, her fury propelled her on. Fear made her certain. If she was to die here tonight, she wasn't going to die alone.

"Let us in!" The boy chanted. "Let us in!"

"Leave me alone!" Ruby shrieked back.

Glass crunched under her boots as she drizzled the linseed oil across the kitchen windowsill. The hands were back, reaching blindly, the shards slicing at their skin. Ruby raced across the room. The scent grew as she sloshed thin trails of the liquid over the couch, the curtains, and along each of the windows. She didn't expect any of the fires to hold. But the sudden flash of burning alcohol might be enough to make them hesitate. Maybe just for a second. Just long enough for her to get a head start. Hoping that her frazzled state would keep the children from seeing the trap, or perhaps make them too enraged to care, she screamed at them again and flung whatever she had on hand in their directions. Everything but the broken flashlight and the remaining linseed oil.

Retreating back, her knuckles strained as she clutched the two items tightly. A hush fell over the world. They were gone. Turning in broken circles, her eyes darting between the windows and door, she tried to catch her breath. The combination of scents on each lungful made her gag. Her head was beginning to swim and her vision blurred around the edges.

A soft gasp of a metal made her spin around. The living room was small, allowing her a clear view of the bedroom door as it gradually creaked open. Slowly, the door swung back, revealing only an endless darkness that consumed the space. A breath of wind stirred the curtains, allowing the thin traces of moonlight to slip through. In that moment, the children stood as blocks of darkness that filled the threshold. The wind died, the curtain stilled, and they bled back into the darkness.

"We won't take long," the boy said.

Ruby fumbled with the bottle of linseed oil. The liquid sloshed from the mouth, sliding down the sides to seep into her gloves. In unison, the three children crept forward. Their eyes caught the faintest traces of light and shone like slick stones. As they neared, she backed up a step and whipped her hand out to form a cross. The linseed oil arched out across the space and splashed against the children. Their only reaction was to take another step closer. All she could hope was that they believed she was really trying to hysterically banish them. That they wouldn't see how deliberately she covered them. That their desire to terrorize her would be enough to keep them in place, just to prove to her how pathetic her attempts to defeat them were.

The bottle ran out. They continued walk forward at a slow pace. She limped back. The empty bottle dropped from her hand and bounced across the floor when the back of her legs collided with the arm of the sofa. Her knees buckled and she barely managed to keep upright. Standing with only a few feet between them, the children watched her in silence. Her stomach churned as she met their cold, glassy gaze. Quickly, she yanked the knife from her pocket and brandished it like a sword.

"Why didn't you let us in?" the boy asked.

Ruby didn't dare look away from them. The soft hiss of the gas served as her answer. To her right, a slight breeze slipped through the shattered frame of the window. *Would it be enough?* Her panicked thoughts filled her. *The windows are broken. Would the gas be enough? Will anything be enough?*

When she couldn't keep her stomach from heaving for a moment longer, Ruby swallowed thickly, tightened her hand on the flashlight, and peeled her fingers from the knife handle. It dropped to the floor, rattling for a moment before it stilled.

The children burst forward like ravenous animals. Ruby held her ground for as long as she dared. Until they reached for her and their fingers raked across her skin. Then she clicked the flashlight on.

The broken bulb sparked as she shoved it into the boy's chest. With a ghastly roar, the tiny flicker claimed the flammable oil and ignited into bright, dancing flames. They lapped over him, spreading by clothes and oil. He released an unholy cry as he tried to extinguish them. Sparks and embers spewed from his hands as he flung them about, catching the traces of alcohol and linseed wherever they landed. The other two leaped for her. Screaming, Ruby kicked the boy into the taller girl as the smaller one fell on top of her and drove her back against the couch.

With two children on fire, it didn't take long for the raging flames to eat away at the walls. Heat pressed against Ruby as she braced her hand against the small girl's chest, lodged her foot against the back of the sofa, and flipped them over. They tumbled over the edge of the sofa and dropped onto the floor. Small hands latched onto Ruby's hair with an unbreakable grip, holding her in place as the fire rushed towards them. Every second pressed against her, coming with the certainty that the next would bring the explosion expected. Clenching her teeth, Ruby hurled herself back. Her hair ripped out from the roots, tearing her scalp apart and freeing blood to pour out over her skin. Ruby didn't hesitate. The moment she was free, she bolted for the window and tossed herself through the wall of fire, protecting her face as best she could.

She made no attempt to break her landing, or limit the pain and damage she inflicted upon herself. She just wanted out before the fire spread and found the lingering gas. The children tried to follow her, but the fire clinging to them caught the remains of the alcohol by the window. There was a sudden burst as the liquor flashed. The heat scorched her back as she landed hard against the earth. Heaving up, she sprinted out into the snow, fleeing the searing flames as she protected her head. The small explosion she had expected from the gas never came, and when she felt she was a safe distance away, she turned to try and catch sight of them once more. The inferno that met her rattled her to the core. It was still spreading, growing, fueled by furniture and bedding until the flames lapped at the low clouds. The heat did nothing against the shivers that shook her.

Ruby watched the fire consume the building until the sight hurt her eyes. The whole time, she kept the knife tight in her hand and hobbled towards the front of the cabin. She was prepared to stab anything that crawled its way out of the flames, but nothing came. Their screams filled the night sky, echoing off the mountains and clinging to the trees as Ruby went around the building. Her ears rang with the sound, but she didn't dare cover them.

The front door was still open. She could see the shadows shifting around within the inferno. Movement caught her gaze. A broken laugh burst from her throat as she saw the dogs trotting around the edges of the meadow. Just like before, they had come back.

A vicious scream ripped from the building and she turned to see the shadows forming. Caution aside, she rushed forward, intent to slam the door shut and keep them trapped. A sudden burst and the building shattered.

Splinters of wood and glass rained down over her as she was forced off her feet. Ruby didn't look back. She crawled, lunged to her feet, then ran as fast as her body would allow. The dogs cowered at the blast but didn't bolt. It didn't feel real when she had her hands around the handle again. She climbed on, clinging tight, and cracked the reins. The dogs lurched forward. Only when they had entered the ring of trees did she allow herself to look back.

As soon as she saw it again, she kept her eyes from it. The distance between them increased and the blaze grew smaller.

Eventually, it faded away into the night.

Chapter 14

The snow had become steady by the time Ruby was able to knock on the front door of the slender house. Then she knocked again. And again, until her knuckles scraped painfully across the wood. Finally, the light turned on. It streamed through the thin curtains that lined the window and spilled out over Main Street.

"I'm not letting you in," Esther's voice called through the wood.

Ruby blinked in surprise.

"It's Ruby. I work for Aaron and Betsy," she yelled back.

The curtain fluttered as Esther snuck a peek outside. Ruby couldn't contemplate what she looked like. Blood caked across her skin, covered in snow and dirt, swaying on her feet as she struggled to stay upright. Despite all that, the door slowly creaked open.

"Ruby?"

"Nugget and Echo are hurt. Can you take care of them?"

Opening the door slightly wider, Esther glanced up and down the street. Eventually, the older woman turned her eyes back onto Ruby and took her in.

"What happened to you?"

Ruby blinked and her mouth opened. But there was too much to explain for any of it to actually pass her lips.

"Ruby, are you alone?"

She nodded. "Mark's dead."

"What?"

"No one came to check on us. I put him in the tent." Pushing down the shock that was threatening to swallow her whole, she turned her head to look at the pups. "They're really hurt. Can you help them?"

Esther took one tentative step outside.

"You brought them all?"

"Yes."

"Help me get them inside," Esther said after a moment of hesitation.

Together, they gathered each of the dogs and brought them into the warm safety of the home. Everything looked surreal. Modern, neat, and covered by the brilliant overhead light. When the pack was inside, and the pups were made as comfortable as possible, Ruby stepped back and let Esther look over the animals.

"They'll be alright," Esther said as last. "The vet doesn't get in until eight in the morning. I'll call them then."

"They're in pain."

"We'll make them comfortable."

Ruby nodded but didn't say anything else. Time slowed and sped up until a thought came crushing into the forefront of her mind.

"I'm not letting you in," she mumbled.

"What was that?"

"You said you wouldn't let me in."

"Yes. But then I saw the state you were in—"

"Or did you check my eyes?" Ruby cut in.

Esther whipped around to face her. Ruby didn't bother to try and piece together the movements of her features. Instead, she asked directly.

"Did you know?"

"Know what? Ruby, you're not making any sense."

"You haven't even asked how Mark died," Ruby shot back. "Doesn't that generally earn a follow-up question?"

"Look, you're obviously in shock."

"Did you know?" Ruby spat out each word, her muscles tensing under her skin.

The long silence that followed gouged out her insides. She could barely keep on her feet for a moment longer, but she didn't so much as flinch towards the sofa.

"What do you think I knew?"

"You warned me about the forest. About the people that went missing. Did you know about the black-eyed children?"

Esther pulled the neckline of her robe closer before she wrapped her arms around her waist.

"They were just urban legends. Local folklore that people tell tourists over campfires."

"Those urban legends killed two people. They tried to kill me."

Esther shook her head. "It's just a story."

"Tell me the story."

It was possible that it was just a trick of her mind, but time seemed to slow as she waited for Esther to response.

"There's nothing to tell, really. Three children show up at your door in the middle of the night. The way most people tell it, the first encounter is at 3 A.M. They try and trick their way in. By most stories, if they're denied, they leave."

"They come back," Ruby said.

Esther nodded. "Three times."

"Only three?"

"They seem to like that number," Esther said. "Three arrive. Three knocks. Three nights."

Gathering her strength, Ruby asked, her voice crackling, "What are they?"

"Most suppose they are demons."

Ruby shook her head. "Suppose? Don't you have anything better than 'suppose'?"

"You're the one that's come face to face with them, not me," Esther said. "I only have the stories to go by. From what I've heard, one of the telltale signs that you are facing a black-eyed child is that they never answer a direct question. At least, not anything that might help you learn anything about them."

Ruby nodded. Then held out her hands to steady herself as she swayed. "That seems true. When does the next train leave town?"

"One comes through town at midnight."

"When's that?"

Esther looked at her watch. "Fifteen minutes."

"East Eagle is the nearest big town, right?"

"Yes."

"Do me a favor? When the police ask, let them know that I'll be dropping by the police station in East Eagle. I assume they'll have a lot of questions for me. I'll answer whatever they want, but I'm never coming back here."

With that, she gave Bannock one last hug goodbye. Like the others, he was too exhausted to do more than lift his head halfheartedly. His tail thumped against the floor. The slight gesture made new tears spill from her eyes. Esther inched closer.

"You should stay. You need medical attention."

"East Eagle is only two days away. I'll go there. I'm sure the train staff know first aid."

On sluggish feet, she headed to the door and pulled it open.

"I can't believe you met them."

"I think I killed them," Ruby said numbly as she opened the door. "But if they come looking for me, don't answer the door."

***

Keeping to the bright glow of the streetlights, she shuffled down the limited distance to the train station. Every cell ached. Her stomach growled even as it rolled. Her head throbbed. Covered by layers of sweat, blood, and dirt, she had never felt so disgusting as she ambled along. But she was just too exhausted to care. Drained in body and mind, she could barely keep her eyes open as she entered the train station. There was only one person on staff and the employee seemed surprised to have anyone appearing at such an hour.

A song played softly through the overhead speakers. The happy tune sounded familiar, but Ruby couldn't begin to place it. The worker's eyes followed her careful as she hobbled through the aisles, snatching up a few bags of chips and a bottle of water. Ruby watched them just as carefully. But her attention was focused solely upon their eyes. She only approached when she was sure that he had patches of white and rings of color.

"Rough night?"

Ruby dumped the items on the table and pulled her wallet out of her pocket.

"Yes. One ticket please."

The woman's eyes kept flicking back up to Ruby as she rung up the items and punched a few buttons.

"Where are you headed?"

"East Eagle."

Ruby presented her debit card and the woman plucked it free from the tattered remains of her gloved fingers.

"Would you like to upgrade to a private sleeper compartment?"

Swaying on her feet, Ruby met the woman's eyes.

"As long as it has a door."

* * *

FREE Bonus Novel!

Wow, I hope you enjoyed this book as much as I did writing it! If you enjoyed the book, please leave a review. Your reviews inspire me to continue writing about the world of spooky and untold horrors!

To really show you my appreciation for purchasing this book, please enjoy a **FREE extra spooky bonus novel.** This will surely leave you running scared!

Visit below to download your bonus novel and to learn about my upcoming releases, future discounts and giveaways: www.ScareStreet.com

FREE books (30 - 60 pages):
Ron Ripley (Ghost Stories)
1. Ghost Stories (Short Story Collection)
   www.scarestreet.com/ghost

A.I. Nasser (Supernatural Suspense)
2. Polly's Haven (Short Story)
   www.scarestreet.com/pollys
3. This is Gonna Hurt (Short Story)
   www.scarestreet.com/thisisgonna

Multi-Author Scare Street Collaboration
4. Horror Stories: A Short Story Collection
   www.scarestreet.com/horror

And experience the full-length novels (150 – 210 pages):
Ron Ripley (Ghost Stories)
1. Sherman's Library Trilogy (FREE via mailing list signup)
   www.scarestreet.com
2. The Boylan House Trilogy
   www.scarestreet.com/boylantri
3. The Blood Contract Trilogy
   www.scarestreet.com/bloodtri

4. The Enfield Horror Trilogy
www.scarestreet.com/enfieldtri

Moving In Series

5. **Moving In Series Box Set Books 1 - 3 (22% off)**
www.scarestreet.com/movinginbox123
6. Moving In (Book 1)
www.scarestreet.com/movingin
7. The Dunewalkers (Moving In Series Book 2)
www.scarestreet.com/dunewalkers
8. Middlebury Sanitarium (Book 3)
www.scarestreet.com/middlebury
9. **Moving In Series Box Set Books 4 - 6 (25% off)**
www.scarestreet.com/movinginbox456
10. The First Church (Book 4)
www.scarestreet.com/firstchurch
11. The Paupers' Crypt (Book 5)
www.scarestreet.com/paupers
12. The Academy (Book 6)
www.scarestreet.com/academy

Berkley Street Series

13. Berkley Street (Book 1)
www.scarestreet.com/berkley
14. The Lighthouse (Book 2)
www.scarestreet.com/lighthouse
15. The Town of Griswold (Book 3)
www.scarestreet.com/griswold
16. Sanford Hospital (Book 4)
www.scarestreet.com/sanford
17. Kurkow Prison (Book 5)
www.scarestreet.com/kurkow
18. Lake Nutaq (Book 6)
www.scarestreet.com/nutaq
19. Slater Mill (Book 7)
www.scarestreet.com/slater
20. Borgin Keep (Book 8)
www.scarestreet.com/borgin
21. Amherst Burial Ground (Book 9)
www.scarestreet.com/amherst

Hungry Ghosts Street Series

22. Hungry Ghosts (Book 1)
www.scarestreet.com/hungry
Haunted Collection Series
23. Collecting Death (Book 1)
www.scarestreet.com/collecting
24. Walter's Rifle (Book 2)
www.scarestreet.com/walter
25. Blood in the Mirror (Book 3)
www.scarestreet.com/bloodmirror

Victor Dark (Supernatural Suspense)
26. Uninvited Guests Trilogy
www.scarestreet.com/uninvitedtri
27. Listen To Me Speak Trilogy
www.scarestreet.com/listentri

A.I. Nasser (Supernatural Suspense)
Slaughter Series
28. Children To The Slaughter (Book 1)
www.scarestreet.com/children
29. Shadow's Embrace (Book 2)
www.scarestreet.com/shadows
30. Copper's Keeper (Book 3)
www.scarestreet.com/coppers
The Sin Series
31. Kurtain Motel (Book 1)
www.scarestreet.com/kurtain
32. Refuge (Book 2)
www.scarestreet.com/refuge
33. Purgatory (Book 3)
www.scarestreet.com/purgatory
The Carnival Series
34. Blood Carousel(Book 1)
www.scarestreet.com/bloodcarousel
Witching Hour Series
35. Witching Hour (Book 1)
www.scarestreet.com/witchinghour
36. Devil's Child (Book 2)
www.scarestreet.com/devilschild

David Longhorn (Supernatural Suspense)
The Sentinels Series

37. Sentinels (Book 1)
    www.scarestreet.com/sentinels
38. The Haunter (Book 2)
    www.scarestreet.com/haunter
39. The Smog (Book 3)
    www.scarestreet.com/smog

Dark Isle Series

40. Dark Isle (Book 1)
    www.scarestreet.com/darkisle
41. White Tower (Book 2)
    www.scarestreet.com/whitetower
42. The Red Chapel (Book 3)
    www.scarestreet.com/redchapel

Ouroboros Series

43. The Sign of Ouroboros (Book 1)
    www.scarestreet.com/ouroboros
44. Fortress of Ghosts (Book 2)
    www.scarestreet.com/fortress
45. Day of The Serpent (Book 3)
    www.scarestreet.com/serpent

Curse of Weyrmouth Series

46. Curse of Weyrmouth (Book 1)
    www.scarestreet.com/weyrmouth
47. Blood of Angels (Book 2)
    www.scarestreet.com/bloodofangels

Eric Whittle (Psychological Horror)
Catharsis Series

48. Catharsis (Book 1)
    www.scarestreet.com/catharsis
49. Mania (Book 2)
    www.scarestreet.com/mania
50. Coffer (Book 3)
    www.scarestreet.com/coffer

Sara Clancy (Supernatural Suspense)
Dark Legacy Series

51. Black Bayou (Book 1)
www.scarestreet.com/bayou
52. Haunted Waterways (Book 2)
www.scarestreet.com/waterways
53. Demon's Tide (Book 3)
www.scarestreet.com/demonstide

Banshee Series

54. Midnight Screams (Book 1)
www.scarestreet.com/midnight
55. Whispering Graves (Book 2)
www.scarestreet.com/whispering
56. Shattered Dreams (Book 3)
www.scarestreet.com/shattered

Black Eyed Children Series

57. Black Eyed Children (Book 1)
www.scarestreet.com/blackeyed
58. Devil's Rise (Book 2)
www.scarestreet.com/rise
59. The Third Knock (Book 3)
www.scarestreet.com/thirdknock

Demonic Games Series

60. Demonic Games (Book 1)
www.scarestreet.com/nesting
61. Buried (Book 2)
www.scarestreet.com/buried

Chelsey Dagner (Supernatural Suspense)
Ghost Mirror Series

62. Ghost Mirror (Book 1)
www.scarestreet.com/ghostmirror
63. The Gatekeeper (Book 2)
www.scarestreet.com/gatekeeper

Keeping it spooky,
Team Scare Street